The HOMEPLACE

Also by Gilbert Morris

Jacob's Way
Jordan's Star
God's Handmaiden
Edge of Honor
The Spider Catcher
Charade

GILBERT MORRIS

The HOMEPLACE

⇒ THE SINGING RIVER SERIES ⇐

BOOK 1

ZONDERVAN™

GRAND RAPIDS, MICHIGAN 49530 USA

ZONDERVAN™

The Homeplace
Copyright © 2005 by Gilbert Morris

Requests for information should be addressed to:
Zondervan, *Grand Rapids, Michigan 49530*

ISBN: 0-7394-5666-0

Published in association with the literary agency of Alive Communications, Inc., 7680 Goddard Street, Suite 200, Colorado Springs, CO 80920.

Interior design by Michelle Espinoza

Printed in the United States of America

To Doug Freeman—
It's good to have one real hero in our family, Buddy.
Thanks for what you and a lot of other guys did at Normandy!

The HOMEPLACE

PART ONE

The Venture

·⇒ CHAPTER I ⇐·

A wedge of pale sunlight slanted through the window to Lanie's left, touching her auburn hair and bringing out a slight golden tint. She bent over the Warm Morning cookstove, opened the firebox, then with quick, economical movements removed the gray ashes with a small shovel, dumping them into a five-gallon can. She reached down into an old apple crate filled with what her dad called "rich pine"— fragments of pine knots so soaked with sap that when lit with a match they would burn like a torch.

Piling several knots onto the grate of the firebox, Lanie took a kitchen match from a box that rested on a shelf and struck the match on the rough strip on the side. She leaned down and held the flame against the wood until the rich pine caught. Quickly she pulled small pieces of pine kindling from a box and put them on top of the blaze. She crisscrossed three smaller sticks of white oak firewood, arranging them expertly so that a draft was formed, causing them to burn evenly. She shut the firebox door and opened the draft on the stovepipe, then paused, listening to the crackle of the flames and the rush of air up the chimney. Satisfied, she turned the knob for the damper partway to slow down the fire.

Lanie Belle Freeman paused, listening to the fire. She tucked a rebellious curl from her forehead behind her ear. At fourteen, Lanie had reached that stage when adolescence gives way to young womanhood. She was thoughtful in most things—cautious and sometimes slow to decide, but moved quickly once she made up her mind. Her faded green dress with a white-flower print revealed the curves of an emerging woman. Her arms suggested a strength unusual for one her age. Sunlight highlighted the curves of her cheeks. Her eyes were large and gray with a hint of green. They were well-shaped, widely spaced, and contemplative, but at times could flash with temper. Her lips were full and expressive, and when she smiled, a dimple appeared on her right cheek.

She moved to a tall wooden kitchen cabinet with a gray-speckled porcelain countertop and pulled open the flour bin. "Plenty of flour," she murmured. A thought came to her and she picked up a Big Chief notebook on the counter and crossed to a table set against the far wall just beside the icebox. As she picked up a pen and sat down at the table in a cane-bottomed chair, a smile turned up the corners of her mouth. Opening the book to a blank page, she began to write. Her handwriting was smooth, even, and neatly executed:

April the 12th, 1928
Lanie Belle Freeman
600 Jefferson Davis Avenue
Fairhope
Stone County
Arkansas
America
North America
Earth
Solar System
Milky Way Galaxy

Lanie studied what she had put down. A quizzical look touched her eyes and she smiled. "There's just one more place to go after that, I reckon." At the bottom of the list she added "Universe," then studied what she had written.

She smiled, then laughed out loud. "Now I reckon I know right where I am."

Closing the book abruptly, she pushed it to the back of the table and put the pen beside it. Suddenly she took a deep breath. "Ice!" she said. Whirling, she walked to the oak icebox and opened the ice compartment. All that was left was a small lump of ice. She shut the door and bent down to check the drip pan. It was almost full. She dashed out of the kitchen and down the long hall that led to the front porch, then turned right into the living room. She caught a glimpse of her brother Cody working with something in the middle of the floor, but ignored him. Going to the window, she reached up on the wall and pulled down a foot-square card that was marked on different sides in large black numbers: "25," "50," "75," and "100." She put the card in the window with the "100" upright to let the iceman know the size ice block she needed.

"Cody," Lanie said, turning to the boy, "go empty the drip pan from under the icebox."

"Aw, shoot, I'm busy, Lanie. You do it."

Cody Freeman did not even look up. He had a screwdriver in one hand and was assembling some sort of apparatus. At the age of eleven he spent most of his waking hours inventing things. Few ever worked, but he had unshakable confidence that someday he would be another Edison.

"You heard what I said, Cody. Now leave that thing alone. You can come back after you empty the drip pan."

Cody grumbled, but got to his feet. He had the same auburn hair and gray-green eyes as Lanie, and there was a liveliness about him. He hurried down the hall, and by the time Lanie got to the kitchen, he had dragged out the drip pan and succeeded in spilling a widening pool of water on the floor.

"You're making a mess, Cody!"

"Well, dang it, I can't help it if the dumb ol' thing's full!"

"If you'd empty it when you're supposed to, it wouldn't get full. Now get it out of here."

"I'm gonna invent something that'll drain this dadgummed ol' icebox so nobody'll have to carry the dumb water out!"

"Well, until you do, just take it out—and stop calling everything *dumb*."

Lanie held the screen door open for Cody, who walked out with the pan, leaving a trail of water behind him. After checking the firebox, Lanie nodded with satisfaction. The rich pine had caught, and the fire was blazing. Straightening, she turned the damper down a little more to lessen the air intake. She had become an expert in building fires in the wood stove and rather liked it.

Glancing at the clock, she saw that it was almost three. She went to her parents' bedroom, where her mother was sitting in a rocker beside an open window, crocheting.

Elizabeth Ann Freeman was thirty-six. Her body was swollen with the child she was expecting, but she had retained much of her early beauty. Her children received most of their looks from her, especially the auburn hair and gray eyes. She had a beautifully shaped face with a short English nose and a slight cleft in her chin.

"Mama, I need to know how to fix fried pies."

She looked up at her daughter. "Fried pies? Don't you know how to do that?"

"I've watched you, Mama, but I never learned how."

"Well, set down here, and I'll tell you."

Lanie sat down on the bed and listened intently as her mother explained the process. She did not write anything down, for she had a phenomenal memory. Lanie noticed how tired her mother looked. Having this baby would be difficult, Lanie knew, for her mother had not borne a child for eleven years. There was a strain about her eyes, and Dr. Givens had left medicine for her. He had also left instructions that Elizabeth was to do no physical work, but should stay in bed as much as possible. Lanie had taken over the housework, with her siblings doing what they could.

"Well, that doesn't sound hard, Mama. I can do it."

Elizabeth smiled. "I know you can, honey. Now tell me about the contest at school. How are you doing?"

Lanie shrugged and made a face. "Oh, I don't know. I'm doing the best I can, but it's gonna be real hard. There are lots of smart kids."

The William McKinley High School had launched a contest to reward the students with the best grades. There were other criteria, too, but grades would count most heavily. The winner in each class would receive a hundred dollars. The grand prize for the overall school winner was two hundred dollars and a silver cup, just like the athletic teams received. Being only a freshman, Lanie did not expect to win the big prize, but her grades had been outstanding in elementary school, and her mother encouraged her to throw herself into the work.

Lanie felt insecure about her abilities. "I might have a chance to win the freshman award, but Roger Langley will win the grand prize." Roger Langley was the son of Otis Langley, the richest man in Fairhope. He was also the idol of every girl in high school—tall, fine-looking, and as good an athlete as he was a student. "I . . . I don't think I can do it, Mama."

"Of course you can! You can do anything you want to, Lanie."

A flush touched Lanie's cheeks. "I can if you help me, Mama." She laughed. "It helps to have a schoolteacher for a mother."

"I haven't taught in a long time, but you and I can do it together."

"I'll do the best I can, Mama. Now I'm going to make Daddy's favorite supper—fried chicken, thickening gravy, fried okra, and fried fruit pies."

"He'll love it!"

Lanie went back to the kitchen and glanced at the clock. She turned on the radio, which was on the table beside the icebox. Her favorite program, *Lum & Abner*, was about to start, and she was pleased to hear the announcer say, "Well, let's see what's going on down in Pine Ridge . . ."

She moved to the cabinet with its porcelain counter and began making the pies. She scooped flour into a bowl, poured salt into her hand and dumped it in, added lard, then mixed everything with her fingers, working the flour into the lard. She added water, working the dough until it formed a soft ball. She rolled out the dough on the counter and used a saucer to cut circles. Quickly she put fruit on one side of each circle. She dipped her fingers in water and wet the edges of the dough. Then she folded the dough in half and crimped the edges together with a fork to seal them.

Lanie used both hands to lift the heavy cast-iron skillet onto the stove. After a few minutes, she heated the grease in the skillet and, using a spatula, carefully put two of the pies in the pan. She watched them fry, peeking under the edge until the crust was brown. Then she carefully turned them over. When they were done, she put the fried pies onto cloth towels made from flour sacks to drain the grease.

She worked quickly and efficiently, frying the rest of the pies, and had just put the last batch into the warming compartment when she heard Beau begin to bark. "That must be Reverend Jones."

She heard footsteps on the porch and went to open the door. "Hello, Reverend."

"Howdy, Miss Lanie. One hundred pounds?" Reverend Jones was a large black man. He had a hundred-pound block of ice on his back, which he held there with a pair of large tongs. His leather cape kept his back dry.

"That's right." Lanie smiled and opened the icebox while Reverend Jones chipped the large block into pieces that would fit inside the metal-lined compartment. He shut the door and smiled at Lanie. "That ought to last you folks a day or two."

"If you've got time, Reverend, I made apple pie yesterday, and I've got some tea."

"Why, that'd go down mighty fine, Miss Lanie." He sat down, his massive form filling the chair. Madison Jones was not only the iceman in Fairhope, he also was pastor of Greater Mount Zion Methodist Episcopal Church, the black church in town. He watched as Lanie pulled a tin plate out of the warming box over the cookstove, cut a generous slice of pie, put it on a saucer, and then set the pie and a fork before him. She opened the icebox and chipped off enough ice to fill a large glass, then poured tea over the ice. "It's already sweetened. We don't have any lemon."

"That be mighty fine, missy. Just the way I likes it."

"How is Melanie doing?"

"Oh, she doing real good! Done got over her mumps, but, of course, the rest of the chil'uns gonna get it too."

Lanie always asked about all eight of the reverend's children and his wife, and that pleased the big man.

"How your mama doin', Miss Lanie?"

"All right, I guess."

"You don't sound too sure 'bout that."

"Well, she hasn't had a baby in a long time, and the doctor doesn't seem to ..."

When Madison Jones saw that she could not finish, he swallowed the pie in his mouth and said gently, "It's gonna be all right. The good Lord's gonna take care of your mama."

"I know He will. But I just worry sometimes."

Madison finished the pie and washed it down with the tea. "I wants to give you a promise verse for today."

"You always do. What is it?"

"The Good Book, it say, 'Our God is in the heavens; he hath done whatsoever he hath pleased.' Dat's in Psalm 115, verse 3. So you see, the good Lord, He's in charge of your mama—and you and me and everybody else."

Lanie smiled. "Thank you, Reverend. I'll remember that."

Madison put out his huge hand, and Lanie put her hand in it. He held her hand in both of his and said, "Me and you, we'll pray for your mama."

After the big man left, Lanie sat at the table. She unfolded a piece of paper she had in her pocket, licked the tip of a pencil, and began to write.

The Iceman
Everyone brings something into our house.
Yesterday Cap'n Brown brought in a dead mouse.
Today our iceman brought in a block of ice

And a Bible verse—which was very nice.
I wish I could believe in God like Reverend Jones,
But sometimes I get scared down to my bones!

Lanie read the verse aloud, then stuffed it into her pocket. "That's not very good, but I can work on it tonight."

Ever since she could write, Lanie had been writing poems, but she didn't show them to anyone. She could say things in poems that she couldn't say to anyone. She glanced toward her parents' bedroom, then shook her head and said, "I've got to kill that dratted chicken."

Her mouth drew down in a look of disgust. Usually one of her parents killed the chickens, but this time it was up to her. Reluctantly, she went to the front door, stepped outside, then descended the steps. For a moment she looked around, taking in the backyard and the fields beyond. Knowing that her family had their own place always gave Lanie a good feeling.

Their property consisted of five acres, which had once been the hub of a large plantation belonging to Jesse and Elma Freeman, her father's great-grandparents. It was parceled off during Reconstruction, and now all that remained were these five acres perched just outside of Fairhope. The front of the two-story house, which was built before the Civil War, faced Jefferson Davis Avenue, the eastern city limit. In the opposite direction, low foothills began to rise a mile away, then the Buffalo Mountains shouldered their way to the sky like dark hump-backed elephants.

Lanie's eyes swept the huge garden, which was just beginning to produce, and she noted the big sorrel, Stonewall, cropping the green grass in the pasture on the farthest edge of the property. The horse was getting old, but Forrest Freeman still used him to break ground in the huge garden he planted every year. She heard the deep, hoarse grunting of their sow, Delilah, inside her fence, and the clucking of a chicken.

Lanie headed toward the chicken yard just as Beau, a huge cinnamon-colored dog, rounded the corner at full speed and lunged at her. Lanie braced herself. His front paws landed on her chest. As he licked her face, she balanced on her left foot and with her right foot trod heavily on his hind paws.

Beau gave a sharp, mournful cry and dropped to all fours. He gave her a hurt look that made Lanie laugh. "You're the only dog I ever saw that could look like his feelings were hurt. If you wouldn't jump up on people, you wouldn't get your toes stomped."

Beau turned and, head down, headed for the house. Whenever his feelings were hurt, Beau found something to face, and this time it was the side of the house. He lay down, staring at the house, and refused to look back. He was a fierce fighter, but any one of the family, just by speaking sharply to him, could drive him to face a wall for half a day. "Well, I'm sorry, Beau, but it's your own fault."

As Lanie walked by the towering walnut tree on the east side of the house, she heard voices and glanced up. Cody had been determined to build a huge tree house on the lower branches, and for the past year he had been collecting lumber with the help of Davis, his older brother. The two of them hauled home every scrap they could find, and now the tree house had a floor, four walls, and a roof. There was even a window. The door was one that Davis had scrounged from the city dump. Lanie looked up. Then she made a quick decision and climbed the ladder all the way to the platform. She could hear Maeva giggling and Cody laughing. When she opened the door, Lanie smelled smoke. Her eyes narrowed and she stepped inside. "Are you two smoking?"

"You bet your boots we are! Come an' have a puff," Maeva said.

Maeva Elizabeth Freeman was a year younger than Lanie, but somehow she seemed older. She was a maverick, afraid of nothing, physically strong, and regularly involved in some sort of problem. She sat there, her green eyes dancing, and stuck the homemade corn-silk cigarette to her lips. She took a drag and blew out the smoke. "You want a smoke, Lanie?"

"No, I don't want a smoke!" Lanie was disgusted with them. Cody looked somewhat ashamed, but not Maeva.

Cody and Maeva had pulled corn silk from the green ears of corn in the garden, spread it out on the tin roof of the barn, and let it dry until it was a crisp brown. Then they rolled it up in real cigarette papers from who knows where. Maeva grinned. "You want to see me blow a smoke ring?"

"No, I don't, and if Daddy finds out what you're doing, you'll get a paddling!"

"You gonna tell him?" Cody asked, a worried look on his face.

"No, I'm not a tattletale, but you two come down from here. Cody, bring in some more wood. Maeva, you've got to help me with supper."

Lanie climbed down, and the two followed her. "You gonna kill a chicken?" Cody asked. He ran his hand through his hair and grinned broadly. "I sure like to see them suckers run when they get their heads wrung off! I wonder how they can run without no head? They can't see where they're goin'."

"That's disgusting! It's not funny to kill something," Lanie said.

"I think it is," Cody said. "I'm gonna watch."

"You can pluck the thing after it's dead if you like dead chickens so much!"

"You know what? I'm gonna invent a chicken plucker." Cody screwed his mouth to one side. "I bet I could make a million dollars."

Maeva snorted in disgust. "You're not gonna invent no chicken plucker!"

"I am too!"

As the two argued, Lanie walked to the chicken yard. It was fenced with wire and had a henhouse on the inside. Even with Beau on guard, it was a constant struggle to keep the foxes, coons, and other varmints out. She opened the gate and went in, and the chickens flocked around her, clucking and bobbing their heads. Her heart sank. She had named every chicken. She loved to name things, but that made the killing more difficult.

"Which one you gonna kill?" Cody demanded.

"It don't make no difference," Maeva said. "They're just chickens."

Lanie made a quick choice. Lucille had not been laying well. She reached down and picked the chicken up by the neck. The chicken squawked out a surprised "cluck-cluck-cluck." Quickly and expertly Lanie twirled the chicken around. The head separated from the body, and Lucille dropped to the ground. She was up at once and began running around exactly as Cody had said. Sickened, Lanie looked down at the head in her hand. The eyes seemed to look at her reproachfully, and she shuddered and dropped the head on the ground.

"Boy, she sure do run, don't she!" Cody said with admiration. "You reckon it hurts the chicken?"

Lanie was disturbed. "Would it hurt you if someone wrung your head off?" She moved toward the hen's now still body.

"Don't feel bad," Maeva said. "God made chickens for us to eat."

"I can't help it. I don't like to kill anything."

Maeva picked up the chicken head and stared at it clinically. Then she pitched it out toward the pasture. She threw like a boy, hard and accurate, and watched the head until it hit the ground. "It don't bother me none. I'll kill the chickens from now on."

᚛᠊ CHAPTER 2 ᠊᚜

Forrest Freeman applied the brakes, and the big logging truck shuddered to a halt. He turned off the ignition, removed the key, and stuck it in his pocket. For a moment he sat behind the wheel, letting the weariness drain from him. After a twelve-hour day of wrestling huge logs to the ground, trimming them, loading them, and hauling them to the sawmill, a man was pretty well ready to quit.

Forrest frowned as the memory of a run-in with Duke Biggins came to him. Biggins, a fellow logger, was a brutal man who bullied smaller men. Duke despised Forrest, who knew it was only a matter of time before he had a fight with the big man because of a standoff they'd had about a year before. Forrest had been loading a huge pine log when he saw Biggins shove Wash Williams, one of the black laborers, and start kicking him. Forrest stepped between the two and for several moments thought Biggins was going to pitch into him too. It didn't happen, but lately he sensed Duke's fuse beginning to smolder and the man had taken to heavy drinking.

But Forrest was not a man to worry about things. He got out of the truck and stretched, the muscles rippling beneath his thin shirt. He was exactly six feet tall and weighed a trim 189 pounds. He had the kind of strength one sees in athletes—which he had been in his youth. Now, at thirty-four, he was still the best catcher the Fairhope Mountaineers could muster. At one time he had thought of playing professional baseball, but he had to make a living for his family—a wife and the children that had started coming almost at once, one a year for four years in a row.

"Hey, Forrest!"

Turning, Forrest saw his neighbor Deoin Jinks crossing Jefferson Davis Avenue. Jinks was the barber and probably, because of his calling, the most talkative man in Fairhope—if not in the county.

"Howdy, Deoin. What's up?"

"Themstinkin'Yankees!" This was said as all one word, for Deoin never referred to the baseball team in any other way. "They won again!"

Deoin's passion was the St. Louis Cardinals, and the team he hated most on the face of the planet was the New York Yankees. He hated them collectively and individually. Deoin could go on for hours about the shortcomings of each player.

Forrest knew better than to get trapped in such a conversation. "Well, they'll probably wear out before the summer's over."

"Themstinkin'Yankees!" Anger distorted Deoin's face. He was a short man with fair hair and dark-blue eyes.

Forrest grinned and started to leave, but Deoin reached out and plucked his sleeve. "Hey, Forrest, I hear that oldest girl of yours is smarter than a tree full of owls! I was cuttin' the math teacher's hair this morning. He said Lanie made a flat A in math. Now think about a girl that could do that!"

"Lanie's a bright girl all right, but there are lots of smart kids in that school. Lots of competition."

Deoin shook his head. "Nope, she's gonna win. I got a feelin' about that."

"You have feelin's about lots of things, but they don't always come true."

"Most of the time they do!"

"Okay, how do you feel about who's gonna be president next November?"

"That no account Yankee Al Smith ain't got a chance! Hoover's gonna win in a landslide."

Herbert Hoover, the Republican nominee, faced Alfred E. Smith, the governor of New York. Smith was an odd choice for 1928. He had affiliations with some pretty shady people, he favored abolishing Prohibition, and he was a Roman Catholic. All of these made him repugnant to the South and most of the West. Still, the Democrats took the plunge, and the race was beginning to heat up.

One reason for the unusual fervor of the race was the economic situation of the United States. The stock market had been rocky, low and then high, then low, for several years, and now it seemed that a strong hand was all that could save the country from economic disaster.

Deoin poked his thumb into Forrest's ribs. "I'll tell you somethin'. You'd better start buyin' up stocks."

"Not me. Them dang things go up and down like an elevator!"

"They ain't goin' to this time, Forrest. You'll get rich." He prodded Forrest again with his thumb. "And you'd better think about buyin' some of them lots down in Florida like I done. They're gonna be worth a fortune."

"You ain't even seen them lots, Deoin. They may be under water."

"No, I seen a picture. They're out of water, all right, palm trees and everything. When I get rich enough, I'm gonna build me a summer house down there where I can take the wife and kids. You'd better grab on or you'll miss the brass ring."

Forrest had heard all this before. He shook his head. "I tried gamblin' when I was a younger man. Lost everything I had."

"But this ain't like poker or dice. This is *business*."

"I don't care what it is. I'm puttin' my money in the bank. Maybe by next year, if things keep going like they have, I'll have enough money to pay off my place and all my logging equipment." Forrest had taken out a loan to pay the hospital bill when his wife fell sick and he now was working long hours to pay off the note. "I'd better get inside and find out how Elizabeth is."

"Are you gonna catch that game for the Mountaineers tomorrow?"

"I guess so."

"Good. We need to beat them smart alecks from Fort Smith." According to Deoin, everybody from Fort Smith, the county seat, was a smart aleck.

Forrest grinned as he left Deoin, but he had not gotten far when Beau, as usual, barked a greeting, reared up on his hind legs, and tried to lick Forrest's face. "Git down, Beau, you're as big as an elephant!" The dog refused to move and, with a sigh, Forrest stepped on his paw. Beau dropped down, gave Forrest a reproachful look, and slumped away, head down, tail tucked between his legs.

Forrest chuckled. "Go on off and pout. It's your own fault." He stepped up on the front porch and as soon as he opened the door and entered the hall, he smelled frying chicken. He walked down the hall and as he was passing the bedroom door, saw Elizabeth sitting in a rocker crocheting. "What are you doing out of bed, honey?" He walked over and put his hand on her shoulder. "You better do like the doctor says."

"I can't stay in bed all day. I'd get bedsores." Elizabeth lifted her face and Forrest bent down and kissed her. "You look tired."

"Fresh as a daisy. Somethin' smells good."

"Lanie's cooking your favorite supper. You brag on it now, no matter if it's not the best."

"Won't be as good as yours." Forrest knelt beside her chair and took her hand in both of his. "How have you been?" He stroked her hand with his callused palm.

"Fine. Just fine."

"You always say that. I don't know when to believe you."

Elizabeth reached out and put her hand on his stubbled cheek. "You forgot to shave this morning."

"I didn't forget. I just didn't see much point in looking pretty for a bunch of pine trees, but I will now." He rose, bent over, and kissed her again. "You'll fall smack dab in love with me when you see how pretty I look." He winked at her and went to the closet. He picked out a pair of pants and a shirt. "Who ironed these?"

"Maeva did. She's real good at that."

"Well, I'll give her a reward."

Forrest went to the bathroom and put the clothes on the hamper. He hesitated, then went to the kitchen. Lanie had her back to him and was turning pieces of chicken in the big iron frying pan. He sneaked up, reached out and grabbed her, and lifted her clear off the floor.

Lanie screamed and wriggled in his arms. "Daddy, put me down!"

"No, I won't do it. You're too dadgummed pretty." Holding her off the floor, he turned in circles until she grew dizzy.

"Daddy, I'll burn the chicken!"

"Well, all right then." He picked up a fork and poked at the chicken. "It looks good to me."

"I'm making you some thickening gravy, too, and fresh biscuits. And then I got a surprise for dessert."

"I do love surprises." He put his hands on her cheeks and held her face for a minute. "You are growin' up, gal. Gettin' pretty as a pair of green shoes with red laces."

"Oh, Daddy!"

"Well, you are. Tell me something. Have any of them fellers at school been tryin' to make up to you?"

"No."

"I bet they have. I bet some of them tried to kiss you."

Lanie loved it when her father teased her, although she tried to pretend indifference. "If they did, I'd bust 'em in the snoot!"

"Good for you, Lanie, and if they need some more of that, you tell me and I'll do it."

Just then Cody ran into the room. Forrest reached over and got his head in the crook of his arm and started rubbing his head with his knuckles. "How about a Dutch rub?"

"Daddy, that hurts!"

Laughing, Forrest released him. "Well, did you invent anything today?"

"I'm gonna invent somethin' to take that dumb ol' water that drips off the ice. Ain't no sense in havin' to empty a pan of water."

"I bet you could do it, too. You're a smart boy. When you get a little older, you're gonna invent somethin' and get rich, and then all I'm gonna do is lie on my back and eat strawberry ice cream every day."

Maeva and Davis walked in. Davis, at twelve, was the tallest of the children. He was lean and athletic and had the same bright greenish gray eyes and auburn hair as the rest of the kids. "Hi, Dad."

"Hey, Davis, you play ball today?"

"Sure did. We played them fellers from Madison. We won too."

"You get any hits?"

"Three for four."

"Good for you. We'll take some battin' practice after supper maybe."

"You gonna catch tomorrow for the Mountaineers?"

"That's what I plan on."

"Let me go with you, Daddy."

"Wouldn't have it no other way."

The children crowded around their father, popping questions at him. He finally reached over and held Maeva by the chin, tilting her face up. "Well, Maeva, have you been a good girl?"

"No, I ain't."

"Well, now, that's comin' right out with it! What'd you do today that was so bad?"

"I made a cigarette out of corn silk and smoked it."

"How'd you like it?"

"I didn't. Bit my tongue like fire. Ain't never gonna smoke one of them things again."

"Maybe you can take up chewin'."

Maeva laughed. "That's nasty. I'd never do that."

"I'm glad to hear it. Nothing hurts a gal's looks like spittin' tobacco."

"Daddy, go get cleaned up," Lanie said. "Supper's almost ready."

"Well, I'm ready for it. Don't you kids get shocked at how pretty I am when I come out."

❦

"Thank you, Lord, for this food, for the hands that prepared it, and thank you for our family. Continue, Lord, to watch over us and keep us safe. In Jesus' name. Amen."

"Amen! Amen! Amen!" Every one of the Freeman family echoed their dad's short blessing.

Forrest took a chicken leg and put it on his plate. "I'd better have both this here chicken's legs. I heard they ain't healthy for young people."

Lanie smiled. She knew her father loved chicken legs best of all the parts.

"I want the liver!" Maeva called out.

"No, I want it!" Cody shouted. "You got it the last time."

"Don't fight over what you get to eat," Elizabeth said. "There's plenty here. I wish a chicken had ten livers."

Indeed there was plenty. In addition to fried chicken, there was a big bowl of thickening gravy to go on fluffy biscuits. The garden had come through so there was not only fried okra but fried squash, crisp radishes and green onions, a big bowl of butter beans, and several kinds of pickles.

Forrest noticed that Elizabeth wasn't eating. She was just pushing at her food, but he said nothing. Finally he picked up one of the drinking glasses, a large green cut-glass affair, and said, "I declare! Things just taste better out of these glasses, and they was free."

"Where'd they come from, Daddy?" Davis asked.

"I get one every time I buy a tank of gas down at the gas station. I'm gonna keep on until we got a whole set."

"I tell you what we ought to do," Maeva said, "we ought to go to the movies."

"What's going to the movies got to do with glasses?" Forrest asked.

"Well, you keep your stub when you go in and they put 'em all in a box, and then they have a draw. The winning stub gets a whole set of dishes."

"Let's go!" Cody said, his eyes glowing. "We ain't been to the movies in a long time, and I hear they got a talkin' picture there."

"A talkin' picture! How can that be?" Elizabeth asked.

"I guess they hook it up to a phonograph," Cody said. "Anyway, they got one. It's Al Jolson in *The Jazz Singer.*"

"I bet Old Man Butterworth won't let 'em show it," Maeva said. "He'll say it's sinful."

Francis Butterworth, the owner of the Rialto Theater, screened his movies carefully. He would not show any film that did not meet his approval, and as a deacon in the Baptist church, his standards were strict.

"Why, that old codger won't even show Buck Jones westerns!" Cody exclaimed. "Ain't nothin' wrong with Buck Jones."

"Well, he does shoot people now and then." Forrest grinned. "How you kids doin' at school?"

As usual, Lanie was doing well. She never made anything less than an A. Maeva's grades went up and down like a thermometer, A's and F's equally spaced. When she was interested in something, she could do it easily, but if not, she made no effort. Cody was good at numbers and figures but not particularly interested in anything else.

Davis didn't say a word, and Forrest didn't press him, because Davis struggled in school. It was a mystery to everyone, including his teachers. He was bright, had a great memory, and was good at math and sports. But reading posed a problem. He finally looked up and said, "I'm flunkin' English, and the coach says I need to get a tutor."

"Well, you won't get a better one than your mama," Forrest said.

"I try the best I can, Daddy, but I just can't get it. Anyway, I'm gonna pitch for the St. Louis Cardinals. You don't have to be smart for that."

Forrest laughed. "I think it takes a little more brains than people think, but not book smarts." He turned to Lanie. "You did a fine job on this meal, honey. Couldn't have been better."

"All the others helped me, Daddy."

"Tell you what. Why don't we all jump in, do these dishes, and then we'll go have a hoedown."

"You and Davis go outside and play catch," Lanie said. "The rest of us will do the dishes."

The light faded slowly. By the time the dishes were washed, and Davis and Forrest had played catch, and all were gathered in the parlor, the light was still murky in the west. Forrest sat down and looked around the room with pleasure. It was his favorite room in the whole house. He had been raised in this house; every inch brought memories of some kind. He glanced at the pictures of his parents and grandparents in their oval frames on the wall, stern-looking men and women afraid to smile for the camera as if there were something sinful about a smile. The furniture was solid walnut and rosewood, bought by his grandfather. Deoin Jinks said once that the furniture was worth a lot of money, but Forrest put the words aside. He had a strong attachment to the land and to the house with its furnishings. The wallpaper was bright and cheerful. Hooked rugs covered the brightly polished pine floors.

A spring breeze came through the open windows. Forrest picked up his fiddle, tucked it under his chin, and drew the bow across the strings gently. The one thing he did better than play baseball was play the fiddle. He played entirely by ear, but after hearing a tune once or twice could play it perfectly. He couldn't read music as Elizabeth could, but as she said once, "It doesn't hurt his playing at all."

The children had all inherited their parents' musical ability. Lanie could play anything with strings. Maeva played the piano with gusto—more gusto than skill at times. Davis could play the mandolin and the dulcimer, and Cody loved the drums.

"What'll it be first?" Forrest asked. He was besieged with song titles and finally said, "All right, Maeva, you first."

She chose "Bye-Bye Blackbird." Forrest launched into it, and the others followed. After that Davis chose "I'm Looking Over a Four-Leaf Clover." Cody called for "When the Red, Red Robin Comes Bob-Bob-Bobbing Along."

They all sang. At chuch they had learned to sing parts with hymns, so they could harmonize on many of the popular songs.

Finally Forrest turned to Elizabeth and said, "What would you like to hear, sweetheart?"

Elizabeth smiled. "I'd like to hear some good hymns."

"Good hymns! There ain't no bad hymns, is there?"

"No, but I like some better than others."

"How about this one?" Forrest began to play and sing "Will the Circle Be Unbroken," and the others joined in, harmonizing. They sang Elizabeth's favorite, "What a Friend We Have in Jesus." Then they sang several about heaven, including "When We All Get to Heaven."

The whole house rang with the sound of the music, and finally Forrest removed the fiddle from under his chin and said, "God has been mighty good to us to give us music. David was a musician, and when old Saul got down in the dumps, he sent for David. And I reckon David would play one of his Psalms."

Elizabeth looked at her family and a lump came to her throat. She had married Forrest against the advice of everyone. She was a school teacher in her second year of teaching, and he was a roughneck lumberjack. But he won her heart with his smile, his music, and his zest for living. She taught him to read and smoothed some of his rough edges, and never once did she regret marrying him.

Finally she said, "We'd better get to bed. We've got to get up early tomorrow."

The kids complained as usual, but they were all tired.

Lanie kissed her mother good-night and then went to her room. The old house had five bedrooms, so each had their own room. Lanie's had a desk that had belonged to her great-great-grandmother. It was made of some exotic dark wood that not even her father could identify. The wood was smooth and hard and had a silky sheen.

Opening a drawer, Lanie took out her journal and dated it April 12, 1928. and began to write:

> *I had to kill Lucille today, and it broke my heart! I hated to do it, but I do admit that she was downright delicious! I fried her for supper and we ate all of her. Mama ate only a little bit of the breast and some of the gravy. I'll be glad when the baby comes and mama is strong again.*
>
> *I wrote a poem about Reverend Jones, but it's not very good . . .*

Lanie had formed the habit of writing everything that happened to her, and she had filled six journals. She kept them well hidden from the family, for her writing exposed her heart. Finally she put her pen down, read what she had written, sighed, and put the notebook back in the drawer under some of her clothing.

She climbed in bed and lay quietly for a while. The earth was cool now, and from far off came the plaintive sound of a coyote, always a lonesome sound to her. She thought about the prize at school, almost prayed to win, but somehow she could not. "God," she finally said, "I'll do my best, and if you'll help me, that's all I ask. And I pray that you let this baby come quick and get Mama strong again."

☞ CHAPTER 3 ☜

The triumphant crowing of Raynard, the rooster, brought Lanie out of sleep. She lay on her stomach, her face turned aside on the feather pillow. Consciousness came back to her a little at a time. The musty smell of the feathers prompted her to roll over and stare at the ceiling. The faint light of dawn peeked through the window, and the smooth texture of the sheets gave her a sense of luxury.

Finally she reached up, pushed her head against the top of the iron bedstead, arched her body, and pointed her toes.

"Ohhhh!" she moaned. She considered rolling over and pushing her face in the pillow and sleeping, but that was impossible. Throwing the covers back, she sat up on the edge of the bed, stretched again, and then stood. A tiny noise caught her attention, something that sounded like *Wow!* It was Cap'n Brown, a tawny tailless manx cat with extra-long hind legs and a huge head that slept with her year round.

Lanie looked down and for a moment could not identify what Cap'n Brown was doing. He had something under his paw that was moving. She leaned down close then ice water seemed to run through her veins.

"A snake!" she screamed, jumping back into the bed and pulling the covers over her head. "A snake! Cap'n Brown, get away from here with that thing!"

She heard the door open and Maeva said, "What's the matter with you? What are you screaming about?"

Lanie poked her head out from under the covers. "A snake! Cap'n Brown brought in a snake!" Now that Maeva was there she felt safer. Maeva was not afraid of snakes—or anything else so far as anyone knew. Lanie got up on her knees and pointed, her voice shaking, "Get . . . get that thing out of here, Maeva!"

Maeva gave Lanie a look of exasperation, reached down, and said, "Gimme that snake, Cap'n Brown." She held it in one hand and stood up, and a mischievous look touched her eyes. She took a step toward the bed. "It's only an old green snake. You want to hold him, sister?"

"Get away from here! Throw him away!"

Maeva laughed. "You'd better be glad he didn't bring you a copperhead. Get up. We got to fix breakfast."

As soon as Maeva left, Lanie picked up Cap'n Brown under his front legs and shook him. "Bad, Cap'n Brown, bad! Don't bring me any more presents, you hear me? No more presents!"

Cap'n Brown yawned, exposing an incredibly red throat and teeth sharper than needles. He wiggled and Lanie put him down and began to dress.

When she got to the kitchen, the warmth from the stove enveloped her, and she saw her dad at the table drinking coffee.

"Daddy, you don't need to drink cold coffee. I'll make you some hot."

Forrest smiled and winked. "The worst cup of coffee I ever had, Muff, was real good." His calling her by his pet nickname pleased Lanie. It gave her a special feeling about him.

"I'll fix you a good breakfast then." She started to turn toward the counter, but Forrest stood up, put his arms around her, and lifted her clean up off the floor. He kissed her heartily on both cheeks.

"Daddy, you need to shave!"

"Nobody's going to see me except a bunch of hillbilly lumberjacks." He put her down, and she began collecting the elements of the breakfast. He sat down and sipped the cold coffee and watched her for a time. Finally he said, "I'm sorry you have to take care of all of us, Muff."

"I don't mind, Daddy."

"Well, it'll be good practice for you when you have your own family."

"Oh, that's a long time off."

"Nothing is as far off as you think. When I was about your age I was wishing I was older. It seemed like I never would grow up." He sipped the coffee again. "Where is that fifteen-year-old boy? Gone forever. Now all that's left of me is this broken-down lumberjack."

"You're not broken down!"

"Maybe not completely. I'll go out and bring in some more wood for you."

"Let the boys do it, Daddy."

"Oh, there's no fun bringing in wood. I want 'em to have as much fun as they can."

Lanie turned from the icebox with a bowl of eggs. She went to him and touched his face. "You're too good to us."

"I hope I always will be. Well, better fix plenty of breakfast. I've got a long day ahead."

<hr/>

After breakfast, as the Freeman siblings left for school, they were joined by Alice and Max Jinks, who lived across the street. Max was twelve, and he and Cody trotted on ahead, talking about what they would do after school. Maeva and Davis followed.

Alice Jinks was fourteen. Her birthday was the same as Lanie's, which made a bond for them. They had spent practically every day of their lives together and shared most of their secrets too. In truth, Alice shared all of hers, but Lanie was more reticent.

"I hope Gerald Pink sits by me in assembly today," Alice said. "I think he's the cutest thing, don't you?"

"He's a nice-looking boy."

Gerald was the son of Harold Pink, the owner of Pink's Drugstore. He worked with his father as a soda jerk and showed his favor for friends of his by giving them extra-thick milkshakes. "When I got a soda yesterday, he winked at me and pinched me."

"Pinched you where?" Lanie asked.

"Oh, just on the arm. Look, it made a little bruise." Alice pulled up her sleeve.

"Do you put up with that?"

"It means he likes me!" Alice protested. She was a plain girl, her chief claim to beauty being her bright-red hair and dark-blue eyes. She hated her freckles, of which she had not a few, and read nothing but *True Romance* magazines, which she kept hidden from her parents. She had let Lanie read a few, but Lanie found them silly.

"You're too young to think about boyfriends, Alice."

"I am not! I'm plenty old enough to have a boyfriend. I will, too! I think it'll be Gerald. He really likes me."

"Alice, you've gone through crushes on boys alphabetically, and now you're down to the Pinks. You don't need to be thinking so much about boys."

"What else am I going to think about? How to diagram a complex sentence?"

"It wouldn't hurt you to study a little harder."

"If I were as smart as you, I wouldn't study at all."

"That doesn't make any sense. I have to study if I'm going to be smart."

The two argued as they cut through the main part of town, passing businesses that were just beginning to open. They came to the Rialto Theater, where Max, Cody, Maeva, and Davis were looking at the posters. Cody was complaining. "Look at this. Another one of those dumb, soupy love stories! They don't ever have anything good here."

Lanie stopped to look at the pictures of Tex Ritter, the cowboy star. Tex's eyes were narrowed, and he was obviously shooting down villains. "You used to like Tex Ritter, Cody."

"That was when I was a little kid. I want to see somethin' better than that."

"Yeah," Max said, "Tommy Franklin said he seen one called *Flesh and the Devil* with Greta Garbo and John Gilbert. He said it was really somethin'."

"It sounds like it," Lanie said with disgust. "You don't need to see a thing like that."

"I don't reckon we will," Davis grumbled. "Old Man Butterworth would say it ain't suitable."

"I tell you what we can do," Cody said. "We can sneak off to Mount Ida and see it next Saturday."

"Mount Ida! How'd we get there?" asked Max.

"We'd hitchhike."

"Hey, that sounds great," Maeva said. "I'll go too."

"None of you are going to sneak off and see that awful movie!" Lanie stated. "Now let's go to school."

"I'll go if I want to," Maeva said, staring at Lanie. "Wouldn't hurt you to go with us. We can tell the folks we're going to see Tex Ritter. They wouldn't mind that."

The argument continued until they reached school. Lanie and Alice went to the large two-story red-brick high school. The others, still grumbling, went to the elementary school.

Lanie walked down the hall to her locker. She put her lunch inside and then walked to room 104.

"Hello, Miss Dunsmore."

Miss Eden Marie Dunsmore was writing on the blackboard, but she turned and smiled. "Good morning, Lanie." She was blond, twenty-two, with large gray eyes. Most of the older male students were half in love with her and spun fantasies about her, though it was rumored that Coach Wilson had recently won her affections. She was especially good to Lanie, and now she whispered, "Work hard now. I want you to win the grand award."

"Oh, I couldn't do that, Miss Dunsmore."

"Yes you can, and I'll help you."

The class filtered in with the usual noises, groanings, and boys flirting with girls and shoving each other around. When the bell rang, Miss Dunsmore said, "Good morning." The class mumbled a "good morning." She picked up the roll book and checked each name, then put the book down and said, "I have your themes ready to hand back."

She moved around the room, handing out papers, and when she handed Helen Langley her paper, Lanie could see a C- written on it. Helen sent up a howl. She sat right next to Lanie and more than once had tried to copy Lanie's work. "A C-! This paper's better than that, Miss Dunsmore!" Helen, a pretty girl with fair hair and blue eyes, was the most spoiled girl in all of Fairhope. Her father gave her everything she wanted. She wore expensive clothes and always had money to spend. "This is a good paper. It ought to be at least a B!"

"Helen, now, you settle down or that C- will become a D+."

Miss Dunsmore put Lanie's paper down on her desk. Helen snatched it and stared. "A+!" She shoved the paper back at Lanie and gave her a venomous glance. "You think you're so smart," Helen whispered, "but my brother Roger's going to win the prize! You can just forget about it!"

Helen's outburst embarrassed Lanie. "I think he probably will," she said.

⚒

Pink's Drugstore was crowded when Lanie and her siblings arrived after school. Roger and Helen Langley were sitting at a table with other students. They were laughing and drinking sodas that were too expensive for the Freemans. All the rich kids who came to Pink's Drugstore wore the latest fashions, and most of the girls had at least one piece of expensive jewelry. The older boys had cars; Roger, who was seventeen, drove a Stutz Bearcat.

"There's the teacher's pet," Helen said. She nudged her brother. "She thinks she's going to beat you out for the grand award, Roger. Isn't that a laugh?"

Roger frowned. "Don't talk so loud. Nobody's deaf." Then he smiled at Lanie. "Hi, Lanie. I hear you're my big competition for the grand award."

"I don't think I'll be much competition," she murmured, then hurried with her brothers and sister to the back of the store, where Mr. Pink was filling prescriptions. He smiled at her. "What can I do for you, Lanie?"

"Mama says we need some paregoric."

"How much?"

"I don't know. Whatever it comes in."

"Well, you can have a gallon if you want." Mr. Pink laughed. "But I guess that'd be a bit much. Somebody got a bellyache?"

"Mama makes us take it every time we get anything," Cody piped up. "I hate the stuff. It tastes awful!"

"Well, don't take too much of it. It'll put you to sleep."

Mr. Pink filled a bottle and handed it to Lanie. "That'll be fifty cents. How's your mother doing?"

"Fine." It was the standard answer. Lanie took the change and said, "Let's get a Coke. Mama said we could."

They sat down at the counter on the tall stools made of heavy wire with red leather cushions, and Harold Pink took their order—small cherry Cokes, all around.

Cody went through his so quickly it disappeared as if by magic. When he hit bottom, his straw made a bubbling noise. "I could drink a dozen of these."

"You don't need a dozen," Davis said.

"When I get rich, I'm gonna get a chocolate soda as big as a number-ten washtub," Maeva proclaimed.

The others tried to make their Cokes last. Lanie was aware that Helen was making remarks about "the farmers," as she liked to call the Freemans, and she was not trying to keep her voice down.

Finally Lanie got off her stool, and the rest followed her. Roger called out, "Take your best shot, Lanie! It's me and you for the big money!"

When they got outside, Maeva said, "He's the best-looking guy in high school. Why don't you get a date with him?"

"Are you crazy? Seniors don't date freshmen."

"I don't see why not. You're better lookin' than some of those ugly old girls he goes around with."

"But they've got money," Cody said. "That makes a difference."

"Look, there's Butcher Knife Annie!" Davis whispered.

Across the street, a tall, gaunt woman wearing a dirty gray dress that came down to her ankles was pulling a wagon loaded with junk. She wore men's big work shoes, a dilapidated straw hat, and had a sinister look on her face.

"I heard she was a witch," Cody said.

"And I heard that the mayor was going to pass an ordinance to keep her out of town," Davis said.

"She's not a witch," Lanie said.

"How do you know?" Cody said. "There's somethin' funny about her, the way she lives all by herself in that old shack and keeps all them cats. I bet she sacrifices them or somethin' awful like that."

"Don't be gossiping about people you don't know!" Lanie said crossly. "She's just a poor old woman."

Indeed, Butcher Knife Annie was a mystery in Fairhope. She pulled her wagon down the alleys, filling it with discards from the various businesses. She paid for what few things she bought with coins, some black with age, or with bills rolled up in a tight wad. No one knew where she got her money except that she got a letter from someone once a year. At least so said the postman, Dan McGibbon.

Rumor had it that she once pulled a butcher knife on a man who cursed her, but no one knew for sure.

"I feel sorry for her," Lanie said.

The four watched long enough to draw attention, and when Annie fixed her fierce eyes on them, Cody said, "Come on. Let's get out of here."

<hr />

"That Helen Langley, I'd have popped her in the mouth if Lanie hadn't stopped me."

"You mustn't be doing that, Maeva." Elizabeth reached out and brushed Maeva's rebellious hair back. "You've got to try to understand people's faults."

"I wish I was more like you, Mama. Who am I like?"

"What do you mean, who are you like?"

"Well," Maeva said thoughtfully, "Lanie's so nice and sweet, and I'm mean as a snake."

Elizabeth laughed and reached out and enfolded the girl in her arms. "You're not mean as a snake."

"I am too. I'm always in trouble."

"You have a great deal of imagination and a very strong will. My brother was exactly the same way."

"Barney?"

"That's him."

"Maybe you should have named me Barney after him."

"Well, it would have been fairly cruel to name a helpless little girl baby Barney, wouldn't it?"

Maeva laughed too and said, "Mama, I worry about you."

"You mean because I'm having trouble with this baby?"

"Yes." She gave her mother a direct stare. "You won't die, will you?"

"No, of course not. I'm just a little bit old to be having a baby."

"You promise you won't die?"

"Yes, I promise. Now, why don't you go fix me some iced tea."

⚬════⊷

After a supper of greens, pork chops, and pot likker, Elizabeth sat out on the porch with Forrest. They rocked and watched the children for a while, then she said, "Maeva's worried about me."

"So am I."

"I'll be all right." She took his hand. "We've got good children, Forrest."

While their parents talked, Cody broached his newest scheme to Maeva and Davis. Keeping an eye on his parents, he said, "I seen them pears in Butcher Knife Annie's orchard. They're just right."

"Well, she wouldn't let you have none of 'em," Maeva said. "Though I don't know what she does with so many."

"She sells them to the store," Davis said.

"Well, I'm gonna go get me some of them pears. Let's all three go," Cody said.

"You mean steal 'em?" Maeva grinned.

"Shoot, they're just gonna rot. We might as well have a few."

"I ain't stealing any pears," Davis said, frowning. "You'd better stay away from there too. I don't reckon she's a witch, but she does have a butcher knife."

"I ain't afraid of Butcher Knife Annie," Cody said. "I'm gonna go and get me some of them pears tomorrow afternoon, just about dark."

"I'll go with you," Maeva said. "Davis, you'll go too, if you're not chicken."

Davis could not refuse a dare. He sighed. "I'd better go along then. You two are bound to get into trouble, and I'll have to be there to pull you out."

━⧯ CHAPTER 4 ⧯━

By the time Maeva, Davis, and Cody reached the edge of Butcher Knife Annie's house, twilight had come, and the low hills to the west turned dark against the sky. It seemed to Davis that the sun dropped with a silent crash of light, and he watched as it seemed to melt into a shapeless crown of gold flames on the faraway hills. He turned to the old woman's shack as the pearl shadows came upon the eaves and lit the soft silver shavings of the dusty path beside it. The evening's peace magnified distant sounds, and he heard the melody of a night bird in the far-off woods. He glanced at Cody and Maeva. "This is crazy! Let's go home."

"No, I'm gettin' me some of them pears," Cody said stubbornly.

"You don't even like pears," Davis retorted. "You just want to be up to mischief."

Maeva was smiling broadly. She took Davis by the arm and shook him. "You ain't gonna chicken out on us, are you, brother?"

"It don't make any sense, Maeva."

"It's adventure." Maeva laughed softly and her eyes danced in the last light of the fading sun. She squeezed his arm. "Come on. Bet I'll fill my sack first."

Davis resisted her pull at first, but finally sighed and shook his head. "All right. Let's get it over with." The three of them entered the ragged orchard. The pear trees were, in fact, very fine, much nicer than the house, and he had tasted their fruit before. More than once he had picked up a ripe pear from the ground and sunk his teeth into the white, juicy flesh. But this was different.

The yellow light of a lantern highlighted the windows of the shack and cast its amber glow across the orchard. Davis found himself holding his breath. He was not afraid, for he was the fastest runner in his age group at William McKinley High School (and in the county for that matter!), and he knew that both Maeva and Cody could outrun the old woman. Not fear, but a distaste for what he was doing troubled him. "This is *dumb*!" he muttered, but it was too late to protest.

Cody was already in a tree, and Maeva was scrambling up another like a boy. The fact that she wore a dress meant nothing to her. He caught a flash of the whiteness of her legs as she shinnied up and began filling her sack. "Come on, Davis," she called in a low voice. "Fill that sack up."

Moving forward, Davis reached up and plucked one of the pears from a low limb. It felt firm, just a little soft, as a ripe pear should. He could not see the color, but he knew it would be that beautiful blend of yellow and orange with dark flecks in it. The flour sack he held would hold at least twenty, and he found plenty on the low branches. Finally they grew scarce, so he pulled himself up and edged out along a limb. He had no sooner gotten there when he heard Cody's shrill warning: "Look out! She's comin'!"

Davis was in an awkward position. He had put his feet on two limbs far apart and was reaching upward when he slipped. One hand held the sack, and he grabbed wildly with the other for the trunk of the tree, but his fingertips barely brushed it. He fell on his stomach, and for a moment the breath left him. Fear rushed in as he tried to breathe. He could hear the fleeing footsteps of Cody and Maeva, and Maeva's voice came floating back faintly, "Come on, Davis! Run!"

He struggled to his feet, still grasping the sack in his right hand. He started to turn and saw the figure of the old woman not ten feet away.

Butcher Knife Annie's face was in the shadows. Her bonnet shaded her eyes, yet not completely. Her eyes seemed to gleam like a cat's or a wolf's, and her lips were in a tight line like a blade. She had something in her hand, and alarm ran along Davis's nerves. A knife!

Reacting instinctively, he grabbed a large pear out of his sack and threw it with all of his might. Davis often pitched for his baseball team, and he never threw a baseball harder. He saw it hit the old woman in the mouth and drive her head backward. She dropped what she was holding, and Davis saw it was a bowl of some kind.

Silence. Davis saw by the last rays of light that Annie's bonnet had fallen off, and he could see her face. Her mouth was bleeding. Her eyes were fixed on him, and suddenly he could not bear to look. He turned, dropped the sack of pears, and dashed out of the orchard, his feet barely touching the ground. When he emerged, he turned down the road and had gone no more than thirty yards when he found Cody and Maeva waiting for him. "Did she pull a knife on you?" Cody demanded.

"No."

"What'd she say to you?" Maeva asked, coming closer and looking at Davis's face.

Davis shook his head. "She didn't say nothin'."

Maeva laughed. "That was fun, wasn't it?"

"No, it wasn't fun!"

"Where's your pears?" Maeva demanded. "Why didn't you bring 'em?"

A disgust that Davis had felt a few times in his life thickened in his throat. He was thoroughly ashamed, and without another word he struck off toward home. He did not want to talk to Maeva or Cody, but the two soon caught up with him and pestered him with questions.

Finally Maeva said, "What's wrong with you, Davis? Why ain't you sayin' nothin'?"

"It was a rotten thing to do!" Davis said.

Maeva stared at him, caught his arm, and pulled him to a stop. "What are you talking about? She's a mean old woman. Maybe a witch."

"That's right." Cody nodded. "Those pears would have rotted anyway."

Davis yanked his arm away from Maeva and took off running. He heard them calling, but he ran as if he were in a race at school. The others had no chance to catch him, and he kept accelerating until the sound of their voices faded. All he could think of was the sight of the old woman's face with blood running from her mouth.

Lanie turned off Oak Street down Stonewall Jackson Avenue and found Pardue Jessup sitting inside the small office working a crossword puzzle. He looked up and winked, "Well, howdy there, missy. Say, what's a three-letter word for a canine?"

"Dog."

"A dog is a canine? Well, why don't they just come out and admit that?" Pardue had his feet up on a desk, though there was scarcely room, for it was covered with paper, advertisements, and *Collier's* magazines, and was probably as neat as the rest of the Sinclair station that he operated. To the right was a door that led to the rack where he greased cars, and out in front two or three older cars waited to be repaired.

"Daddy asked me to come by and pick up the carburetor for his Model T."

"It come in on the bus this mornin'. I reckon he can put it in himself." Pardue stood up and scratched his head. He was a tall, well-built man in his mid-thirties. He had the blackest hair that Lanie had ever seen and dark eyes. She had always admired his rough good looks and heard rumors that grown women did too. She had seen him several times at dances, for he could play a fiddle, and at social events he was always either fiddling or dancing.

Pardue was also the sheriff. He was wearing a work shirt now that was fairly clean of grease, but he wore another shirt when he was on duty. It was hanging up in the corner along with the pants to match it. Sometimes he wore his old Sinclair uniform to make arrests, but he never serviced cars in his uniform. "Where you headed for, honey?" Pardue asked, holding the box with the carburetor.

"I'm going down to the library to get some books, and then I'm going home."

"The library?" Pardue's eyebrows shot up, and he grinned broadly. He looked vaguely like a rough sort of Clark Gable with the same kind of dimple in his cheek. "You don't need to be carrying this heavy carburetor. I'll just take you down there myself."

"Why, Sheriff, you don't need to take me. I can carry it."

"No, young folks don't need to be overburdened." Still grinning, Pardue walked over to the door and opened it and said, "Hey, Boo, I'm going to take me a young lady to the library and then home. You watch out they don't steal everything that ain't tied down."

Boo Findley slid out from under a car, covered with black grease. "Why shore, Shurf. I'll take keer of it. Howdy, Miss Lanie."

"Hello, Boo."

Boo had just graduated from high school and was friendly enough, more than most of the older students. "You gonna win that grand prize, ain't cha now?" he grinned.

"I might win one of the little ones, but I don't think the big one."

"Shoot, that ain't no way to talk." Boo smiled. "You can do it. You can beat 'em all."

"Come along, sweetheart. I'll take you down to that library." Pardue grabbed the wide-brimmed straw hat that he often wore and walked out to his car. He drove a big Oldsmobile which he had rebuilt from the ground up after a Yankee from St. Louis wrecked it.

As soon as Lanie was settled, he put the carburetor on the floorboard and said, "Now, let's go to that library. Maybe I'll get a book myself."

"You like to read, Sheriff?"

"Not particularly. I read the sports page every day and the comics. I bet you do, though."

"I like to read all right."

The Oldsmobile exploded to life, and Sheriff Jessup drove like there was no one else on the highway. He roared off down Stonewall Jackson Boulevard to Elm, took a right, and at the end of the block, right next to Robert E. Lee Boulevard, he pulled the Bearcat in front of the red-brick library. "It may take me a while, Sheriff," Lanie said as she got out and started down the walk. The yard was beautifully cultured and tailored with flowers, and she admired it as she always did.

The sheriff caught up with her, and Lanie said, "Are you going inside?"

"Oh, sure. I might catch a criminal in there."

The sheriff opened the door and Lanie walked inside. She saw Miss Pruitt behind the desk. Cassandra Sue Pruitt was in her early thirties, and Lanie had always liked the way she looked. She was perfectly groomed with her dark hair always in place. Today she wore a tailored dress. As Lanie approached, she took off her glasses and smiled. "Hello, Lanie. You've already read those books?"

"Yes, ma'am, I have. I'd like to get some more if you don't mind."

"Why, of course not. You go right ahead."

"I think I might get me a book too," Sheriff Jessup said.

Cassandra Sue Pruitt had to look up at the sheriff, for he was six-two in his stocking feet, and he was wearing boots. She was not a short woman, but she felt somehow fragile in front of the sheriff's broad shoulders and deep chest. "What kind of book would you like, Sheriff?" she said primly.

"I reckon I'd like me a romance book. You probably got lots of them."

A faint flush touched the librarian's cheeks. "Of course, we have all kinds of romances. Do you have any special author?"

"No, to tell the truth, Miss Cassandra, I ain't never read one, but I thought I might ought to. Maybe it'll make me be a little bit more romantic."

"From what I hear, you don't need any lessons."

"Oh, shucks! Now who have you been talkin' to telling stories on me like that?" Sheriff Jessup leaned over the counter until his face was close to the librarian's. "You don't want to listen to all them things. I'm just an innocent boy."

"I . . . I'll get you a book if you wait here."

"I don't mind going with you now."

"No, I'll be right back."

Lanie was fascinated. She had never seen Miss Pruitt disturbed, and something about the big man did bother her. "I think you embarrassed her, Sheriff," she whispered.

"Embarrassed her! Why in the blue-eyed world would she be embarrassed?"

"You know. You asking for a romance book. I don't think she has any romance much in her."

"Well, she ort to. I pure hate to see a fine-lookin' woman wasted." He grinned and winked and looked more like Clark Gable than ever. "I'm gonna ask her to a dance."

Lanie stared at him. "She never goes to dances."

"About time she started then." Pardue Jessup stood a bit straighter as Cassandra walked back and laid the book down on the counter.

"You might like this one. It's romantic, so I hear," she said.

It took Lanie ten minutes to find the books she wanted. When she came out of the stacks, Pardue Jessup was still leaning there against the counter and talking softly, his hands moving expressively. Cassandra Pruitt was listening, fascinated. She was startled when Lanie put the books down.

"Oh! Those are the ones you want!" She stamped the books with the date due and pushed them over toward Lanie, but her eyes were on the sheriff.

"I'm not givin' up on that dance. I'll tell you what. A man gets lonesome around here. Needs company. If I'm gonna start readin' books and be a literary fellow, I'm gonna need some help. How about it, Miss Librarian, would you give a fellow a hand?" He stuck out his big hand, and before Cassandra Pruitt knew what she was doing, she had taken it. Pardue's big hand closed on her hand. He grinned. "You think about it. I'll come by every day to be sure it's on your mind." He looked at Lanie. "You ready to go, sweetie?"

"Yes, sir."

The two walked out of the library, and as they got into the Bearcat, Lanie said, "You can't treat Miss Pruitt like you do other women."

"Why not?"

"Because she's a college graduate."

"Don't they have feelings like other people?"

"Well, I suppose—"

"Shore they do, sweetie."

"But it doesn't make any sense."

"Romance never does make sense. You just don't see enough movies, Lanie."

"I don't get my ideas from the movies."

"That's a good idea." Pardue reached over and squeezed her earlobe and winked at her when she turned around. "Come on. I'll take you and that carburetor home. Maybe I'll even help your pa put it in."

⊶⟢

There was never any question about whether the Freemans would go to church. That issue had been settled before Lanie was born. They went to church every Sunday morning and Sunday night and Wednesday night, and every night during revival meetings, even if they lasted for six weeks.

Ordinarily, Davis rather enjoyed church. He had a fine Sunday school teacher. Matthew Sixkiller was the town veterinarian and a full-blooded Cherokee Indian. He had played semi-pro baseball and was the best hunter and fisherman in the entire state as far as anyone could tell. He was also the best Sunday school teacher Davis ever had, for he could make the Bible come alive. On this particular morning, Davis wished Mr. Sixkiller wasn't quite so good at it.

"The lesson this morning is taken from the book of Joshua. You remember last Sunday we studied how Joshua defeated the men of Jericho. How many of you remember how he won that battle?"

"By tootin' horns," Cody said eagerly. "They walked around the city and tooted on their trumpets until the walls fell down."

A smile creased the face of Mr. Sixkiller, and he nodded. "That's right. Well, this morning I'm going to read to you from the seventh chapter of the book of Joshua. Get your Bibles out."

Davis's Bible had been a gift from his mother and was signed by her on the front page. He followed along as Mr. Sixkiller read the story, and then he heard a serious note in the teacher's voice.

"You fellows see what happened?"

"They got whupped!" Cody piped up.

"That's right. After defeating a big city and a powerful army within walls, the Israelites took a pounding. Do any of you know why?" He waited and looked around and then said, "It's in the first verse. 'But the children of Israel committed a trespass in the accursed thing: for Achan, the son of Carmi, the son of Zabdi, the son of Zerah, of the tribe of Judah, took of the accursed thing: and the anger of the LORD was kindled against the children of Israel.'"

Benny Oz, the son of Harry Oz, who owned the hardware store, said, "What's the accursed thing, Mr. Sixkiller?"

"God had told them not to take anything from Jericho, which He destroyed utterly, but this man Achan disobeyed God, and you heard the story. He hid it in his tent, buried it I suppose. And you know, boys, Achan probably thought, 'Well, it's gonna be all right. Nobody knows about it. I'm gonna make it fine.' But as we've heard, he didn't. I heard a preacher once preach on this in a sermon called 'The Curse of Hidden Sins.' It scared me half to death."

"What sin did you have hidden?" Cody asked.

Mr. Sixkiller grinned. "That's my business and God's, but it really doesn't matter. The fact is you can hide your sins from your daddy or your mama. You can hide 'em from the sheriff, maybe, but you can't hide 'em from God."

The lesson continued until finally Achan and his sons and his daughters were taken, and Mr. Sixkiller read how the people stoned him and then buried him with stones, along with all of his sons and daughters and everything he had.

"That's a pretty rough deal," Buddy Stockwell said. "To kill 'em just for takin' somethin'."

"It's not about how big a thing you take, Buddy," Mr. Sixkiller said quietly. "It's about disobeying God. When you steal a dollar, you're in the same class as Al Capone, who steals millions of dollars. I want you boys to listen to this. If you've got a sin hidden in your life, sooner or later it's gonna hurt you. You know what a time bomb is?"

"Sure, I seen one in the movies. It's got a clock attached. You set it and when it reaches whatever time you set, it goes off," Cody said.

"That's right. If you've got a hidden sin, something that you know is wrong before God, your clock is ticking. And one of these days it'll blow up."

Buddy said, "What do you do about it?"

"Get it out of your life. If you harm somebody, confess it to 'em. Ask for their forgiveness. Don't do it anymore. That's what's called repentance, and that's what I'd like for you boys to get out of this lesson."

The bell rang soon after, and Davis left with the others to sit with his family in the sanctuary. During the song service, Davis sang mechanically. His mind wasn't on it. Nor did he hear a word of the sermon. All he could think of was that time bomb inside of him, about to blow him up.

⊷⊷

Lanie stared at Davis. He had told her to meet him behind the barn. She had never seen him so troubled. His lips trembled as he told her about stealing the fruit and hitting Butcher Knife Annie with a pear, and she suddenly had an insight.

"You didn't go alone, did you, Davis?"

Davis looked down at the ground and refused to answer.

"Maeva and Cody were with you, weren't they?"

"They didn't force me to go. But I feel terrible. Mr. Sixkiller talked about what happens when you do wrong things and try to cover 'em up." Davis looked up, and Lanie saw the pain in his eyes. "I can't stand it, Lanie," he whispered. "I just can't stand it!"

"Well, you don't have to," Lanie said.

"But what can I do?"

"I'll tell you what we can do," Lanie said. "I baked a chocolate cake for supper tonight, but we're not eating that cake. You and me and Maeva and Cody are going over, and we're going to give it to Annie."

Davis stared at her for a long time and then nodded. "That's what we'll do, Lanie, and I'll tell her how sorry I am. Cody and Maeva maybe won't want to go."

"That's up to them," Lanie said firmly. "You and I'll go, and they can come if they want to."

⊷⊷

As the four Freeman youngsters approached Annie's house, Maeva grunted, "I don't know why we're having to do this."

"Because what we done was a rotten thing to do!" Davis snapped. "Now hush up or leave!"

Cody had not said a word since agreeing to come. He looked nervously at Lanie, who was carrying the cake draped with a thin towel. "I don't wanna do this, Lanie."

"Then leave," Lanie said.

Cody looked at Maeva, who sniffed at him. "Go on if you're scared! I'm gonna face up to her. I ain't afraid of her nor her butcher knife neither."

"She doesn't have a butcher knife!" Lanie said. "That's all gossip. Now come on!"

They approached the house, but there was no sign of Annie.

"Maybe she ain't home," Cody whispered. "We can come back later."

Ignoring him, Lanie knocked on the door. She heard someone moving inside, and then the door opened. Annie stood before them dressed in the same dress that it seemed she always wore. She didn't say one word but stared at the four children.

"Miss Annie," Lanie said, "my brother Davis has something to say to you if you don't mind."

"What is it?" The old woman's voice seemed creaky like a hinge that needed oiling. She stared at Davis, and her face was set in a stern frown.

"Miss Annie, I . . . I want to tell you," Davis said, forcing the words out, "I'm right sorry for what I done. I'm sorry I stole your pears, and I'm sorry I hit you with one of them. If you want to hit me back, it'll be all right with me. But I had to say I'm sorry."

The four Freeman youngsters scarcely breathed. Annie was glaring at them almost wildly. Maeva stepped forward and said, "I'm sorry too, Miss Annie. I shouldn't have stole them pears. I'm sorry, and I'll do anything you want to make it right."

"Me too," Cody said quickly. "If you need some work done around here, you just tell us what it is, and we'll do it."

"That's right," Lanie said. She held the cake out and smiled at the old woman. "I baked this cake, and all of us want you to have it. I'm not the best cook in the world, but I think it's fairly good."

Annie stared at them and something changed in her expression. They saw her lips move slightly, and then she said, "What you doin' this for?"

It was Davis who answered. "Miss Annie, that was a rotten thing I did. I . . . I wish you'd hit me with a stick of stove wood! It'd make me feel better."

"Ain't no need for that. What do you want?"

Davis swallowed hard and looked down at his feet for a moment, then he looked up and said, "I guess, Miss Annie, I just want us to be friends."

Butcher Knife Annie stared at the four children, and for a moment Lanie thought she was going to scream and run them off. But she smiled. There was snuff in the corners of her mouth, and she was dirty and wearing clothes that should have been thrown away. Yet there was something strange and wonderful in the smile that came to her thin lips.

"I reckon I'd like that cake. Maybe you young'uns can come in and help me eat it."

Davis took a deep breath and said with a shaky voice, "Be right proud to, Miss Annie, and after that we'll figure out some way to work out what we done."

Lanie walked inside. There were cats everywhere. "You must love cats, Miss Annie."

"People dump 'em off here. I can't let 'em starve."

"I've got a cat. His name's Cap'n Brown."

"I got me eighteen of 'em now. I'll have some more when that 'un there has kittens."

The smell of the place was terrible, but the four Freeman children ate the cake, which Annie cut with a butcher knife. As she was cutting it, she saw them watching her. "That's right. This is the butcher knife I use. They call me Butcher Knife Annie, but I don't mind. I been called worse."

Lanie saw Annie's loneliness, and tears came to her eyes. She silently made a vow that the old woman would never be lonely again.

⚬══✦══

Lanie put her pen down and reread the poem she had written. For several days she had thought of Butcher Knife Annie and finally decided to write a poem about what happened. Though she wasn't there when Davis hit the old woman with the pear, Lanie had the gift of putting herself inside other people. Why, she'd even written a poem from the point of view of Cap'n Brown trying to catch a mouse!

She'd seen the guilt in Davis's eyes and tried to write a poem that expressed his feelings. Now she read it aloud, whispering the words softly so no one could hear.

Butcher Knife Annie lived in a tar paper shack
With cats inside and pear trees in the back.
    Every day she combed the alleys, filling
     A warped red wagon with empty bottles, spilling
Juices on its wobbly track.

She swapped at Kroger's for snuff and day-old bread,
Stopped at Bell's for a fifth of Dago Red,
    Then shuffled back to her cats and trees, weaving
     A bit from either wine or age, breathing
Heavily, plodding toward her flimsy shed.

One memory of Annie presses on me hard—
That day one spring I broke into her yard
    And started eating stolen fruit, squeezing
     Juicy nectar from sweet pears—freezing
When Annie came and caught me off my guard.

Mindless with guilt and fear, I seized a pear,
With all my might I heaved it hard and fair.
    It struck her mouth, she gave one cry—then stood
     Without a word, and so did I—like wood.
The world was mute. Just she and I alone.

In that wink of time, I saw her eyes
And knew a loneliness without disguise
    Then for the first time in my life I wept
     For another than myself—then swept
Away—but still in dreams I see old Annie's eyes.

Lanie stared at the poem, then whispered, "I can never show this to anyone. It would shame Davis." She put it with the other poems she'd written about the people in her life, hid the notebook under her mattress, then got into bed and went to sleep.

☙ CHAPTER 5 ❧

Elizabeth moved clumsily across the room and felt a wave of discouragement. This pregnancy was different from her others. It seemed all four of her children had been born with great ease. Of course eleven years had passed since Cody's arrival, and memories of the pain and discomfort of childbirth faded, as hard things sometimes do. Still, she could not remember having difficulties as she had now.

She heard the sound of a vehicle approaching and, moving carefully, went over to the window. Her eyes widened with surprise when she saw Forrest drive up in the log truck. It was not loaded, and she wondered if something was wrong. He usually worked like a machine, not stopping until he delivered a certain number of logs to the mill. She watched as he leaped out of the door and ran for the house. He appeared excited but not disturbed.

He's like a little boy getting excited about things.

She turned and heard him bound up the porch steps, open the screen door, and let it slam behind him, and then he appeared, his eyes bright and his ball cap pushed back on his head.

"What is it, Forrest?"

He walked over to her in long strides, smiling. He put his arms around her, handling her gently as if she were a precious treasure, and then kissed her. "I've got a surprise for you."

Whenever Forrest got excited, his eyes seemed to dance, and he could not keep still. His feet were twitching even now, and he patted her back as he held her. "Come on over here and sit down. What are you doing up anyway?"

"I get tired of lying down and sitting down."

Even so, she allowed him to walk her over to the couch and ease her down, and then he plopped himself down beside her. He leaned forward so he could look into her face and said, "I've been working on something. I didn't want to tell you about it until it happened, but by golly it's come true now!"

"What's come true?"

"I've been thinkin' for a long time, Elizabeth, about how we're not gettin' anywhere."

"We're doing all right! We haven't missed a meal yet."

"No, but we had to postpone one or two. The kids are growing up, and they're going to be more expensive, so I've been thinkin' of a way that we could better ourselves."

"What is it? You're not thinking of getting out of the logging business, are you?"

"No, I'm thinkin' of getting into it bigger."

"Bigger? In what way?"

"Well, I've been doing all right with the one truck, but it's about had it, Elizabeth. You know I have to spend as much time working on it as I do using it. What I need is some new equipment. So I went in and talked to Mr. Langley about those big tracts of first-growth timber over by Elmore. He owns a lot of land over there, and I heard a rumor that he was gonna start logging it. Well, there'll be a lot of fellas tryin' to get that job, but I went to see him this morning. I walked right into his office and asked to see him."

Elizabeth saw that Forrest was proud of himself. She took his hand and held it. "What did he say? And what did you say? Now, don't just tell me the headlines like men do. I want the fine print."

"Well, I'll give you the headline first. I've got the job of cutting most of that timber, but it's a big job, and I'm going to have to have at least two trucks and hire some extra men."

"But that will take a lot of money, won't it, Forrest?"

"Yep, it will. We're gonna have to borrow. But it's the chance of a lifetime!"

Elizabeth was glad to see the excitement in her husband's eyes. He had always been this way, excited about opportunities, whether small or large, and his eagerness had drawn her to him in the first place.

But she was the cautious one, and now she said gently, "But where are we going to get the money to do all that?"

"I'm going into the bank to borrow it tomorrow. Too late today."

"But this seems like a bad time for a thing like this."

Forrest lifted his eyebrows with surprise. "A bad time? No, it's a great time! This opportunity is right before us, sweetheart, and I need to grab it. I may never get another chance to get into the big time."

Elizabeth kept her tone gentle. "But things are so unsteady. There's something in the paper almost every day about the market going up and then coming down. No one knows what's going to happen."

"No matter what happens to those stocks and bonds, we're going to need lumber, and I can make enough in a year if I get more equipment and hire some good men. I could pay it off quick and then I'll have money to do some things for you."

"I don't need anything. Really."

"Don't need anything?! Why, you need one of those new gas cookstoves," Forrest said. "I'm tired of watchin' you struggle with all those heavy chunks of wood."

"You know I don't mind that."

"I know you don't, but I hate to see you have to work so hard. And like I said, the kids are going to need things too. Clothes for school, and first thing you know, Lanie'll be needing to go to college, and we couldn't afford to send her the way things are." He squeezed her hand. "It's gonna be great, Elizabeth, you'll see."

Elizabeth saw that he was caught up with the thing. "Maybe we need to think about it, not rush into it."

"There are two more guys waiting to jump on this contract with Mr. Langley. First come, first served."

Weariness settled over Elizabeth. Fatigue was not a familiar part of her life. She worked hard, bore her children, and had always been blessed with strength, but this child she carried sapped all her energy. She smiled as best she could and put her hand on Forrest's cheek. "Well, I see you want to do this thing. We'll just pray that it will work out."

"It'll work out," Forrest said. "Now where's Lanie?"

"I think she's outside gathering vegetables."

"I'm going to tell her about this. And I'm going to take her to the bank with me tomorrow."

"To the bank?"

"Yes. I want to start doing more things with the kids."

Forrest jumped up and left the room, and Elizabeth watched him go, not sure Forrest's plan was the right thing to do.

School lasted for an eternity, or so it seemed to Lanie. She wore her best dress, and many people noticed. Victor Sixkiller, the vet's son, grinned at her, his teeth white against his copper skin. "You look all dressed up to go to a funeral, Lanie. What's the occasion?"

"My daddy's taking me out to eat at the restaurant. We're going out to do some business," she said importantly.

Victor's eyes widened. "The only time my dad lets me help him is to clean up the mess there at his office."

In English class, Miss Dunsmore stared at her for a moment and then smiled. "You look so pretty, Lanie. Is that a new dress?"

"Oh, no, I've had it a while. I'm leaving school at noon today. Daddy and I are going to do some things and then going out to eat together."

"That's wonderful! Is it a reward of some kind?"

"No, he said it was because I've worked so hard all this year."

"Well, he's exactly right. You have worked hard."

Helen Langley rolled her eyes at Lanie but said nothing about her dress. Her brother Roger looked at Lanie and winked. "You're lookin' good today, Lanie."

"Thank you, Roger."

"You still pushing me with those grades? Now, you don't want to beat me for the grand award. It wouldn't look right for a freshman to beat a senior." He saw Lanie's smile disappear and he laughed. "That's all right. You do your best, Lanie."

She finally got through her classes and at noon went outside, where her father was waiting. "I cleaned up the seat of the old truck so it wouldn't get your dress dirty," he said as she got in. "Try to look as smart as you can because we've got to convince Miss Effie to let us have a bunch of money."

"Do you think she will?"

"We won't know until we try, but I think we've got a good chance."

Planter's Bank was located on the corner of North Bedford Forest Avenue and Main Street. The sturdy-looking red-brick building had been built right after the Civil War. It stood opposite the town square and the courthouse.

As the two of them entered, Lanie looked around the bank. Along one side of the open floor was a row of tellers' cages, each shielded by a thin grillwork. To the right were tall tables, containing inkwells and pens. Several desks for the loan officers sat to the left. A door had a placard on it that said "President."

"Hello, Lanie." Lanie turned to see Cora Johnson smiling at her. She was sitting at one of the desks and got up at once. "It's so good to see you."

"Hello, Miss Johnson." Cora Johnson was once Lanie's Sunday school teacher, and Lanie had always liked her. Cora was the younger sister of the bank's president, Effie Johnson. Their father died when Cora was just a baby, and Effie took over the bank and kept it running.

"How are you, Mr. Freeman?"

"Fine. We'd like to see Miss Effie if she's not busy."

"I don't think she is. Let me go check."

Cora walked to the back. She was an attractive woman of thirty-five with light brown hair and soft brown eyes. Lanie had always envied Cora's beautiful complexion, but not the ugly clothes that hid the woman's trim figure.

Cora soon returned. "Come in, Mr. Forrest, and you too, Lanie."

The two entered, and Cora closed the door behind them. "Howdy, Miss Effie," Forrest said. "I see you know my oldest girl, Lanie."

"Of course I do. I see her every Sunday at church." Effie Johnson was a tall woman, gaunt and stern. She had steel gray hair, and her eyes were sharp and quick. She was all business as a rule. She was also a staunch Baptist. If she had been a man, she would have been a deacon, but since Baptists didn't allow women to be deacons, she pretty well managed church things without any office. She was on every committee, and because she was smarter than most of the men, she usually got what she wanted. It was fortunate for the church that she was a good woman, always on the side of right. "I hear you're setting records at school, Lanie. I'm always glad to hear that."

"Thank you, Miss Johnson. I'm trying hard."

A rare smile touched Effie Johnson's face. "All of us at the church are very proud of you. Hope you win the grand award."

Then Effie's face resumed its stern expression. She motioned for them to sit. "What can I do for you today, Brother Freeman?"

Forrest began nervously. He twisted his hat around in his big hands and talked, describing his good opportunity. When he had laid it all out, he said, "So I need to borrow enough money to buy some new equipment and to hire some new hands. It's really a great opportunity, Miss Effie."

"Well, Brother Freeman, this is not the best time to plunge into a new venture. You've read the papers. Things are very unsteady in the business world."

"Yes, ma'am, I know that, but this is a sure thing. You know Mr. Langley. He's not going to let anything bad happen. Those trees are solid enough, and there's always going to be a market for lumber. Mr. Langley wouldn't be paying to cut them down if he didn't think he could sell the timber."

"I'm sure Mr. Langley knows his business, but as I see it, he's not risking anything, and you would be risking almost everything."

"I don't understand you, Miss Effie."

"Well, this is a large sum of money you're talking about. Do you have any collateral?"

"Just my place."

"But that could be dangerous. You could lose it. You've got about five acres there, haven't you?"

"Yes, ma'am, that's right."

"Why don't you sell it all off except the lot that your house is on? The town is expanding that way. You could chop it into lots and sell them off individually."

Forrest's discomfort showed in his hat, now nearly wrung into uselessness. "I don't think I'd care to do that, ma'am. You see, that's the last of the plantation that my great-grandpa owned. He had to start sellin' it off after the war, and now all we've got left of it is the five acres."

Effie Johnson studied the man and the girl. She knew the family well. They were good people, and it was for this reason she hesitated. She knew the world of business and was disturbed about the economic winds blowing across the country. No one in Fairhope knew better than she how fragile was the structure that held the economic side of America together. Finally she said, "I would advise against this, Brother Freeman. Things could turn very bad."

Forrest looked down at his feet, and when he looked up, anxiety creased his face. "I would appreciate it if you would help me with this, Miss Effie. A fellow like me doesn't have many chances, and this is the only one that I see comin' my way."

Effie Johnson sighed. "Very well. I'll have the papers drawn up. I'll have the survey done on your property. You'll have to sign a paper, and you know that if you can't make your payments, we would have to take action. It's not something I'd like to do, especially with a fellow believer, but I'm responsible to the depositors."

"You won't have to worry about that," Forrest said with relief. "We can do it! I'm a hard worker, Miss Effie, you know that."

"I know that, Brother Freeman, otherwise I wouldn't even consider the loan. Well, come back tomorrow, and I'll have the papers ready. I think I can get Mr. Bruten to do the survey. It's a simple enough matter."

"I sure do thank you, ma'am. I really do."

"I hope I'm doing you a favor," Effie said. She rose and extended her hand. Her hand was swallowed by Forrest's, and she felt the strength and the hardness of his palm. *Lord, I hope I'm doing the right thing.* "You keep up the good work, Lanie. I'm very proud of you."

"Thank you, ma'am," Lanie said.

Forrest and Lanie left the office. "Everything go all right?" Cora asked from her desk.

"Just fine." Forrest smiled down at her. "Me and this girl are going to go into business in a big way."

"I'm glad to hear it." Cora smiled, and her whole face lit up.

The Dew Drop Inn occupied the corner of Robert E. Lee Avenue and Main Street. Windows lined two sides and red-and-white-checkered cloths covered the tables. As it was the only place to eat in Fairhope, it did a brisk business.

Forrest and Lanie were greeted by Myrtle Poindexter—Sister Myrtle as she was called by everyone in Fairhope, a title given to her as pastor of the Fire Baptized Pentecostal Church on the edge of town. She was a big woman with leather lungs who greeted strangers with, "Well, sister or brother, have you been saved, sanctified, and filled with the Holy Ghost?"

Many first-time visitors to the Dew Drop Inn were shocked beyond bounds, but none of this troubled Sister Myrtle.

"Well, praise God, praise the Lord O my soul, if it ain't Brother Forrest and Sister Lanie! Come in and set down and tell me what the good Lord's done for you today."

Forrest grinned and said, "The Lord's been real good to us today, Sister Myrtle. I'm bringin' this pretty young lady out to celebrate."

"Well, you set yourselves down right here." Sister Myrtle's voice filled the café so that the other customers were part of the conversation whether they joined in or not.

"Howdy, Forrest!" Charlie Poindexter came out of the kitchen wearing a white apron and a St. Louis Cardinals baseball cap. "What's happenin'?" Charlie, a thin man with long legs and arms, was a fine cook. He and Myrtle started the café with her doing the cooking and him waiting on tables, but that didn't last long, for she was a notoriously terrible cook.

"Howdy, Charlie. Just doing some celebrating. We want the best you got today."

"You name it, and I'll cook it."

"Praise God, the special is good today," Sister Myrtle said. "Roast beef, mashed potatoes and gravy, and green beans and squash."

"How does that sound, Lanie?" Forrest said.

"Good, Daddy."

"We'll have that then and some big red soda pops."

Forrest carried on a conversation with Sheriff Jessup, seated at the next table. When Forrest mentioned that he was getting new vehicles, Jessup winked and said, "Well, you won't have to put an ad in the paper. Everything that's said in this place gets told around. I wonder who does all that gossipin'?"

Sister Myrtle came out with two large red Nehi sodas and plunked them down on the table in front of Forrest and Lanie harder than usual. She glanced at the sheriff and said, "I wouldn't be castin' no stones about gossipin' if I was you, Pardue! You got a tongue long enough to sit in the livin' room and lick the skillet back in the kitchen."

Pardue laughed. "I reckon you're right about that, Sister. Reckon if I come over to your church you can straighten me out?"

Sister Myrtle's eyes gleamed. She walked over and put her heavy hand on Pardue's shoulder. "We can get you sanctified in no time, young man. A law enforcement officer ought to be a sanctified feller."

"Why, I think I'm a pretty good Christian."

Sister Myrtle sniffed. "Pride goeth before a fall. You think I don't know about you carryin' on with Minnie Sellings?"

"We're just good friends." Pardue winked again at Forrest, who was amused by the conversation.

"Good friends my foot! Don't you know the Bible says that a strange woman leads a man straight down into the pit?"

All the customers were, at that point, subjected to a sermon on the horrors of strange women and what they could do to men. She made several trips to the kitchen to bring out food, but when she stepped into the kitchen, she simply raised her voice.

"She can holler loud enough to make your hair fall out," Sheriff Jessup said, smiling.

"Good woman," Forrest said.

"Yes, she is. Need more like her."

Forrest and Lanie enjoyed their meal. Such outings were rare for the Freeman family, and Forrest said once, "When our ship really comes in, we're going to eat out, the whole bunch of us, once a week, right here."

"The other kids won't like it that you've brought just me here today."

"I'm going to do something fun with all the others too. It's my New Year's resolution."

"But it's not New Year's. It's only May."

"I know, but I'm making mine early. I'm going to take Davis to St. Louis to see the Cardinals play. Then I'm going to take Maeva to that circus in Fort Smith. I'll have to go over there to pick up a new truck anyway, and then Cody and me will go on an overnight campin' trip."

"But can we afford all that, Daddy?"

"I'll tell you, honey, the good times are just about to start."

Charlie brought in two dishes of fresh strawberries. "I think you're gonna like this," he said. "I'm doin' it different. It's my own special way of servin' strawberry shortcake."

"What's this?" Forrest asked.

"Them long strips is pie crust. Crumble 'em up in that bowl and dump you some of these juicy strawberries in there. Let the juice kind of saturate and swish around. Then you put a big dollop of whipped cream right on top of it."

Lanie and her father followed the instructions, and when Lanie tasted her first bite, she cried out, "This is so good, Mr. Charlie!"

"Strawberries ain't fit to eat no other way but with pie crust broke up like that," Charlie announced. "So you're gettin' into the big time, buyin' more trucks. That right, Forrest?"

"Yep, that's it."

"But don't that take a lot of money?"

"Already taken care of. Lanie and me just arranged a loan with Miss Effie down at the Planter's Bank."

Sister Myrtle came to stand over the two eating their strawberries. "Brother, have you fasted and prayed about gettin' into this business?"

"Why, I figure it's an opportunity."

Sister Myrtle frowned. "I don't hold with borrowing money."

"You have to borrow money to make money, Sister Myrtle," Forrest protested.

"Well, I won't meddle," Sister Myrtle said.

"Won't meddle!" Charlie stared at her and laughed out loud. "Why, you meddle all the time!"

"I'd like to know when."

"You've been meddlin' with me ever since you first talked me into marryin' you."

All the men in the café laughed, and Sister Myrtle's face turned red. "You chased me for a year before I'd even let you set on my front porch, Charlie Poindexter! Now, you behave!"

"Well, I will, but you meddle all the time."

Sister Myrtle's face assumed a pious look. "Maybe I do, but it's for their own good. Now, get back in the kitchen. I'll handle these customers."

Forrest was gone most of the time during the month of May, busy with two new trucks, hired hands, and Otis Langley's lumber. But he came in early on May 26, graduation night at McKinley High School.

Despite Lanie's protests, everyone was certain that she would win the scholar's award for the freshman class, so they all washed and put on their best clothes. Elizabeth could not go, but she insisted that Forrest not stay home with her.

The Freemans happened to reach the front doors of the high school at the same time as the Langley family did. Mr. Langley was a big man with brown hair and dark eyes. "Hello, Forrest," he said. "That cutting is going good, isn't it?"

"Yes, sir, it sure is."

Langley looked down at Lanie. "I hear you're quite a scholar, young lady."

"She sure is, Dad." Roger Langley said. He grinned. "She's the smartest kid in school."

"Now, Roger," Mr. Langley said, "I'd never forgive you if you let a freshman beat you, but I hope you win the freshman award, young lady."

They all walked in, and Roger rushed off to put on his robe. The Freemans took their seats, and Lanie had a hard time sitting still. Some of her classmates came over to whisper that she was sure to win, but their confidence did not calm her.

Finally the graduating seniors marched in wearing bright red gowns and mortarboards. The ceremony commenced with songs and speeches that seemed to go on forever before the principal, Silas Pringle, said, "We are now going to have the awards for the various classes. The winner of each class will receive a monetary award and a cup. The first award is for the freshman class." He looked down at the paper in his hand and then smiled and hesitated for a moment.

Lanie was clenching her hands tightly together.

Mr. Pringle looked out at the audience. "And the winner is—Lanie Belle Freeman!"

Applause broke out, and Lanie could hardly breathe for a moment. She felt her dad's hand on her back patting her and he said, "Get up, honey. Go get that award."

Lanie got out of the seat and walked down the center aisle. The walk seemed like a hundred miles, and when she took the small cup and the check from Mr. Pringle, he said, "Say a few words, Lanie."

Lanie turned around and almost had difficulty speaking. "I want to thank my parents, who helped me, and my teachers, who helped me too. Thank you very much."

She went back and took her seat. Cody grabbed at the cup, and she let him have it. He read the inscription: "'Prize Scholar, Freshman Class.'" Davis and Maeva pulled at the cup then, and Lanie felt her father's hand on her neck, squeezing it gently, and heard him say, "I'm so proud of you I could bust, and your mama will be too!"

The awards for the other classes—sophomore, junior, and senior— were given out. Roger Langley was the senior class winner.

Then it was time for the big moment. "And now, the grand award for the best scholar at William McKinley High School for the year 1928. This award is based on two things. One is grade-point average, and the other is character. The faculty of William McKinley High School recognizes that both of these are important." He took the envelope from the school coach, opened it, and said, "No one except the faculty knows who the winner is, not even I." He pulled out a slip of paper. For a moment he seemed stunned, and then he looked out over the audience. "And the winner is Lanie Belle Freeman of the freshman class!"

There were two kinds of cries then, cries of disappointment from the losers and cries of excitement from the freshman class, and it was

Maeva who yelled, "That's the way to go, Lanie!" her voice rising above the applause.

Once again Lanie's legs barely carried her up to the stage to receive the reward. She shook Mr. Pringle's hand, took the big cup in her left hand and held the check in her right. She knew she was expected to make some sort of speech. "I've already said how much I owe to my family and to my teachers. I don't think I can say anything more than that, but I want to thank especially Miss Dunsmore, who encouraged me every day of the school year. The other teachers, too, have been so good to me." Tears came to her eyes and she choked up. "Thank you." She looked out at the audience and her eyes fell on Mr. Langley, who was pale and obviously angry. For some reason this frightened her. She had to walk past the seniors who were lined up on the stage, and suddenly someone was standing in front of her. Roger Langley was smiling at her and he put out his hand. "Congratulations, Lanie. You deserve it."

A round of applause went up as Roger made his gracious acknowledgment, and Lanie whispered, "Thank you, Roger," and went back to her seat.

The rest of the evening passed in a blur. The seniors received their diplomas, and Lanie remained stunned by her achievement. As the family filed out, they saw Mr. Langley, his face drawn tight into a scowl, talking to Roger. Maeva whispered, "Look, Old Man Langley doesn't like it that you beat his boy. He looks mad as a hornet."

"I wish he wouldn't be that way," Lanie said. She walked out with her family and tried to put Mr. Langley out of her mind. She focused instead on Roger, who brought her a warm feeling. It must have hurt him to lose to a girl, and a freshman at that, but he had been so sweet.

CHAPTER 6

Ten more minutes until closing, Effie Johnson thought as she looked out the window of her office. She thought about how she and her sister would spend the next day at the county fair and sighed. Effie didn't particularly enjoy going to the fair, but Cora loved their Independence Day tradition. Effie had to admit that she took secret joy in the fact that Cora always took awards in the baked and canned goods competitions she entered. *She has more ribbons than we do customers!*

Once again Effie sighed. *I hope we still own the bank next year.* Effie was fifty-five years old and had never married. Over the years she had plenty of suitors, but none that could reach the standard her father had encouraged her to set for herself. "Better to not be married than to be in a bad marriage," he always told Effie. Unfortunately, he died young. With a heart already weakened by rheumatic fever, his wife's death in childbirth was too much for his frail body.

Effie moved to the window and caught a reflection of herself. She took no pride in her appearance, and as she stood there, bitter memories overcame her. She remembered the one man she had loved—Harold Simms. She was delirious with joy until she learned from a distant relative how Harold bragged that he was only after her money. When she confronted him, he shouted, "You think any man would marry you except for money?" He struck her in the face. A few days later he left town. Effie's face healed, but her spirit was broken and she swore off men.

Effie caught sight of Forrest hurrying across the street toward the bank. She liked his family. She stepped back from the window, checked her hair and dress in a mirror, and sat down at her desk, as if she were terribly busy.

"Howdy, Miss Johnson!" Forrest said as he entered the office.

Effie stood and nodded a greeting as he walked over to her desk. "Have a seat, Brother Freeman. Can I get you a glass of sweet tea?"

"Miss Johnson, I'd like a glass, but I promised Elizabeth and the kids I'd be home right soon."

Effie smiled, "I understand." She sat down in her chair and motioned to Forrest to sit down. "When's that baby due?"

"'Bout another month. Elizabeth's had a mighty hard time. Between the swelling and the headaches and . . ."

"And what?"

"And the bleeding."

"Oh my."

"Yes, ma'am. Sometimes it's right heavy. But the doc says there's nothing to do but pray about it and keep her at bed rest as much as possible."

"Well, Brother Freeman, rest assured that you and your family have been and will be in our prayers."

"Thank you, ma'am. Elizabeth and me both need your prayers. I've been working mighty hard to get some money put aside, but it's not easy with Langley."

"What's the matter with Mr. Langley?" Effie considered it her business to know of matters involving the bank's board chairman.

Forrest seemed to weigh his response. "Well . . . I don't really know where to begin, but to be frank, Langley is making my life miserable."

"I'm sorry to hear that."

"Yes, ma'am. Well, I just wanted to bring by this month's payment." Forrest pulled a wad of bills from his pocket.

Effie counted the money and wrote a receipt for Forrest. "Brother Freeman, I must be careful what I say." Effie lowered her voice so Forrest had to lean in to hear her. "Let me warn you. Don't fail in your payments. Don't even miss one! Mr. Langley is a proud and arrogant man, and he cannot bear to be crossed. Even though he attends the Presbyterian Church, it doesn't seem to make any difference."

"I *can* make the payments, Miss Johnson, and I will!" Forrest quickly stood, walked to the door, and then left the bank. Effie slowly shook her head as her eyes filled with tears. *I wish I had never made that loan to Forrest. I may end up being responsible for his downfall.*

As Forrest approached his house, he heard a voice shouting at him from across the street. "Hey, Freeman!"

Deoin Jinks stepped off his porch and walked toward him. "Glad I caught you, Forrest. Me and Agnes are taking the kids to the county fair tomorrow. There are going to be some new rides, and the city is putting on a spectacular fireworks display. Me and the missus would love to take your kids with us, if that would be okay with you."

Forrest liked Deoin, but he was never one to be a burden to others. "I appreciate your invitation, Deoin, but it might be better for the children to be with their mama."

Deoin threw his head back in laughter. "Forrest, you old hardhead! You *know* your kids would love to go to the fair. Max and Cody enjoy the rides and the girls get pleasure from the crafts and cooking, and since we're already planning on going, it'll be no trouble at all."

Forrest wasn't sure how to respond. Before he could say another word, Deoin said, "Besides, Forrest, I cut the fair manager's hair, and he gives me a handful of free passes. If you don't let me take your kids, then those passes are just going to go to waste. A good Christian man like you wouldn't want me to squander a gift, would you?"

Now it was Forrest's turn to smile. The barber had him. "Well, Deoin, I suspect the children would enjoy the day, and I sure wouldn't mind some quiet time with Elizabeth. Are you sure it's no trouble?"

Deoin smiled. "Trouble? You kiddin' me? Agnes and I love your kids like they were our own. It'll be a great day. How about you send the kids over to our house just after lunch, and we'll have them home after the fireworks."

"You're a good friend, Deoin. Thanks."

Deoin lowered his head. "Forrest, the folks at our church have been praying for you and Elizabeth. We know the pregnancy has been real hard on Elizabeth and you, and I just want you to know we're praying."

Forrest could only whisper "Thanks," then quickly turned and walked toward his home.

❦

As they approached the fairgrounds, the children's excitement grew. By the time Deoin parked his Oldsmobile, they were bubbling with anticipation. The boys wanted to run ahead, but Deoin made them walk. As they approached the gate, he said, "Come here, kids, and listen up." As the children gathered around him, he dispensed their marching orders. "We'll meet back at the gate right after the fireworks. When that last firework goes off, you each best be heading right for this exit gate. Okay?" The children all nodded their heads. "Davis, you're in charge of Cody and Max. Your job is to be with them at all times and to keep them out of trouble. All right?"

Davis nodded. "Yes, sir."

"Lanie, I want you to be in charge of the girls."

"Why not *me*, Pa?" complained Alice.

"'Cause Lanie is the oldest."

"But only by three hours," Alice protested.

Deoin smiled. "Okay, Alice, you *and* Lanie will be in charge of Maeva. You all stick together at all times. I don't want you separating for any reason. Understood?"

The three girls nodded. "Now, let me give you the passes for the admission. I also want you to have some money for rides and food. We're going to have a swell time today. That's for sure!"

Lanie looked up at Deoin. "Mr. Jinks, that's real kind of you, but I've got some money for the rides for our family."

"You sure, Lanie? I know things have been a bit tight for you all."

"I'm sure, Mr. Jinks, but I sure do appreciate the kind thought!" Then Lanie reached into her pocket and pulled out four five-dollar bills, handed one to each of her siblings and kept one for herself. "You all be careful how you spend your money now, you hear?"

Davis whispered a series of questions to her in rapid sequence. "Lanie, did Pa give you that money? Where'd he get it? He's having trouble making the payments as it is! Maybe we best not use it for this."

"You just hush up, Davis Freeman. This is *my* money from the school contest, and I want to share it with each of you." She smiled at him and said, "It's my gift and there are *no* strings attached. You just have a good time, you hear?"

Davis gave her a hug. "Come on, you guys! Whoopee!"

Lanie smiled as the boys ran off. She, Maeva, and Alice had plenty to explore, and there was no reason to have any old boys around to bother them.

⚬━✦⚬

The afternoon was glorious. First the girls attended the 4-H exhibits. Lanie enjoyed petting the lambs, while Alice liked the crafts. Maeva's eyes grew big as sunflowers when she saw the giant vegetables that had been grown in the county. The girls ate cotton candy and caramel pop-corn as they wandered through the livestock sheds. The large work horses were Lanie's favorites, the other girls enjoyed the cattle.

After a dinner of hamburgers and fried potatoes, the girls splurged on ice cream with chocolate sauce before skipping to the carnival rides. Lanie rode the Ferris wheel three times. Each time she reached the top, she would look as far as she could see and imagine she was a bird. She loved the feeling of freedom. *One day I'll be able to fly away from this old town. I'll be free!* Then the rapid trip down made her gasp and squeal.

Maeva and Alice both loved the carousel. They pretended to be maids in distress as they rode their horses at a rapid clip, trying to escape the desperados chasing them on horseback. True, the bandits and villains looked remarkably like their brothers! Lanie rode in a car-riage on the carousel, imagining her knight in white armor riding up to ask for her hand in marriage. Of course she imagined playing *very* hard to get!

While the boys went to compete for prizes at the carnival booths, the girls settled onto a small patch of grass to listen to the barbershop quartet contest. The songs about motherhood, home, Dixie, automo-biles, boys and girls, and courtship all made her feel good. She loved all the Tin Pan Alley greats such as Harry von Tilzer, George M. Cohan, Gus Edwards, Ernest Ball, Al Piantadosi, and Irving Berlin. Lanie joined the crowd in clapping as another four men with handlebar moustaches, wearing striped vests, began singing a cappella. Lanie closed her eyes and hummed as the group sang her favorite song in nearly perfect harmony:

Let me call you Sweetheart,
I'm in love with you.
Let me hear you whisper that you love me too.
Keep the love light glowing in your eyes so true,
Let me call you Sweetheart,
I'm in love with you!

Before they knew it, the sun began to set. The girls made one last stop at the candy booth and purchased a small bag of salt-water taffy to enjoy while they waited for the fireworks, sitting on a patch of cool green grass, laughing and telling stories.

Lanie had not had so much fun in a long time. She was so stuffed she didn't think she would *ever* be able to eat again. She lay back on the cool grass and looked up at the clear blue sky. She took in a slow deep breath, closed her eyes, and smiled. This was about as perfect a day as she could imagine!

On the way home, Mr. and Mrs. Jinks sat in the front seat of their Oldsmobile touring car, and the children crowded onto the large over-stuffed back seat. While the boys talked over an idea they had hatched to build an even more elaborate tree house in the woods near their home, Alice, Lanie, and Maeva sang songs in the round:

Row, row, row your boat,
Gently down the stream,
Merrily, merrily, merrily, merrily,
Life is but a dream.

After each verse the girls would giggle and laugh while their brothers scowled at them.

"You boys are far too serious," scolded Alice.

Cody glared at them. "You girls are just plain silly. We're planning a fantastic tree fort and don't have no time for dumb ol' songs. We've got more important things to do."

Lanie countered with, "Your forts will rot someday, but music lasts forever. The Bible says that we're going to sing and worship in glory right beside the angels. It doesn't say anything about building forts."

"Oh yeah?" Max said. "Well Jesus said, 'And into whatsoever house ye enter, first say, Peace be to this house.' So while you girls are wasting your time singing, me and Cody are gonna be making a tree house where we can have some peace."

"Oh no!" Maeva cried.

Lanie turned to see what Maeva was looking at.

"Lanie, look—the doctor's car is at our house! And there's Pastor William's car and Sister Myrtle's car. Lanie, what's happening?"

A sudden fear gripped Lanie, and she could not say a word.

Deoin pulled into his driveway, but Maeva and Lanie leaped out before he could bring the car to a complete stop. They crossed the street and the yard and burst in the front door of their house. They ran to the parlor, and Lanie saw their pastor, Brother Prince, and his wife, Ellen, sitting on one sofa. Sister Myrtle and her husband, Charlie, were on another sofa. Standing in the corner of the parlor was Madison Jones, the black pastor, and his wife, Ethel. The others stood when the children entered the room.

"What's wrong, Brother Prince?" Lanie asked. The pastor tried to smile, but it was not a good smile.

Max and Cody burst through the door and stopped. "What's the matter?" Max blurted out. "Is Mama sick?"

Lanie glared at him.

Pastor William bent down on one knee. "Kids, the baby decided she was going to come early."

"She?" Cody asked.

"Yep, she. A little girl came into the world this afternoon. She's beautiful and Doc Givens says that she's as healthy as can be."

"Then *why* are you all still here?" Lanie said. "And why didn't someone send for us?"

Pastor William cleared his throat. "Lanie, the baby came real fast. And like I said, she's fine. But your ma is having some problems. Your dad and Doc Givens are in there, along with Doc's nurse. They're doing everything they can to help your ma, and we're out here praying as hard as we can."

Lanie felt the panic beginning to well up in her heart. "What are they doing? And what are you all having to pray about?"

He paused for a few seconds. "I'm not sure I know all the whys and what fors. Your dad only said Elizabeth hasn't been doing well."

"But she's going to be all right, isn't she, Pastor?"

Pastor William looked at the floor and shook his head. "I don't know, Lanie Belle. I just don't know."

A wave of panic crashed over Lanie. Her throat was so tight she couldn't speak, and she turned her face away so that Pastor William wouldn't see the tears she couldn't hold back. *No, God! Don't let my mama die!*

⟾⊷

The clock on the sitting room wall slowly ticked off the minutes. It chimed at each quarter hour. To Lanie it seemed that each quarter hour passed more slowly than the one before. Her thoughts bounced back and forth from fear to confident prayer that the Lord would make all things right. At times she would sit, and at other times she paced.

The bedroom door squeaked and opened. Lanie heard footsteps coming down the hall. When Dr. Givens and her daddy entered the parlor, Lanie knew something was terribly wrong! She sensed that her dad had been crying. His eyes were puffy and swollen. Doc Givens' usually spry and happy demeanor had given way to gloom. His coarse salt-and-pepper hair looked more gray than usual, and his old-fashioned moustache seemed to droop in sadness.

Forrest cleared his throat. "Children, your mama is in a bad way. The baby is fine . . . she's a beautiful little girl, but . . ." Forrest's voice broke as his lips trembled and tears began to run down his cheeks. He slumped into a chair with his head in his hands and began to sob.

Forrest's tears shocked everyone into an awkward silence. Lanie clasped her hand to her open mouth and slowly sank into a chair.

Dr. Givens put his hand on Forrest's shoulder. "Children, you'd better go to your mother."

Forrest slowly stood and then held out his hand. Lanie took it and, with the other children trailing them, they left the parlor and walked toward the bedroom.

⌐══×⊢

"Elizabeth, the children are here."

Her eyes slowly opened and then she focused on the children and whispered, "Children, come here." Lanie let her brothers and sister go first. She watched her mother whisper something to each of them and then hug them, and Lanie wished she could escape this terrible nightmare.

Doc Givens quietly entered the room and closed the door behind him. He stood against the door as Forrest gestured to Lanie that it was her turn. She walked toward the side of her mother's bed, her shoes lead on her feet. She sat by her mother, who looked up at her and smiled. Almost instinctively, Lanie leaned over, kissed her mother softly on the cheek, and then whispered, "Mama, you can't leave us now! We all need you so much, and so does the baby."

"Oh, precious, I don't want to go. But the doctor says I don't have a say in this."

"What's that doctor know?" Lanie said with trembling lips.

Elizabeth smiled and reached up to stroke Lanie's hair. "Well, precious, if he's wrong, I'll be the happiest person in the whole world, but if the Lord has chosen today to take me to glory, to be with Him forever, we've just got to accept that, don't we?"

Lanie nodded, hot tears warming her icy cheeks.

Her mother smiled. "Lanie Belle, you'll have to take my place. You're the steady one and I need you to be strong and dependable for your dad and the younger children. Will you?"

"I will, Mama! I will!"

Elizabeth smiled again. "Lanie, I need to talk to your dad."

Lanie gave her mother a long, sobbing hug. Finally she released her, stood, and walked to the foot of the bed to stand by the other children. Elizabeth gestured to Forrest, who took her hand.

"Forrest, bring me the baby, will you?"

Lanie watched her dad walk over to the crib and gently lift the sleeping child. He placed her beside Elizabeth. When Lanie saw that her mother was too weak to even hold the baby, she felt a chill go through her body. Then her mother bowed her head and her voice was faint as she prayed.

"Dear Lord, I . . . I want to thank you for the gift of this precious child. Her safe arrival is a direct answer to our prayers. Lord, I know I won't be here to be her mother, so I ask you to give Forrest . . . a special measure of strength to be her daddy." Elizabeth's voice was very faint, and her lips scarcely seemed to move.

"I ask that you would give Lanie . . . the patience and energy to care for this little one. And give her a special love for her little sister, to raise and nurture her. Lord, please give a special grace to my family and to this most special little baby. In Jesus' name I pray. Amen."

Lanie looked up. Her father's face was streaked with tears. Elizabeth laid her head back on the pillow and smiled as she looked up at him. "Oh, Forrest, you've been"—her voice broke, but she reached out her hand for his—"a fine husband and a wonderful father for our children. I've never loved anyone . . . as much as I love you . . ."

"I love you, too, sweetheart," Forrest whispered.

Lanie thought that her mother was radiant and her smile was angelic. "One day," her mother whispered so faintly that Lanie could barely hear the words, "one day . . . we'll all be together again."

Her mother's eyes closed. After a final sigh, she breathed her last, a smile on her lips.

Lanie ran around the bed. "Mama!" But her dad stopped her. He placed his arms around her and pulled her to his chest. Lanie sobbed uncontrollably, and Forrest gestured to the other children to come. He held them all close as they wept—and then he began to sob with them.

PART TWO

The Accident

CHAPTER 7

The snowy white blanket of snow that carpeted the school yard did not touch Lanie with its pristine beauty. As a rule, she loved to see the ground carpeted white with snow, but all she could think of now was that her mother's grave was underneath this same blanket. Involuntarily the picture of the grave flashed in her mind's eye, and she quickly turned away from Miss Dunsmore's classroom window, pressing her lips together and blinking her eyes to keep back the tears. Someone had told her that "time heals all wounds," but in the six months since her mother died, she had not found the saying to be true. She glanced at Miss Dunsmore, who was saying good-bye to the last of the students on this last day of school before Christmas vacation. The sounds of laughter and shouting in the hall came to her as the door opened, but she felt none of the joy.

Miss Dunsmore closed the door, came over to where she was standing, and smiled. "I wanted to say a special merry Christmas to you, Lanie, although I'll be seeing you at church." Miss Dunsmore wore a white dress that reached just below her knees, a lime-green belt, and a light-gray sweater to take the chill off. "I hope you have a good Christmas," she said warmly.

The words tumbled out of Lanie before she could stop them. "Miss Dunsmore, I'm right sorry I didn't do well in your class. I didn't even deserve the C you gave me."

When she had received her report card and saw her low grades, especially in English class, Lanie had cried herself to sleep. Always before she had made nothing but A's, but taking care of an infant and keeping the rest of the house going had sapped her strength. To her horror, she felt tears running down her cheeks. She snatched a handkerchief out of her pocket and wiped them away. "I don't . . . mean to be a crybaby, but it's been so hard since Mama died!"

"I know it has, dear."

"Daddy . . . he's been working until dark, and we had to hire Madison Jones' mother, Delilah, to take care of baby Corliss while I'm in school."

"I know it's been hard for you, Lanie, but things are bound to get better. Are you keeping up with your writing at all?"

"No, ma'am, I don't have time for anything like that."

Miss Dunsmore slipped her arm around the girl's shoulders and hugged her. She had grieved over Lanie Freeman's fall from top student to average one. More than once she had offered to give her special help, but Lanie had no time even for that. She gave the girl a squeeze and said, "Next semester we'll work out something." She tried to think of something positive to say. "I was surprised that you won't be in the Christmas pageant at church."

"I just didn't have time, ma'am, but Maeva, Davis, and Cody are all in it." Lanie gathered up her books.

"Yes, I know, but I especially wanted you to be in it. I think—"

The door opened and Dempsey Wilson, the school basketball coach, came in. "Merry Christmas to you, Lanie."

"Thank you, Mr. Wilson." She didn't want the coach to see that she'd been crying, so she mumbled, "I have to go now."

"If I don't see you before Christmas, watch out and don't let Santa Claus burn up when he comes down through your chimney," Dempsey said cheerfully.

"No, sir, I won't," Lanie answered, but could not muster a smile. "Good-bye, Miss Dunsmore. Merry Christmas." And she slipped out as quickly as she could.

⌖

Lanie entered the house and took off her coat and cap and gloves. Her face was red from the cold. Going over to the potbellied stove in the living room, she put her hands out and flexed her fingers. "It's downright cold out there, Delilah. I hope you wore a heavy coat."

Delilah Jones was sitting in the rocking chair with Corliss in her lap. She wore a faded light blue dress that reached down to her ankles. As mother of the pastor of the Methodist Episcopal Church, she took things seriously. "Of course I brought a long coat! God gave me sense to wear clothes—which is more than I kin say for some of these young girls."

Lanie was accustomed to Delilah's preaching. She had said once, "Delilah does more preaching than her son, and louder too." She reached down and picked up Corliss, who looked up cross-eyed for a moment, then straightened out her sight and chortled. Lanie squeezed her until she protested, then kissed her cheek. "I don't know what we'd do without you, Delilah."

"I don't neither." Delilah got up, moving slowly and stiffly, for she had rheumatism. She was a round woman in body and face. Her black moon face with warm, brown eyes could look sharp or kindly as her mood struck her. She pulled her lips together in a disapproving way and said, "I got to talk to you 'bout somethin', Miss Lanie."

"Well, go ahead."

"You needs to get this here girl chil' baptized."

Lanie smiled. "We've been over that. We're Baptist, Delilah. We don't baptize babies."

"Well, shame on you! You ort to! Now we Methodist folk knows how to take keer of dat." She leaned forward and with a conspiratorial whisper said, "I'll tell you what. Why don't you lemme take this here young'un to church with me Sunday. I'll sneak her in and Madison will baptize her. Then she'll be baptized right."

Lanie laughed. "I don't think we could do that. We just feel differently about the business of baptizing."

Delilah drew herself up and said primly, "Well, be it on your own head, Lanie Freeman! I'm goin' home now."

Lanie went with Delilah until she put on her heavy coat and pulled a hat down almost over her ears. She pulled on a pair of heavy work gloves and said, "I'll be here in the mornin'."

"Thank you, Delilah. Like I've said, we couldn't do without you."

"You certainly couldn't—and lemme tell you dis: We may not agree on baptizin', but I'm gonna pray that you'll be enlightened"— she paused—"but I wants you to make them other chil'uns help you with the work. They's lazy to the bone!"

"Oh, they're not really lazy, Delilah. They're just young."

"Ha! That no-'count Maeva is jes one year younger than you is— and stronger! You make her do some work, you hear me! Cut a switch to 'er!"

"I don't think that would work. She can whip me any day."

"Then get your pappy to do it."

"No, I couldn't tell Daddy about Maeva or the boys. We'll work it out."

"Where is they anyways? Lemme wait around. I'll tell 'em how the cow ate the cabbage!"

"They had to stop by the church and meet with the preacher's wife, something about the pageant. But they'll be home pretty soon."

"Huh, I'll bet dey will! You put 'em to work. It ain't gonna hurt 'em none."

"I will, Delilah. I'll see you tomorrow morning."

As soon as Lanie closed the door behind Delilah, she put Corliss Jeanne in the baby bed, which was in the warm living room, and squeezed her fat cheek. "You stay right here, honey. You be good now and talk to your powder can." She placed an empty Mennen's talcum powder can beside the infant's head, and at once Corliss began cooing at it. When all else failed to quiet Corliss, the can worked like magic!

For the next twenty minutes Lanie busied herself cleaning the house. In all truth, it never got fully clean no matter how hard she tried.

When she heard the door slam, she went downstairs to find Maeva standing over by the fire warming her hands. "Where's Cody and Davis?" she asked.

"They went huntin'."

"Hunting? Oh no they're not!" Lanie ran to the door just as the boys were headed out of the yard. They had an old twenty-two single shot that they took turns using and did manage to get squirrels and rabbits now and then.

"Davis! Cody! You come right back here!"

Both boys turned, and Cody said stubbornly, "We're goin' huntin'. We need some squirrels."

"We don't need squirrels. We need some work done. You come in the house right now!"

"Aw, come on, Lanie!" Davis said. "We're out of school. Let us have a break."

"You can go hunting when the work's done."

"It'll be dark then."

"Then you can go tomorrow. Now both wood boxes are empty. You two go split enough wood to fill both of them, in the kitchen and in the living room. And those wood crates Daddy brought need to be split into kindling too. And the stock has to be fed, and the cow has to be milked. Now get to it!"

"Shoot!" Cody kicked the snow. "A fella never has any fun."

Davis shook his head. "We'd better get to it, I guess."

"I sure hope there ain't no wood to be split in heaven," Cody grumbled.

"What are you talking about? Of course there won't be no wood to be split in heaven!"

"How'd you know? You ain't never been there."

"Well, I know there ain't nothin' in the Bible about it."

Cody would argue with a stump, especially on theological matters. "It's bound to get cold in heaven and somebody's got to build a fire."

Davis gave Cody a disgusted look. "You have the dumbest ideas I ever heard, Cody! What makes you think it'll be cold in heaven?"

The two went to the woodpile and began splitting wood, Cody's voice getting louder as he argued about the temperature in heavenly places.

By the time Lanie got back in the house, she saw that Maeva had escaped. Corliss needed changing and was crying. Lanie had become expert at this. It was not a job that she cared for, but she had grown accustomed to it. When she got a fresh diaper on Corliss and pulled the baby's pajamas back on, she put her back in the crib with her powder can. "Here's your powder can. Now you can sing to it."

Lanie ran upstairs and threw open the door to Maeva's room.

"What do you want? You're supposed to knock before you come into my room!" Maeva was lying on the bed reading a copy of *True Romance*.

"You haven't got time to read that romance junk. Where'd you get it anyhow?"

"I got it from Alice Jinks, and I've got three more too."

"You don't have any business reading them."

"I'll read what I please!" Maeva said. "You read the books you want. I'll read what I want."

Lanie took a deep breath. As mildly as she could, she said, "Corliss is almost out of diapers. You go down and wash them while I cook supper."

"I don't want to wash them diapers. They stink."

"They have to be done, and you know it, Maeva, so don't argue about it."

Maeva threw the magazine down and got off the bed. "You're not gonna make a slave out of me!"

"I'm not making a slave out of anybody."

"You are too! Let me tell you somethin'. You're not my mama!"

Lanie's temper snapped. "If Mama were here, she wouldn't be having this discussion with you! I can't fix supper and wash clothes and clean the house all at the same time. Now you get down there and wash those diapers!"

"What are you going to do if I won't?" Maeva taunted. "You can't whip me."

Maeva was right about that. She was strong and active, and in fights with larger girls always came out on top. "Maybe I can't whip you, but I know somebody who can, and he'll be home in plenty of time to do any whipping necessary."

"You ain't nothin' but a danged ol' tattletale!" Maeva yelled. She ran out of the room, slamming the door.

Lanie listened to her sister's feet pound down the hall, then go down the stairs. She sat down on the bed, suddenly weak, barely resisting an overwhelming temptation to cry—she hated nagging the other kids.

She struggled to regain her composure, and her eyes fell on the copy of *True Romance*. She picked it up and saw that a beautiful woman on the cover was smiling, and a man was holding her. The title of the story was "All a Woman Needs Is a Man."

Lanie got up, stared at the magazine, and threw it on the bed. "Well, I don't need a man! Unless he can wash diapers."

She went downstairs. Maeva had left the house, as Lanie knew she would. She started dividing her time between washing the diapers, trying to get something cooked for supper, and going back to check on Corliss. "I get so tired of all this, but I've got to keep going." She picked up Corliss, who was laughing, and smiled ruefully. "I wish I didn't have any more problems than you have, sweetheart!"

Forrest swirled the brush around in the shaving mug, lathered up a thick cream, and started pulling his razor down his cheeks. He had a tough beard, and his eyes watered, but he shaved quickly. The blade was dull, but safety razor blades cost money, so he made do. He had formed the habit of shaving at night, for it was easier to do it in the warm evening bathroom than in the cold morning one. When he finished, he washed the razor and the brush, put them in the medicine cabinet, and went into the bedroom. He paused and looked at the bed that he had shared with Elizabeth for so many years, then quickly turned away to the closet. He picked a long-sleeved warm shirt, slipped it on, and left the tail hanging out. Leaving the bedroom, he smelled the aroma of cooking food. When he got to the kitchen, he said, "You kids are ready to eat, I see, and I'm starved."

As Forrest took his seat, he saw that the faces around the table were unhappy. "Well, you ought to feel good gettin' out of school for vacation. Aren't you happy?"

"Sure, Daddy." Cody nodded. "It'll give me time to do some worthwhile stuff."

Forrest laughed. "You don't think school's worthwhile?"

"Shoot no! What do I have to study that old geography for? I ain't ever goin' to China."

It was an old argument, so Forrest didn't pursue it. "What's the matter with you, Maeva? You look like you bit into a bad apple."

"Nothin's wrong with me."

Lanie brought a platter and a large bowl to the table. She set them down and took her place without saying anything.

"Well, this looks downright good. I'll just say the blessing over it myself." He prayed quickly and then began to pile the food on his plate. "The roast is burned," Maeva said. "I don't think even Beau would eat it."

"It sure is burnt!" Cody exclaimed. "Can't hardly stick a fork in it. Why'd you burn it like this?"

"You leave your sister alone," Forrest said. "Everybody burns food once in a while."

"I can't eat this old burnt roast!" Maeva exclaimed. She had tried cutting it with a knife, and truly the roast was in bad shape. "It stinks."

Cody opened a baked potato. "Hey, this here tater ain't cooked! How come you burnt the roast and didn't cook the potatoes enough, Lanie?"

"That's enough from you, Cody," Forrest said sternly. He saw that Lanie had her head down. "Don't you worry about it, Muff. Everybody has bad days. I've had enough of 'em myself."

When Lanie lifted her head, Forrest saw misery on her face. "I'm sorry supper's so bad, Daddy. I just didn't have time to cook a good meal."

Davis cut off a chunk of beef and was chewing it manfully. He picked up one of the biscuits left over from the day before and said, "If you didn't spend so much time washing clothes, you could have done better."

Suddenly Forrest turned and looked at Maeva. She met his look for a moment, then looked down. "Maeva, did you wash the clothes today?"

"No. I hate to wash clothes."

Forrest felt the heat of anger. "And you think your sister enjoys it?"

Maeva looked up and glared at Lanie. "I don't have to mind her! She ain't my boss!"

Forrest's fist hit the table. "Yes she is! And you boys get this! We've lost your mama, and somebody has to take over around here. I can't be here because I'm out makin' a living. When Delilah is here, she's the boss. When she's not here and Lanie is, you mind Lanie just like she was your mama."

The misery on Lanie's face trickled into her words. "Don't say that, Daddy. I'm not their mama."

"There's no other way, Muff," Forrest said. "We've got a tough row to hoe." He looked around the table. "And everybody's got to pull his weight. Maeva, from now on you do the washing, and I'd better not hear about any complaining."

Lanie saw the stubbornness and anger on Maeva's face and knew that trouble would come from her. "I can help her, Daddy."

"No. You do the cooking and the ironing and most of the rest of the house cleaning. "That's your job—and washing is Maeva's." Maeva looked up and saw an expression that troubled her. Her father was a happy man, always smiling, but he wasn't smiling now.

"I want all of you," Forrest said, "to take care of Corliss. She won't have a mama's love like the rest of you had so"—his voice seemed to break, and he reached over and caressed the baby's silky hair—"we've all got to be sure she gets lots of love."

A quiet fell across the table, and Forrest got up. He went around to Maeva and pulled her to her feet and put his arms around her. "I sound hard, but we've all got to pull together. You're a tough egg, daughter, and I need you."

Maeva grabbed him and held him fiercely. "I'll wash the stupid ol' diapers, Daddy!"

"That's my girl. Now let's sit down and let's fix up a breakfast."

"But it's supper time."

"I know, but let's me and you, Maeva, fix up eggs and ham and we'll make some toast."

"What'll we do with this roast?" Lanie said.

"We'll do this." Forrest picked up a piece of roast from his plate and tossed it to Beau, who gulped it down and began to whine for more. They all threw meat at him, and soon they were all laughing. Cap'n Brown appeared and Lanie began to feed him small portions of the meat.

"You're nothing but a glutton, Beau!" Forrest said. His stern tone hurt Beau's feelings, so he turned and lay down in the corner with his face to the wall.

"Now, while we fix this breakfast, you all tell me about what you're doing in the pageant. What parts are you playing?"

"I'm the star," Maeva said proudly. "I'm the Virgin Mary."

"And me and Davis are dumb ol' shepherds!" Cody said with disgust. "I wanted to bring in real sheep and cows, but the preacher's wife she said it would be dangerous."

"Dangerous! You mean they'd bite somebody?"

"Heck no!" Cody yelped. "She was scared they'd poop right in the middle of the pageant!"

His words amused the others, and they laughed as they cracked eggs and fried ham. Forrest managed to laugh with the kids, but his sober thoughts lay just beneath the levity. *It's too hard on these kids—especially Lanie—but there ain't no other way.*

The fire had gone down in the stove so the coals no longer glowed red. Lanie gave Corliss a bath in an oversized dishpan placed on the library table, which her dad had dragged close to the stove. Corliss was having a fine time splashing the water and giggling.

Forrest put down his newspaper and went over to run his hand over the infant's back. "You know, I reckon the smoothest thing in this world is a baby's skin."

"I think you're right, Daddy." Lanie looked at her father. "You need to go to bed now. You're tired."

"You sound like your mama." Forrest smiled. "She was always bossing me around. Now you're starting."

"Well, you work too hard. How's the cutting going?"

"All right. Good timber, but some of it's hard to get to. It's hard to find good help," he added, "and I'm not much of a bookkeeper."

"Maybe I can help you."

"You already do more than your share, Muff." He looked at her. "I'm sorry your grades went down. It wasn't your fault."

"Oh, it doesn't matter."

"Yes it does, but I'll try to make things easier for you."

"Don't worry about it, Daddy."

"Maybe I'll hire a woman to come in and do the housework."

"We can't afford that."

"I've been trying to get a payment or two ahead at the bank." He was running his hand over Corliss's back, savoring the smooth feel of her rosy skin. He looked up, worry in his eyes. "I wish I'd never borrowed that money on our place here. This new President Hoover—I know he's a smart man, but the markets are still going up and down. Nobody knows which way it's going, not even the smart guys."

Lanie put her arm around his waist and looked up at him. "It'll be all right, Daddy. The Lord will take care of us."

"You're just like your mama," Forrest marveled. He leaned over and kissed her, then kissed the baby on the top of the head. "I am going to bed. You know, Muff, I'm really looking forward to that Christmas pageant."

"It'll be good."

Forrest had reached the door, but he turned around and smiled. "Something's funny about the way they chose Maeva to play the Virgin Mary."

"She'll do a good job."

"You'd think they'd want a real sweet girl for that."

"Maeva can be sweet."

"She can be meaner than a snake too. I hope she gets through that play without embarrassing all of us. Good night, sweetheart."

"Good night, Daddy."

~→ CHAPTER 8 ←~

The acrid smell of wood smoke laced the thin winter air, and a breeze stirred the sweet and musty and pungent odors of the earth. Forrest Freeman paused to watch a cloud of blackbirds wheeling into the falling darkness. The moon, a pale silver disk, beamed from the sky, and Forrest remembered how Lanie had always reached up for it as a baby. The memory made him laugh and he savored it for a time.

Forrest walked slowly around the perimeter of his five acres. He paused briefly when a small squirrel streaking from one tree to another with the usual calamitous air of such creatures stopped and looked at him. The squirrel reared up on his hind legs and tucked his front legs tightly against his chest. He looked like some kind of a priest saying prayers. Forrest smiled, stomped the ground, and watched the squirrel scurry away and fly up a tree as if it were flat earth.

This small plot was to Forrest Freeman the closest thing to holy ground that he had ever known. He had never known any home but this one, and he remembered with keen, strong waves of memory his father and his mother and his grandparents. He did not believe in the spirits of the dead haunting the earth, but somehow the memories brought them back almost as clearly as if he could see them.

Twilight softness and silence lay on the earth, and he looked up into the heavens. Far off to the west, Venus twinkled. He knew it was Venus because on his first date with Elizabeth she had pointed out the star and said, "That's Venus." When he asked how she knew, she laughed and said, "My father told me, and now we both know."

The thought of Elizabeth brought a pang as it always did. "Lord, I guess I can only see through a glass darkly." The sound of his voice was loud, and he shook his head ruefully. "I'm like Jacob wrestling with the angel. You know that I got awful mad at You when You took Elizabeth from me, but I know You're the Lord. And as much as it hurts, You know best. I won't question You again."

He turned abruptly and headed toward the house. Behind him the trees stood in disorganized ranks, laying their shadows on the ground in long lines. The big walnut tree shouldered the moon out of the way as he reached the porch. He heard the children inside and murmured, "Thank you, Lord, that You left me my kids. And I pray You'll keep 'em safe and keep us all together as a family."

He stepped into the house, went through the kitchen, and found the children in the living room listening to the radio. Lanie was in the big, overstuffed rocker holding Corliss. Maeva, Davis, and Cody were all seated cross-legged Indian fashion on the floor before the radio. He watched them for a moment, then said, "You kids better get to bed."

They all looked at him with surprise, and it was Cody who said, "Shoot, Daddy, it's only nine o'clock, and we don't have to get up in the morning."

"Yes you do."

"What for?" Davis protested. "There ain't no school tomorrow."

"Your mom would have told you to say 'There *isn't* any school tomorrow,' but we've got somethin' better than school." He grinned. "I'm takin' you boys hunting. We're going out to get a deer apiece."

The boys jumped up and fired questions at their father. He held up his hand and laughed. "There's a bit of timber we've been cutting with a creek to it. There's more deer tracks, big ones, around there than you've ever seen in your life. So tomorrow mornin' at daybreak we'll be sittin' there. We'll have to get up maybe at three o'clock."

"I want to go too, Daddy!" Maeva said.

"Huntin' ain't for girls!" Cody said.

"It is too! Take me, Daddy!" Maeva pulled at Forrest's sleeve.

"All right. I reckon so. What about you, Lanie? You want to go too? We'll get Delilah over here to keep Corliss."

"No, I don't like to kill things, but I'll get up and cook breakfast for you. Then Corliss and me will have the day all to ourselves."

"We'll be back by noon with three big fat deer. And tomorrow night's the Christmas pageant, so you actors will have to get ready for your parts."

"It don't take no actin' to wear a bathrobe and a towel wrapped around your head and tote a crooked stick," Cody said. "I wanted them to let me be the angel, but Miz Prince, she wouldn't do it."

"Too bad they didn't need a devil," Davis said, winking at his father. "You'd have been great for that part."

"That's enough of that," Forrest said sharply. "Everybody to bed."

Cody, Davis, and Maeva scampered off, and Forrest winked at Lanie. "I found a secret how to make 'em go to bed without arguin'. Tell 'em I'll take 'em deer huntin'." He laid his hand on the smooth crown of Lanie's hair. "You've got pretty hair just like your mama. You sure you don't want to go?"

"I don't want to kill one of those beautiful deer."

Forrest leaned down and kissed her cheek. "You eat 'em though, that nice tender venison." He laughed. "Here, let me have my girl baby. You go on to bed. I'll get you up in the mornin'. You can cook us a great breakfast."

Lanie did go to bed, but not to sleep. A poem, a sonnet, had been forming in her mind. Miss Dunsmore had taught the class how sonnets worked before the Christmas break. "A sonnet is very regular," she had said. "Every sonnet has fourteen lines. If it has one more or one less, it's not a sonnet. And every sonnet has three quatrains and one couplet. A quatrain is four lines and a couplet is two. Each of the three quatrains say one thing, and the couplet sums up the whole poem."

For several days now, in the absence of other schoolwork, Lanie's creative ideas had begun to reassert themselves. Carefully Lanie began writing.

Lost Things

When I was four, a Raggedy Ann doll was my treasure.
I loved her dearly and shared with her my bed.
She was my childhood friend and dearest pleasure—
But she got lost on a picnic, and now is dead.
When I was six, my present was a book all filled
With pictures of lovely ladies and knights.
My delight was in the Table Round—until
A leaky roof drowned all my delight.
I thought I'd lose nothing I loved more
Than these. But when my mama left us all,
The world turned black and from my heart tore
Itself in two. I found how deep a heart can fall.
The sun and moon and stars you keep in place,
Then why, O Lord, withhold from me your grace?

For a long moment Lanie stared at the words, then crumpled the paper and threw it on the floor. She buried her face in the pillow and wept.

⊷⊶

The next morning the four older Freeman children stumbled into the kitchen sleepy-eyed, the boys and Maeva pulling on their heavy clothing and Lanie in a heavy chenille robe that had been her mother's. It was cut down to fit her, and it brought a twinge of regret to Forrest, who was up and had the fire going in the stove. He said only, "We need a big meal here, kids. I reckon about four or five eggs ought to be plenty for me with a little of that fried ham and some grits."

Lanie had made preparations the night before, and since the fire was ready it took almost no time to cook breakfast. As she cooked, she listened as her father instructed all three in guns. The boys had shot already, but Maeva had not.

"I'm gonna let you have this shotgun, honey," he said, holding it carefully. "I'll see that we get close enough where you can't miss."

"Daddy, she's liable to shoot us all with that thing!" Davis said.

"No she won't. It'll be fine. Now, is that breakfast ready, Lanie?"

"Yes, Daddy."

"Then let's lay our ears back and buck right into it."

Lanie watched them eat hurriedly, listening all the while for Corliss's cry. She had learned to hear the baby's crying even when she was in a sound sleep. When they all got up to leave, Forrest hugged her and whispered, "We'll be back by noon. Don't worry about cookin' anything. I'll take care of that."

"All right, Daddy."

Forrest looked at his boys and Maeva and said, "Well, I guess we're like Nimrod in the Bible. We're mighty hunters before the Lord."

"Can Beau go with us?" Davis asked.

"No, he'd scare every deer in ten miles. Come on. Let's go."

Lanie watched them go, and then she sat down in front of the kitchen stove and drank a cup of coffee. She left the door of the stove open so she could hear the crackling of the firewood as it snapped and popped. Finally she went upstairs, got a notebook, and returned to the kitchen table. Cap'n Brown jumped up into her lap and purred like a small engine.

She turned to a blank page, ready in the quiet hours before Corliss awoke to attempt a different kind of poem. In addition to the sonnet, Miss Dunsmore had also been teaching her class about dramatic monologue. "It's a poem spoken by one person," Lanie recalled her saying, "and the poem tells you what that person is really like on the inside. Most of the time we don't let people know what we're going through, but in this kind of poem, the character speaks without regard for what people will think."

As she sat before the fire, Lanie became consumed with a desire to write a poem like that. But who would be her character? Not anyone she knew; they might be offended if her efforts were discovered.

"Why, I could write a poem about some character in the Bible!" Mary, perhaps, because it was almost Christmas. The idea excited her so much that she jumped up and fetched the family Bible to read the story again, though she knew it well.

Mary wasn't married—but she was going to have a baby. She was the only one who knew the baby was from God, and she knew everyone would think she had been a sinful girl. And she was engaged to Joseph. How would she tell him? It would be so hard!

Lanie began to write and was surprised to find out how quickly the ideas came to her. She worked on the poem for a long time and changed it more than once. Now, as dawn tiptoed through the windows, she somehow knew that what she was doing was right! Finally she put her pencil down.

Mary

Three days I've waited here, but Joseph's smile
Has silenced me. I could not speak my heart
Beside this sunlit well with strangers close.
But now so late he works the sky is veiled—
Except for rose-tints from the dying sun,
And even now they fade. I hear his steps;
Tonight I must tell him I am with child.

He is a child himself (though older far
Than I) and nothing knows of women's ways.
More like a father than a husband, Joseph
Seems to me. Could it be that God
Foresaw the peril of a young man
(Blinded by a hotly jealous heart)

Gave me instead to one made temperate
By the slowing pace of older blood?

I see him now in those dark sycamores
Feeling his way along the stony path.
His is the right by law to cast me off—
But how I fear to walk this road alone!
O God, if Joseph will but keep me close
Despite the public shame—I'll say your hand
Has moved the two of us to your own ends!

For a long time Lanie studied her work, and a warmth came to her. She thought of how she had tried to put herself in Mary's place in that most difficult time, and how the tears had come to her eyes, so caught up she was with that ancient event.

Finally she closed the notebook with a sense of satisfaction. And even as she did, a thought came to her: *I could write a whole lot of poems like this! I could pick out the people who met the Lord Jesus and write what they were thinking and saying about Him!*

The thought startled her, but at the same time she felt a sense of rightness in it. *I can't preach, but I can write poems about the Savior!* Her own daring stunned her, but then she prayed, "Lord, I'd like to do this for You. Even if nobody ever sees the poems but me, I'd like to do this to say how much I love You."

Corliss cried out. Carefully Lanie closed the notebook and put the pencil with it and went to pick up the baby. "We're gonna have a fine day, just me and you, Corliss. All those noisy people are out killing innocent little deer, but you and me are going to have fun. I may even write a poem about you!"

She found a great joy taking care of Corliss, and after she changed the girl's diaper and put warm pajamas on her, she sat in the chair and poked at Corliss's cheeks, which delighted the baby. When Corliss grew fussy, Lanie put her on her stomach on the floor with the talcum powder can just out of reach. She could not get to it, for she swam on her stomach, getting nowhere.

"Come on, you can do it! Crawl!"

At ten o'clock Lanie heard a slight knock at the door. "Who can that be?" she muttered. She glanced over at Corliss, who was playing in the crib. Lanie went to the front door and opened it. There was no one there. She stepped outside and saw a package in red paper with a bow on it right in front of the door. She bent over, picked it up, and went back in the house. Shutting the door, she studied the present. It was about eight inches square and obviously a Christmas present. A little tag was on it, and when she held it up to the light she saw written very faintly with a pen her own name. "For me? Who could have brought that?" Curiosity touched her. She had the impulse to leave it until Christmas morning, but she couldn't wait. Carefully removing the paper, she unveiled a box that said: "Winter Wonderland."

"Winter Wonderland? What's that?" Carefully she opened the box and pulled out a round glass globe. Inside was a tiny nativity scene with Joseph and Mary and the baby Jesus in a manger. They were made out of some sort of glittering material, and when she stirred the ball, white flakes flew up.

"How beautiful!" Lanie exclaimed. She shook it and watched the flakes swirl. "It's the same one that I looked at in the drugstore, but it cost ten whole dollars." She ran her hand over the smooth surface of the glass, wondering who would have done such a thing. Then she noticed a small piece of white paper in the box. She pulled it out: "Mery Cristmus. You ar a kind gurl."

"Who in the world? Somebody who couldn't spell very well. And why didn't they wait for me to answer the door?" She took the ball over to where Corliss was playing on the floor, picked Corliss up, then spun the ball so that the flakes swirled. "Isn't that pretty, Corliss? You see how pretty the snow is?" Corliss agreed, for she gurgled and beat the ball with her fists.

"I don't think I'll tell Daddy and the others about this. It's a secret thing."

⌾⟞⟝⟞⌾

At eleven thirty Lanie heard the truck roaring and went outside. The log truck came into view, two big deer with heavy antlers laid across the hood. The horn was blowing, and when her dad stopped the truck, the kids boiled out, shouting. "I got the big one!" Davis yelled.

"And I got the other one!" Maeva cried. "That one right there. You see, Lanie?"

They grabbed Lanie and pulled her up to the truck, and she tried to express her admiration, but dead deer didn't thrill her all that much.

She felt a sadness when she saw their stiffened bodies, but she made herself say brightly, "They are certainly wonderful. Where's the third?"

"Well, shoot! That dumb ol' gun don't shoot right. I would have hit him if I had another shot, but he got away," Cody said. "Besides that, I don't think the ammunition was any good, and the light wasn't too good either."

"I guess that's about enough excuses for one missed deer," Forrest said. The tall, young son of Reverend Madison Jones stood next to him, grinning his agreement.

"Hello, Bascom, did you go hunting too?" Lanie said.

"No, Missy, I ain't studyin' no huntin', but yo' daddy says if I help dress them two deer that he's gonna give one of 'em to my family."

"Oh, that's wonderful! I bet you like venison, don't you, Bascom?"

"I'se 'specially fond of it, Miss Lanie, 'specially fond!"

"You kids go on and practice on your parts," Forrest said. "Me and Bascom will dress out these here deer."

"You look up in the balcony tonight," Bascom called after the kids. "Our whole church is comin' to watch you do your Christmas pageant. You do real good now, you hear?"

"You watch me," Maeva said. "I'll be the best Virgin Mary you've ever saw!"

Bascom hooted and said, "I'm mighty curious about why the preacher's wife picked Miss Maeva to be the star."

Forrest winked at him. "Why, I guess she thought that Maeva was the sweetest, most gentle girl in all Fairhope."

Bascom winked back and laughed. "I reckon she is if you say so, Mr. Freeman. Now, you let me clean them two deer. You go in and play with dat girl baby of yours."

⚬—×—

Davis went into town alone to look at the decorations. He had precious little money, and it wasn't time to go to the rehearsal at the church, so he just walked up and down the streets looking in the windows and enjoying the displays. He knew most everybody in Fairhope and stopped to talk with his friends and greeted others he knew.

He walked in front of the courthouse and then down to the Dew Drop Inn, where he was greeted by Sister Myrtle and Charlie. The place was packed, but Sister Myrtle said in her big booming voice, "Well, praise God, alleluia, Davis! Come in here and let me set you down a big meal."

"All I got's enough for a hamburger, Sister Myrtle."

"It's on the house. My Christmas present. Charlie, you go fix this young man a hamburger, a good 'un, and some of them french fries. You set right down there, Davis. Do you want an RC Cola or a Nehi strawberry?"

"Either one, Sister Myrtle."

Davis enjoyed the warmth and the conversation of this place. He heard someone call his name, and he turned around to see the lawyer Orrin Pierce sitting at a table with Mamie Dorr, who owned the beauty parlor. "Howdy, Mr. Pierce. How are you, Miss Dorr?"

"We're mighty fine," Mamie said. Mamie Dorr was a beauty. She was a widow, and it was whispered that her husband had killed himself. Secretly Davis had always thought she was the prettiest woman in town. Even though women gossiped about her and said she wore too much makeup and her clothes were too tight and her dresses were too short and she was too free with men, he still liked her.

"Are you all ready for the great production, Davis?" Orrin smiled. He had dark hair and light blue eyes that seemed to look right through a body. He was a heavy drinker, and some were appalled to hear that Mrs. Prince had chosen him to read the narration from the Bible for the pageant. Of course, he did have a deep baritone voice, but still he was, more or less, a drunkard, and Mrs. Prince had come under fire for her choice.

Mamie smiled at Davis. "You're shootin' up like a weed, boy! You're gonna be as tall and good-lookin' as your pa the first thing you know."

Davis flushed. "I hope I'll be as good a man as he is."

Orrin sipped his coffee and a smile touched his lips. "That's the way, Davis. Always hold up for your folks." He took another sip of coffee. "I still can't figure out why I'm involved in a Christmas play."

"Because you're such a saint, of course," Mamie said. She reached over and ran her finger over the back of Orrin's hand. "That's why I'm goin' tonight. I hope the roof doesn't fall in. I haven't been to church since I was fourteen, but I'm lookin' forward to it." She turned to Davis with a smile.

"Here's your hamburger." Sister Myrtle set down his hamburger and a pile of french fries.

Davis said, "I like the way you read the Bible, Mr. Pierce. It sounds just beautiful."

"It'd sound more beautiful if you stopped wearing them sinful neckties," Sister Myrtle said.

Orrin began to laugh, and Mamie laughed with him. Mamie finally said, "If that's the worst thing Orrin Pierce ever does, he's sure for heaven."

Sister Myrtle sniffed. "You both need to come to my church."

"Maybe we'll do that," Orrin said. "I'm sure we'll hear somethin' worth hearing."

Davis ate his hamburger and french fries and washed it all down with a Nehi soda and an RC, both of which Sister Myrtle had put in front of him. When he was finished, he thanked Sister Myrtle. "That was the best hamburger I ever had."

"I'll see you in that play tonight. I don't hold with theatricals, but I'm makin' an exception just because I like you folks."

"I'll watch for you, Sister Myrtle."

Davis left the Dew Drop Inn and started back down Robert E. Lee Boulevard for the house. When he passed the alley in the middle of the block, a movement caught his eye, and he saw Butcher Knife Annie dragging her wagon with the wobbly wheels. It was piled high with junk of one kind or another. The wind was not blowing, but still it was cold and a touch of remorse came to Davis as he saw her. In truth he had never forgiven himself completely for hitting her in the mouth with a pear. He and the other kids had gone by occasionally to take her bowls of food or fresh baked bread, and Davis and Cody worked half a day once propping up her old barn that was about to fall down. Annie had not even said "Thank you," but that hadn't mattered.

Turning to go, something touched Davis almost as palpable as a hand. He did not understand what it was, but he stopped dead still, turned around slowly and watched as Annie moved through the alley. She shuffled slowly, stiff with the cold. She didn't have gloves on. He could see how red and raw her hands were and, without planning to, he walked toward her. By the time he reached her, he knew what to say. "Hello, Annie."

"Howdy."

"Good to see you again." She did not answer, so he said, "What are you going to do tonight, Annie?"

Annie stared at him strangely. "Do? I ain't gonna do nothin'."

"We're having a Christmas pageant, and me and Cody and Maeva are in it. Everybody'll be there. Why don't you come?"

"Church ain't for me."

"Sure it is! Church is for everybody."

Annie blew on her hands and shook her head. Though he expected her reticence, Davis made one more try. "Look, it'll be fun. I'll come by and walk you to church, and you can sit with Daddy and Lanie, and you can see the baby."

"They won't like it."

"Who won't like it?"

"People. They don't want me."

Davis took a deep breath. "Well, I want you, so will you come?"

Annie looked at the ground for so long that Davis felt she had forgotten his question. Finally she mumbled, "I reckon so." Then without another word she picked up the handle of the wagon and hobbled down the alley.

"Well, I'm glad you're so excited about it," Davis mumbled, wondering how he would tell his family what he had just done.

⌖

Davis did not tell anyone about inviting Annie until it was time for the actors to leave. He startled them all when he said, "Maeva, you and Cody go on."

"You're coming with us, aren't you?" Maeva said.

"No, I've got to go by and get Annie." They all stared at him, including Lanie and his father, and he blurted out, "I asked her to go to the Christmas pageant."

"You asked Butcher Knife Annie!" Cody exclaimed. "Why'd you do a crazy thing like that?"

"I don't think it's crazy," Lanie said quickly. "I think it's sweet."

"That was a thoughtful thing to do, son. I should have thought of it myself," Forrest said. "You run along and get her. Lanie and me will get some good seats down front. When you get there, you just bring Annie to sit with us."

Warmth flooded Davis and he smiled. "Thanks, Daddy."

Davis left at once, and Maeva muttered, "Well, I hope he washes her down before he brings her in. You can smell her a block away."

"You never mind that, Maeva," Forrest said. "Remember, you're the Virgin Mary now. Start actin' like her."

☞⋆

Lanie and her father found places up in the front, but the church was filling up fast. Holding Corliss, Lanie kept glancing back at the door. "I don't think they're coming, Daddy," she said.

"Doesn't look like it. Look at how many people there are here. Look up in the balcony. I think every member of Reverend Jones' church is here."

Lanie did look up in the balcony then. It was packed with members of the Methodist Church. She saw Bascom Jones grinning at her and waving, and she waved back and smiled at him.

"Daddy, do you think that black people will ever be able to sit in the same room with white people?"

Forrest sighed. "I don't know, Muff. It don't look like it unless things change a lot, but then—" He broke off and said, "Look, there comes Davis with Annie."

Lanie turned and saw that Davis had just walked in. Annie was beside him. "Daddy, she hasn't cleaned up or anything!"

Indeed, Butcher Knife Annie wore the same tattered coat, the same heavy brogans, and the same ratty old shawl wrapped around her neck. She wore a man's hat, full of holes, and she stared around defiantly. If Annie was looking defiant, the congregation at the First Baptist Church of Fairhope, Arkansas, was having their look as well.

"Everybody's staring at her, Daddy!"

Forrest Freeman stood up and waved. "Over here, Davis," he said loudly. "Bring Annie down. We've saved a seat for her."

Relief crossed Davis's face. "Come on, Annie," he whispered. "There's Daddy and Lanie."

The two walked right down the aisle, then Annie hesitated. There were three people between her and the Freemans, and they stared at Annie with undisguised disgust.

"Come right on in, Annie," Forrest said. "We're about ready to start."

Annie looked around wildly, and for a moment she looked ready to bolt, but Davis whispered, "Go on, Annie, they're waiting for you."

Annie moved past the three people and sat down beside Lanie. Lanie reached out and squeezed her arm. "I'm so glad you could come. Look, you haven't seen Corliss. She's growing every day."

Forrest leaned forward and said to her, "Glad you could come, Annie. This ought to be good."

Annie did not say a word. She did reach out and touch the baby on the cheek. Corliss stared at her and then suddenly chortled. She had this strange laugh that seemed to begin way down deep in her stomach and then bubble over.

"She likes you, Annie," Lanie whispered.

The overhead lights went out, and two spotlights from the balcony focused on the stage. The rostrum had been transformed into a pastoral set that could be quickly changed. The sound of Orrin Pierce's smooth baritone voice broke the silence. "And it came to pass in those days, that there went out a decree from Caesar Augustus, that all the world should be taxed . . ."

As the old story was told again, Lanie held Corliss firmly. She hoped the baby wouldn't decide to sing or to cry. Instead, Corliss seemed fascinated by the lights pointed at the stage.

From time to time Lanie glanced at Annie. The old woman was leaning forward, intent upon the wise men and the shepherds. This was Cody's and Davis's part. They took their place on the stage and listened as Orrin read. "And there were in the same country shepherds abiding in the field, keeping watch over their flocks by night. And, lo, the angel of the Lord came upon them, and the glory of the Lord shone round about them: and they were sore afraid."

At this moment the lights brightened, and Lanie was horrified to see Cody fall flat on his back, covering his face up as if he had been shot.

"That's a bad case of overacting," Forrest whispered, humor in his voice.

"He's just awful!"

The play went on, and finally Joseph brought Mary to the inn. Maeva and Cody had both argued that Mary should come in riding a real donkey, since there were plenty of them around, but Mrs. Prince had put the quietus on that idea.

As Mary and Joseph stood before the door that had been built of pine, Maeva looked absolutely beautiful. Her face looked innocent and sweet, and Lanie felt her dad take her hand and squeeze it hard. She squeezed it back and noticed that Annie was hardly breathing.

Joseph knocked on the door and said, "Innkeeper, are you there?"

That was Lowell Stockwell's cue. Lowell was a tall, heavy boy with a round face, and not the smartest boy in Fairhope, to put it kindly. At fifteen his voice had already changed. But he had begged so hard to have a part in the pageant that Mrs. Prince couldn't refuse him.

"What do you want?" he howled.

"Please. We need a room for the night," Joseph said.

"There's no room. Now be off with you!"

Joseph argued, and Lowell Stockwell got rougher with each moment. He was reveling in the part, and the audience appreciated good acting when they saw it.

Finally it was Maeva's turn. She did not turn all the way around but let the light fall across her profile. Her cheeks were smooth, and she let the hood fall back so that her red hair glistened. Her voice was soft as she whispered, "Oh please, sir, we need a place to sleep!"

"I tell you there is no place! I don't have room for you!"

Mary stepped forward, and she looked very small compared to the bulky form of Lowell Stockwell. "I hate to ask for favors, but you see, I'm going to have a baby, and if you could find just any place at all, my husband and I would be so grateful to you."

Lowell Stockwell could not get his next line out.

Lowell cleared his throat and couldn't seem to get the words out, and when he did speak, his voice had risen in kind of a frantic tone. "Well, I . . . I don't think there's room."

Maeva took one step forward and looked up into Lowell's face. He watched her, fascinated, unable to turn away.

"Oh, please, sir, I can tell you're a kind man. Please find us some place."

Everyone in the house saw tears come into Lowell Stockwell's eyes. They ran down his cheeks, and the lights picked up the glitter as they left a track. He opened his mouth to speak two or three times but could not find the words.

"Oh, please help us!" Maeva whispered.

Then something happened that became a legend in Fairhope.

Butcher Knife Annie stood up and shouted in a voice that made everyone in the audience and on the stage jump convulsively.

"Let 'er in, you dummy! What kind of a feller are you to act like a blasted devil! Now, you let that poor girl in, you hear me?"

A thick silence seemed to blanket the spectators, and then suddenly Joseph shouted, "She's right! Lowell, you take her in the house!"

Lowell, totally confused, was even more shaken when the audience exploded with laughter and spontaneous applause. Everyone started standing up, and the applause filled the auditorium of First Baptist Church.

Pastor William Prince was standing stock still, and his wife's mouth was open as if she were frozen. William Prince started laughing, and at first his wife looked at him angrily, but then she giggled. The two of them hugged each other, still laughing, then Pastor William Prince walked up on the stage.

He took his place beside Lowell and dropped a hand on the boy's shoulder. He held up his other hand for silence and with a broad smile said, "I think this time we're going to have the Christmas pageant done the way we wish it could have been—not the way it happened. Just think what an opportunity that innkeeper missed! He could have had the honor of being the host of the Savior of the world—but he turned it down. I am made to wonder just how many times we have an opportunity like this—to do good to one of God's creatures, and refuse to do it. I think I'd like to be more alert to the needs of people, and I'd like to be quick this year to take people who need help into my heart and into my home and into my church!"

Applause broke out, and there were many "Amens" and "Praise the Lords." But it was Sister Mrytle Poindexter's charismatic voice that drowned out all the others: "Well, glory to God! The Lord has spoken—and I'm plum ashamed He had to come to this here Baptist church to get heard! Lord, touch the hearts of ever' born-again, sanctified child of God! Cause us all to open the doors and let the Lord Jesus come in!"

Pastor William Prince, after the benediction, made straight for Butcher Knife Annie. He took her hand and said warmly, "Sister Annie, thanks for standing up for the Lord. You've made this a Christmas that will never be forgotten in Fairhope!"

Annie was overwhelmed by the pastor's words. She dropped her head for a moment, then lifted her eyes to meet those of the pastor. "Well, preacher, I jist couldn't stand fer that gal to get left out."

"You did just right, Annie." Prince smiled. "The Lord Jesus never wants anyone to be left out."

⇜ CHAPTER 9 ⇝

Corliss was sound asleep, lying on her stomach in the baby bed, both fists clenched tightly. Lanie smiled at the sight of the powder can that apparently could not only entertain Corliss but also put her to sleep.

The house was strangely quiet. Cody, Davis, and Maeva had gone off after lunch to take in the Saturday matinee at the Rialto. The picture featured the Cisco Kid, starring Warner Baxter. Lanie didn't care for westerns, and it had been no sacrifice to tell the others that she would stay home and take care of Corliss.

Sitting at the kitchen table with the Big Chief notebook in front of her and a jelly glass full of pencils all sharpened and ready, Lanie studied the pages that she had written. She had thought long and hard about the assignment for English, the big assignment that would count for 25 percent of her grade. She had weighed her options thoughtfully and finally decided to write a story, but no ideas came.

Suddenly she sat straight up. "I could write a poem about the innkeeper! Everybody is still thinking about the nativity play at church. And I've already written a poem about Mary. What would the innkeeper be like? A pretty tough fellow, I'll bet!" Ideas began to flow, and for over an hour she wrote and scratched out lines—and finally took a deep breath and put her pen down. "I don't know if it's any good, but I'm going to hand it in." She ran her fingers over the paper.

Innkeeper
All right—all right! Don't smash the door!
What's that you say? You want a room?
There is no room; they're on the floor
As you can see by light of moon.

This whole town's stacked with Jews from every nation;
You should have made an early reservation.

Who's that behind you in the dark?
   Your wife? You say her time is near?
Well I can tell you that's no lark!
   Why did you drag her here this time of year?
No! No! There's no room—but listen stranger,
You two can stay tonight in yonder manger.

Now, back to bed—it's cold tonight.
   That girl will freeze in that old stable!
There's some will swear I've been too tight,
   But I must do my business able.
My bills don't stop—not even for a birth.
Besides—that pair? Why, they're of little worth!

She took a silent delight in studying the poem. Miss Dunsmore had taught her how to make good rhymes, and also how to make up the rhyme schemes. She could not have done it without Miss Dunsmore! Putting away the poetry, she pulled out her journal and leafed through it. She stopped at the entry marked two years ago to the day, March the thirteenth, and read aloud.

"Today I am thirteen years old, a genuine teenager. It has been wonderful! Mama made me a cake, and she also made me a beautiful dress out of real store-bought material, not flour sacks. Everybody had a gift for me, and we played until late at night. I hugged Mama and Daddy as hard as I could, and Daddy said, 'Well, we've got a grown young woman on our hands here. No more little girl.' And I said, 'I'll always be your little girl, Daddy.' And then I saw that Mama was looking like she wanted to cry, and I asked her what was the matter. 'It's sad to see children grow up. They have to, of course, but it reminds me of the day when we won't be together. You'll be off with a home of your own, and I'll be the creakity old grandma.'

"'You never will be,' I told her. 'You'll always be beautiful like you are now.'"

Slowly Lanie closed the book and felt the touch of sorrow that had come so often since her mother died. She had her daddy, but she missed her mama more than she had ever known she could miss anyone. They were so close, and she had not even known it! Cap'n Brown jumped into her lap with one of those expert leaps that cats can make, and then Beau nudged her with his nose.

"You can't get up in my lap, Beau," she said, stroking his head. "There's not room for you." Beau laid his head on her lap next to Cap'n Brown, and all was quiet except for the rhythmic ticking of the great-grandfather clock out in the living room. Its ticking filled the house and it seemed to say, "Hap-py Birth-day! Hap-py Birth-day! Hap-py Birth-day!"

The disappointment that had been lurking in Lanie all day broke the surface. "Nobody even mentioned my birthday, Cap'n Brown. They could have mentioned it at least." She put her hand on Beau's head and stroked it. "Well, maybe Daddy will bring me a present when he comes home from work."

⌖

Forrest's legs trembled slightly, for it had been a hard morning. He stood in front of the bookkeeper and took the check that the old man handed him. *I'm gettin' old. When I was twenty I could have worked three times this long.*

"Thanks a lot, Mr. Hudson."

"Sure thing, Forrest."

"The Biggins boys been through with their load yet?"

"No, sir. Ain't seen hide nor hair of 'em s'morning."

Forrest sighed. "Well, I'll see to it then."

He walked to his truck, staring at the check, then folded it and put it in his pocket. He glanced at the huge pile of logs offloaded from his flatbed. Most of them he had hauled himself. Every day seemed longer than the one before. He cut the timber, loaded it, went to the sawmill, dumped it, and went right back for another load. The Biggins brothers' regular truancy didn't help him out at all. Maybe he'd start cutting their pay.

He started the big truck and pulled out of the sawmill yard, waving at some of the hands. He stepped on the gas. The truck was running well, and he nudged at the speed limit slightly as he went out Highway 82 toward the logging road. The truck bumped and jounced over the ruts, and finally he had to stop, for this was the last place to turn around. Still no sign of his other truck, which the Bigginses would have used. Reaching over, he opened the glove compartment, picked out the thirty-eight and stuck it in his belt. He had seen enough rattlers in the deep woods to make him jumpy.

As he walked, he didn't hear the sound of men cutting lumber, and he knew something was wrong.

At the place where the last trees had been cut the day before, he stepped over a tree trunk two feet thick. When his foot hit, it struck something round, something softer than solid ground, and at the same time he heard the sound he hated worst in all the world—the deadly buzzing sound of a rattler. He threw himself over but felt something strike his boot just above the ankle. Yanking the thirty-eight from his belt, he turned and saw one of the largest rattlers he had ever seen in his life rearing back to strike again. He leveled and fired the weapon, missed, and then fired three more times. The last shot struck the rattler in the middle of the body just below the head, and the reptile fell over twitching.

"Wow! That was a close one!" Forrest could not control the trembling in his hands, and he walked over to the log and sat down, looking first for a mate. He felt weak as dishwater and sat there for five minutes until the weakness passed away. He got up, took a deep breath, and cut the rattles from the snake. It was a huge one, and if it had struck his leg above the boot instead of below, he would have had little chance. He couldn't understand timbermen who wore low-quartered shoes and wouldn't have done it himself for anything. The shots had not stirred anybody, and he discovered by walking another thirty yards that no one was there. Several trees were down, but they hadn't been trimmed or cut to length. A grim mood seized him. He walked rapidly back toward the truck, got in and started it, turned around, and headed for the Bigginses' house in the foothills.

⌑

The sight of his own logging truck parked in front of the shack brought a cold rage to Forrest. He'd had reservations about hiring the Biggins brothers, but they were the best he could find. He marched up to the door and banged on it. "Duke, Alvin, get out here!"

The door did not open for a long time, and when it did, Ethel Crawford, Duke's live-in girlfriend, emerged. She was wearing a short dress, faded and thin, and obviously with nothing under it. She was a sultry woman with red hair and blue eyes, and Forrest saw a discoloration on the left side of her face. Duke was no doubt responsible for that, he thought grimly.

"Where's Duke?"

"He ain't here."

"I know that. Where'd he and Alvin go?"

"They went in to the Green Door to get drunk."

"How'd they get there without using the truck?"

"Duke's cousin Willie came by in that old car of his."

At that moment Forrest saw something change in Ethel's eyes. She would be fat one day, but now beauty was still hers, and her full lips turned upward in a smile. "Why don't you come on in, Forrest, and have a little drink."

"No thanks, Ethel."

Ethel stepped out and squeezed his arm. "Oh, come on. You're not in any big hurry. We could have us a little party."

Ethel probably got her bruise for taking up with another man. She had put her eyes on him before, but he always ignored her. Now he pulled away. "I'm going and find those two."

"What's the matter? I'm not good enough for you?" The smile turned to a grim twisting of the lips. "You think you're better than I am! Is that it?"

"You tell 'em that I'm lookin' for 'em. I'm not payin' them to get drunk at a juke joint!" Forrest walked away, conscious of her stream of profanity as she cursed him. He shook his head as he got into the truck. *I'll have to go get Bascom to get the truck back. I'm not lettin' those clowns get in it again until I'm sure they're gonna be sober—which may be never.*

⟊⟊ CHAPTER 10 ⟊⟊

Sunlight ran fresh and fine through the trees that surrounded the small cemetery. It flashed against the sheen of the new polished stones and cut long, dark shadows on the velvet green carpet of grass. As Lanie knelt beside the grave of her mother, plucking the tiny weeds that grew there, a queer memory rose in her, a stray current out of her past. Her mother had been dead for exactly one year, for this was July the fourth, and for her that year had been as long as anything she could imagine. The days marked the time for her like the ticking of a clock that had no face or hands. At times it was difficult to remember what life had been like when her mother had been there with her cheerful smile and her quick laughter, but it came back now, and Lanie had to struggle to keep her composure. Across the grave, Maeva stood, fists clenched, and she looked ready to attack someone. Her attitude had not changed in the year that had passed. She still resented God for taking their mother from them.

"The cemetery's beautiful this time of the year, isn't it, Maeva?"

"It's all right."

"It's more than that. Look how green the grass is! There are so many birds out here. Look, there's a mockingbird flashing his wings. I wonder why they do that?" She was not really particularly interested in the mockingbird, but she wanted to soften Maeva. She got to her feet and looked at the grave, which was still mounded. Other graves were flat, having long ago sunk. She didn't want to think about that and said, "Come on. Let's go back to the house."

Lanie tried to keep up a bright conversation and pointed out a tombstone that had always amused her. It was very old and barely decipherable. "Look what that one says." She stopped and bent to read the inscription.

To the memory of Caleb Jones.
Accidentally shot April 1844
As a mark of affection
From his brother.

She smiled as she always did. "It sounds like Caleb's brother shot him as a mark of affection. I think there's a misplaced modifier or something." She watched Maeva's face, but Maeva simply shrugged and said, "Hurry up. I don't like this place."

Lanie had to quicken her pace to stay up with Maeva. Lanie finally said, "I know how much we both miss Mama, but we have to—"

"God didn't have to take her. I'm mad at Him!"

Lanie had never heard anyone say that they were mad at God, and for her own sister to say it frightened her a little bit. "You mustn't say that, Maeva."

"Why not? It's true enough. You believe in telling the truth, don't you?"

"Well, sure I do, but it worries me because God loves us so much."

Maeva shot her a glance and set her lips in a white line, tight and hard. She did not speak, and Lanie said finally, "We'll see Mama again."

Maeva stopped, turned, and planted herself as if getting ready for a battle. "I want to see her now, Lanie, not fifty years from now in heaven! Don't talk to me anymore about it." She turned and ran away at full speed.

Lanie made no attempt to catch her. "Lord," she prayed, "don't let her feel this way. She's hurt and so am I, but I know You love her, and I'm asking You to soften her heart." She moved on past the tombstones surrounded by the emerald-green grass, which seemed a strange mockery among the dead stones.

Maeva went to see the fireworks along with the others. The show was exciting enough, but she was still upset over her visit to the cemetery. She wandered away from Lanie and her two brothers, and Ralph Delaughter, the son of the mayor, joined her. "Hi, Maeva."

"Hello, Ralph."

"The fireworks were pretty neat, huh?"

"They were all right."

Ralph was two years older than Maeva, a large boy and not particularly attractive, but he had always been smitten with Maeva. She never offered him encouragement, but allowed him now to follow and chatter, and she made an answer from time to time.

Finally Ralph said, "Have you ever seen the light, Maeva?"

"You mean in church? That's the way some people ask if you've ever been saved."

"No, I don't mean that." Ralph shook his head. "I mean the Phantom Brakeman's light."

"Oh, there ain't nothin' to that, Ralph!"

"Sure there is!" Ralph nodded furiously. "I know lots of people that have seen it."

"They're just talking. There's no such thing as ghosts."

"There is!" Ralph insisted. "It all happened back a long time ago. A brakeman with the Rock Island Railroad had a pretty wife, and one of the other fellows that worked for the railroad wanted her, so he knocked the brakeman off the train and he was run over. Killed him dead."

"That'll do it." Maeva grinned briefly.

"Well, it happened, and he still walks the tracks at night. You can see the light, but when you go toward it, it disappears."

"You'd better go tell Cody about it then. He believes stuff like that."

"I'm goin' out to see him tonight."

"You won't see anything."

"You come with me, Maeva."

Maeva stopped and stared at Ralph. "Me? My daddy would whip me with a switch if I did a thing like that!"

"Don't tell him. I'm goin' late, about midnight. Stay awake and sneak out of the house. I'll meet you down by the water tower. We can walk out, and I bet you we see the light."

Maeva ordinarily would have scoffed at Ralph, but suddenly she felt rebellious and wanted to do something to shock God. "All right. I'll meet you there at midnight."

Ralph waved her off. "Ah, you won't come. You'll be scared!"

"You ever know me to be afraid of anything?"

Ralph scratched his head. "No, I never did. To tell you the truth, I'd be kind of afraid to go by myself. But I asked my cousin to go with me."

"Who's that?"

"Phil Dixon. He's seventeen. He's seen the light his own self. He'll be there with me."

"All right. I'll see you then," Maeva said. She left and found her family and was quiet for the rest of the evening.

The stars sparkled in the sky, and the moon was a huge yellow disk as Maeva walked toward the water tower. As she had anticipated, sneaking out was no problem. Her father slept soundly, and so did the rest of the family. Now the warm breath of the summer night was on her, and the water tower stood like a sentinel just ahead. No sign of Ralph. *He'd be just chicken enough not to show after getting me up in the middle of the night.*

The thought just passed her mind when she heard her name called. "Maeva! Over here!"

Turning quickly, Maeva saw Ralph step out with a boy she had not seen before. He was taller than Ralph and had a cap pulled down over his face. "This here's my cousin Phil. Phil, this is Maeva Freeman."

"Hello," Maeva said.

"I never thought a girl would come out to see a spook." Phil moved closer and shoved the ball cap back on his head. The moonlight revealed a freckled face and loose, smiling lips.

"I ain't afraid of any ghosts because I don't believe in such things!"

"You will after tonight." Phil pulled a flat bottle from his hip pocket. "Got a little somethin' to give us some nerve."

"Is that bootleg liquor?" Maeva said.

"Sure is. We make it at our place. Good stuff too." He took a swig and shoved it out toward Maeva. "Try a sip."

"I don't want any!"

"I'll try some," Ralph said. He took the bottle, tilted it, then went into a fit of coughing.

Phil grabbed the bottle to keep it from falling and laughed. "Why, you're no man, Ralph! I should have brought me a drinkin' buddy instead of a guy that can't hold his liquor and a girl that's afraid to try it."

"Who said I'm afraid?" Maeva said. She had never tasted liquor, and now she was feeling rash and restless. "Give me that bottle!" She took the bottle and sipped. It burned all the way down, but she forced herself to hand it back, saying, "I don't see what all the fuss is about."

"Well," Phil said in surprise, "I've known grown men that couldn't do as good as you done, Maeva." He took another drink and considered her. "Of course I wouldn't want to get you drunk. That might get us in trouble."

"I'm not getting drunk!"

"That's the way to talk." Phil laughed. He took another sip and handed it to Maeva. She had hated the taste of it but drank anyway. She suppressed the shudder that went through her and handed the bottle back. "Let's go see this famous ghost. You say you've seen it, Phil?"

"Sure have. Me and my brother Amos came out about this time last year. We seen it too."

"Let's go," Ralph said. "We can't stand here all night."

The three turned and started walking down the tracks, which made for difficult walking. The ties were too short for a single step, but too long for a double. Maeva tried walking on the rail awhile, for she had good balance, but it was difficult. Phil talked constantly, taking sips out of the bottle and insisting that Maeva join in. He even got Ralph to take a few sips.

A burst of delight grew in Maeva for her daring in stealing out of the house and then in drinking whiskey. She knew Lanie had never done anything like this, and that gave her a sense of pride. *She's older than I am, but she ain't got my nerve.*

They walked for fifteen minutes until finally the faint lights of town had almost faded. Maeva found herself feeling quite able to do anything. She nagged Phil about the light, accusing him of making it up, and twice more she sampled the raw white lightning from the flat bottle.

Phil shook his head with admiration. "I never saw a girl could hold her liquor like you do! You're some punkin', Maeva!"

"Well, the punkin' wants to see the light!"

"I reckon we'll see it any minute."

They walked along another five minutes and then suddenly Maeva said, "Look, what's that?"

All three of them stopped dead still, and there far off in the distance was a light of some sort. It was dim and had a bluish quality to it.

"That's it!" Phil whispered. "That's the Phantom Brakeman!"

"What we do now?" Ralph said.

"Why, we go try to catch him."

Ralph looked with alarm at Phil. "I don't want to catch him!"

"I didn't figure you would." Phil laughed. "What about you, Maeva?"

"You won't have to wait for me if you want to catch some old haunt."

Phil laughed. "All right. One more drink and we'll catch him." He and Maeva shared another sip. By this time Maeva's legs were tingling. She took two steps, but her legs would not go where she wanted them to. She tripped and went down. The rocks between the ties should have hurt, but she felt numb. She suddenly found it terribly funny that she had fallen down.

Phil was laughing too, and Ralph joined them. "Here, help me pick her up, Ralph," Phil said. "Can you walk?"

"'Course I can walk! Where is that brakeman? I'll take his durn lantern away from him!"

They staggered on down the tracks when suddenly Ralph cried out, "That ain't no brakeman! That's the incoming freight!"

Indeed it was!

"I'll tell you what," Phil said. "It looks like the brakeman ain't walkin' tonight. Let's hop this freight and ride it back to town."

"Hop it! What do you mean?" Ralph said.

"It always slows down about here. All we have to do is catch the ladder on the side and pull ourselves onto one of the flat cars. Get us a free ride. Are you game?"

"Sounds dangerous to me," Ralph said.

"I'll do it," Maeva shouted. "Where is that dadgummed old train?"

"Now wait a minute. You got to be careful, Maeva," Phil said. "If you miss, you could fall under the wheels. That wouldn't do you no good. You'd be the Phantom Schoolgirl then."

"I'm ridin' that train back. You two do what you want to."

"That's the way to talk," Phil said. "It'll be movin' pretty slow when it gets this close to town. They will probably want to stop for water. We have to get out of sight though so the engineer don't see us. Let's get over here on this side of the tracks. The fireman, he won't be lookin'."

Sure enough, when the train approached, it was moving very slowly. They waited until the engine passed, and then Phil shouted, "Look, there's some flat cars. Let's go!"

Maeva started running. She was filled with excitement, and when the front of one of the cars was close by, she made a wild grab and caught it. It pulled her off her feet, but she was able to hoist herself on. She shouted, "Come on, get on this here train!"

The two boys ran hard, and both of them jumped on. They sat down beside Maeva, and Phil said, "Ain't much left in this bottle. Might as well finish it." He took two swallows, and Maeva took a sip and then Ralph took some. "That's all she wrote," Ralph said. He threw the bottle out and laughed.

"You shouldn't of did that! We could have filled it up again."

The three of them sat there thrilled with their accomplishment. Finally the train slowed further. Phil said, "We'd better not ride 'er all the way into town. We better jump for it."

"Not me. I'm goin' all the way in," Maeva said.

The three sat there in the moonlight, the wheels clanking over the rails rhythmically. They pulled by the water tower and then into the siding. They heard the brakes being thrown, and then the clanging as the cars began to bang into each other. Maeva was caught off guard and fell flat, but she only laughed.

She heard Ralph shout, "Look out, there comes the brakeman!"

"Come on," Phil said, "we've got to get out of here!"

Maeva tried to get up, but her legs wouldn't work. She saw the two boys leap off the train, and as the train moved on, they were lost in the darkness. A dark form swung aboard the car, and then she heard a voice and felt a strong hand grab her arm. "What are you doin' here, girl?"

"Turn loose of me!"

"I'll turn loose of you! I'm gonna turn you over to the sheriff is what I'm gonna do! You crazy kids! You could have been killed. Your daddy oughtta be whipped for lettin' you out like this."

"You shut your mouth about my daddy! He's worth ten of you!"

The brakeman guffawed. "Well, I like a kid that stands up for her family, but you're goin' to see the sheriff anyway. He'll probably put you in jail."

"No he won't! He's a friend of mine!"

"He'd better be."

⚬⚬⚬

The sound of a car pulling up to the house awakened Forrest. He rolled out of bed, and by the time he got his pants on he heard a knock on the door. He moved out barefooted and found Lanie already there, holding Corliss. "Who is it, Daddy?"

"I don't know who it could be this time of the night."

Cody and Davis emerged in their underwear. Forrest hesitated, then flipped on the porch light and opened the door. "Why, Sheriff, what are you doin' here?" Then his eyes fell on Maeva. Pardue was holding her lightly by the arm, and he said, "Had a little trouble here, Forrest. Need to talk to you."

Unable to speak for a moment, Forrest finally said, "Sure. Come on in." He kept his eyes on Maeva as the sheriff led her inside. "Come on into the living room," he said, leading the way. "What's all this about, Pardue?"

"Well, Maeva here—"

"I'll tell 'im my ownself!" Maeva said. "I snuck out and went to see the Phantom Brakeman." She glared at Lanie and her brothers and then faced her father. "And I drunk some whiskey, too—so go on and whup me if you want to. I don't care."

"She was with a couple of others, boys I think, but she won't tell who they are."

"You say you've been drinkin' whiskey?"

"Yes, I have."

"Well, I'll leave you folks. This ain't no arrestin' matter. I just wanted to be sure she got home. I know you'll take care of it, Forrest."

"Sure, and thanks a lot, Pardue."

"It'll turn out all right. Kids do foolish things. I did, and I expect you did."

"I'm not sure I ever did anything this foolish," Forrest muttered. He watched as the sheriff left. Then he turned around and said, "All right, tell me all about it."

"There ain't nothin' to tell except I snuck off and went to see the Phantom Brakeman with two boys. One of them had some whiskey, and I drunk a little of it. We hopped a freight, and the brakeman caught us. The boys left, but they caught me and took me to Sheriff Jessup. That's all there is to it."

Forrest stared at this daughter of his so unlike either him or his wife or any of their other children. He saw these four all staring at her. "Well, the rest of you go back to bed. I'll need to talk to Maeva."

Without a word, but with backward glances, the three left.

"Sit down, Maeva, we'll talk."

"I don't want to be talked to. You get your belt and whup me. I know you're going to."

"I don't want to do that, Maeva. I just want to talk to you. Now sit down."

Forrest did not know how to begin. He wished that Elizabeth were there, for she would know. He asked God to give him words, but even as he spoke, he saw the hard glint in Maeva's eyes. After a time he said, "I love you, Maeva, and so do your brothers and your sister. Now go to bed."

"You ain't gonna whup me?"

"No, I'm not. I'll give you some kind of punishment, maybe doing extra work, but I don't feel like taking a belt to you."

"I wisht you would. I know I deserve it."

"I guess I deserved lots of whippins I didn't get." Forrest put his arms around Maeva. She stiffened, but he kissed her cheek. "Go on to bed, honey. It's not the end of the world."

He watched as she went upstairs and thought he saw a sign of remorse in her face, but he couldn't be sure. He went back to bed, but did not sleep. All he could do was pray, "Oh, Lord, what am I going to do with this girl?"

❧

Day after day, Forrest grew more morose. He became short-tempered and irritable with his family and with the crews that worked for him. Everyone was aware of it, and one man said, "Better stay away from the boss man. He's touchy as a bear with a sore tail."

Perhaps if Forrest had been in a better mood the thing would never have happened, but when he went out to check on the Biggins brothers and found that they were gone yet again, he blew his stack.

"That's it!" he said aloud, his face twisted with anger. "I won't put up with those worthless Bigginses any longer!"

He got into his truck and went on a hunt for the brothers. He went first to the Green Door, where Clara Richter, who owned the place, was wiping down the counter. "Clara, have the Biggins boys been here?"

"Sure were, Forrest." Clara was a big woman with a rough voice and a face that spoke of hard living. "I threw 'em out, dead drunk. Duke an' Alvin had to carry that cousin o' theirs. I hope they don't wreck your truck. You don't need that kind workin' for you, Forrest."

"They won't be anymore. I feel like I could shoot 'em both!"

"Well, they'll probably wind up in somebody else's place until they get so drunk they can't drive."

"Thanks, Clara."

Forrest drove to the Bigginses' shack not expecting to find them and was surprised to see his truck parked in front. It was jackknifed in front of the house, half-loaded with logs.

Forrest jumped out of the car and went to the door. He was furious, as angry as he had ever been in his life. He banged on the door, and there was no answer. He continued to bang and shout and eventually heard someone cursing from the inside. "Get away!"

"Open this door, Duke!"

There was talk inside and then the door opened. Duke Biggins wore a pair of overalls but no shirt. His eyes were red with drinking, and he smelled like a brewery. "What do you want?"

"I want the keys to the truck."

"I'll bring the truck back tomorrow."

"No you won't. You give me the keys right now. You're through, Duke. You and Alvin both."

Duke began to curse. Forrest shoved him backward and entered the house. Alvin, slouching at the table, was in about the same shape as his brother. Ethel Crawford, as drunk as the other two, had backed up against the wall cursing with the rest. The Bigginses' cousin, Willie, dozed on the sofa. Or maybe he was passed out.

"There'll be no talk here. Just give me the keys, and you don't need bother to come to work anymore."

Duke lunged, so drunk he could hardly stand, but he was a big, powerful man, and his blow caught Forrest in the chest. It drove him backward, but he set himself and hit Duke in the face with a solid right fist. The force of the blow drove the big man backward into the table, which collapsed.

A movement caught Forrest's eye, and he saw that Alvin Biggins had drawn a knife and was coming at him. Forrest pulled out his thirty-eight and leveled it at Alvin. "Put that knife down, Alvin." Alvin started walking toward him. Ethel screamed and cursed, but Alvin ignored her. Forrest heard Duke scrambling to his feet, but his eyes were on Alvin. Duke struck him from the back and sent him to the floor, his big hand clamped down on Forrest's wrist. "Gimme that gun! I'll make you eat it!"

The two men wrestled, and Alvin and Ethel circled, yelling at Duke to kill him.

Duke was the bigger man, but Forrest was equally strong. He twisted around, and Duke fell on him, trapping the pistol between the two bodies. Duke struck out and dealt Forrest a blow to the temple. The pistol fired. It made a muffled sound, and Forrest heard Duke cry out wildly. Duke sat up, blood streaming from his chest. "You done kilt me!"

Willie stirred on the sofa. Forrest stared at Duke's wound and knew it was serious. "We've got to get a doctor!" He started to get up.

He never made it up, for he had not seen Alvin pick up a chair and lift it high. It struck him on the head, and all he saw were thousands of tiny pinpoints of light.

Somehow, as soon as Sheriff Jessup came to the house, Maeva knew that something was wrong. "Have you come to arrest me for ridin' that train?"

"No, I haven't, Maeva. Where's Lanie?"

"She's in the house."

"Are the boys there?"

"Yes, they're here. What's wrong?"

Pardue shook his head. "I'll tell you all at once. Call 'em out."

Maeva felt a cold chill. She ran to the house and opened the door. "Lanie, Cody, Davis, you all come out here!" The three came to the porch. All four of them stared at the sheriff, whose roughly handsome face was drawn into a tense expression.

"What's wrong, Sheriff?" Lanie said in a frightened voice.

"Your daddy's got into some trouble."

"What kind of trouble?" Maeva asked, finding it hard to catch her breath.

"He got into a fight with Duke Biggins and shot him."

"Is he . . . is he dead?" Cody whispered.

"I'm afraid he is, boy. I had to arrest your daddy on a charge of murder. I hate to be the one to tell you this. There'll have to be a trial, but I want you to know, all of you, that I'll do all I can for you. And the church folks will too."

Maeva did not hear another word. *It's my fault! God's doing this to me because I drunk whiskey.* She sat down hard on the porch steps, for her legs would not hold her up. She began to cry, and the sheriff sat down and put his big arm around her. "Well, you go ahead and cry, sweetheart, and after you get through crying we'll talk some more about this."

⟫ CHAPTER 11 ⟪

After Forrest repeated his side of the story, Orrin Pierce pushed his chair back from the table, stood, and looked out the jailhouse window. His eyes were bloodshot and Forrest suspected he'd been into the bourbon. "Forrest, I believe you. I really do. But with the Biggins boys stickin' to their story, it's gonna make it hard for us to convince the jury otherwise."

"It's them against me, ain't it?" Forrest asked.

"It is."

"And it don't mean anything that the boys are no-'count?"

The attorney stared out the window without responding.

Forrest pulled his handkerchief out and wiped the sweat from his brow. "I need to get back to the house. When will I know about bail?"

Pierce kept looking out the window. "Forrest, this is a first-degree murder charge you got. There won't be bail."

"My kids need me, Orrin. You know that and so does the judge."

"I know, Forrest, but the law's clear on this one." Pierce returned to the table and sat in his chair. "Forrest, I need to be honest with you."

"I'd expect nothing else from you."

Pierce nodded. "I don't know if I have what you need to beat this one, my friend. I know you're innocent, but I'm not sure I've got the theatrical skills needed to convince the jury."

Forrest's face began to flush. "Theater skills? What are you talking about, Orrin? I need an attorney, not an actor. You know that!"

Pierce smiled. "Forrest, it surprises most folks to learn that sometimes it takes more than truth to win a criminal case. Sometimes how the case is presented and how those that are testifying are questioned makes all the difference. A skilled criminal defense lawyer can raise little nuggets of doubt in the witnesses and jury alike. Then he'll weave a story in a way that moves the jurors with the emotion of it all. All he has to do is convince them of doubt, even *some* doubt, in the evidence. I've seen the good ones work magic in the courtroom. And, my friend, barring a miracle here, we're gonna need some tricks up our sleeves, I'll tell you that."

Forrest just stared at his friend. "You sayin' you can't do that for me?"

"You know I'll do my best, but Forrest, if I were you I'd want a whole lot better criminal defense lawyer than me."

"Who?"

"Well," replied the attorney, "I know a real good one in Little Rock."

"Bet he costs a pretty penny."

"Yes, his charges are mighty high, but just having him would give the prosecutor's office a fit. They would know this case was in trouble, for sure."

Forrest wiped his forehead again. "Orrin, you know I ain't got that much money, and if I have to pay a big, fancy attorney, I won't be able to meet my loan payments."

Pierce took a deep breath and then leaned forward on the table. "It boils down to this: you either lose your place and gain your freedom, or you lose your place and you lose your freedom."

Forrest gaped in disbelief. "What are you saying?"

"Without the help of God or one real good attorney, you're going up the river for a lifelong stay—and that's only if they don't execute you. Without you, your kids won't be able to keep up the payments. And then what? They could easily end up in an orphanage in Little Rock. If we don't get you the best attorney there is, you're gonna lose it all."

Forrest's head dropped into his hands. He thought deep and long. Finally he looked back up. "Counselor, you say I need the help of the Lord or an attorney I can't afford, right?"

The attorney nodded.

Forrest sighed. "Well, I can afford the Lord. And I can't afford not to trust Him with my place, my kids, and my life."

Pierce nodded. "If that's your choice, then I've only got one other recommendation."

"What's that?"

Pierce pushed back from the table and stood up. "While you're talking to the Lord, I'll head over to the prosecutor's office and talk to him."

"About what?"

"About some kind of deal or plea bargain. It's the only prayer we got, Forrest. The only one."

⟜⟞

Lanie awoke with a start. She had been having a nightmare but could not remember what it was. She rubbed the goose flesh on her arms as she sat up and looked out the window. She could hear the birds singing and could already feel the heat radiating in through her window. After bowing her head and saying a morning prayer, Lanie went downstairs to fix breakfast.

Silently the other children filtered into the kitchen. Maeva set the table as Davis poured a glass of milk for each of them. Cody just sat at the table. As Lanie served their plates, she could see the worry on Cody's face. *That boy's never been afraid of a thing. But now he sure is.* When everyone was served, Lanie sat down and bowed her head. "Lord, we thank Thee for this day and for this food. May it strengthen us to serve You. Keep us from fear, O Lord. Give us hope for the future. And bless our daddy today and bring him home to us soon. I pray this in the name of Jesus. Amen."

The family ate in silence for several minutes until Davis finally put down his fork and said, "Lanie, you can pray all day for us not to be afraid, but I got to tell you that I'm scared for Daddy."

"Me too!" exclaimed Maeva.

"I'm scared too," added Cody. "And I'm scared for all of us, Lanie."

Lanie slowly put down her fork and wiped her lips with a napkin as she thought about what to say. "Well, I'd be less than honest if I didn't admit to being fearful myself. In fact, I've been having night-mares lately."

"I have too," Maeva said.

Lanie smiled at her. "Maeva, I suspect most anyone in our situation would be afraid, but we've just got to trust the Lord. After all, what else can we do?"

Davis nodded. "I'll tell you what we can do. We can take care of each other, and we can *never* let Daddy see that we're scared. He needs us so much."

A knock sounded on the kitchen door. Lanie turned to see Madison Jones. "Hi, Reverend! Come on in!"

"Good morning, children." Madison entered the kitchen, followed by his son Bascom.

"Davis, you and Cody pull up two chairs," Lanie said. "Madison, you and Bascom have a seat. Can I get you some breakfast?"

Madison smiled as he and Bascom sat in the chairs the boys had pulled up to the table. "We done already had breakfuss, but I appreciates the offer. We just come by to say that all the folks around know that your daddy is innocent and we all been prayin'."

Lanie nodded. "Thanks, Madison, that's sure appreciated."

Then Madison said, "Bascom done come to me with an idea. And I want you children to hear it." Madison turned to his son. "Tell them what you told me, son."

"I knows that your daddy's work needs to go on. If'n it don't, you all gonna lose the business and lose your home."

Lanie put her fork down. Her mouth began to feel dry.

"Your daddy has one good crew, but that still leaves two trucks not working. I been working with your daddy for two years now, and I think he trusts me. So this here's my idea." All eyes were glued on him. "What I'd like to do is take over his truck and get my brother Luke to help me."

Lanie and Davis nodded as they thought about the idea. Bascom seemed to get more enthusiastic. "And you know my sister Fannie married Josh Simpson. He's real good in the woods and he's got common sense. And he's good with trucks and driving. I was thinking he could run the other truck and I could help him find some good hands." Bascom paused a second to let his comments seep in. "That's my idea."

Lanie continued to nod as she looked down and thought about Bascom's scheme. Everyone was staring at her. Finally she looked up, smiled at Bascom, and then looked at Madison. "Madison, I'd say your son's idea sounds pretty good."

Madison's smile seemed to light up the room. "Well, I'm a might proud to hear that. I think Bascom done come up with one fine plan." Then he became more serious. "But, Miss Lanie, you gotta realize that some folks might not like it."

"What's not to like?" Davis interjected.

Madison looked at him. "Well, Davis, there's folks would take offense about letting black men take over the jobs of white men."

"Well, rain on 'em!" Maeva exclaimed. "I don't see nobody else standing in line to help us!"

Lanie and Davis laughed. "Maeva's right!" Lanie declared. "I say let's go see what Daddy says!"

"Hooray!" shouted Cody and Davis in unison. Lanie and Madison laughed together, and for the first time in days, she felt some hope.

⌐━━•⊱

The heat in the jail cell was oppressive. A deputy had placed a floor fan just outside Forrest's cell, but it really only circulated the hot, muggy air, which made his mood even worse than it already was.

"Forrest!" called the sheriff. "You've got visitors."

Forrest sat up to see Sister Myrtle and Brother Prince walking toward the cell, smiling, and he stood to welcome them. "Well, to what do I owe a visit from two pastors at once?"

Brother Prince began. "Morning, Forrest. Just came by to see how you're doing."

Myrtle nodded. "We want you to know that we've got our churches fasting and praying for you."

"Of course," Brother Prince said, "I'm expecting our prayers to be answered sooner than those of Sister Myrtle's church."

Forrest smiled as he saw the gleam in Brother Prince's eyes.

Sister Myrtle said, "Ain't no truth to that, Brother Forrest. When you expect God to do a miracle, like you be needing, then it be best to have the brothers and sisters at the Fire Baptized Pentecostal Church praying and fasting. And that's the truth."

"I'll tell you what the truth is," said Brother Prince. "It's that we all be praying for you, Brother Forrest."

"Amen," said Forrest.

Myrtle asked, "You need anything?"

"Tell you what, Sister. If any of your folks want to cook up a cake or pie and bring it down here, me and the sheriff would appreciate it. The jail cooks seem to forget to do dessert from time to time. Ain't that right, Sheriff?"

"That's sure enough true!" called the Sheriff.

"Consider it done, Forrest!" Myrtle smiled and looked over her shoulder and lowered her voice. "I'll have the sisters put a hacksaw blade in the cake to help you escape."

Sheriff Jessup stood, smiled, and walked over to the two pastors. "Sister Myrtle, no need to do that."

"Why not?"

"'Cause I'm betting on your prayers to give us that miracle we're all hoping for!"

Sister Myrtle pretended to scowl at him, "Now, Sheriff, don't you know it's a sin to gamble?"

"Not when I'm betting on your prayers, Sister."

⌌══⌐

The Dew Drop Inn bustled with activity. Dr. Oscar Givens was eating at a booth with Orrin Pierce and Sheriff Jessup. Jessup leaned forward toward the men sitting across the table from him. "You hear what happened at Mamie Dorr's today?"

"At the beauty shop?" asked Orrin.

"Yep."

Both men shook their heads.

"Mrs. Langley was there getting her hair done and said some fairly nasty things about Forrest and his kids. Mamie threatened her with a big pair of scissors and then threw her out of the shop. Cassandra Pruitt was there and saw the whole thing."

"I'm not sure it was wise to rile that old crow," Orrin said.

Doc Givens laughed. "You're probably right, Orrin, but I'd a paid a month's wages to have seen that. Probably the first time that lady's been put in her place in some time."

Pardue laughed and each of the men took a bite of his dinner. The door swung open and Alvin Biggins and his cousin Willie, along with Ethel Crawford, walked in and sat at the counter.

"There's trouble here," Pardue mumbled. Orrin and the doctor looked over their shoulders to see the unwelcome company.

Sister Myrtle was in the back picking up an order. When she didn't appear right away, Alvin cried out, "Hey! Anybody back there to take my order?"

Myrtle stuck her head out the kitchen door. "Be right with you!"

Alvin scowled. "How 'bout you drop what you're doin' and come take our order."

Myrtle stuck her head out again. Everyone in the café had turned their attention toward the counter. "What did you say?" Sister Myrtle asked. Pardue could see that her eyes were fiery.

"You get out here and take my order! Now!"

Myrtle let the kitchen door slam behind her and slowly walked to the counter just in front of Alvin. "The Good Book tells me that patience is a virtue, Mr. Biggins. Maybe you should try to get a little. Might make you a bit more pleasant." She smiled at him.

"Why don't you shut up and take our order?"

The kitchen door opened again and now Charlie walked out. His apron was greasy and dirty, and he rubbed the blade of a butcher knife across his abdomen.

Alvin looked at him and back at Sister Myrtle. "What I need from you is three cheeseburgers and three Cokes. And this time, why don't you put a bit more ice in 'em. You hear? And don't keep me and my friends waitin'."

As Charlie took a step toward the counter, Pardue bounded out of his booth and took a seat by Alvin.

"Alvin, I can't believe you're ordering cheeseburgers."

"Why not?"

"Why, me and my friends just got the last three. So maybe you all best order your cheeseburgers somewhere else. All right?"

Alvin turned on the stool to face the sheriff and leaned forward until his nose was only inches from Pardue's. "I got a right to eat here."

"You'd best go find another café, Biggins."

Snickers rippled around the café as Alvin glowered.

Ethel spoke up. "Come on, boys. Let's go get us some good grub. Sure won't find it in this here rat hole!"

She and Willie stood and left. Alvin was still staring at the sheriff.

"You gonna be smart like your friends, or are you gonna give me the pleasure of dragging your no-good self to my jail?"

Alvin smiled. "Sheriff, the only no-good around here is that lyin' murderer what's already locked up in your jail. And pretty soon that slime ball's gonna be rotting in the state pen—that is, if he's not swinging from the end of the hangman's noose."

Alvin stood and turned to leave.

"Biggins!" Pardue called out.

The man turned slowly.

"The only way that man's going to prison is if you and Ethel place your hands on God's Holy Bible, swear to tell the truth, the whole truth, and nothing but the truth, and then sit in the witness stand and lie to God and the good people of Fairhope."

An evil smile spread across Alvin's lips, revealing his yellow teeth. Then he turned and left the inn.

The sheriff watched the door for a moment, and Charlie put his arm around his wife. The doc and Orrin stood and walked over to the sheriff, who spun around on the counter stool to face Myrtle and Charlie. "You are good people. I'm not gonna let you be mistreated."

"Thanks, Sheriff," said Charlie. "I was afraid I was gonna have to filet that gook."

"Wouldn't have been a good thing, my friend. But if he or any of his gang gives you any further trouble, you let me know, you hear?"

"I was afraid they were going to jump you, Pardue," Doc Givens said. "Then what would you have done?"

The sheriff smiled. "Well, I know you two would have jumped in the fray, and I suspect Charlie here would have commenced to cut some slices of meat. Right, Charlie?"

Charlie's smile spread across his face. "Sheriff, there would have been ears a flying, just like in the Garden of Gethsemane, I'll tell you that."

The men laughed, but Myrtle was still shaking and staring at the door.

"You all right, Myrtle?" Pardue asked.

"That man scares me, Sheriff. He's pure, unadulterated evil, and he's gonna get in that witness box and lie his pants off. I best have my church fast and pray during the entire trial."

Orrin looked at Myrtle. "I think you're right, Sister."

"Then why not join us, Mr. Pierce? We would love to have you praying with us!"

"Sister, it's times like these that I wish I had a line to God, but I don't. So I guess it's up to you people who do."

Myrtle smiled at the silver-haired attorney and then reached across the counter to pat his forearm. "One day you will. I think that old hound of heaven's got you in his scent, so I'm gonna be praying for Forrest and for his attorney."

⇒ CHAPTER 12 ⇐

The trial of Forrest Freeman was set for September the fourth at nine o'clock. At seven Delilah Jones came over to the Freeman house to take care of Corliss. She helped Lanie fix breakfast, and after the youngsters all sat down, she said, "We gonna pray over dis heah food, and we gonna pray over your daddy. You want to do it, Miss Lanie, or do you wants me to?"

"You do it, Delilah," Lanie said. She could barely speak, for her throat was closed with fear. She had slept spasmodically throughout the night, and now that the time had come, she could not see how she could go through the trial.

Delilah said, "You chil'uns all reach out and hold hands." She took Lanie's hand and Cody's on the other side, then said, "Lord, You knowed all 'bout dis problem before these chil'uns was even born, before this world was even made. You knows all 'bout us. There ain't nothin' we can hide from You, and, Lord, this mornin' I wants to put this precious father in Your hands. The judge, he think Mr. Forrest is in his hands, but he ain't. He's in Your hands. So now, Lord, I'm askin' You to show Your everlastin' tender mercies and to take keer of these chil'uns and to take care of Mr. Forrest. In Jesus' name." She lifted her head and said, "Now, you eat."

"I'm not hungry," Maeva said in a small voice.

"You eat anyway. Dat trial they say could last several days, so you're gonna need to keep your strength up."

The children had little to say, so Delilah kept speaking about how God performs miracles, and they ate what they could. Finally Lanie lifted her head at the sound of a motor. "There's the car," she said. "That's probably Mr. Jinks to take us to the courthouse." She leaned over and kissed Corliss, who chortled happily and doubled up her fists and struck herself in the eye. "You be a good girl, Corliss."

"She always be a good girl. Don't you worry 'bout her, Miss Lanie. I'll be right here."

"Thank you, Delilah. You're a comfort."

Deoin Jinks and his wife were waiting in their big Oldsmobile, and the four Freemans squeezed together in the back seat. "Are Alice and Max going?" Lanie asked.

Agnes Jinks turned around. "They've already gone. They walked." She reached out her hand, and when Lanie took it, she said, "You poor things, I bet you didn't sleep a wink last night."

"Not much, ma'am."

"Well, it'll be all right."

"Of course it will," Deoin said with as much force as he could muster. "Everybody knows what sorry trash the Biggins brothers are. It was an accident, that's what it was."

"That's not what Alvin Biggins says, or that woman Ethel Crawford," Maeva said, her voice hard. "They're gonna swear that Daddy did wrong."

"How do you know that?" Agnes Jinks asked in surprise.

"Because Alvin Biggins has been goin' around tellin' it. He thinks he's big. Well, he ain't nothin' but a big liar!"

"Don't get yourself stirred up, Maeva," Lanie said. "We've got to face this thing, and it doesn't do any good to get mad at Alvin Biggins."

Maeva didn't answer, and there was silence in the car until they turned down Main Street and headed toward the courthouse square.

"My land, look at the cars!" Deoin exclaimed. "I ain't seen this many cars since election day!"

The parking places around the courthouse were all taken, filled with pickups and farm trucks. Agnes said, "All the country people have come to town. Why didn't they stay home? This isn't a show!"

"You know how it is with a big trial," Deoin said. He frowned. "We'll have to park several blocks away and walk back."

As they walked the three blocks to the courthouse, Lanie and the others were intensely aware of people casting curious glances their way. Many of them were friends, and more than one said, "We're praying for you kids."

But as soon as they reached the courthouse steps, a man with a camera jumped in front of them, held it up, and flashed a light in their face. "My name's Simpson. I'm with the *Arkansas Democrat*. I'd like to talk to you kids."

Simpson planted himself in the way. He was a small man with scanty sandy hair and a pair of thick glasses. "What do you kids think about that Judge Lawrence Simons? He's the one they call the hangin' judge, you know."

Suddenly the newspaperman seemed to rise up. He let out an alarmed cry, "Ow! What are you doin'?"

Coach Dempsey Wilson had appeared from nowhere. He was a strong young man, and he simply turned Simpson around, saying, "There'll be no interviews of these children. Now let me help you out of here."

Lanie felt relief as the teacher hauled Simpson off.

Inside, the chief of police, Ed Hathcock, was waiting. "I got you children some seats up front. Come along." He led them to the front, and they sat down on the left side. Doc Givens was sitting on the bench, and he put his hand on Lanie's arm and said, "How are you feeling, Lanie?"

"Not very good, Dr. Givens."

Givens seemed to struggle for something to say. He had cigar ashes on the front of his shirt, and the shirt itself was not too clean. He pulled at his whiskers and ran his hand through his salt-and-pepper hair. "It'll be all right," he said.

Lanie watched as a small, rather fierce-looking man turned around. He was sitting at a table just beyond the railing that separated the audience from the area where the lawyers and the judge sat. "Who's he, Dr. Givens?"

"That's Carlton Hobbs. He's the prosecuting attorney. Turned down Mr. Pierce's plea bargain."

"He looks mean," Cody said. "What's wrong with him?"

Myrtle Poindexter, seated with Charlie right behind the Freeman family, leaned forward and said in a voice that could be heard by all, "He's runnin' for office, and he wants to make a showin'. God help us when we got men like that in our courtroom!"

Hobbs gave the woman a hard look, but he got nothing off Myrtle, who returned the expression.

"Look," Davis said, "there's Daddy!"

Everyone in the courtroom turned to look as the police chief came out leading Forrest. Forrest stepped inside the big courtroom and saw his children at once. He tried to smile, but the bags under his eyes seemed to stop it.

Cody said, "Daddy looks plum peaked, don't he? He's real worried."

Orrin Pierce spoke rapidly to Forrest for the next five minutes, and Lanie felt herself choke up again with fear. This place was like a machine that had caught her father up and was pulling him in, where he would be mangled.

Suddenly a big man with black eyes and dark hair stood up and said, "Oyez, oyez, this court is now in session, Judge Lawrence Simons presiding."

The judge was a small man with brown hair and steady, gray eyes. He did not smile, and when he said, "You may be seated," Lanie sat down weakly.

"He's the one they call the hanging judge," Cody whispered.

"Be quiet," Davis said. "You're not supposed to talk in here."

Judge Simons looked at the paper in front of him and then out over the crowd. "This case involves the State against Forrest Wayne Freeman on the charge of first-degree murder." He said more that Lanie did not understand, but the words *first-degree murder* chilled her. Everyone spoke of the shooting as *the accident*, but the judge had not minced words. Now he said, "The prosecution may make the opening statement."

Carlton Hobbs leaped to his feet, a dapper man wearing a gray suit and a blue tie. His hair was carefully cut, and his voice was loud and penetrating for a small man. "This case is clear. The defendant, Forrest Wayne Freeman, took a gun to the home of Marvin Biggins, better known as 'Duke,' and killed him in cold blood. The State will prove that there was bad blood between the two men. They had trouble in the past on more than one occasion. The State will also produce eyewitnesses who will testify that they saw the defendant pull his revolver and shoot the victim without provocation."

The speech went on for some ten minutes, and finally Judge Simons leaned forward and said, "I think that is enough, Mr. Hobbs."

"Of course, Your Honor. I just wanted to make it clear that this is a simple case."

"Suppose you present your evidence and let me decide whether it's simple or not."

"Of course, Your Honor."

"The defense may make an opening statement."

Orrin Pierce rose and began to speak. He was a much finer-looking man than Hobbs—tall, good-looking, well educated. He had a drinking problem, but it was not evident this day. His voice was clear, as were his eyes. "We will prove that the defendant, Forrest Wayne Freeman, has never been a violent man. We will show that Duke Biggins was indeed a violent man. We will prove he made threats against the defendant on many occasions, and we will prove that the witnesses are all prejudiced."

The speech went on for a long time, and hope rose in Lanie. It all sounded so clear the way Pierce put it. Finally he sat down, and the judge said, "The prosecution will present its evidence."

Hobbs rose at once and said, "Your Honor, I am interested in making this case short in the interest of saving time."

Judge Simons lifted one eyebrow and stared at Hobbs. "Mr. Hobbs, the court is more interested in justice being done."

Hobbs swallowed hard and blushed. "Yes, Your Honor. The prosecution calls Willie Biggins."

Willie Biggins came forward. He was a tall, shambling man in his early twenties dressed in an ill-fitting suit obviously new and bought for the occasion. He had tow-colored hair, watery blue eyes, and could hardly raise his voice above a whisper because he was so nervous. He continually pulled at his tie, and after he was sworn in he stared at Forrest as if he had never seen him before. He dropped his head quickly when Forrest met his gaze.

"Mr. Biggins, you were present when the murder was committed."

"I object," Pierce said. "You have not proved yet that it was murder, Mr. Hobbs."

"Objection sustained," the judge said.

"Well," Hobbs said, "let me put it this way. When the shooting took place, you were in the room?"

"Yes, sir, I was."

"Would you please tell the jury what happened."

"Well, we was all in the house, and suddenly there was a bangin' on the door. And when Duke went to the door, he came right in."

"Who came right in? Be specific, please."

"Him. Forrest Freeman."

"The defendant right over there."

"Yeah, him. He came in and he had a gun in his hand, and he was mad."

"Did he say anything?"

"He began cussin', and when Duke tried to talk to him, he just lifted that pistol and shot him right where he stood."

"There was no provocation?"

"No what?"

"Your cousin did not do anything to make the defendant angry?"

"He didn't do nothin' except try to talk to him. Freeman, he just shot Duke for no reason. He never did like him no how."

"Objection!" Pierce said.

"Objection sustained."

Hobbs made Willie Biggins go over his story twice, then he said, "No more questions."

Judge Simons said, "You may question the witness, Mr. Pierce."

Pierce rose. "May I approach the witness, Your Honor?"

"Yes, you may."

Pierce positioned himself directly in front of Willie Biggins. He held the man's gaze for a moment, and Biggins dropped his eyes. "Were you drunk when this scene took place?"

"Objection!" Hobbs said. "That has no bearing."

"I believe it does, Your Honor. It makes a difference whether a witness is drunk or sober."

"Objection denied. Continue, Mr. Pierce."

"Were you drunk?"

"We had a little bit to drink."

"I can call witnesses from the saloon, the Green Door, who will testify that you were so drunk that your cousin and his brother had to carry you out."

"Well, I reckon maybe I was drunk."

"So drunk that you couldn't see straight?"

"I seen what he done all right." Willie Biggins began to squirm.

"How is it that the defendant, Mr. Freeman, was knocked unconscious? He had a gun in his hand. You say he shot Duke Biggins, and yet he was knocked unconscious."

"Alvin got behind him and hit him with a chair after he shot Duke."

The questioning went on for some time, and Willie's nervousness grew worse. Finally Pierce said, "I think the jury can see what kind of a witness you are. You were drunk, so drunk you had to be carried out of the saloon, and now you're expecting this jury to believe that you saw all this."

"I seen what I seen!"

"I have no more questions, Your Honor."

Hobbs stood up and said, "I call Ethel Crawford to the stand."

Ethel Crawford looked better than anyone had ever seen her. Doc Givens whispered hoarsely, "Hobbs took her and got her all cleaned up. Bought her new clothes and got her hair fixed. She hasn't looked that respectable in her whole life."

"You were in the room when the shooting took place, Miss Crawford?"

"Yes, I was." Ethel Crawford stared defiantly at Forrest. "I seen it all."

"Will you tell the jury, please, what you saw."

Ethel Crawford basically repeated Willie's story. Her voice rose, and she said, "He killed him. He's nothin' but a murderer!"

"Objection, Your Honor," Orrin Pierce said.

"Sustained. You will keep your remarks to yourself, Miss Crawford."

"Yes, Your Honor."

"I have no further questions," Hobbs said. "Your witness, Counselor."

Pierce studied the woman. She glared at him defiantly, and he said, "It is Miss Crawford, isn't it?"

Ethel stared at him. "Yes, that's right."

"So, you are not the wife of the dead man."

"N-no, I ain't."

"But you lived with him."

"We . . . we was good friends." A twitter went over the room. "There ain't nothin' funny about that!" Ethel said to the court.

"Your Honor, please instruct the witness to answer the questions and refrain from personal remarks."

"You will answer the questions, Miss Crawford, nothing else."

Ethel Crawford dropped her head, and then, for the next twenty minutes, Pierce stripped her bare. She had lived with more than one man, which she denied until he offered to have them testify, and in each case she said, "Maybe I did stay with them a little bit."

"Oh, so you stayed with them a little bit. That means you lived with them out of wedlock."

"I guess that's right."

"You guess that's right! You know it's right, don't you?"

"All right then. It's right."

"Did you ever have any trouble with Forrest Freeman?"

"He never liked me."

"It is true," Pierce said quietly, "that you made advances toward him and he rejected you."

"That's a filthy lie! I never did!"

"I can bring witnesses who will testify that you did."

Ethel suddenly seemed to collapse. "I liked him, I guess, but he wouldn't have nothin' to do with me." She glared at him. "He thought he was too good for me."

"I have no more questions, Your Honor."

"You may step down, Miss Crawford."

The jury watched Ethel Crawford leave the stand. She could not look up, and Lanie saw her give her father a look of bitter hatred.

"I now call Alvin Biggins to the stand."

Alvin Biggins was sworn in. He, too, was wearing a new suit and was shaved for a change. He told the same story, and when Hobbs was through and said, "Your witness," Alvin looked with some trepidation at Pierce.

"You had a fight once with the defendant, didn't you?"

"He hit me when I wasn't lookin'. I wasn't doin' nothin'."

"Several witnesses say you were attempting to molest his young daughter."

"That's a lie! I was just being nice to her."

"I can bring witnesses who will testify that you did make improper advances to Mr. Freeman's daughter."

"Well, mebby it looked that ways."

"Have you ever been in jail?"

"In jail?"

"Yes, in jail. Is that too hard for you? Have you ever been in jail?"

"I reckon."

"How many times?"

"Two or three."

Pierce walked over to the table and picked up a piece of paper. "I have a record here that you've been in jail sixteen times. Would you care to have me read them?"

"Uh, I didn't know it was that many."

"I object," Hobbs shouted. "The witness's criminal record has nothing to do with this testimony."

"I believe the jury may have different ideas about that," Pierce said.

Lanie sat on the edge of the bench through eight hours of testimony, with an hour out for lunch. When the judge ended the day, she asked Doc Givens, "How long will it take?"

"I don't know, honey." The grandfatherly man patted her shoulder. "Maybe a long time. Lawyers like to drag things out."

"I don't think I can stand it."

"You'll have to, honey. We all have to."

⌁⋆⋆

The defense began on the third day. Orrin Pierce had warned them that the only defense they had was Forrest's good record and his word against the bad record of Duke's allies.

Before Forrest took the stand, Pierce brought eight character witnesses forward, all giving the same testimony: Forrest had never given anyone any trouble and never shown a violent streak.

Finally Forrest himself took the stand. He told his story in a straightforward fashion, and Lanie kept her hands clasped together for the duration. "How could anybody not believe him?" she whispered. She watched the jury but could not read their faces.

When Hobbs got up to cross-examine, he seemed to be a man beside himself. "Do you carry a gun, Mr. Freeman?"

"I have a gun."

"I didn't ask if you had a gun. I asked if you carried it?"

"I carry it when I go to the woods. I've shot many a snake with that gun."

"Do you carry it when you're not in the woods?"

"Not as a rule."

"Not as a rule," Hobbs sneered. "But you were carrying it when you went to the home of the murdered man."

"I had been in the woods, and it was in my belt. I simply forgot about it."

"Oh, you forgot about it!" Hobbs glanced at the jury. "I find that difficult to believe."

"It's the truth though."

"You'd had trouble with Duke Biggins before."

"Quite a few times. He worked for me, and he was unreliable. I had to stay on him constantly."

Hobbs continued to hammer on the fact that Forrest had a gun, and finally he said, "I think the jury understands clearly what has happened. You had a gun, you were angry, and you went in the house and shot the man dead."

Forrest did not answer, for there was no question.

"Is that true or not?"

"I've told you. Alvin Biggins drew a knife. I pulled the gun to stop him from stabbing me. Duke grabbed me from behind and wrestled me to the floor. The gun went off, and he was shot accidentally."

"But three witnesses have sworn that you are lying."

"They can swear all they want to, but they're the liars."

❦

The trial dragged on for another day, but eventually both sides reached the end of their presentations. Both Hobbs and Pierce made their final statements, and the judge said, "The jury will now retire. They will find the verdict before they return to this courtroom. Court is recessed."

Lanie looked around in confusion. "What do we do now?"

Orrin came over and said, "Are you kids all right?"

"What do we do now, Mr. Pierce?" Cody said. "How long will it be?"

"Nobody knows that, son. We just have to hang around and wait. I know it's hard, but there's no other way."

The jury did not return by five o'clock, and the judge declared that the court would not reconvene until the next day, if then.

"Come on. I'll take you kids home," Doc Givens said.

"Oh, we'll do it," Mr. Jinks said. "We got that big car of ours."

"All right, Deoin." The doctor looked at the four youngsters. "I know this is hard, but you're going to have to be strong." When he walked away, his shoulders were slumped.

Maeva stared after him. "He thinks Daddy's going to be found guilty."

"Come on," Deoin said. "Let's don't hang around this place."

❦

"I got a good supper fixed," Delilah said when they walked in the house.

"I don't want nothin'," Maeva said. She turned and ran up the stairs.

"I ain't hungry either," Cody said.

"You got to eat. We all do," Lanie said. "Delilah fixed a good supper, and we've got to eat it. Has Corliss been good?"

"As good as gold."

Lanie forced herself to eat, and after Delilah left she spent the evening taking care of Corliss. She got on the floor with her and played with her until bedtime. She put her in the bed, got her to sleep, then went to her own bedroom. She knelt down beside her bed and prayed for a long time for her father to be found innocent. She began crying somewhere in the middle of her prayer and simply got into bed. Cap'n Brown hopped up and pushed himself against her. She rubbed his silky fur. "Cap'n Brown, I couldn't stand it if my daddy had to go to jail."

Cap'n Brown began to purr.

"The jury's back," Orrin Pierce said. He'd brought the children to a special room, and his eyes were bloodshot and droopy.

"How does it look, Mr. Pierce?" Davis asked.

"You never know about a jury, but I think we've got a good chance. Come on. Let's go back."

In the crowded courtroom, people whispered until the judge came out. They all rose, and when the judge sat down, they took their seats again.

Judge Simons was silent for a time. He looked down at Forrest, who had been brought in by the police chief and was sitting beside Pierce. He said, "Will the defendant please rise?" Judge Simons turned to the jury. "Have you reached a verdict?"

Tom Maddox stood up. He was a farmer from east of town and said, "Yes, Judge, we have."

"How do you find?"

"We do not find the defendant guilty of murder in the first degree."

A wave of joy went through Lanie, and she clutched Maeva's arm.

"We find him guilty of manslaughter."

Lanie's skin turned cold, and she could not move.

Judge Simons said, "I thank the jury for their work. It's the court's duty to make the world see that anyone who takes a life pays for it. I therefore sentence you, Forrest Wayne Freeman, to the maximum sentence for the crime of manslaughter. You will be delivered to the State Penitentiary at Cummings and serve for ten years at that institution."

Maeva jumped up and shouted, "You're a bad man, Judge! I hope you die!"

Judge Simons flinched and stared at the young girl glaring at him with a fierce hatred. He chose to ignore her.

Lanie put her arm around Maeva, trying not to cry, but when she saw her daddy being taken away, his shoulders bent, she couldn't help it. She turned blindly and stumbled into the arms of Miss Eden Marie Dunsmore, her English teacher, and began to weep.

PART THREE

The Miracle

⋙ CHAPTER 13 ⋘

F ar in the east a milky whiteness announced the rising of the sun.
Lanie, unable to sleep, got up, dressed, and went down to the kitchen.
She started a fire in the stove, for the September weather was cold for
Arkansas, and fixed a pot of coffee. Even this simple act was difficult, for
it reminded her that this was the first thing she had done when she fixed
breakfast for her father.

Pulling a sweater off a peg by the door, she slipped it on, picked up
the mug of coffee, and went outside. For a time she stood on the front
porch noting the gray spirals of smoke that rose from the stoves and fire-
places in Fairhope. She wondered how many of the families in those
houses were thinking of the Freemans. A touch on the back of her legs
startled her, and she turned to see Beau standing there. She knelt down
and, holding the coffee in her left hand, put her arm around him. "Good
morning, Beau," she whispered. "How are you this morning?"

The big dog whined and licked her face. He gazed at her out of
his mismatched eyes, one robin's-egg blue, the other a warm brown.
For a few moments Lanie fought back the tears, as she did every morning since she had said good-bye to her father. In this early cobwebby
time of the day, the sadness seemed to well up in her. She cleared her
throat and said as best as she could, "I haven't got time for you, Beau.
I've got to fix breakfast."

Going back into the house, she started the routine. Her mind and
hands worked quickly. At seven o'clock, she went upstairs and woke
the boys and Maeva. By the time she got back downstairs, Corliss was
awake, and she quickly changed her diaper and pulled the bed into the
cooking area where it was warm. She heard the footsteps, and the boys
came in with their hair wild and uncombed.

"You can't go to school like that!" Lanie said.

"I don't want to go to school, and Maeva says she ain't goin'!" Cody proclaimed.

"What are you talking about? You've got to go to school! Here, you hold Corliss while I go talk to Maeva."

She mounted the stairs and found Maeva staring at her defiantly from the bed. "Get out of that bed, Maeva! You've got to go to school."

"I ain't goin'!"

"Of course you're going. You got to go. It's the law. Now don't make things any worse than they are."

Maeva glared at Lanie but finally threw back the covers and got out of bed and began pulling off her flannel gown. "Well, I'll go to the dumb old school—but I ain't gonna learn nothin'!"

"You just hurry up and get downstairs. You've got chores to do."

Lanie knew that it was going to be up to her to put the pressure on Maeva and her brothers. Davis would be no trouble, but Cody and Maeva would be. Her lips tightened as she went back into the kitchen. "You two go get washed up. I'll have breakfast on the table by the time you get back."

Cody grumbled, but the two of them went. Lanie finished the breakfast of scrambled eggs, fried ham, red-eye gravy, and biscuits left over from the day before. As they sat down to eat, she did not wait, but bowed her head and began praying. "Lord, bless this food and keep us safe. Be with Daddy, Lord, and we're asking You to get him out of that place. In Jesus' name. Amen."

The boys began shoveling the scrambled eggs into small mounds, breaking their biscuits and pouring gravy over them. Maeva shook her head rebelliously. "There ain't no sense in prayin' to get Daddy out of Cummings Prison."

"Yes there is. God can do anything. Eat your breakfast and then go out and do your chores."

Delilah came early, and as the children left the house, she said, "You do good now—and mind you keep your head up high. Don't let nobody give you no sass. God's gonna rare back and do a miracle with yo' daddy."

"Thank you, Delilah. That's what I like to hear," Lanie said. She left the house with the others, and they were joined by Alice and Max Jinks, who were bundled up against the cool fall air. Neither of them said a word about the trial, and Lanie was fairly certain their parents had strictly warned them against it. Max, Davis, and Cody ran on ahead while the three girls followed. Others joined them on the way, and not a one of them mentioned the fate of Forrest Freeman.

By the time they arrived at school, Lanie had steeled herself against what she considered to be an ordeal. She spoke to several of her friends and was aware that people cast secret glances at her. She remembered what Delilah had said, and she kept her head up high and managed to keep a semblance of a smile on her face. Helen Langley met her glance and held it for a moment, then put her head up and walked away.

Lanie's first class was math, and she walked into Mr. Dixon's room and took her seat without speaking to anybody. Mr. Dixon was already at the board putting problems on it, and Lowell Stockwell, who had revolutionized the role of the innkeeper in the Christmas pageant, whispered from behind Lanie. "I can't work none of these problems, Lanie. You gotta let me see your answers."

Lanie did not respond. Lowell could never pass math anyway, so everyone in the class let him copy. Mr. Dixon was aware of this, but said nothing. The math class passed without incident except that when she left, Mr. Dixon happened to put himself by the door as the students moved out. As Lanie passed, he put his hand on her shoulder, startling her. He winked at her and smiled. "You're lookin' good this morning, Lanie."

The compliment flustered Lanie. "Why . . . thank you, Mr. Dixon. You look good too."

"We make a good-looking couple." He squeezed her shoulder, and Lanie knew that he was on her side at least.

The morning went quickly, and Lanie got through it hoping that Maeva and the boys had not gotten into trouble. The elementary students had less sophistication and, perhaps, were less kind than older students. She was tense all morning expecting the principal to come tell her that Maeva had punched somebody in the eye.

When she went into the cafeteria carrying her lunch, the Sixkiller twins, Dawn and Victor, approached her on each side. "Hey, come on and let's eat. Maybe I'll swap sandwiches with you," Vic said.

Dawn winked at her. "Don't trade with him. He's already tried to swap with half a dozen people."

They sat down, and Vic said, "I'll go get the milk. You girls just sit here. Don't be monkeyin' with my lunch."

Dawn turned to Lanie. "Why don't you come home with me after school today? Daddy's taking care of some brand-new collie puppies. They're the cutest things you ever saw."

"Oh, I'd love to, Dawn, but I have to get home and take care of Corliss."

"Well, maybe you can come later."

Lanie was aware that the girl was trying to show her sympathy, and she was grateful for it. When Vic came back with three glasses of milk, spilling some in the process, he said, "What kind of a sandwich you got?"

"Ham and cheese."

"All I got's a dumb old tuna fish. I hate tuna fish."

"Here. You can have mine. I'll trade you."

Vic snatched at the sandwich and shook his head. "You're not very smart, Lanie, trading good old ham and cheese for tuna fish." He stuffed his mouth full and talked constantly. "You know, if it was the good old days, me and Dawn would be eatin' buffalo tongue or maybe the liver. Those were the days." He shook his head woefully and turned his eyes up and feigned sorrow. "No dumb school. Just huntin' and scalpin' the white eyes. Your scalp would be real good, Lanie." He reached out and grabbed Lanie by the hair and gave it a pull.

"Let her alone or I'll scalp you!" Dawn said.

"Well, she has got the prettiest hair I ever saw. Sure would make a nice-lookin' scalp hanging from my tepee."

As the three ate, others came by, and several managed to offer Lanie a cheerful word. She knew they were showing their support and thought, *Maybe I can make it. Most people are so kind!*

⊙━⋋⊱

Doc Givens stepped inside the Dew Drop Inn, paused for a moment, and ran his eye around the crowd. Mamie Dorr, the beauty operator, was talking with Zeno Bruten, the mortician. They made an odd-looking pair, Mamie flushed and full of life, and Zeno Bruten looking like one of his own deceased clients, thin, lanky, and pale.

Doc Givens took the table next to the couple, and Mamie turned and flashed a smile at him. "Hi, Doc."

"Good day, Mamie."

"You know, you don't need to be eatin' in this restaurant all the time. Not good for your stomach."

Givens glanced at her. "I only eat here at lunch time and then not very often."

"What you need is a good wife, Doc, and I need a rich husband. Why don't you come courtin' me?"

"I'm not rich!"

Mamie shook her head and gave him a lewd wink. "All doctors are rich."

Sister Myrtle appeared at that moment. "What'll you have, Doctor?"

"The special, I guess."

Without moving from where she stood or turning her head, Sister Myrtle bellowed, "A special for Doc Givens, Charlie!"

Irritation made its mark on the doctor's face. "Did it ever occur to you, Sister Myrtle, that some people might not like the other customers knowing what they order?"

"They ort not to eat things they're ashamed of," Sister Myrtle said firmly. "Besides, this ain't a big place. Everybody can see what everybody else is eatin'."

Zeno Bruten was looking at the paper. "I can't believe this! On the first of September the New York stock market hit an all-time high." He shook his head woefully. "The next day the thing nose-dived. What do you think about all this, Doc?"

"I never bought a share of stock in my life. My money's in land. People are fools to put their money into paper that might not be worth a nickel the next day."

"But good times is a-comin'," Zeno insisted. "Why, Henry Ford is the smartest man in America, I guess, and he raised all his workers from six to seven dollars a day."

"Ford can afford to make a mistake. You can't, Zeno. This get-rich-quick mentality is going to ruin the country."

"You're right about that, Doctor," Sister Myrtle boomed. "It's the root of all evil, money is."

"Well, I wish I had more of the root." Zeno shook his head sadly.

The door opened, and Sheriff Pardue Jessup came in followed by Ed Hathcock, the chief of police. When Sister Myrtle asked for their order, Pardue winked at Ed and said, "I think I'll have some pig lips."

"We ain't got no pig lips! You know that, Sheriff. Now quit your foolishness."

"All right. I'll have the special."

"What's the special today, Sister Myrtle?" Ed asked.

"Meat loaf, green beans, and cornbread, same as it is every Tuesday."

"Guess I'll have a cheeseburger with fries," Ed said.

Mamie stopped eating long enough to say, "Who's catching criminals with both of our lawmen eating lunch?"

Pardue leaned back and winked at Mamie. He liked the beautician a great deal and was not particular about the rumors about her moral character. "I put a sign up: NO CRIME ALLOWED UNTIL AFTER LUNCH."

Mamie laughed and said loudly enough for every customer to hear, "How's your social life, Pardue?"

"Come to a dead stop. How about me and you goin' over to the dance at Cedar Grove Saturday night?"

"Sure thing." Mamie smiled. "I'll wear that green dress you like so much."

Ed Hathcock stared at Pardue Jessup. "I thought you was sparkin' Cassandra Pruitt."

"No, I'm too rough around the edges. She's too fine for me."

"She's a woman, ain't she?" Mamie jeered. "All that book learning don't change that."

"That's right, Sheriff," Zeno Bruten said and grinned. "The colonel's lady and Judy O'Brady are sisters under the skin."

"Who in the cat hair are them two?" Ed Hathcock asked.

"Oh, that's from a poem by a fellow named Kipling. Pretty much says that all women are the same."

"I might read some of that poetry," Mamie said and grinned.

The food finally came for Pardue and Ed, and it was Hathcock who brought the subject of the Freeman youngsters up. "I don't know what's gonna happen to those poor kids, their daddy in Cummings. Who's gonna take care of 'em?"

Sister Myrtle was taking a pot of coffee around refilling cups. "The good Lord's gonna take care of 'em. That's who."

"I reckon He'll have to." Pardue shook his head. "They can't take care of themselves. How are they gonna pay their bills?"

The talk went around the cafe while Doc Givens finished his meal. "This place is a regular gossip parlor," he said. "Everybody knows everybody else's business." He walked over to the counter and fished his billfold out and laid a dollar down. Sister Myrtle took it and said, "I want you to come to church Sunday, Doctor."

Givens stared at the woman with exasperation. "You've been askin' me that for fifteen years, Myrtle. When are you going to give up on an old sinner?"

"Never!" Myrtle said.

The doctor snorted, turned, and walked out. As soon as he left, Pardue said, allowing admiration to shade his voice, "I purely admire a firm woman, Sister Myrtle. One of these days I'm gonna come to your church and hit the glory trail."

"Well, I declare you need it, Pardue Jessup, and let me tell you—" The sound of squealing tires and a loud yell cut her off. Myrtle went to the window and looked out. "It's Doc Givens, he's been hit by a car!"

The whole crowd rushed out, and others were gathering. Dr. Givens was lying in the street, and the car that had hit him sped away. Ed Hathcock yelled, "I'll get him! You know that car, Pardue?"

"No, it must be a stranger."

Pardue knelt down and said, "Doc, are you hurt bad?"

Givens murmured, "My leg—"

Gerald Pink, the pharmacist, came across the street from his drugstore. He knelt down and studied the leg without touching it. "That's a bad compound fracture. We're gonna have to take you to Fort Smith, Doc. I'll go get somethin' to help with the pain."

As Pink left, Pardue called out, "Call the hospital in Forth Smith! Tell them I'm bringin' Doc Givens in."

"Why, you can't take him in a car with that leg," Zeno Bruten said.

"Nope, I'll have to borrow your hearse, Zeno."

"That'll be okay, Pardue. There's no funerals today."

⌖

Ten minutes later Pardue and two other men carefully loaded Dr. Givens in the back of the black hearse. It was a painful thing, and the doctor moaned. Pardue heard him say, "I never thought I'd be alive when I rode in this blasted thing!"

"You take it easy, Doc," Pardue said. "You're gonna be all right."

"I'll have to call Memphis and get another doctor down here."

"You can call when they get you all put together," Pardue said. "Now, you folks clear the way." He got up, closed the door on the hearse, and started the engine. As he drove off, Orrin Pierce, who had arrived late, said, "Well, we got no police protection and no medical help."

Sister Myrtle stared at him, then said loudly, "Well, we got God, ain't we?"

≈ CHAPTER 14 ≈

A harsh-looking woman with gray hair and dark eyes opened the door and frowned. "What is it?" she demanded. "We ain't buyin' nothing."

"I'm Dr. Owen Merritt. I've come to see Dr. Givens."

The woman wore an apron over her sixty-something frame and wiped her hands on it now. "Oh, well, I reckon it's all right for you to come in! Come on back to the bedroom. I'm Matilda Satterfield, Dr. Givens' housekeeper."

"How's he doing, Mrs. Satterfield?"

"He's about the worst patient I ever saw! He'd kill any patient of his that acts like he does. My lands, you think a man his age would have enough sense to look before crossing the street!"

Merritt followed the tall woman down the hall into a bedroom. "Dr. Givens, this here is your new assistant."

Merritt walked up to the bed and said, "Hello, Dr. Givens."

"Well, you took your time gettin' here."

Merritt grinned suddenly. "Couldn't go any faster than the train, I'm afraid. How's that leg?"

"It hurts like the devil!" Doc Givens had a tray on his lap. "I'm havin' lunch. Matilda, bring the doctor some fried chicken and butter beans."

"Oh, you don't have to do that, Dr. Givens."

Givens waved his protest aside and pointed to a chair by the bed. "Do what I tell you, Matilda. Now set down there and tell me about yourself."

Sitting, Owen Merritt began to speak of his background. He had grown up in Memphis, Tennessee, and finished medical school at Baptist Hospital, where he was fulfilling his residency.

"Not much experience," Givens grumbled, nibbling at a chicken leg. "About what I figured. How old are you?"

"Twenty-seven."

"How'd you get out of medical school so quick?"

"I graduated from high school a couple of years early." Merritt shrugged. He picked up the drumstick from the plate that Matilda had brought and tasted it. "This is good chicken."

Givens grunted. "So you're a city man?"

"Yes, sir, all in Memphis."

"Well, what works in a big city won't work in a small town."

"I expect I'll have a lot to learn, Doctor."

Givens brushed the crumbs from the front of his robe and stared at the younger man. "I'm not one for the new-fangled, fly-by-night medicine, but I'll give you a try. If it don't work out, you'll have to go. You got a car?"

"No, sir."

"Well, you can use mine—and you be careful of it, you hear?"

"That's kind of you. I'll have to find a place to stay—"

"You'll stay right here," Givens said. "Plenty of room in this big old house up on the second floor. Have your own bath up there. I can't get up there with this leg. Matilda's a good cook—better than anyone else in this town."

Owen Merritt instinctively resisted this order. The old man was crusty enough, and to be stuck with him constantly was not to his liking. But Givens had his mind made up.

"That will be very handy, Dr. Givens."

Givens scowled. "I won't be able to come to the office for quite a while, but I'll sit by the telephone. You can call me when you run into somethin' you don't know how to handle."

"That would be very convenient."

"You'll take your meals here at night. After dinner we can go over the cases."

It sounded like some form of slavery to Owen Merritt, but he was grateful for the opportunity. The offer had come at a good time, and he knew that Givens was right. Practice in a small town was different from a large hospital in a big city.

"Matilda, show the doctor his room—and be sure his sheets are changed."

Matilda sniffed. "You think I don't know how to keep a house!" She went out huffing. Merritt followed her, grinning.

The afternoon was busy enough. Word of Merritt's arrival spread quickly, and he suspected that many who dropped by the office came just to look the new doctor over.

Dr. Givens' nurse, Bertha Pickens, had her own ways. She handled the office as if she were the doctor, and before admitting any patient, she would give Owen a complete medical history, including the patient's ancestry back to the great-great-grandparents. Nurse Pickens was a short, stocky woman. A Pentecostal, she let him know instantly. "I'm Pentecost at any cost," is the way she put it.

By five o'clock Owen Merritt felt that the traffic had slowed down, and Nurse Pickens stepped inside and shut the door behind her. "The oldest Freeman girl's outside."

"Who's she?"

"Her name is Lanie Freeman. Her dad just got sent to Cummings Prison Farm for shooting a man."

"What's wrong with her?"

"She won't say," Nurse Pickens snipped. "You don't have to see her. I'm sure she doesn't have any money."

"Oh, I think I'd better. Have her come in, Nurse."

Owen got to his feet. When the young woman, or girl, came into the office, he saw that she was frightened. "Well, hello there." He smiled. "My name is Dr. Merritt. And what's yours?"

"I'm Lanie Freeman."

"Well, would you care to sit down here and tell me your problem, Miss Lanie?" He tried to estimate her age, but found it rather difficult. He put her at fifteen or perhaps a year older. Her best features were her eyes, deep-set, widely spaced and beautifully shaped. "Are you having some kind of sickness?"

"No, sir, it's not me. It's a friend of mine. She's cut herself, and she won't come to the doctor. I'm afraid for her."

"Why won't she come to a doctor?"

"She . . . she won't have much to do with anybody in town."

"Well, if she won't come to the doctor, the doctor will have to go to her. What's her name?"

"Everybody calls her Butcher Knife Annie."

"That's an odd name. Why do they call her that?"

"I don't know, Doctor, but she needs you awful bad."

"All right. Let me get my bag, and we'll take a look."

As the two passed through the outer office, Owen said, "I'll see you in the morning, Nurse."

"Where are you going, Doctor?"

"Have a house call to make. Thanks for all of your excellent help."

Owen opened the door of Dr. Givens' big Oldsmobile and saw Lanie look at him with surprise. "Thank you," she murmured as she got in. Merritt shut the door, walked around, tossed his bag in, then cranked the engine up. "One of these days they're going to put a starter in a car so you won't have to crank the fool thing." He climbed in. "Now, which way?"

"Right down this street and then turn left."

As Owen Merritt drove down the street, he took in the town, which seemed nice enough. But he was mostly interested in Lanie Freeman. He thought it best not to ask about her father, but he did say, "Do you have brothers and sisters?"

"Two sisters and two brothers."

"Older than you?"

"No, sir, I'm the oldest."

Something about the girl's tone warned Owen Merritt that this was no time to question her. She seemed sensitive enough, if extremely nervous. When she directed him to a ramshackle house on the edge of town, he pulled up and without comment got out.

"Dr. Merritt, she might not be—"

"She might not be what?"

"She might not be too nice. Annie's not good with people."

"Well, I'll try to make my best impression. You go first, Lanie."

The two went into the shack, and Merritt was struck by the awful odor of the place. Cats prowled the house—white cats, yellow cats, gray cats—all sorts of cats, but he hid his shock. The living area was large enough, but was cluttered with all sorts of junk. Old calendar pictures and others cut out of periodicals covered the walls. He did not have time to look long, for a woman came out. She was about the dirtiest woman he had ever seen. Lanie said, "Annie, I brought Dr. Merritt by to look at that cut."

"I ain't needin' no doctor!"

"Oh, come on now, Miss Annie. Now that I'm here let me take a look."

It took some persuasion, but finally Lanie talked Annie into sitting down at the kitchen table. Her arm was wrapped in a crusty bandage, and when Merritt unwrapped it, he said at once, "You're going to need some stitches here, Annie. It will hurt a little bit."

"You have to do it, Annie," Lanie said. "The doctor just wants to help you."

Merritt dressed the arm quickly and noticed that the old woman did not flinch. She had a stern face and would have been presentable if she were not so dirty. A scarf covered her iron-gray hair, and her dress appeared never to have been washed. "Probably a good thing I came by. That arm could have gotten infected."

"How much money do you want?" Annie demanded.

"Well, this is my first day of doctoring in Fairhope, so I'm giving a bargain price today. It's on me."

"I don't take no charity."

"Not charity. Just a bonus." Merritt got up and repacked his bag. "I'll drop by in a couple of days and change that dressing. Try not to bang it if you can help it."

Merritt started for the door, but Lanie stayed behind and patted Annie on the shoulder. She whispered something he could not hear, and when they got outside, Merritt said, "It's getting dark. I'd better take you home."

"I can walk, Doctor."

"No need of that. That's what this car's for."

The two got in the car, and she directed him to her house. When they pulled up outside, she turned to him and said, "Doctor, I'd like to pay you for treating Annie."

"Why no, Lanie. You heard what I said. My first day. It's all free work."

Lanie smiled at him and he realized she was a pretty young girl. "If it's free, would you come in and look at my baby sister?"

"Sure, I will. What's wrong with her?"

"I don't know. She's been crying a lot and I'm worried."

"What does your mother say?"

"She . . . died a year ago."

Merritt saw that the girl's face was tense. "I'll be glad to look at her."

"If you won't let me pay you, I made some fudge this morning. Would you like some of it?"

"Fudge! I can resist anything except fudge and temptation!"

"Come in, and I'll fix you up a sack of it."

Merritt got out of the car and followed the girl into the house. They were met on the steps by a huge cinnamon-colored dog who growled at Merritt but then decided he was friendly. He reared up, and Merritt was staggered by the weight of the dog who put his paws on his chest.

"Just step on his toes, Dr. Merritt. He's just friendly."

Merritt did as instructed, and the dog yelped. Then he plopped down by the wall, staring at the doctor reproachfully.

"I think I hurt his feelings."

"He's got real tender feelings, Dr. Merritt. Come on in."

Merritt stepped inside and saw that the kitchen was occupied. Four youngsters were there, a young girl holding a baby, and two boys.

"This is my sister Maeva and my new sister Corliss Jeanne, and these are my brothers Cody and Davis."

"Well, I'm glad to meet you all. Let me have a look at this young lady." Walking over, he reached out his arms and took the child. She began crying at once, and Maeva said, "She ain't done nothin' but cry. She must be sick."

"She doesn't have any fever." Merritt examined the child, and finally he stuck his finger in her mouth, and she clamped down on it. "There's the trouble. Look, she's cutting a tooth."

Lanie smiled with relief. "I've been so worried about her, Doctor."

"I think she's just as healthy and pretty as a baby should be."

Dr. Merritt handed the baby back and spoke to the two boys. When Lanie gave him the paper sack full of candy, he said, "Thank you, Lanie. I promise to eat every bite of it."

"Thank you for taking care of Annie, Dr. Merritt."

"No problem. I'll check on her in a couple of days. Nice to meet all of you," he said.

As soon as he was out of the room, Maeva said, "He's better lookin' than any doctor I've ever seen."

"You never seen any but ol' Doc Givens!" Cody said.

"I expect all the women will be chasin' after him." Maeva grinned. "If you was a couple years older, Lanie, you might catch him."

"Don't be foolish! Now, let me get supper started."

☞✦☜

Lanie was caught up in the poems she was writing about the birth of Jesus. After the others went to bed, she took up her poem about

Herod. It had come to her that not everyone had been glad to see Jesus come to earth, and she struggled to write a poem about the cruel king who had the babies slain. She finally put down her pen, flexed her fingers, and read the poem aloud, whispering softly:

Herod

Centurion! Centurion! See here,
*   A message from the troops we sent to find*
Those snoopers from the East — remember them?
*   "Where is the newborn King?" they asked — of me!*

Those fools you sent have let them slip away,
*   So now we must take measures desperate.*
Take your troops to Bethlehem, kill every babe —
*   Oh, spare me your protest — you've killed before!*

I've dealt before with this kingly infection.
*   Kill it not — it spreads itself like plague!*
And who'd be first to go if a Jewish king
*   Arrived? Me — then you — then Rome itself!*

We'll crush this infant threat to Roman power.
*   I'll have his blood! Centurion, begone!*
My name will live and long remembered be
*   When this child's name is wiped from memory!*

Slowly Lanie closed her notebook, put it away, then went to bed. "Nobody will ever read it, but it makes me feel good to write about the Lord Jesus." She closed her eyes, then dropped off to sleep.

CHAPTER 15

As Lanie exited from the high school, she looked with a sense of delight around her. The snow, which had been falling all afternoon, had coated the landscape with a blanket of pristine white, and the late afternoon sun made the surface glitter like millions of diamonds. Caught up in the rush of escaping students, Lanie ran across the unbroken snow, gleefully leaving new tracks in the surface. She heard her name called and looked up to see Maeva and her brothers running toward her from the elementary school.

"Hey, how about this snow!" Maeva yelled. Reaching down, she scooped up a double handful and caked it into a ball. She threw it at Lanie, who ducked and yelled back, "You couldn't hit the broad side of a barn!" She made her own snowball, and soon the school yard was filled with flying missiles. Lanie caught one in her ear, but she had on a knit cap so it stung only a little.

Cody, yelling like a wild Indian, jumped on Max Jinks and brought him down. He scooped up a handful of snow and began washing his face, yelling, "You need a bath, Jinks, you stink!"

For a time the novelty of the snow kept the students of both schools occupied, but finally Lanie called out, "Come on. We've got to get home." She left the school yard with her siblings and headed down Oak Street. "It's beautiful, isn't it?" she said, her eyes glowing as she studied the houses. "It looks like a fairy town." The snow had put smooth, unbroken roofs on all of the houses, transforming the sharp angles into curving frosted shapes.

The Fairhope business center, too, was coated with the sparkling snow and did not seem to be itself. The four Freemans made their way past the statue in the square, and they passed by the office of the Fairhope

Sentinel, the town's newspaper. A woman in a thin coat was shoveling snow. Lanie smiled at her. "Hi, Miss Patton. You don't need to be shoveling that old snow. Let us do it."

Elspeth Patton, staunch Baptist and publisher of the *Sentinel,* turned to face them. She was a small woman with beautifully shaped silver hair and a pair of fine gray eyes. At sixty-one she was still an attractive woman. "I expect you could do a better job than I could. Here." She held out the shovel, and Davis grabbed it and began making the snow fly. Miss Patton got out of the way. "Come on in the office, Lanie. Let these hoodlums do the work. Boys, as soon as you get through, come inside. I'll have something you'll like." She walked into the building. Lanie followed, but Maeva stayed outside, insisting on taking her turn with the shovel.

The smell of ink and paper was strong in the outer office, a large room with desks scattered about. Cork bulletin boards filled with notices, pictures, and stories from past issues covered the walls. From the back came the clanking sound of the press running and a man's voice singing "Yes, We Have No Bananas."

"Let's make up a big pot of cocoa. I've got some cookies here that I baked last night." Elspeth moved toward a hot plate and began making the cocoa. She was silent for a time, and there was concern in her eyes as she glanced toward Lanie. "Have you heard from your father?"

Lanie turned from a bulletin board. "Yes, ma'am. I write to him almost every day. Of course I don't mail the letters every day, but I date them. Sometimes I'll have three or four in one envelope."

Miss Patton was a straightforward woman. Her father founded the Fairhope *Sentinel,* and she had taken on the calling after he died. She was also a compassionate woman. She stooped down and picked up a big Persian cat and sat down. Stroking its fur, she said, "Daisy, stop that!"—then to Lanie—"She loves to dig her claws into me."

"Our cat does that too. I wonder why?"

"I have no idea. Cats are mysterious creatures."

A short balding man with an ink-stained apron burst out of the back room. The sound of the presses intensified, and he shouted, "How's this, Miss Patton?"

Taking the sheet of paper from the printer, she examined it, and Lanie saw something change in her expression. "That's very good."

"It ain't very good news, but that's the way it is."

"Okay. Run it like this, Harry."

"Yes, ma'am."

As soon as the printer closed the door, muting the sound, Elspeth turned the sheet around so Lanie could see it. "Bad news. The very worst kind."

Lanie read the headline, which was in bold black letters: "STOCK MARKET FALLS." She looked up. "I've been hearing about that. I don't understand it."

"I don't think even the men who operate the stock market understand it. It's like some kind of black magic. But it's bad news, Harry's right about that."

"What do you think it means? Won't there be any stock market after today?"

"Oh, they'll keep on doing business, but it's going to be a hard time for this country. A lot of businesses are going to go under, Lanie. People have been chasing rainbows for years now. You must have heard about it. People using their life's savings to buy land in Florida they've never even seen, hoping the value will triple or go even higher. Gambling on stocks in companies they never even heard of on the advice of some man they don't even know. Some people are always trying to get something for nothing."

A slight fear touched Lanie then, and she thought of the note at the bank and of the trucks her father had bought. "But people will still have to have things. I mean, the grocery stores won't close, will they?"

"Some of them will." Looking at Lanie, she said, "You're worrying about your note at the bank, aren't you?"

"How did you know about that?"

"No secrets in a small town." She winked and smiled. "Besides, I'm on the board of the bank."

"Well, I am a bit worried, Miss Patton, but Mr. Langley has got lots of money. He won't go broke, will he?"

"No one can say about that. I don't want to alarm you, but it looks serious."

The two sat there, and Lanie listened as Elspeth Patton explained some of the intricacies of Wall Street. The door burst open, and Maeva and the boys came thundering in, their faces flushed. "All done, Miss Patton," Cody said.

"All right. How about some cocoa and cookies?"

Lanie helped pour the cocoa and divided the cookies, and the children scarfed them down and sputtered and blew on the hot cocoa, which was too hot to drink right down.

After all the cups were empty, Lanie said, "We've got to go. We'll be late. Thanks for the cookies and the cocoa, Miss Patton."

"Thanks for doing my sidewalk. I'll see you in church Sunday." She watched the four go, and a touch of sadness came to her. "It's going to go hard with those youngsters," she murmured.

Bascom Jones was on the porch waiting for them. As soon as Lanie saw his face, her heart sank. "What is it, Bascom? Come in out of the cold."

Lanie opened the door and Bascom stepped inside, pulled his cap off, and stood in the hall. "I got some real bad news, Miss Lanie. I really hates to give it to you."

"What is it? Did one of the trucks break down?"

"No, ma'am, it's worse than that. We took a load of logs to the mill today, and the boss man there, he say the company ain't buyin' no more logs—at least not from us."

Lanie tried to keep her face from showing what she felt, but panic had its way with her. "They won't buy logs? But Mr. Langley had a deal with Daddy."

"Yes, ma'am. I didn't talk to Mr. Langley, of course, but Mr. Jones, the sawmill boss, he say for us not to bring no mo'. I don't rightly know what to do with them logs on the truck now."

Lanie thought quickly. "I'll go talk to Mr. Langley."

"Yes, ma'am. What'll I do about the logs?"

"Just leave them for now. Surely he won't close the sawmill down."

"I don't know, miss. Things are powerful bad. Everything's goin' to pieces, seems like."

"I'll see about it, Bascom."

"I'd like to see Mr. Langley if I could, please."

The secretary stared at Lanie with hard brown eyes. "What is your business?"

"I'd really rather tell Mr. Langley, if you don't mind."

"What's your name?"

"Lanie Freeman."

"Mr. Langley's a very busy man, but I'll see if he can make a moment for you."

Lanie stood there, her legs so weak that she wanted to sit. Otis Langley was the richest and most important man in Fairhope. She had spoken to him only a few times, and she remembered his anger when she beat his son Roger for the grand prize.

The secretary came out and held the door open. "You can see Mr. Langley for a few minutes."

"Thank you, ma'am."

Lanie walked inside and took one quick frightened look around. There was carpet on the floor and a big desk in the middle of the room, behind which sat Mr. Langley. He looked at her with a steady expression. "Hello, Lanie."

"Hello, Mr. Langley."

"What can I do for you today?"

Lanie swallowed hard and found that she was twisting her hands together. She pulled them apart and willed them steady at her sides. "One of the men who drives my daddy's trucks said that the sawmill wouldn't buy the logs anymore."

Langley leaned back in his chair. He was a big man with an abundant crown of brown hair and an air of confidence. He extended his hands, spread his fingers, and tapped his fingertips together. "You know what's going on in this country, don't you, Lanie?"

"You mean the stock market?"

"That's right. Everything is different now. It's the hardest time this country has ever seen, I think, except perhaps during the war." He looked out the window for a moment and lowered his voice. "Though it may get worse than that before it's over." He turned back to Lanie. "I'm sorry, but I'm shutting the mill down, for the most part, for a time."

"You're not buying any logs at all?"

"That will be up to the manager, but you can't count on our buying any more from your men."

Lanie's mouth went dry. A big hole seemed to have opened up before her, and panic threatened to swallow her. "But we have to sell logs, sir."

"I know it's hard for you, especially with your father in prison, but this Depression is not going to be over in a hurry." He leaned forward. "I was going to ask you to come in and see me, Lanie."

"You were?"

"Yes, I was. I have a proposition to make."

Hope came to Lanie. "I'll do anything. If we have to come down on our prices for the hauling—"

"No, that's over, at least for a while. I'm on the board at the bank, and I know about the note that your father owes there. It's unfortunate, but you understand that if that note isn't paid, the bank will have to foreclose."

Lanie could not think of a single thing to say. She had been frightened in her life a few times, but never like this!

Finally Langley said, "It's going to be very difficult, if not impossible, for you to hang onto your place with that note hanging over you like it is. It has to be paid every month. I'm sure you know that. And with your father unable to work, I just don't think you're going to be able to do it."

"But we've got to do something!"

"Yes, you do, and here's what I propose: You have five acres and a house. I'd like to buy that property from you. I think, Lanie, that I could offer you enough to pay off your note at the bank, and you'll have some money left over."

"But where would we live, Mr. Langley?"

"Well, that's a problem you're going to have to solve, I'm afraid. Don't you have any relatives that can take you in?"

"No, sir. No close relatives."

"Well, something will have to be worked out." Langley stood up, and he seemed big and ominous to Lanie. She had to look up to face him. "This is the best thing for you, young lady. No property is worth as much as it was with the way prices are dropping. But I'll guarantee that you'll be clear of the loan at the bank and that you'll have enough money, perhaps, to buy a smaller place."

Lanie knew what she had to do. "Thank you, Mr. Langley, but we've got to hang onto the place. It's all Daddy has. When he gets out of prison, he's got to have some place to come home to."

"Be reasonable, child," Langley said impatiently. "It's going to be a long time before your father gets out of the penitentiary. By that time you'll be grown, and your brothers and sisters will be grown. Everything will be changed. But you must remember that the note is due, and if it isn't paid, then the bank will foreclose."

Lanie could not stand being in the office for another moment. She said faintly, "Thank you, Mr. Langley," and turned to leave.

As she opened the door, he called out, "You think it over, Lanie, and you'll see it's the best thing to do."

Outside, the cold struck Lanie, but she did not feel it.

"I've got to talk to Miss Effie," she said aloud.

⟜✦⟜

Lanie was grateful to sit, for her legs were weaker than ever. Her voice was unsteady as she told Effie Johnson about her meeting with Mr. Langley.

Finally she said, "I don't know what to do, Miss Johnson. I just don't know. We can't lose our place. We just can't!"

Effie Johnson exchanged glances with Cora, who was standing beside Lanie's chair. "We'll do something. We Baptists have to stick together, don't we?"

"I'm so scared! I don't know what to do."

Effie Johnson had the reputation of being one of the most hard-nosed women in Fairhope. Those who tried to best her in business found themselves faced with a carnivore of sorts. But now her voice was soft. "I've been thinking about what to do ever since the stock market fell. I saw this coming."

"Please, ma'am, I don't understand it, but we've got to keep our place."

Effie Johnson folded her hands and set them in her lap. "All right. Here's what we'll do. We'll sell the equipment for whatever it will bring. I'll get the very best prices for you. Bob Haynes will help me. It's still valuable equipment. It won't bring what your father paid for it new, but it'll bring the note down to about a hundred dollars a month."

"A hundred dollars! That's a lot of money."

"I know it is, but it's the best we can do now. We'll make out a new note. It won't be due for a month. You have enough money in your account to pay a note of a hundred dollars a month for at least three or four months. By that time something will have to be worked out."

Lanie's eyes filled with tears. She whispered, "Thank you, Miss Johnson. I don't know what I'd do without you."

"You go on home now, and don't you worry about this."

Lanie suddenly went over to Effie and put her arms around her. "Thank you," she whispered.

Effie Johnson had not received many caresses, and Lanie's gesture startled her. She awkwardly put her arms around the girl, patted her, and said huskily, "You go on now. Remember, you've got friends and you've got the Lord Jesus."

⌖

Effie left the bank and walked directly to Orrin Pierce's office. He was sitting in a chair, leaning back, staring at the ceiling. He got up at once. "Hello, Effie, what's going on?"

"Bad news." Effie, without sitting down, told Orrin the story. "We've got to help those children."

A scowl marred Orrin's handsome face. "You know what it's all about, don't you?"

"I've got a good idea. Langley's out to get the Freeman place."

"That's right. He's always been mad about Lanie winning the grand prize over Roger."

"Yes, and he knows that one day those five acres will be a valuable property. It'll be right in the center of town if Fairhope grows."

They rapidly laid out plans, and finally Orrin nodded. "I'm glad you're on the side of those children." Pain filled his eyes. "You know, times like this I wish I were a praying man."

"You could be, Orrin."

"I don't know about that. I may have missed my chance."

Effie Johnson stared at him. "God's always at home. All you have to do is invite Him in."

"Maybe sometime I will, Effie, but we can't wait for that. Let's stay on top of this thing. Forrest is a good man, and he's helpless."

Effie left the office, and Orrin looked back at the ceiling. "If I were a praying man, I'd pray for Otis Langley to break his neck!"

⌖

"That's just the way it is. We've got to work and make a hundred dollars a month in addition to what it takes to live on." Lanie had told her siblings the whole story, and now she said briskly, "And I have to tell you something else. I'm not going back to school. I'm going to stay home and take care of Corliss and the house—and try to think of some ways to make more money. We've got maybe four months, and by that time we have to find a way to make the payment."

Cody stared at her and swallowed hard. "I . . . I don't think we can do it."

Maeva stood up and glared at him. "Sure we can do it! I ain't afraid."

Lanie put her arm around Maeva. "You're a tough egg, Maeva, and I think that's what we're going to need from here on out."

⤖ CHAPTER 16 ⤖

As Lanie walked toward the courthouse, the sights and smells of spring surrounded her. The birds had come back from wherever they had been, and their morning twitter and clatter, their shrill cries and whistles came to her as she made her way along the streets. The crabapple trees in many yards flung out pink and white flowers toward the sun, and the hawthornes and the wild haw trees put little white flowers out beside their brittle thorns and sent a sweet scent with the wind.

The chill of winter had faded from the earth, but the Depression that gripped America with an iron grasp seemed even worse. Leaving school had brought an ache to Lanie's breast that no one knew about. She made light of it, but more than once at night she cried herself to sleep, for she loved learning and school itself. But the note payment hung over the family like a dark cloud. They had just enough money to make two more payments and then, despite cutting every expense and all of their efforts to make money at odd jobs, a shadow larger than a mountain loomed over them.

All of them had tried to make extra money selling eggs, chopping wood, cleaning up at the *Sentinel*. But in Fairhope, two stores had already closed their doors, and men were out of work, so there was little opportunity for children to make money.

Lanie reached the courthouse steps, nodded and spoke to Billy Henderson, the county clerk who went to her church, then entered the building. She had been here only twice before, both times with her father. It was an old building and smelled of old wood and paper and sweat and perfume. She turned down the hallway and went to an office at the end of the hall. Stepping inside, she saw Fred Stevenson bent over a desk writing something. "Hello, Mr. Stevenson."

"Hello, Lanie." Mr. Stevenson was a tall, lanky man with an engaging grin. He had two children about Lanie's age, and she asked about them, and he answered. Then she said, "I've got to have a driver's license, Mr. Stevenson."

Stevenson blinked with surprise. "Well, you have to be sixteen, Lanie."

"I'm sixteen years old today. March thirteenth."

"It's your birthday?"

"Yes, sir."

Fred ran his hands through his hair. "I think you still need an adult to vouch for you if you're not twenty-one."

"Just any adult?"

"Well, it's usually somebody in your family, but in your case somebody from church might do. The pastor maybe. Here's the form." Fred opened a drawer and pulled out a sheet of paper. "Just have him sign it at the bottom, then bring it back here." He hesitated. "Can you drive? You have to pass a driver's test and a written test too."

"I can drive," Lanie said.

⟜⊷⟜

Dr. Oscar Givens stared over his spectacles at his young colleague. The fact that he had to delegate much of his work to Dr. Owen Merritt was a hard pill for the old man to swallow. He had handled the health of his patients in Fairhope for years without help, and it galled him that he could not do what he once could.

"Did you go by and see Harriett Rumpler?"

"Sure did, Doctor. Nothing serious, just gas," Owen said cheerfully. He sat opposite the older man, his fingers laced behind his head, smiling. At first Doc Givens had been critical of everything he did, and at night he insisted on going over the history of every patient that Merritt treated. Merritt survived, however, and learned to respect Givens in the process. His elder was not up on the modern techniques, which could not be expected, but underneath his crusty exterior was a deep love for the people he treated. Merritt answered Givens' questions and finally, when the old man ran down, he said, "Something interesting from England. A fellow named Alexander Fleming."

"Who's he?"

"He's a doctor at Saint Mary's Hospital in London. He developed something called penicillin. According to all I hear it's pretty much a miracle drug. It destroys the staphylococci. You know what that would mean, Doctor. Why, we'd save lots of patients if we could kill off those varmints."

"They're always coming up with some miracle drug. I don't believe a word of it until I try it myself."

"I think it's going to work. Fleming has a good reputation. I just wish we had a stock of that new penicillin right now."

It aggravated Givens that his assistant had time to read a great deal about new developments. He himself relied on the old tried-and-true methods.

"Something else. There's a doctor at Harvard named Levine. He did a study and found out that sixty out of a hundred and forty-five heart attack patients have high blood pressure."

"And the others who died don't have high blood pressure. You can make statistics say anything you want to."

"I don't know, Dr. Givens. I've noticed that people with high blood pressure seem to have more heart trouble than others. Something to think about."

The door opened, and Nurse Pickens stuck her head inside. "Lanie Freeman's here. Do you want to see her?"

"Sure, Bertha, send her in." Merritt got up, but the old man, favoring his leg, kept his seat. Lately he managed to come to the office and work half days, though his injury prevented him from making outside calls.

"Hello, Lanie," Merritt said. "Are you sick? Some of your family maybe?"

"No, sir, we're all fine, but I've got to get a driver's license, and Mr. Stevenson says an adult has to sign my application. I was wondering if you would sign for me."

"Why, I sure would. You got it with you?"

"Yes, sir. It's right here."

Givens watched as Merritt took the paper and signed it. "How's that baby sister of yours doin'? She getting over the croup?"

"Oh, yes, Dr. Givens. She's fine. We're all doing real well."

"I'm glad to hear it. You hear from your daddy pretty often?"

"Yes, sir, and I'm going to visit him. That's why I need a driver's license."

"You going to drive all the way down to Cummings? That's a long drive," Merritt said. He held the paper a minute and said, "What kind of car does your daddy have?"

"It's a Model T."

"You know that's a long trip for a young woman. The car might break down."

"I've got to go, Doctor. They won't let prisoners have any visitors for the first three months. That was up the day before yesterday. I've just got to go."

Merritt reached into his pocket, pulled out his billfold, and took out a bill. "Going to be expensive. You'll probably have to stay all night in a hotel there, and then there's gas. Maybe this will help."

Lanie stared at the bill and shook her head. "I couldn't take it, but thank you."

"Don't be foolish." Reaching out, he took Lanie's hand, opened it, put the bill inside, and then closed her fingers. He winked at her. "You can cut my grass if I ever get any grass to cut. When you come back, stop by and tell me about your visit."

☞⌐

Maeva surprised Lanie after supper when she said, "We're gonna have a party."

"A birthday party!" Cody grinned. "Davis and me are gonna make ice cream, and Maeva made a cake."

"And Annie's coming. She said she'd bring something to eat too."

"I'd hate to eat anything she cooked, dirty as she is!" Maeva sniffed. "Might poison me."

"Don't you say a word," Davis warned. "She'll do the best she can."

Annie arrived thirty minutes later, and she received a big welcome. Maeva whispered, "Why, I think she's even had a bath and washed her dress!"

Annie did look somewhat better, at least cleaner. She had brought a paper sack full of oatmeal cookies, and Lanie made over them a great deal. "These are the best cookies I've ever had in my life!"

Annie offered a rare smile at that. "My ma taught me how to cook."

"I got my license today, and I'm going to see Daddy tomorrow, Annie," Lanie said. "I'll take him some of your cookies."

Annie stared at Lanie, then said, "Tell the poor feller I feel for 'im."

"I'll tell him." Lanie winked at Annie. "You keep an eye on this bunch while I'm gone. No telling what they might get into without me here to watch them!"

Maeva stared at her, then laughed. "I reckon we'll be fine. And you tell Daddy the next time we're all comin' to see him!"

⁓

The next morning, when Lanie walked out of the house, Sheriff Jessup was sitting in a cane-bottomed chair on the front porch. He was wearing his uniform and looked roughly handsome. "Why, hello, Sheriff. What are you doing here?"

"The doc and I figure you might need a mechanic along. I'm gettin' tired of workin' so I thought I'd take the day off."

Relief washed over Lanie. "That would be nice. I wouldn't know how to fix the car if it quit."

"Well, that's what I'm for. Besides that, it won't hurt to have a little official push to get you in to see your daddy. Come on. Let's get started."

⁓

The Cummings Prison Farm was not at all impressive. Set in the middle of flat Arkansas delta land, the prison consisted of long buildings that looked like barracks surrounded by barbed wire fences.

At the entrance, a fat officer with small, piggish eyes glared at Lanie. "You're supposed to write and get a permit to see an inmate."

"I didn't know that, but I need to see my daddy."

"You got to have a permit."

Pardue stood behind Lanie. "Reckon I'd better talk to Warden Gladden about this."

"You know the warden?"

"Oh, yeah. Me and him's old buddies. We used to hunt together in the hills just outside of Jasper where we grew up."

"Well, you can ask him. I can't let you in without a permit."

"Where's his office?"

"Right down that hall."

"Come along, Lanie. We'll go get us that permit."

Warden Potter Gladden was happy enough to see his old friend. He was a tall, rangy man with clear blue eyes and a ready smile. "Glad to see you again, buddy. How about stayin' over for a few days, and we'll go out and get us a couple of bucks."

"Reckon I'll have to come back for that, Potter, but this little lady here needs a permit. She didn't know you had to write ahead. I'd appreciate it if you could help her out."

"Nothin' easier. Who is your daddy?"

"Forrest Freeman, sir."

"Oh, yes. He's doin' well." Gladden got a paper, scribbled on it, and handed it to her.

"Warden, could I sometimes bring my brothers and sisters so Daddy could see all of us?"

"Well, it ain't regulation, but seeing as you're a friend of this ugly galoot here, I guess I'll have to say yes."

"Thanks a lot, Potter," Pardue said. "I appreciate it. I'll come back next time and we'll get them bucks."

Pardue and Lanie walked down the hall and gave the paper to the fat guard, who shrugged. "I'll bring him in. You can wait in there. Coffee, if you want it, over on the table."

Lanie grew nervous as she waited. She was somehow frightened too. Pardue realized she was tense. "I'll just stay long enough to say hello to your daddy, and then I'll let you two visit."

Ten minutes later Forrest walked in. He wore a faded khaki uniform of sorts and had evidently been working, for his hands were grimy and he was covered with sweat. As soon as he stepped inside, Lanie flew to him. "Daddy!" She threw her arms around him and hugged him fiercely.

"Lanie, you look so good to me!" Forrest said, kissing the top of her head. He looked up and said, "Pardue, did you bring Lanie down?"

"She's got her own license now, Forrest, but I thought that car might need a little work on the way so I come along for the ride. Good to see you." He put out his hand. "I just wanted to say hello. The warden's good friend of mine. He treatin' you right?"

Forrest shook hands with Pardue. "All right."

"Good. Look, I'm going to be outside. You stay as long as you want, Lanie. I'll see you next time, Forrest."

"Thanks, Pardue."

Lanie could not take her eyes off her father. She had not known how much she missed him, and now she ached, somehow, with love for him. Tears stung her eyes, for he looked worn and tired, not at all like himself. "I brought a bunch of things, Daddy. They're in the boxes." She flew to the door and said, "Sheriff, would you bring the boxes in?"

"Sure will, honey!"

Ten minutes later Lanie was unloading the treasures—cakes, cookies, and shelled pecans. "This shaving stuff is from Mr. Pink, and here's a box from Harry Oz."

"This is all good. I've missed your cookin', honey."

"Look, I got these pictures. Mr. Jinks took them with his camera."

Forrest grabbed at the pictures and fastened his eyes on them. "Look at Corliss, she's a beauty! So fat and pretty . . . and look at the boys. They're gettin' so big! It seems like I haven't seen 'em in a year."

Lanie bent over the pictures with her father and saw how he devoured them. She sat close to him, and he put his arm around her as he shuffled the pictures around on the table. They talked about each one for a long time, and finally he said, "Tell me all that's going on, honey. Everything."

Lanie had worried about this. She did not want her father to know how serious things were. She had practiced a speech, and she spent a great deal of time telling him of inconsequential details. She had already told him about selling the logging equipment to pay off most of the note at the bank.

"I hate that you had to drop out of school."

"Oh, that's all right, Daddy. I'm studying a lot at home now. I really think I'm learning more at home than I did at school. I don't mind."

"It's not right, sweetheart," Forrest said, and a gloom descended upon him. His arm was around her, and he squeezed her. "I'd give anything if you could go back to school. If I could just be there to take care of you and the others."

"You will one day, Daddy. You wait and see."

"You really believe that, Lanie?"

"Yes. All of us pray every night, and the church prays, too, that somehow you'll get out of this place."

"It doesn't seem likely, but I'm glad you're prayin' for that."

Lanie felt they'd been talking for only a few minutes when Pardue came in and said, "They tell me it's time to go, Lanie."

Lanie hugged her father. His arms came around her, and he bent over to kiss her. She held his head, put her arms around his neck, and whispered in his ear. "Don't give up hope, Daddy. God will open the door to this place one day, and you'll just walk out of here and come home to all of us." She kissed him on the cheek. "We'll be back soon, and the warden says I can bring the other kids too. We'll have a party."

Forrest Freeman had never wanted to cry so much in his life. He knew the sacrifices Lanie had made, so he made himself smile and wave as they walked away. "I'll look forward to that. You drive careful. Thanks again, Pardue."

Alone in the room, a sense of hopelessness overcame Forrest. Still, the words of Lanie were fixed in his mind. *One day you'll walk out and come home to all of us.* He straightened his shoulders and breathed a quick prayer.

CHAPTER 17

L anie stared at the bank book in dismay. The balance was practically at rock bottom. They had not had enough money to make the last payment, and Miss Effie allowed them to pay just the interest, but that could not go on forever.

Leaning back in her chair, Lanie closed her eyes. She could hear Cap'n Brown purring, for he had come to perch on the table next to her Big Chief notebook. He sounded as if he had a tiny motor running inside, and Lanie felt a touch of envy. "I wish I didn't have any more worries than you have, Cap'n Brown."

The sun shone through the windows this quiet Saturday morning. She and Corliss had the house to themselves. The other three Freemans had gone out to try to make a few dollars. Beau lay facing the wall, for Lanie had hurt his feelings by speaking sharply to him. "You're the only dog I ever knew that had touchy feelings, Beau." Beau turned to face her and somehow managed to look reproachful. He sniffed once and then turned back to face the wall.

Steps sounded on the front porch and the door banged. Maeva never allowed a door to close softly, but seemed to delight in the banging. Her eyes were alive with excitement when she came into the kitchen. The sun glinted on her red hair. "Look what I got here! I got seven dollars, and I made it all this mornin'!"

Lanie reached out and took the bills. They were old and crumpled, but they would spend. "Seven dollars in one morning! How'd you do it, Maeva?"

Maeva pranced around the kitchen. She patted Beau on the head, and he got up and reared up on her. She stepped on his toes. "Get off of me, Beau, you're too big and heavy!" Beau at once resumed his position staring at the wall. "I found a way to make some money that nobody ever thought of."

"What is it?"

"Nobody thinks much about old bottles—but I did. I went around town, collected them from the alleys, and most people throw 'em out around their houses. I got a whole wagonful, then I sold 'em to Old Man Jenkins."

"Old Man Jenkins? Why, he's a moonshiner!"

"I reckon he does make shine, and maybe that's why he wanted the bottles."

Lanie stared at Maeva in despair. "We can't sell bottles to moonshiners!"

"There ain't nothin' wrong with it."

"It's against the law to make moonshine!"

"It's not against the law to sell bottles. It's none of my business what he does with them."

"You got to stop it, Maeva."

"Well, I ain't going to. We're gonna keep this place, no matter what we have to do. You said that your own self, Lanie. Now, I'm goin' out to get more bottles." She dashed out of the room without another word.

Lanie looked down at the seven dollars. "Lord, I reckon it's wrong, but I don't know how to stop her. Just watch out for her and don't let her get hurt."

❦

The bank's board consisted of seven members. As they sat around the long table in the conference room of Planter's Bank, Effie Johnson studied each one carefully. As she had expected, Otis Langley had proposed as the first item of business that the bank foreclose on the Freeman property.

"We'd be within our rights," Langley said. "They didn't make their last payment, so I'm proposing that we take action at once."

A fairly hot and heavy discussion ensued. The lawyer Orrin Pierce, *Sentinel* owner Elspeth Patton, and Mayor Phineas Delaughter stood with Effie against the motion. Mortician Zeno Bruten and theater owner Francis Butterworth, dependent upon Langley's financial support, sided with Langley.

When Effie saw that a vote would favor Lanie's family, she said, "All in favor of extending clemency to the Freeman children, raise your hand."

As she had expected, Orrin, Elspeth, and Phineas raised their hands. "No sense taking another vote. It's four to three."

Otis Langley disliked being crossed. His face grew red, and he stared at the three members of the board who had voted to show mercy. "We're a business here, not a charity! I'm sorry for the Freeman children, but they've got to face the facts."

"The fact is," Orrin said vehemently, "that those kids are practically orphans. I'm not a Christian myself, but I know what the Bible says about anybody who picks on widows and orphans, and I won't have any part of it!"

"This is business, Orrin!" Langley insisted.

"We've got to give them all the leeway we can, Otis," Elspeth said. "It's not going to break this bank to extend the loan a little bit. They've paid the interest. That's more than others have done, isn't it, Effie?"

"Yes, it is. They're trying hard."

"Trying won't do it!" Langley said. "You know and I know that with their father in prison, they can't make enough money to live on, much less pay this note. Now, I've offered to buy their place, and I'll pay them enough to pay off the note and have some cash left!"

"Where would they live?" Elspeth demanded. "We can't take their home away from them."

Langley managed to lower his voice. "I don't want to be hard about this, but you know what's happening in this country. A lot of good people are losing their homes. A lot of businesses are closing, and it's going to get worse. Their best chance is to take my offer, and I think those of you who know them should encourage them to take the money they can get."

"I'll never change my vote," Orrin said.

Langley looked at Phineas, and the mayor became flustered. "We'll just have to see how it comes out," he said.

After the meeting was over, Orrin whispered to Effie, "He'll try to put the pressure on Phineas. If he can get him to change his vote, he'll get his way."

Effie sighed. "We'll have to convince Phineas to stand firm."

━◦━

"All right, everybody, listen to me," Cody said. He had come home with a flat square box in his hand, which he set aside until after supper.

When the dishes were washed, Cody put the box on the table and grinned from ear to ear. "Our worries are over! We're gonna make it fine with my new invention."

"What is it this time?" Maeva said wearily. "A perpetual motion machine?"

"No, it's something practical, and it's all my idea."

"What is it, Cody?" Lanie asked. She had little hope that Cody's idea would be as great as he thought. "What have you got in that box?"

"What I've got in this box is what's going to save this place."

"What is it?" Davis said. "You been walking around grinning like a possum for two or three days now."

"I've been getting it just right and now I've got it." He pulled the lid off the box and pulled out a white object. "This is it, folks." He put it down on the table. "Feast your eyes!"

Maeva reached out and touched it. "It's a round piece of wood with a hole in the middle. What's it for?"

The object was oval and painted white. It was smooth and rounded on top, but as Lanie picked it up she saw that it was flat underneath. "It's a seat of some kind."

"That's exactly what it is, but what kind of a seat? Can't you see? That's what makes a genius. We see stuff other people can't."

"Well, what kind of stuff? Are you gonna make a chair for it to fit in?" Maeva asked, a puzzled look on her face.

"No. Just look at it. Can't you tell what it fits?"

"I can't tell anything about it. What is it?" Davis said with some irritation.

"It fits your bottom. That's what it fits."

"What are you talking about?" Lanie exclaimed. "You shouldn't be talking like that at the table."

"Well, we ain't eatin' and it don't matter anyway. You all know what outhouses are like, a flat board with maybe two holes in it, and most of the time those boards are rough and got splinters. What this is is an outhouse seat. You fasten it down over the hole with screws. See how smooth it is and how much better it'd be to sit on this thing than on those old splintery boards."

Maeva began to laugh. "You are crazy, Cody! I'll admit it might be a little more comfortable, but how is this going to make us rich?"

"We're gonna sell 'em!" Cody announced. "How many houses are there in Fairhope?"

"I have no idea," Lanie said, "but we can't—"

"There must be at least five hundred, and every one of 'em has got an outhouse, and most of 'em are two-holers. That's a thousand seats it would take, and you can't tell me people won't spend a few dollars once they see the advantages of it."

"You know, your ideas are usually nutty, but this one may have somethin'," Davis said. He took the seat and ran his hand over the smooth surface. "How'd you make this thing anyway? How'd you get the hole in it and make it so smooth and round?"

"Well, I got this idea—that's what geniuses do, you know. Then I got some scrap lumber from the mill and glued it up until it was as wide as a seat. When it was all dry, I went to Mr. Schwartz's carpentry shop and told him what I wanted. He let me use his band saw, and I sawed it out into an oval, and he showed me how to cut the center out. Then he showed me how to shape it, make it all nice and round. At first we used hand planes, don't you know, then Mr. Schwartz figured out a way to use one of his machines to round it off. The hard part's sandin' 'em to make 'em smooth. He's got a sander there that's just right."

"We can't do a thing like that!" Lanie protested. "It's not genteel."

"Genteel my foot!" Maeva said, and her eyes flashed. "I think Cody's got a good thing here. Don't tell me you like to put your bare bottom on them old splintery boards, Lanie."

"I wish you'd stop talkin' like that. It's not nice," Lanie said weakly.

"You don't have to worry about sellin' 'em. I already sold six. I'm makin' 'em right now," Cody said. "I'm gettin' four dollars apiece. I have to pay Mr. Schwartz a dollar apiece for using his machinery."

"Who'd you sell 'em to?" Maeva demanded.

"Mr. Pink, Mr. Stockwell, and Chief Hathcock. They were tickled with 'em. They all got two-holers, and they each ordered two. So there you are. We're in business!"

"Those were all men!" Lanie said in disgust. "You couldn't talk to a lady about this."

"Well, shoot, I can!" Maeva said. "I can go to the women, and Davis and Cody can go to the men."

"You'll all have to help me make 'em. They take lots of fine sanding and then we have to paint 'em. We'll have to set up a place out in the barn or somewhere where the paint will be nice and smooth." Cody overflowed with ideas, and Lanie watched Maeva and Davis get caught up in them.

Finally Maeva dealt Cody a sharp blow on the shoulder. "Brother," she said, "I'll never say anything about your inventions again. We're in business!"

Lanie could not believe this was happening. She protested feebly. "We can't sell seats for outhouses. It wouldn't be decent."

"Sure it would," Cody said. "Maybe we can borrow some money and buy our own equipment so we don't have to pay Mr. Schwartz."

Lanie stamped her foot. "No, we're not borrowing any more money!" She looked around and saw the three staring at her and knew she was defeated. "All right, but I mean it about the money. You just wait. You know what they'll be calling us, don't you?"

"What?" Cody demanded.

"Probably 'The Outhouse Kids.'"

"I don't care what they call us as long as we make enough money to keep our place," Cody said.

Lanie began to laugh. "All right. You did good, Cody." She gave him a big hug. "We might be called worse, but if it'll keep our place, I don't care."

The room was full of talk, Cody expounding on the production, and Maeva talking about getting samples to show. She said, "When we get all of Fairhope supplied, we can go on over to Rosewood. They got as many outhouses as we have. Why, the world is full of outhouses!"

Lanie found herself smiling.

Lanie's eyes were red with fatigue, but she felt a surge of pride. "This is the longest poem I ever wrote," she whispered. She read over the lines with pleasure, for it was not only the longest poem she'd ever written but maybe the best. She read it softly, dramatizing the lines she had labored over for a week.

shepherd

Well, here's Jerusalem, and I am home.
That shop I left last year for good, will
Be my tomb. But then, it's not a bad old box,
And since I've done my fifty years and two
Enclosed within those peeling walls, just let
Them bury me right here when time wags out.

It's late, and there's my window in the shadow.
Almost I see myself spinning endless rugs
Forever there—but no, I need not see a ghost
So many stranger things I've seen of late.

Tomorrow Tychicus will jibe at me:
Well, well, our wealthy herdsman is returned!
But where is the gold those sheep were going to bring?
He never understood it was not money
Which bade me close my shop, turn all my cash
To sheep, and drove me from my buried life.
My city-cluttered eyes I craved to rest
Just once on clear, unbroken desert space
Sweeping off to hidden continents
While sweet, unbroken silence touched my ears.

For months my eyes were washed by canyons burnt
To crimson cinders, daubed with smears of
Yellow blooms. I saw the searing pale-blue skies
Of noon grow coolly dark, then turn to sheets
Of purple silk across the glittering sky.

If I cannot explain my going forth
Much less then my return. For who'd
Believe I've seen the heavens peopled
Thick as Jerusalem itself at noon.
Shouting wildly, "Glory to God in the highest!"
Oh, how that cry shook heaven, earth—and me!
Or who'd believe the brightest of the host
Gave me command: "Go find the Christ of God!"

I heard, obeyed, and stumbling on these legs
So shrunk with age, outran my lad until
We found the child, then breathless fell
Struck sudden dumb by what that stable held!

When we returned, the wild Judean dogs
Had slaughtered every sheep and every lamb.
So I am back. Tomorrow I'll begin
My little life, and some will laugh. But yet

There's always this—it isn't every birth
That brings the angels overhead to shout!

Some sheep I lost, but had I stayed for them
All else were lost — but now my treasure's sure:
One night — just for a while — I saw the King!

Lanie sighed, for her life was now so hard, but she found pleasure in working on her poems. She closed her eyes and prayed, "Lord, I hope you like my poem. I did it for You."

CHAPTER 18

As they sat down for the evening meal, Cody offered to give thanks. "Dear Lord, we thank You for our new business. Lord, this idea come from You. And, Lord, we all thank You . . . for the money and for how much better it feels to sit down in the outhouse."

"Cody!" exclaimed Lanie as Maeva and Davis chuckled, "you can't pray like that."

"It's what I think, and I mean it, Lanie!"

"You just use better language at the table, young man."

Cody bowed his head and continued, "Anyway, Lord, thanks for this here food. Bless Lanie's hands for making it. Amen."

"Lanie," Davis chided, as he scooped mashed potatoes onto his plate, "you gotta admit, them seats do make the outhouse comfortable."

"What I *will* admit is that I'm still surprised that they are selling so well."

"Yep," said Cody, putting gravy on his potatoes. "And not just here, but in nearby towns."

"I can't wait to tell Daddy about the business!" Lanie declared.

"You ain't wrote and told him about The Outhouse Gang?" Davis asked, surprised.

"No, I want to tell him in person. And"—Lanie looked at Cody— "I want to take one to show him."

"Heck, we all ought to go. After all, we're *all* in the gang," Cody remarked. "Seems like we all ought to tell him."

"I don't know about that," Lanie countered.

"Well, I do," retorted Davis as he ladled gravy on his potatoes. "I vote we all go with you this month. You're driving really good, Lanie, and there's enough room if we all squeeze in."

"I'll need to pray about that before I decide. All right?"

Maeva placed a piece of pot roast on her plate and passed the meat plate to Davis. "I think Daddy's going to be plum excited to know about the business and that it's allowing us to pay more and more each month on the note."

Lanie put her fork down.

"What's the matter, Lanie?" asked Davis. "You look like you just heard something bad."

"I don't know if I should tell you all."

"What?" cried the children in unison.

Lanie wiped her mouth with her napkin. "I saw Miss Johnson at the store today. She told me the board is getting more and more nervous about our paying interest only. She suggested we do everything we can to make the full note in July. If we don't, she can't guarantee us that Mr. Langley won't foreclose."

Dr. Owen Merritt wiped his mouth and neatly trimmed beard with the embroidered linen napkin. "Mrs. Langley, you've outdone yourself. That has to be the finest meal I've had since I arrived in Fairhope."

"We're so glad you could join us, Dr. Merritt," Martha Langley said. Owen thought that her clear blue eyes and beautiful smile gave her a classy appearance. He had enjoyed getting to know her as he had begun to court her daughter Louise. The rumors around town weren't really of any bother to him—after all, he wasn't sure he'd be here that much longer anyway. He glanced at Louise, who was smiling at him. She had her mother's eyes and fair skin, but was blond. Louise taught music in Fort Smith and had access to the finer families in the area.

"Miss Langley, do you think you'll return to Fort Smith to teach this fall?" Owen asked.

Louise put her napkin on her plate and furrowed her brow. "Well, I do need to discuss this with my mother and father, but I'm thinking of relocating to New York City to continue my training."

"Hear, hear," snorted Mr. Langley. "Louise, I think that would be fabulous. I have a friend at the music conservatory there. The training is world class, as is your voice."

Louise smiled at Owen. "Daddy's just too kind."

"No, no! It's true, Dr. Merritt. This lady's voice is the envy of the angels," he said, his chest puffed out in pride.

Mrs. Langley took a sip of water. "Otis, I'm not sure it's proper for a single woman to travel to such a big city. It might not look right."

Mr. Langley reached over and patted her forearm. "Now, now, darling. It's more and more common in these modern times. Besides, the conservatory has a dorm for the women with houseparents and very strict rules. Not that our Louise would need rules."

Louise's brother Roger said, "I'm not sure it's safe for a single woman to travel alone on the train these days—not even in a private compartment."

"Hogwash, son!" exclaimed his father. "Nothing could be further from the truth. Why just last year Cassandra Sue Pruitt traveled to New York City to study at the city library. Remember?"

Everyone nodded and he continued, "She took a private compartment and said she felt safe every inch of the trip. And Henrietta Green took the train to Memphis to get her phone company training."

"I must admit," added Owen, "I found the train from Memphis to be very comfortable. The Pullman car was nice. I'd recommend it."

"Well," added Helen, "The train may be safe, but not all of the roads around here are."

"I think they are," Owen observed.

"Not the one to the prison," Helen replied.

Helen's father laughed. "Honey, your sister isn't going to prison."

"I know that!" Helen reacted with obvious irritation. "I'm talking abut Lanie Freeman. She drives that old car of her father's all the way to the prison."

"What!" exclaimed Louise. "What a wild idea!"

"It sure is. And now that she has her driver's license, she's decided to drive over this month with all of her brothers and sisters."

"She's not taking that baby on a road trip, is she?" asked Mrs. Langley.

"No, but she's taking Davis, Maeva, and Cody."

Mr. Langley frowned. "Sounds to me like just one more piece of evidence that the girl does not have the maturity to care for those children. It's about time someone reported them to the State. They all need to be in an orphanage, if you ask me!"

"Do they keep up their payments on their place, Dad?" Roger asked.

"No, and I'm here to tell you that they simply will not be able to hang on to it much longer. They can barely pay the interest on the note. The last time the board met, we were closely divided on calling it in.

But their inability to pay is like a millstone around their neck. Pretty soon, they're going to sink."

Roger looked at his father in disbelief. "Father, I think you need to be very careful how you deal with those children."

Mr. Langley raised his eyebrows. "And why is that, Roger?"

"Because Jesus said, 'But whoso shall offend one of these little ones which believe in me, it were better for him that a millstone were hanged about his neck, and that he were drowned in the depth of the sea.'"

Louise jumped in, knowing that Roger had stirred their father's anger. "Well, I'll tell you this: Driving halfway across the state in an old Model T is just foolhardy. Why, it could break down halfway there. Then where would they be?"

Neither Owen nor Roger laughed. Owen could see that Mr. Langley's attitude hurt Roger. *He's a better man than his father—and I like him for it.*

On the way back to Doc Givens' home, Owen Merritt couldn't get the Freeman family out of his mind. *What a terrible situation! And what a sacrifice Lanie is making. She's quit school to take care of a business and a baby and a family. She doesn't deserve the scorn of uppity folks like the Langleys—she deserves a medal!*

An idea crossed his mind, and so he drove toward the Freeman home. He got out of the car and walked up to the porch. After standing there a while to gather his thoughts, he knocked on the door. After a moment, the porch light flickered on, and Lanie opened the door. The surprise on her face was obvious, even through the screen.

"Hi, Lanie."

"Good evening, Dr. Merritt. What brings you out this time of night?"

Owen could see the fatigue in her face and his heart went out to her. "I heard you were driving your family to Cummings to see your father tomorrow."

"Yes, we are. We're leaving early in the morning. Why?"

"Well"—Owen stammered for a moment—"Dr. Givens has given me the day off tomorrow and I've been wanting to see a bit of the countryside, so I hoped I might go to Cummings with you."

Lanie smiled at him. "Dr. Merritt, there's no room in our little car. We'll be packed like sardines as it is."

Owen laughed. "Oh, that's not what I meant. Dr. Givens is thinking of selling me his big old car. I thought it might be wise to take it out for a test drive. If you'd be willing, I'd like to drive you over to the prison."

Lanie smiled, and he could tell she liked the idea. He suspected that she was happy to have a man taking them, and with her brothers present she'd feel safe and avoid any impropriety. She finally nodded her assent. "We'll need to leave by five in the morning to get over there in time for visitation. That all right?"

"Your driver will be here at five minutes before the hour."

"Will my driver be needing coffee?"

It was Owen's turn to smile. "Your driver would love a big cup of black coffee."

"See you in the morning, Dr. Merritt. And thank you."

The visit went much faster than Lanie expected. Her daddy was shocked beyond belief to see the younger children. He hugged the three of them so hard that she thought they might suffocate, and he was very glad to meet Dr. Owen Merritt. Lanie was pleased when her daddy said how much he appreciated Dr. Merritt's kindness to his children.

Dr. Merritt took a walk to give the family privacy, a gesture Lanie considered thoughtful. When the time came for the visit to end, her father said good-bye to the younger children, sent them out, then turned to Lanie and held out his arms. She ran into them and he held her tight.

"Lanie," he whispered, "I know it's hard."

"It's harder than anything I could ever imagine. Every day is so difficult."

"I know, precious. I know."

"Daddy, I appreciate Mama more now than ever, and I miss her so much."

"Me too, Lanie, but this is the path the Lord has laid before us."

"I don't know if I can make it, Daddy."

Forrest held her at arm's length. "Lanie, you can make it."

"But how?"

"Lanie, don't ever forget the words of St. Paul. He told the Philippian church, 'I can do all things through Christ which strengtheneth me.' And, Lanie, so can you."

"I can't imagine even trying to walk this path without Him. Every morning I try to get up early enough to read the Word and to pray. And you're right. He has given me the strength I need, but I'm gonna need so much more."

"He's only promised enough grace for each day—for each step of each day. No more, no less. Lanie, Paul also told the Philippians exactly what I want to now tell you." He looked into her eyes. "Lanie Belle Freeman, notwithstanding, ye have well done."

Lanie smiled. Her dad's kind words gave her a new strength. She pulled him close and hugged him long.

"Visit's over!" bellowed the guard.

"I love you, Daddy!"

"I love you too, Muff. You are precious to me. And, Lanie Belle, you are precious to our Lord. Keep strong!"

⌀═✦►

After leaving Cummings, Owen parked the car outside a roadside diner and treated the Freemans to lunch. Lanie protested, but he refused to take her money.

"I owe you," he said.

"For what?"

"For giving me a free tour of this part of the country and for the privilege of meeting your dad. Lanie, I could see in his eyes and in the way he loves you all that he's a good man."

On the way home, the boys and Maeva fell asleep. Lanie looked at the back seat and smiled. Davis was leaning against the door, with Maeva leaning on him and Cody on her. They looked so peaceful. She sighed and faced forward.

"Penny for your thoughts, Lanie."

"Just thinking that it's nice to relax for a bit." She sighed again. "Dr. Merritt, I really appreciate you offering to drive us."

"It's a pleasure, Lanie. It really is."

"I just worry about Dad's old Model T. I'm half expecting it to break down most any day. So I confess I was worried about this trip."

"You've got an awful lot on your shoulders, young lady."

She knew he was trying to comfort her, but his calling her a young lady somehow stung. With all of her responsibilities, she felt more grown up than that.

He saw her almost imperceptible frown. "Lanie, I apologize."

"For what?"

"For calling you a young lady. With the load that you are carrying and the way you are running a family—not to mention having to oversee The Outhouse Gang—well, it's remarkable. I don't know many grown women who could do what you're doing, and I don't know *any* men that could do it half as well!"

She smiled. "I doubt that."

"I heard what a good student you were, and I heard about the award you won. Folks say you could be a doctor or an engineer. Others say you could write books or magazine articles. Most say you're brilliant and that you gave up your future to make one for your brothers and sisters."

Lanie was quiet.

"Lanie, when the man that the Lord has picked for you finds you . . . well, I'll tell you what. He's going to find himself a real treasure."

"How many men do you know want to marry a girl who has four children to care for?"

"They'll be gone before you know it!"

"How about Corliss? I have another decade and a half before she'll be ready to leave. I'll be an old maid before I'm free again."

It was Owen's turn to laugh.

"What you laughing at?" Lanie asked, irritated.

"Tell you what, Lanie. I don't think you're *ever* going to be an old maid."

By the time they arrived at the Freeman home, all the children were awake and chattering about the day. As they unloaded, the younger children all ran inside, yelling back their thanks to Dr. Merritt.

The doctor came around the car to open Lanie's door. As she got out, she apologized. "Please excuse them, Dr. Merritt. They go wild sometimes."

"They're just children." He smiled at her. "Lanie, thanks again for allowing me to drive you today. I'm delighted to get to know all of you."

"We're the ones who owe you a great debt. Especially me! You saved me a long drive and a lot of fretting. I appreciate it so much!"

Before she knew it, he reached out and gave her a hug. She knew it was *not* a romantic hug, but more like a hug her pastor or the sheriff would give her. She also knew he thought of her as a child. Even so, her heart was thrilled.

As he released her, he kept his hands on her shoulders. "Lanie Freeman, I want to tell you something."

He seemed very serious.

"This doctor is committing to help you all. If there's ever anything I can do for you, at least until you get solidly on your feet, then I'm ready and willing. Will you let me know?"

Lanie nodded. Her admiration for the young physician soared. "There's no way I can thank you for that, Dr. Merritt."

"Yes, there is."

"How?"

"I'll take a sample of one of those outhouse seats I've been hearing about. That will be payment plenty from the famous Outhouse Gang."

Lanie smiled at him. "I'll hand deliver your payment tomorrow."

"Thank you, Lanie."

Lanie watched him drive away, her heart confident that this young man was going to have a special place in the future of the Freemans.

⟿ CHAPTER 19 ⟸

Cody burst through the back door. "Lanie! Lanie!" Lanie was at the sink, peeling potatoes for dinner. She whirled around in alarm.

"What's the matter, Cody?"

"Looky here! Looky here!" Cody skidded to a halt in front of her, holding a small tin.

"What is it?"

"Just look, Lanie." Cody opened the tin, which was full of wadded-up bills. "It's nearly thirteen dollars in bills and coins."

"Where'd you get this money, Cody? If you've stolen it, then you're in for a whippin'!"

"It's from sales of the outhouse seats, Lanie, and I've already paid all my expenses for this month. This here's what's left."

Then Maeva burst through the door. When she saw Lanie looking at the money she was angry. "How come you didn't wait for me, you bumpkin! I helped as much as you and I wanted to show Lanie!"

Lanie smiled. "I'm so proud of you both. You've really done a good job."

Cody and Maeva both smiled.

"Now go wash your hands and come help me fix supper, you hear?"

⟿⟸

After supper, Lanie pulled out the coffee can. Her rule was simple: The money would not be counted until after supper on the eve of the payment's due date. Before that night, the family would work and pray each day. Lanie felt that knowing the amount in the can would only be a root of worry and concern. "Let's just do our best and leave the results to God," she said.

The excitement around the table was palpable. With the sale of Maeva's jars and Cody's toilet seats, all believed not only that the note would be met but that there would be funds for a good start on the next month's payment.

When Lanie finished counting, there was a collective sigh. "Oh, no!" Davis exclaimed.

"Drats!" agreed Cody.

"Oh, murder!" moaned Maeva. "It's hopeless."

Lanie recounted the money. "We're four dollars and fifty cents short."

Davis stood up, red-faced. "How'd that happen? Someone musta stole some!"

"Davis, sit down." Lanie commanded. "No one stole anything! It's just that our expenses were more this month. We had to buy sugar and salt."

"It's hopeless!" Maeva said again.

"No, it's not hopeless!" Cody cried out. "It'll more than cover the interest."

"The bank ain't gonna take interest only anymore, Cody," Maeva snapped. "Miss Johnson told us we better have the whole amount this month or Mr. Langley would have the votes to take our home. Now we're short and we're gonna lose our home. There ain't no hope!"

Lanie tried to put on a brave face. "Maeva, it's never hopeless when we serve God. He knows our needs, and His Word says He'll meet them. Let's just take a minute to pray."

Davis pointed his finger at Lanie. "It ain't gonna do no good to pray. We're short. Can't you see that, Lanie? We're gonna lose it all." He turned and ran out of the room.

Lanie bowed her head while Maeva and Cody looked on. "Dear Lord, You know we're short for a full payment to the bank. You know our full note is due tomorrow. Lord, I ask You to provide for the need of your children. Lord, when you do, we'll be sure to give You the thanks. In Jesus' name. Amen." She raised her head and said with all the confidence she could muster, "God is going to do a miracle." But inside she didn't know if she believed it herself.

The next morning, when Maeva walked into the kitchen, Lanie was preparing breakfast. A cup of coffee and her open Bible were on the kitchen table.

"Morning, Lanie," Maeva muttered. She had not slept well. Lanie's prayer echoed in her mind all night. *How could she have so much faith?* Maeva had asked herself.

"Need me to fetch the milk?" Maeva asked.

"Oh dear, yes. Would you? I completely forgot that today was milk day."

Maeva stepped out the back door and walked over to the cooler where the delivery man left their milk twice a week. To her surprise, she found a small tin next to the cooler. She opened it and her eyes widened. "Hey! Everybody come look!"

"What's the matter?" Lanie cried as she rushed out the door.

Maeva beamed. "Money!" She held out the tin and Lanie pulled out five crisp one-dollar bills and a small piece of paper, which bore a penciled message in childlike block letters: "A GIFT FROM THE LORD."

Lanie held the money and looked around at the others. "It's a five-dollar miracle, isn't it?" She began to dance and was joined by three other Freemans.

Otis Langley was reviewing some accounts with Effie Johnson when the door of her office opened and the Freeman children hurried in.

"Here it is, Miss Johnson. Our whole payment!"

"The whole thing?" asked Effie. "Well, I'm happy for you all!"

"We are too!" shouted Cody. "We're going to the Dew Drop Inn for a celebration soda. We got more money than we know what to do with!"

"You hush, Cody!" commanded Lanie. "Actually, Miss Johnson, this payment is somewhat of a miracle. It's a direct answer to prayer."

"Oh, I have no doubt, child. Prayer's a mighty thing."

"It is! Especially when the Lord answers it specifically. Good day, Miss Johnson."

"Good day, Lanie. You enjoy your sodas."

"Good day, Mr. Langley," Lanie said as she left with the others.

Effie looked at Otis. "Why, Mr. Langley, you look irritated."

"I most certainly am not!" Langley exclaimed.

"Are you upset the children met their obligation?"

Langley's face softened. "Of course not. I just happen to know that they will not be able to continue this level of debt payment. It's impossible. They'll fail. I'll tell you that!"

⊂══⊷

A small crowd gathered around the Freeman children at the Dew Drop Inn, listening as Lanie told the story again.

"That's amazing!" exclaimed Pardue.

"It ain't amazing, Sheriff," Sister Myrtle said. "It's a miracle!"

"Well, whatever it is, I'd have given a month's salary to see Old Man Langley's face when you kids paid that debt. Must have been one fine moment, I'll tell you that."

"Cheers," agreed Harry Oz. "You children done good!"

Murmurs of agreement swept across the small crowd.

"Tell you what, these sodas are on me!" Sister Myrtle declared to a round of applause. "Won't have you children spending your hard-earned money here. Besides, my bottom end is much less calloused and splintered than usual because of that fine invention of Cody Freeman's."

"In that case, Sister Myrtle, can I have me a complimentary cherry to go in my soda?" Cody asked.

All laughed, and Harry Oz spoke up, "You should know we're rootin' for you! You've done a great thing!"

Applause went up across the room. "Speech, speech!" someone shouted.

"Go ahead," Sister Myrtle told Lanie.

Lanie smiled and the crowd got quiet. "Thanks, everyone, but we shouldn't get any credit. It's Jesus who's done it all."

"Amen to that!" several said.

Sister Myrtle smiled. "These are some of the heartiest amens I've ever heard to one of the sweetest and shortest sermons I've ever heard." Then she laughed out loud and began a praise of thanksgiving to the Lord as she dropped cherries in each of the children's sodas.

PART FOUR

The Revenge

↠ CHAPTER 20 ↞

F all had come and with it the cool, sharp breezes of September. As
Lanie stood in front of the window, she thought she could almost
feel the change in the earth. A gray squirrel ran along a limb of the
pecan tree at the side of the house. He moved like one who had serious business but stopped abruptly when Lanie raised the window and
leaned outside and said, "Hello, Frisky."

The squirrel seemed astonished. He popped up into a sitting position and folded his paws, looking at that instant like a monk folding
his hands in prayer. His bright black eyes stayed open, however, and
his nose twitched furiously. He began to chatter angrily before he finally
disappeared behind the bulk of the tree.

Lanie smiled at the squirrel's antics, then closed the window and
turned to put on the faded dress that she had finished ironing. She held
it for a moment, and a brief touch of sadness came over her, for it was
the last dress her mother had made. She held it up to her cheek and
thought of the day her mother gave it to her. "It'll be too big for you
now, but you'll grow into it, daughter."

With a swift motion she lifted the dress, slipped her arms into it,
and tried to work it down. She had not worn the dress for a year. Now
she realized that it was much too small. She tugged at it, but it stuck
to her like skin on a grape.

"If I took a deep breath, I'd bust out every seam," she said aloud.
She turned to look in the mirror, and it was obvious that the dress
would not do. She had been conscious of a swelling bosom and the
broadening of her hips, but the sight of herself about to pop out of the
dress startled her.

"Where is that little girl who wore this dress?" she said. Even as she said it, the idea for putting the experience into a poem came to her. She stood still for a moment, her eyes half-closed and unseeing, as the lines seemed to march out and arrange themselves. Sometimes a poem came to her like this, born whole and complete, needing only a little change. She reached down and with great difficulty pulled the dress up over her head. She looked at it woefully. "I guess Maeva will get this one. She'd still fit in it, I bet."

She returned the dress to its hanger, then pulled out her green dress. She had made it herself, and she was not the seamstress her mother was. "Well, it's big enough at least, even if it's not pretty."

She was troubled, somehow, by the realization that she had crossed a line without really being aware of it. She remembered crossing the state line from Arkansas into Oklahoma without having noticed. It had been a shock to be told she was in Oklahoma. She remembered how her mother had once told stories of her childhood. Now the little girl that became her mother was gone, and so was the woman. "Everything changes, I guess," she whispered.

She heard the sound of steps on the porch. She looked out the window and saw Annie mounting the steps with difficulty. Lanie ran downstairs, almost stumbling over Cap'n Brown, who meowed at her and then followed. She ran to the door and opened it. "Annie, come on in."

"I brought you some pears and some flour sacks."

"Oh, we can use those pears! They're the best in the country. Come on in."

She led Annie into the kitchen and made much of the pears and held up the patterned flour sacks. "You can never get enough flour sacks, Annie. I'll be making Cody and Davis shirts out of these. I can't sew like Mama did though."

Annie sat herself down carefully in one of the kitchen chairs and smiled briefly as Lanie kept the conversation going. Annie finally asked, "How's Cody doin' with them toilet seats he was a makin'?"

A disappointed note touched Lanie's voice. "Well, we did real well with them at first, but only rich people can afford them, and you know there aren't many rich people in Fairhope."

"That's a fact. It's too bad."

"Yes, a lot of people started making their own, and then a man over at Pine View started making them. A cabinet maker. He can make them real cheap, and he's started selling them to stores. So I guess you could say he put us out of business."

"I reckon that didn't help any in payin' that note," Annie said. Her eyes were bright, and she smacked her lips as she sipped the sassafras tea. "Are you gonna make it all right this month?"

"I don't know. Last month we were short thirty-two dollars, but it was all right. The angel came and left it in a jar on the front porch."

Annie grinned. She had snuff at the corners of her mouth and a black-gum snuff stick in her mouth. She shifted the brush around and grinned. "You still believin' in angels?"

"We call him the Angel of Fairhope. He's left money three times, and I think he's the one that left the earrings that I showed you for my birthday."

Annie cackled now, her laugh sounding harsh. "Well, now, if you ever see him, you tell him to stop by old Annie's house. I could use a few dollars myself."

Still chuckling, Annie turned to Corliss, who was asleep on a pallet on the floor. She went to the child and bent over painfully. She stroked the toddler's silky hair and said, "This here is the angel."

"Yes, she is." Lanie stared at Annie's withered hand on the fresh baby hair of Corliss. There was a poem on this, and she made a note to write it sometime. "We'll be going to church tonight. It's prayer meeting. Why don't you come and go with us?"

"I reckon I'm past all that."

"Nobody ever gets past that." Lanie wiped her hands on her apron, checked the stew that was simmering on top of the stove, and stirred it. "Annie, have you ever been saved?"

"Saved? Saved from what?"

"You know, saved by the Lord."

"I don't reckon so." Annie returned to her sassafras tea and swirled it around. She stared into the cup long and hard, as if it contained her future—or more likely her past. She said quietly, "I had a hard time, Lanie. I had a husband and two babies. My husband died in a mine accident in West Virginia. The boy, he died of diphtheria. Our daughter, her name was Heddie, after my mama. She took up with a bad man. He got her with a baby, and she died during childbirth."

"What about the baby?"

"It was a boy, and the man she was livin' with, he took him away and moved somewhere up north. I never did know where. Since then I guess I've been all by myself. No family and no God. No nothin'."

Lanie went over to Annie, her heart touched by the story. Putting her arm around the old woman, she hugged her firmly and said, "You do have a family, Annie. Remember that. All of us Freemans are your family, and I want you to find Jesus."

"He ain't interested in me, child. Not after the way I lived."

"Yes, He is, and I'm going to pray that you find Him like I have." She kept her arm around the old woman and prayed silently for her. Annie was looking at her with an odd expression, but she smiled. "You might tell that angel to stop by my place if he ain't got nothin' better to do."

⊨⊷

"Hey, Lanie, got to talk to you."

Ralph Delaughter, the mayor's son, caught up to Lanie on the street. "What is it, Ralph?"

"I got an invite for you."

"An invite? To do what?"

"There's gonna be a dance over at Cedar Grove next week. You know that new bridge they just built over the Buffalo River? They finally finished it. They're gonna have a big christening."

Lanie smiled. "I didn't know you christened bridges. I thought you only christened ships."

"Well, whatever. There's gonna be free food and speeches. It's almost election time, you know. All the politicians will be there. There'll be barbecue and soft drinks. Lots of good stuff."

"Oh, I don't really think I could go, Ralph."

"Shoot yes you can go!" Ralph grinned and winked at her. "You need to get out and have some fun. All you do is work."

This was so true that Lanie made a face. She liked Ralph, although she didn't know him very well. He continued to persuade her until she finally said, "All right, Ralph."

"Good! I'll get my dad's car. I'll pick you up at five o'clock. We'll have a great time."

At home, Maeva greeted Lanie with an announcement. "Charlie Young asked me to go to that dance on the bridge."

"You're too young to go to that dance. Besides, Charlie is wild."

Maeva's face clouded over, and her voice rose. "I'll bet you're goin'!"

"That's different. I'm going with Ralph Delaughter."

"Well, Ralph ain't no angel from what I've heard."

The argument proceeded for the rest of the evening. At bedtime, Lanie gave up. "All right. You can go, but you'll have to go with Ralph and me."

Maeva gave Lanie a hug. "We'll have us a good old time. And if we get tired of Ralph and Charlie, we'll find somebody better at the dance."

Lanie laughed. "You're awful, Maeva!"

"No I ain't. I just got good sense. If you bite into an apple and find out it's bad, you don't eat the whole apple." She danced around the room and turned to face Lanie with a wicked grin on her lips. "We may find some better apples than them two old boys!"

CHAPTER 21

After dinner, Louise Langley took Owen Merritt into the larger of the Langley's two parlors to listen to the latest recordings on the new electric record player. They listened to a new song called "Stardust," which Owen liked very much, and then "Honeysuckle Rose" by Fats Waller. When the record ran down, Owen said, "You know, black people are really great singers."

Louise stared at him. "You mean that was a black man singing?"

"Sure. Fats Waller is one of the leaders in jazz music. Most of it comes out of New Orleans. You didn't know?"

Louise frowned. "No," she said, "but I don't care for it." She rose from the horsehair couch, opened a drawer, and put the record in it. Owen suspected that that was the last of that record for the Langley household. "Here's one I really like," Louise said. Her pale blue organdy dress showed off her lissome figure. As she bent over to put the record on, Owen said, "Is it one we can dance to?"

"No, I think this is the listening kind. It's called 'Wedding Bells Are Breaking Up That Old Gang of Mine.'" She returned to Owen's side and sat closer than she would have if her parents had been in the room. He took her hand, and she smiled at him as they listened to the song. When it was over, she said, "You want to dance?"

"Sure, but not any of that Charleston stuff. Something nice and slow for an old man."

"You're not an old man." Louise put her hand on his cheek. "You're just the right age for a doctor. Young enough to be energetic and old enough to have some authority." She walked to the record player and selected a new album. "This one ought to be good to dance to."

The music started, and Owen put his arm around her and then took her hand. "'You Were Meant for Me.' I like it."

"It is nice, isn't it?"

The two moved across the carpet. "I'm going to a dance this Saturday," Owen said.

"A dance? I haven't heard of any dances."

"The government finally finished that bridge over the Buffalo River down by Cedar Grove. They named it after some politician who probably didn't have anything to do with the bridge. The election's coming up, so there'll be flag-waving speeches. But they're going to have a dance and all kinds of music and singing—and free food."

"Oh, that'll just be the country people with their fiddles and banjos."

"Hey now, I kind of like mountain music."

"They'll just be square dancing."

Owen smiled. "I take it you don't want to go."

"Not really. It's not my kind of thing. Owen, you can't imagine how I miss going into the big hotels with the big bands in Chicago."

"Well, I think I'll take it in." Mischief danced in Owen's eyes. "As a matter of fact, Mamie Dorr has promised to teach me about square dancing."

"Mamie Dorr? Don't tell me you'd go with that awful woman!"

"Mamie's not so bad."

"She'll chase anything that wears pants!" Louise said. "I forbid you to go with her!"

Owen laughed. Louise amused him at times. He liked her, but he could not deny that she had a strong independent streak. She was accustomed to having her own way and usually he gave in, but not tonight. "Well, there's only one woman who can forbid me to go to a dance."

"And who's that?"

"My mother. But she wouldn't mind. As a matter of fact, she'd probably enjoy going herself."

"I doubt your mother would like square dancing."

"You're wrong about that. She's quite a gal. She was even a flapper for a time, although she was a bit old for it."

The song ended, and Louise turned the record player off.

"No more music or dancing?" Owen asked, lifting one eyebrow. "Is this your way of sending me home?"

Louise appeared to be thinking hard, and then she smiled. "You know, that dance might be fun. I used to go listen to the mountain music on the courthouse square when I was a little girl. Haven't done that in a long time. Yes, I think I will go with you."

"Good! Better wear something warm. It'll be kind of chilly. I'll be going now. You've been so nice to me to have me over for dinner, sparing me some of Dr. Givens' nightly interrogations."

Owen moved closer and put his arms around her. She turned to him and lifted her face. Bending his head, Owen kissed her, and she returned his kiss. She was a beautiful woman, and her fragrance and softness stirred him. He broke away first. "That's all the affection you get tonight. You can hope for more on Saturday if you're a good girl."

Louise struck him in the chest with her fist. "You are a beast!" she cried. "See if you get any more kisses out of me!"

"It has been a good evening. I'll look forward to Saturday."

She walked with him to the door, handed him his coat, and when he settled his hat, she squeezed his arm. "It was fun. I'll look forward to Saturday too."

After the door closed, she walked to the small parlor where her mother sat reading a book.

"Owen's gone home?"

"Yes." Sitting next to her mother, Louise said, "I didn't know doctors could be so much fun. Owen is, though."

Martha examined Louise more closely. "Are you serious about Owen?"

"I might be. He's nice."

"He'll never be rich," Martha warned. "Small-town doctors work hard and usually don't get paid much—especially in these times."

Louise ran her hand through her hair. "He could have a profitable practice if he went to a big city like Chicago."

"You may be right." Martha examined her daughter's expression. "Is he thinking of marriage?"

Louise smiled and then laughed out loud. "Not now, but I think I could persuade him."

Martha chuckled. "You sound like a hunter going out after a deer."

"It's not like that." Louise shrugged. "Anyway, I've got to go to this horrible dance out on some bridge over the Buffalo on Saturday night. It'll be awful!"

"Why are you going then?"

"Because he said he'll take Mamie Dorr if I don't go."

"Mamie Dorr! Why, that woman's notorious!"

"I think he was teasing me. And anyway, it might be fun." She yawned and stood. "Good-night, mother."

"Good-night." Martha watched her daughter leave and felt a sense of satisfaction. Owen might be a very good thing. Owen might become a successful doctor in a big city.

⚬══⊶

"I really don't think I should go to the dance."

Maeva looked up at Lanie with a startled expression. "Not go to the dance? Why, you've got to go! We've worked like slaves on these dresses!"

"I know, but Corliss has a fever. I hate to go off and leave her."

Davis said, "Don't worry about it, sis. Cody and I can take care of Corliss." He was holding Corliss on his lap and put his cheek next to hers. "She doesn't feel too hot. Probably cutting another tooth."

Cody grinned at Lanie. "Yeah, sis, you look great! I'd dance with you myself if I was gonna be there."

Lanie saw that Maeva looked disappointed. The two of them had worked frantically to finish their dresses. They found some leftover material in their mother's cedar chest and traded some ginseng roots to the general store for the rest of the material. Although neither of the girls could sew as well as their mother, together they rose to the challenge. Maeva's dark-green skirt fell halfway between her knees and ankles and was topped by a frilly white blouse. The outfit accented her trim form. "You do look so nice, Maeva," Lanie said.

"So do you. I think your dress is prettier than mine."

Lanie's one-piece dress, made of soft wool, was a rich wine color decorated with white embroidery. She had cut down a wool jacket of her mother's to fit, and both girls also found silk stockings and low-quarter shoes among their mother's things.

"Hey, here comes somebody!" Davis said. He raced to the window and peered out. "It's Ralph in that fancy car of his dad's . . . and there's Charlie right behind him in that old Ford of his."

"I'll get the door!" Cody yelled. He ran out and they heard him say, "Hey, you two guys look great. If you drop dead, we won't have to do anything to you 'cept stick a lily in your hands."

Charlie and Ralph came in, and both of them bragged on the appearance of their dates. "You girls ready?" Ralph said eagerly. "We're gonna have a great time."

"We're all ready," Lanie said. She leaned over and kissed Corliss. Maeva slipped on her coat. "Charlie, you got to behave yourself tonight. We've got two chaperones."

"Who? I didn't agree to any chaperones."

"Lanie and Ralph. They're gonna keep an eye on us." Maeva winked.

Charlie laughed. "We'll probably have to keep an eye on them. You know how wild they are."

⌁

The new bridge over the Buffalo River was packed, and the air was filled with the sound of fiddles, banjos, mandolins, and throbbing bass fiddles. The long tables arranged on both sides of the bridge were filled with food, mostly barbecued. Lanie thoroughly enjoyed the evening, for she loved square dancing, and Ralph wasn't bad—although he wasn't as good as she was. Bright overhead lights illuminated the crowd, and even though the cold breeze was sharp, she didn't mind. But when Ralph withdrew a bottle, poorly concealed in a brown sack, and laced his drink with liquor, her joy wavered.

"You shouldn't be drinking, Ralph."

"Aw, don't be such a bluenose, Lanie. Just try it. It'll liven you up—and warm you up too." He pushed the bottle toward Lanie, but she shook her head.

"You know I don't drink, and I'm surprised at you."

"What are you, some kind of Holy Roller?" He tilted the bottle, swallowed several times, then shivered and stamped his feet, catching his breath. "Wow! That's strong stuff! Better try some."

Lanie crossed her arms. "No, and I wish you wouldn't."

Lanie's protests did little to influence Ralph, so she allowed herself to drift. She danced with several of her old friends and noticed that Dr. Merritt had come with Louise Langley. Louise, she thought, looked out of place. She wore a dress far too formal for square dancing, but she appeared to be having a good time. Lanie wondered about the talk she had heard about the two getting serious.

He'll probably marry her, but I don't think she's his kind.

⌁

"You having a good time, Louise?"

Louise looked up at Owen as they danced to the mountain music. "Oh, it's all right, I suppose."

"I really like this sort of thing. I used to go down to Beale Street in Memphis and listen to the jazz musicians. Boy can they play those trumpets and pound those pianos! But these folks do pretty well with their fiddles and banjos, don't they?"

The two danced until the music ended and the master of ceremonies announced, "Folks, we've got a real treat fer you tonight. Two of Forrest Freeman's girls are here, and ya'll know that that whole family is about as musical as folks can git. I'm gonna ask 'em to come up and entertain us. Come on, Lanie, and you too, Maeva, let's have a good one!"

"Well, that's something," Owen said. "I didn't know they were musical."

"Oh, the Freemans have always been that way. Their father could play just about anything."

The two watched as Lanie and Maeva went to the front. Lanie appeared embarrassed, but Maeva was grinning. "We're gonna sing for you 'The Wabash Cannonball.'"

Lanie sang clear soprano, and Maeva harmonized perfectly with a low alto. The girls received loud applause and requests to sing another number, "The Great Speckled Bird."

Applauding heartily as the girls stepped down, Owen said, "Why, those two are good enough to go professional!"

"Yes, they do very well," Louise said. At that moment Harold Pinnock asked Louise for a dance, and she accepted. Owen moved toward Lanie. "I think this is our dance—but I warn you to watch out for your feet. I'm not very good."

Lanie smiled, and they joined the other couples.

"I liked your singing very much. I didn't know you could sing like that." He stumbled, and his weight fell on Lanie's shoulders. "There," he said with a rueful laugh, "I warned you."

"I'll bet you're more used to fancy ballrooms with orchestras."

"I like this much better. It's the real thing. It's different listening to a bunch of paid performers. These people are playing because they love it."

"Why, that's right!" Lanie said with surprise. "I'd never thought of it like that."

"There's a reality to mountain music. It comes from the earth, so to speak. I was telling Louise that you and your sister could become professionals."

"Oh, we're not that good."

"Never know. One of these days I might be listening to you on the radio." He put his head back and said, "And now, ladies and gentlemen,

I present to you the songbirds of the South—the Freeman sisters." He grinned. "How was that for an introduction?"

Lanie laughed. "It would be nice, but I doubt it will ever happen."

❦

Ralph held onto the wheel with both hands, but the car weaved across the road in an alarming fashion. "I don't see why we had to leave!" he complained. "I was havin' a good time." His words were slurred, and he took his eyes off the road to look at Lanie. "Come on over here and sit close to me."

"You watch where you're going, Ralph! Keep your eyes on the road!" The car swerved toward the ditch, and Lanie grabbed the wheel just in time to straighten it out. Ralph laughed, released the wheel with his right hand, threw it around her shoulder, and pulled her close. He tried to kiss her, but she yanked herself away. "Ralph, take me home!" She was humiliated and angry, for Ralph had made a spectacle of himself. She'd had no idea that he was so wild. At school he was loud and boisterous, but his behavior at the dance was terrible!

Ralph pulled off to the side of the road. He left the engine running but moved over and threw his arms around her. "Come on. Let's have a little lovin'." His breath was rank with alcohol, and before Lanie could move he kissed her noisily just in front of the ear.

"Leave me alone, Ralph! Take me home right now!" Ralph appeared not to hear. "Keep your hands off me, Ralph, or I'll bust you in the jaw!"

Ralph merely laughed, but when he moved toward her again, she gave him a resounding slap on the face. "Hey, what are you doin'?" he yelled.

"If you don't take me home, I'll get out and walk!"

Ralph glared at her and shouted, "Why don't you then! That's all you're good for, Miss High and Mighty!"

Lanie yanked at the door handle and stepped outside of the Oldsmobile. As she began walking, she heard the car roar. Ralph yelled something she could not understand, then the car moved away, weaving and throwing gravel. She watched as the taillights of the Oldsmobile disappeared in the distance. Anger surged through her. She walked fast under the bright moon, holding her jacket closed, for the night had grown very cold.

Five minutes later she heard a car approaching and turned around to see headlights. She did not know whether to ask for a ride or not, but the car pulled up, and she heard Maeva's voice. "What in the blue-eyed world are you doin' out here, Lanie? You have a fight with Ralph?"

Lanie walked up to Maeva's window. "Yes. Can I ride with you, Charlie?"

"Why, sure. Get in, Lanie." Lanie opened the door and sat next to Maeva. Charlie stepped on the gas. "Ralph get out of line?"

"He certainly did!"

"He does that when he drinks. He thinks he's some Romeo."

"I didn't know he drank."

"Yeah, he started about a year ago. He doesn't know when to quit."

"I wish I had known."

◦◦◦ CHAPTER 22 ◦◦◦

The three boys had been running and laughing. They stopped to pick up rocks, and they all took a shot at a large gray squirrel that chattered angrily at them from a low branch of a hickory tree. Cody and Max missed by a broad margin, but Davis's rock struck the limb right over the creature's head. The squirrel turned an acrobatic backflip, caught another branch, then scampered to the top, disappearing into the upper branches.

"You nearly got him, Davis!" Cody cried.

"You sure can chuck rocks. Guess that's why you're such a good pitcher," Max said, admiration shading his tone. "You sure showed them guys from Pine Grove how to play baseball!"

Davis grinned, picked up another rock, and sent it into the tree with a deceptively free and easy motion. He always began his windup with a high kick in the air and threw with a leisurely sidearm. When the ball left his fingers, however, it appeared to pick up explosive speed.

"That was a good game," Davis said. "They had some pretty fair hitters."

"Shoot, they couldn't touch you!" Cody boasted. "A couple of years from now I'm gonna be your manager and get you a contract with the Saint Louis Cardinals. We'll be millionaires!"

Davis laughed at his brother's scheme. "Do you ever dream of anything practical, Cody? I'm not going to make a million dollars playing baseball. Hundreds of guys can pitch better than I can."

"Well, kiss my foot, you're only fifteen! Wait two or three more years until you get your growth," Max said.

They reached the foot of Macy's Ridge, a long outcropping that bordered Fairhope to the south. It rose at first in a gentle slope and then crested sharply some two hundred feet in the air. The land beneath was thickly wooded, and the boys started up the trail. "Hey, look at that!" Cody yelled.

Davis looked. "That's an old tractor tire, a big one too!"

Cody was already at the tire, trying to lift it up. "This is great! I'm taking it home with me."

"You can't take that thing home," Max scoffed. "You can't even pick it up!"

"All of us can. Come on, grab hold."

"What would you want an old worn-out tractor tire for?" Davis asked.

"Lots of things. I might put a lining in it and make a fish pond out of it and paint it blue and sell it. I'll find somethin' to use it for."

Davis grumbled, but the three of them tugged and pushed until they got the tire upright. Davis glanced up the slope and shook his head. "It'll be a chore gettin' this thing up that hill."

"But think how easy it'll be gettin' it down!" Cody said. "Come on now. Let's go."

The monumental struggle to get the huge tractor tire up to the top of the ridge took all the boys' strength. By the time they reached the crest, all of them were gasping. Cody said, "Well, we ... made it ... now it'll be ... easy."

The three guided the tire over the crest, and then the downhill slope began to pull at the tire.

"Hang onto it!" Max warned. "Look out, don't let it get away!"

But the huge tire did get away. Davis's feet slipped, and when he fell, Cody was unable to hold it. The big tire rolled rapidly away.

"Well, ain't that a pretty come off!" Cody yelped, then took off running. "Come on, let's catch that dumb ol' tire!"

"I hope it don't hit none of them apple trees," Max said. "That's Old Man Langley's place down there. He'll have us all put in jail if we done anything to it."

The three boys ran after the tire, but it had gathered momentum and was bounding straight down the hill. "Dad gum it!" Davis groaned. "It's gonna hit Mr. Langley's fence!" All three stopped to watch.

"Hope it don't bust it," Max whispered.

But the tire struck the white picket fence, flattened a section, and plunged straight toward the saplings.

"It's gonna hit his apple trees!" Cody yelped. "He loves them dumb ol' trees. He boasted to everybody how much he spent on that orchard."

Otis Langley had planted a beautiful apple orchard the year before in neat, organized rows. The trees were only saplings, but they were the best money could buy. All three of the boys leaned to the left as if that effort would pull the bounding, rushing tire between the rows.

"It's gonna hit 'em!" Cody swallowed hard. "It's gonna knock 'em down!"

The big tire hit the first apple tree, snapped it off—then the second—then the third. *Snap! Snap! Snap! Snap!* The tire seemed guided by some unseen malevolent force! The trees were planted at least thirty feet apart, and if the tire had gone down the middle, all would have been well. But by the time it reached the end of the row it had destroyed at least twenty of the young saplings.

Davis watched as the tire crashed through the far side of the picket fence and then hit the side of the Langley house with a crash.

"Come on," Max cried, "let's get out of here!"

"Yeah," Cody said. "We'll go back and come in from the west. Nobody will ever know who done it."

A sickness came to Davis as he saw the wreckage from the huge tire. He could understand Mr. Langley's love for the orchard, for the trees were beautiful, so straight and true—and now a whole row of them lay crushed. He turned around and ran after the two as they fled down the far side of the ridge. When they reached the safety of the woods, Davis said flatly, "That was a bad thing."

"Aw, shoot, what's a few trees to Ol' Man Langley?" Cody said. "He's rich enough to buy all the trees in the world. We're lucky nobody seen us do it. Come on. We don't say anything to anybody, right?"

"Well, I ain't talkin'," Max said. "I don't want no trouble with that man for sure."

Davis did not speak, but a misery formed within him, and he knew it would not be easy to forget what he had just seen.

○══✦══

By the next day most of the town had heard of the fate of Otis Langley's apple trees. Most of them found it funny that the richest man in town could suffer a loss even as the rest of them did. Others worried about the vandalism.

Langley stormed into the office of the police chief, Ed Hathcock. He shouted about the damage and ended by saying, "Ed, I want you to find the thugs that ruined my orchard. I'm going to prosecute!"

"Well now, Mr. Langley, that ain't gonna be too easy."

"I don't care whether it's easy or hard! You get out there and hunt for them. Somebody must have seen those hoodlums, whoever they were, with a big tire like that."

Hathcock scratched his neck. "Well, I'll sure try, Mr. Langley, but it don't look too promisin'. I been askin' around, but nobody saw a thing."

"If you want to hang onto your job, Ed, you'd better find those criminals quick!" Langley slammed the door behind him when he left.

⌖

"Who did you say is here?"

Helen Langley said, "It's one of those Freeman children. His name is Davis."

"What does he want?"

"He wouldn't tell me, Daddy."

"Well, have him come on in."

Langley leaned back in the chair. It was Sunday afternoon, and he had returned from church in a bad mood. The sermon had been titled "Love Thy Neighbor," but he felt little love at the moment. He glanced out the window and winced at the wreckage of his orchard. Davis entered. "What is it you want, boy?"

Davis had been struggling with his conscience ever since the disaster. Max and Cody had written the whole thing off, but Davis was unable to sleep. At church that morning he had been miserable. The sermon was not particularly abusive, for Brother Prince wasn't that kind of a preacher, but he spoke with conviction about being fair and honest as Jesus was.

Davis went home after the service saying almost nothing, but by one o'clock he knew he couldn't carry his burden any longer. Without a word to anyone, he left the house and went to the Langleys' place.

His voice was thin and reedy. "I . . . I got to tell you something, Mr. Langley."

"What is it? Speak up. I have things to do."

"Well . . . I have to tell you that . . ." For a moment Davis could not finish. "I was the one who let that tire wreck all your trees." He saw Mr. Langley's face turn red. "I didn't mean to do it, sir. It was an accident, and I'll work, and I'll pay you back for the—"

Langley stood up. "Work it out? You know what those trees cost, boy?"

"No, sir, but—"

"Seven dollars apiece. That's a hundred and forty dollars worth of trees for twenty! There'll be no working it out!"

Horror came to Davis then. He could never get that much money together. "Please, sir, I'll do anything! I'll cut your grass or paint. I'm a hard worker."

"Get out of this house, boy, and I'll tell you right now! I'm telling Chief Hathcock about this. You'll be sorry for this trick!"

Davis left the house, his heart filled with fear. He knew that he had to tell his family. He dreaded that as much as anything, but it had to be done.

Langley did not wait until Monday. He got in his car and went to Ed Hathcock's house.

"What is it, Mr. Langley?" Hathcock looked alarmed.

"I know who destroyed my trees. It was that oldest Freeman boy."

"Are you sure? Davis is a mighty good boy. Never been in trouble."

"He confessed. I want you to arrest him, Ed."

"Why, I can't do that, Mr. Langley. It was an accident, wasn't it? The boy sure didn't mean to do it on purpose."

"He did it, and that's what counts! It's destruction of property."

"Look here, Mr. Langley. I realize you're mad, but we can't do this. You can charge the boy for the trees. He'll probably have to work it out."

"I don't want it worked out! I want him arrested!"

"Well, I just plain can't do it."

Langley slapped his hat against his thigh. "I think you're due for an early retirement, Ed. If you won't do your job, we'll find somebody who will!" He turned without another word and walked out, slamming the door. Ed walked slowly back to the kitchen, where his wife Laverne was fixing dinner.

"Well, you done the right thing," she said. "That poor family don't need any more trouble."

Ed sighed and looked toward the door. "Well, you know Otis. He's like a bear with a sore tail when he's crossed. I'm thinkin' he'll make it harder than ever on them Freeman kids."

⊂══×~

Lanie listened silently to Davis, and when he finished his confession, she put her arms around him. "You did the right thing. It'll be all right."

"No it won't. He's gonna have me arrested," Davis whispered. "I-I'm scared, sis. I don't want to go to jail."

"You're not going to go to jail."

"Those trees cost a hundred and forty dollars. How will I ever pay it?"

"We won't worry about that. We've been studying in church about faith. Now, if God can make a highway in the Red Sea, He can take care of a few apple trees. Don't you worry about it."

"Well, rats! It was my fault!" Cody said. "I was the one who wanted to get that old tire." He stood up. "I'm going to go tell 'im it was my fault."

"No," Davis said, "it wouldn't do any good. You just keep quiet about it."

"I wish it had wrecked all of his dumb ol' trees!" Cody muttered.

"No, you don't," Lanie said. "Now we'll just be quiet. We pray about this, and it will be all right." She smoothed Davis's rebellious hair back from his forehead. "Times like these we realize how much we need Jesus, don't we, Davis?"

Davis nodded numbly. "I wisht I'd never seen that dumb old tire!"

⊂══×~

Within two days everyone knew the story of Davis Freeman and the tire and the wrecked apple trees, and most people expected an explosion from Otis Langley.

To everyone's surprise, nothing seemed to happen. Since Langley was not a man to take things lying down, this puzzled the town. No one dared to ask him about the situation. He kept his own counsel, and finally Orrin Pierce said to Sheriff Jessup, "I guess the old man has decided to let it go."

Pardue shook his head. "Nope, I'm thinkin' he's just waitin' for something. I don't know what it is, but that man don't ever forget a wrong. He's still sore because Lanie won that grand prize instead of his boy Roger. You can see it when he looks at her. I'm afraid he's going to get even this time."

"We can't let them prosecute that boy. I'd defend him for nothing."

"I hope it don't come to that, Orrin, but it might."

⌒

When Lanie opened the door, a stranger greeted her. He wore a dark suit and took off his hat at once. He had light blue eyes and fair hair, and he was obviously from the city. "I'm looking for the Freeman place."

"I'm Lanie Freeman. Can I help you?"

"My name's Millard Gamble, Miss Freeman. I work for the State. I expect I'd better come in and talk to you."

A touch of fear ran along Lanie's nerves. "Come on in, Mr. Gamble."

Lanie led the man into the living room, and when he sat down, she perched herself on the edge of the chair, tension in her eyes.

"I work for the Department of Child Welfare, Miss Freeman." Reaching down, he opened his briefcase and pulled out some papers. He looked at them briefly. "I understand your mother is not living."

"No, sir, she's not."

"And your father. He's incarcerated—in prison, that is?"

"Yes, sir."

"And how old are you, Miss Freeman?"

"Sixteen."

"No adults in the house?"

"No. Not now."

Mr. Gamble tightened his lips and ran his eyes along the paper. "I'm afraid I've got some bad news for you."

"Bad news? Is it about my father?"

"No, it's about you and your brothers and sisters. You see, we've had a complaint, and I've been ordered to make an investigation."

"Investigation of what?"

"Of your situation here. My department sees to it that children are taken care of, and I must tell you that your situation is not acceptable."

Fear fluttered in Lanie's breast, and she felt light-headed. "What do you mean? What have we done wrong?"

"You haven't done anything wrong. It's just that you have five children living alone without an adult or any means of support." Gamble looked through some papers and said, "Do you have any relatives that might come and live with you?"

"No, sir, we don't have anybody like that."

"Well, I'm afraid my recommendation is going to seem a little harsh to you. But we can't have infants and very young children living on their own. There has to be adult supervision."

"What . . . what's going to happen?"

"I think it's likely that the five of you will be placed in foster homes."

Lanie jumped to her feet, and her eyes were wide open. "No, you can't do that! You can't separate us like that, you can't!"

Mr. Gamble got to his feet and put the papers back in his briefcase. "I knew this would be hard for you. I'll finish my report and turn it in to my office. A committee will examine it and make the decision, but you should prepare yourself and your siblings to be moved to a foster home. I'm sorry to give you this bad news, Miss Freeman. You'll be seeing me later."

The man left the house, and Lanie stared after him. She seemed unable to move. Once she had been struck in the stomach while playing a game at school. It had knocked the wind out of her, and she was unable to breathe for a brief period. This was like that in a way. Finally she sat down abruptly in the chair and buried her face in her hands. "Oh, God, don't let this happen! Please don't let this happen to us!"

CHAPTER 23

Effie Johnson entered the law office of Orrin Pierce and said without preamble, "Orrin, I'm worried about this business with the Freeman children. How serious do you think it is?"

"I just made a call to the capital, Effie," Orrin said, and his tone was shaded with doubt. He came to stand beside her. "From what I can pick up, they mean business."

"You know where it all started, don't you?"

"Of course I do." Orrin snorted with disgust. "Langley's behind the whole thing. You have to understand, Effie, that those people at the capital don't know anything about the human side of these problems. All they've got is a piece of paper, and that piece of paper says that there are five children, one of them a mere toddler, living alone in a house without any means of support—and whose father is in prison. You have to admit that sounds pretty bad."

Anger flared in Effie's eyes. "Well, I see the human side of it, and so do you!" She caught the smell of liquor on Orrin's breath and gave him a sharp look. "It's too early in the mornin' for you to be drinkin', Orrin. As a matter of fact, you don't need to be drinkin' at all."

Pierce looked down at the small woman, who returned his gaze with such severity that he had to drop his head. "It's just the way I am, Effie. Nobody knows it better than I do."

"You can't stop drinking by yourself, Orrin. You need help."

"I think I'm about past that."

"Past it!" Effie sniffed. "Fiddlesticks! You're not past God's help." She liked this tall man. He had strength, good looks, and intelligence. He could go anywhere, but booze tied him down. Her tone softened and she put her hand on his arm. "The good Lord doesn't see anyone as being past help." She waited for him to reply, and when he didn't, she withdrew her hand. "All right, we'll have to do something."

"I think it's God who will have to do something. You know how the State is, Effie." Effie's words stung, but he knew she had a good heart. "I'll talk to some people. We'll see." When she turned to leave the room, he added, "Don't give up on me, Effie."

Turning to face him, Effie said, "I wouldn't do that, Orrin. You're too good a man to be wasted."

⚬⚬⚬

The Wednesday-night prayer meeting at First Baptist Church of Fairhope was usually a rather regimented affair. The small crowd began to filter in a few minutes before seven. At the urging of the pastor, William Prince, they took the front seats so that he could speak to them more easily. They came bundled up, and most of them kept their coats on. To save money, the church wasn't heated during the week.

Prince met Deoin and Agnes Jinks as they entered, shaking hands with both of them and smiling. "Well, you two are always faithful on Wednesday night. I appreciate your coming."

"You know what they say." Deoin winked. His face was pale from the cold, but he was always a cheerful man. "Those that love the Lord come on Sunday morning, and those that love the church come on Sunday night—and those that love the preacher come on Wednesday night."

Prince smiled. He had heard Jinks say this regularly for the past two years. "You may be right about that. It looks like we're going to have a small crowd tonight." He remained at the door until seven, then walked to the front of the church. Cora Johnson was seated at the piano, and he smiled at her. "I hope your fingers aren't too cold to play."

"No, it's not bad, Brother Prince." Cora smiled at him, and he thought again what an attractive woman she would be if only she would take some care of herself. *Why, she looks like a Pentecostal lady—no makeup, no jewelry, hair tied back.* "Well, it looks like I'll have to lead the singing, as Brother Barnes isn't here tonight. What about 'Love Lifted Me'? That's a peppy one."

"That's fine, Brother Prince." Cora knew all the hymns in the Broadman hymnal by heart. She was an excellent musician and began to play with vigor.

Prince abandoned the platform and stood directly in front of the twenty or so people present. "Let's all stand and sing this song as if we really mean it." He led the hymn, and the singing was rather ragged. After two more hymns, Prince prayed, then said, "All right, you can be seated." Prince took his Bible from where it lay on the front pew and opened it. "Tonight we're going to continue our study in the book of Colossians."

For the next ten minutes the pastor taught his small flock. He was an excellent teacher, well read and still young enough to be hopeful that God would move greatly in this small church in this small Arkansas community. So far his stay in Fairhope had been effective, but hardly dramatic. At times he had to encourage himself in the Lord to believe that his work here was worth all the effort it had taken him to get through Bible school and Fort Worth Baptist Seminary.

He spoke for half an hour. "And so we see that these Christians in the Colossian church faced the same problems that we face today, and there's never—"

The sound of voices came to the sanctuary, and the preacher stopped abruptly. Everyone turned to look, and Sister Myrtle and her husband, Charlie, came bursting through the door, followed by a small crowd.

"That's Sister Myrtle," Davis whispered to Lanie, "and it looks like she brought her whole church with her."

Sister Myrtle and Charlie came marching up the aisle followed by about twenty-five other people.

"Well, Brother Prince, we've come to your prayer meeting." Sister Myrtle's voice seemed to rattle the windows, and she nodded with obvious satisfaction. "I brought my folks along. We've come to help you folks pray for the Freeman family."

"Why, that's very gracious of you, Sister Myrtle," Prince said, amused by the invasion. He had long ago given up being shocked at anything Sister Myrtle Poindexter did or said. She was loud, impulsive, and possessed the confidence of an iron bar, and she had one of the best hearts Prince had ever known. Noting that his congregation was stunned, he said, "We were just closing our study, so I think it's about time to start praying."

"Well, praise God! Hallelujah! Glory to the Lamb!" Sister Myrtle bellowed. "Let's get started then." She rubbed her hands together. "Nothin' I like better than a good fight with the devil—that red-legged rascal! We're gonna put the run on him tonight, Brother!"

"Amen and amen! Glory to God and the Lamb forever!"

The deep bass voice seemed to come from the back of the church, as if from heaven, and everyone turned and craned their necks and looked up to the balcony. Lanie's eyes opened wide, and she whispered to Davis, "Look. That's Madison Jones and his church members."

The balcony was filling at a rapid rate. The massive figure of the iceman/preacher Madison Jones stood at the rail looking down, his black face shining. Behind him, Bascom and the rest of Madison's children filed in, along with Faye and Sally Dupont, the black couple who owned the laundry, and a crowd of other folks.

"Sister Myrtle done come by and told me to pray at our prayer meeting," Reverend Jones boomed. "And I allowed as how we'd come over here and join with you. We wants to add our petition to the prayers going up to God for these chil'uns."

"It's so good to have you folks," Brother Prince called out, smiling. A thrill had gone through him, for nothing like this had ever happened in Fairhope before. He had a deep and intense desire to tell the black congregation to come down and join with the others, but this was Arkansas, 1930. Such things might happen in the future, but they had not come to that place yet.

"I don't know how you Baptist folks pray," Sister Myrtle said, "but we Pentecostal folks believe in lettin' God know we mean business."

"I believe you do, sister," Brother Prince said, "and I think right now we'll just begin. I'm a little bit tired of plans and programs." The words came unbidden, and Prince was surprised at himself. "Tonight we're just going to seek God, and we're going to find Him."

The amens and the hallelujahs rolled down from the balcony and rose up from Sister Myrtle, seeming to meet somewhere in the air. A few of the bolder Baptists joined in rather feebly, and Brother Prince could see that some of his deacons were apprehensive. "I think the first thing we need to do is to get you and your brothers and sisters up here, Lanie."

"Amen! We'll lay hands on 'em and let the Almighty know that we're serious!" Sister Myrtle boomed.

Lanie was shocked, but at the same time her heart was warmed. The arrival of Madison, whom she had known all her life, and of Sister Myrtle, whom she truly admired, cheered her. "Come on," she said, urging Davis, Maeva, and Cody to follow her to the platform.

"Bring that young'un out of the nursery!" Sister Myrtle said. "She's gonna be prayed for too." She waited until Lena Pranger brought baby

Corliss out and gave her to Lanie. Sister Myrtle put her hands lightly on Lanie's head. Her grip tightened when she began to pray. Lanie noticed that others had put their hands on her siblings, and she was pleased to see Ellen Prince touching Corliss. She also saw that her former teacher Miss Dunsmore stood nearby. Her eyes caught Lanie's. "God bless you, Lanie. God's here tonight."

And so the praying began, and the First Baptist Church of Fairhope, Arkansas, had seldom, if ever, heard such praise and prayer. Lanie bowed her head and felt Sister Myrtle's hands holding her. She felt a sense of security, and she squeezed Corliss until the little girl protested with a squeal.

Finally the noise died down, and Sister Myrtle said, "All right. I reckon as how that'll get us started. Now, everybody find a place. It don't make no difference where it is. Go up on the roof if you want to, walk the aisles, get under a bench. But get somewhere and grab hold of God's coattails, and don't let Him go until He says what you want to hear!"

❦

Nothing quite like this Wednesday prayer meeting had ever happened at this First Baptist Church! As a rule, the Wednesday prayer sessions lasted no longer than fifteen or twenty minutes.

But on the evening of November 19, nine o'clock came and passed, then ten, and the prayers went on. At ten fifteen, Morley Daman, a Baptist deacon who had the reputation of being a mossy-backed, fussy old man, decided to put a stop to it. "Now folks, this has been fine, but I'll now pronounce the benediction."

Sister Myrtle laughed. "You benedict all you want to, my dear brother, then you go on home. But I'm wrestling the devil here, and I'm not lettin' that varmint go until he's flat on his back!"

The deacon stared at her openmouthed. Then, to the amazement of his pastor, Morley Daman went to the front pew, fell on his knees, and began praying loudly.

❦

Elspeth Patton, the publisher of the *Sentinel*, had just finished breakfast when she got a call about some unusual goings-on down at the Baptist church and decided to investigate. When she arrived, the parking lot was full, with more cars still arriving. She went into the church, then stopped dead still. She was a Presbyterian and by nature a reserved woman, but there was nothing reserved about what was going on in the First Baptist Church of Fairhope! Some people were sitting in the pews, leaning forward with their heads pressed against the back of the next pew. As she entered cautiously, she glanced back over her shoulder to see that the balcony was packed with black people, and she heard the deep bass voice of Madison Jones rumbling as he spoke to God.

All through the auditorium there was movement. Some were walking the aisles praying, many lifting their hands, and Elspeth, who knew everybody in Fairhope, saw that the Pentecostals had invaded Baptist territory! She took a seat and for the next twenty minutes simply sat there. She was joined by Cassandra Pruitt, the librarian. "Have you been here long, Cassandra?"

"I came in about two hours ago. I'm so worried about the Freeman children." She looked around, her eyes wide, and said, "I don't know what to make of all this, Miss Patton."

"Well, it's not a typical Baptist meeting—or Presbyterian either."

"Do you think it's a good thing?"

Elspeth Patton loved the order of the Presbyterian service and was often appalled by what she considered the excesses of other groups—particularly Pentecostals—but today she saw people with tears running down their faces, and up on the rostrum the chairman of the Baptist deacons was stretched flat on his face before God. She whispered, "I think it's a very good thing, Cassandra, indeed I do!"

Elspeth Patton stayed all morning. Some of the supplicants left, but their places were quickly taken by others. She knew most of the people who came through the door and saw curiosity on their faces. The news had evidently spread even to the farming community, for men came in worn overalls, and a few country women wore their homespun dresses and thin coats.

Elspeth was composing the story in her mind when she saw Lanie crossing the room. Rising, she caught Lanie in the hall. "Lanie, I'm a little bit stunned by all this."

"Oh, Miss Patton, so am I! Isn't it wonderful? I was just going down to check on Corliss."

"I'll go with you." The two walked to the nursery and found that Corliss was sound asleep. "If you're getting tired, Miss Pickens, I'll take the baby," Lanie said.

Bertha Pickens, Doc Givens' nurse, was a staunch member of Sister Myrtle's Fire Baptized Pentecostal Church. She held Corliss in her lap, rocking back and forth. "Not a bit tired. How could a body get tired to see God working like this? Never thought to see the day! Makes me think a heap better of you Baptist folks."

Elspeth smiled and nodded. "I would have to say the same thing. A thing like this can't be planned, I don't think."

"Yes, it just seemed to happen," Lanie said. "Of course, Sister Myrtle and Reverend Jones had a lot to do with it." The two returned to the auditorium, and the voices of prayer comforted Lanie. "Look, there's Mamie Dorr."

"Well, that's probably the first time Mamie's been to a church in many a year," Elspeth remarked. "And there's the sheriff with her."

"I'm going to say hello to them," Lanie said. She moved down the aisle and smiled. "Hello, Miss Dorr. Hello, Sheriff."

Mamie looked like an exotic bird among a bunch of doves. As always she wore flashy, colorful clothes, and her makeup was excessive. She swallowed hard and with somewhat less than her usual brashness said, "Well, I ain't a prayin' woman, Lanie, but I heard about this and I came over to see what was happenin'."

"I'm glad you came, Miss Dorr."

Elspeth, who had joined them, reached out toward Mamie, and Mamie took her hand. "I'm glad to see you too, Mamie. I think this is real."

"You going to make a story about this, Elspeth?" Pardue asked. He wore his mechanics jumper, stained with oil and grease.

"I think so. I believe it deserves a headline."

Mamie shook her head. "I never saw anything like this."

"I don't think most of us have," Lanie said. "Not in our church anyway."

"It's a good thing," Pardue said. "If things like this keep happening, I reckon I'll have to hit the glory road myself."

"I wish you would, Sheriff," Lanie said.

"You've got a good heart, honey," Pardue said. He reached out and squeezed her arm. "With this many people praying for you, something great is going to happen."

At noon, Lanie's eyes were gritty from lack of sleep, and the voice of Reverend Madison Jones rose above the crowd. The praying had more or less died down to a murmur, and the vibrancy of Jones seemed to fill the auditorium from floor to roof. "The Lord has spoken to me, and He has said, 'I am pleased with my people. I have heard your cries, and I will answer your prayers. Thus sayeth the Lord!'"

Sister Myrtle bellowed, "Amen and hallelujah!" She walked over to Lanie, put her arms around the young woman, and began to dance around the floor. Confused, Lanie hung on with all her might.

"It's gonna be all right, honey," Sister Myrtle cried. "The Lord has given a word to Reverend Jones, and it's settled in heaven. You won't be going to no foster home."

The meeting began to break up, but one small group lingered. The Episcopal priest, Father Roy Jefferson, had lain for a time weeping flat on his face up on the rostrum next to the chairman of the Baptist board of deacons. He joined William Prince, Sister Myrtle, and Father Douglas, the burly Catholic priest from Springdale with an Irish face. When Sister Myrtle took Father Douglas's hand and pumped it, he smiled. "I wish you'd bring some of this to my parish, Sister."

"Be glad to come anytime."

Brother Prince said, "You know, we Baptists like to keep things under control. It seems to me we draw a circle around things, but I think last night God jumped out of it and the rest of us had to follow."

Father Jefferson, an insignificant-looking man with intense blue eyes, nodded vigorously. "I love to see the work of God get out of control—out of *our* control, that is."

Later that day, after the crowds had left, William Prince and his wife, Ellen, stood together in the sanctuary. They were both exhausted.

"Bill, I never saw anything like that."

"I think that was the way things happened when Jesus was on earth. Crowds followed Him and pushed and shoved to get to Him. There was excitement, and things were happening. I think we got a little taste of that."

"I really feel that God's going to do something for the Freemans."

"He'll have to. We've got His word that it's all right."

"You believe what Madison Jones said was some kind of prophecy?"

"It sounded real to me. I'm going to believe it until somebody convinces me different—and that'll be hard to do, honey!"

⚬═══⚬

"You really believe all that stuff that happened at the church, Lanie?" Maeva was gathering her books for school. Though typically skeptical, the unusual prayer meeting had made an impact on her.

Lanie stared straight at her and saw that Cody and Davis were also waiting for her reply. "Yes, Maeva. I believe it was God, and I don't think we have a thing to worry about."

Cody winked at Lanie. "If they'd have more prayer meetings like that, it'd be fun, wouldn't it?"

"Yes, it would. Now you go on to school."

Lanie shut the door and watched through the window as they were joined by the Jinks children. As soon as they were out of sight, she checked on Corliss, who was chattering at her powder can. "I declare I don't know what it is you see in that powder can! If all other children were so fascinated, that company would make a lot of money just selling empty cans."

Leaving Corliss in her play crib, Lanie went to her parents' bedroom and pulled down a shoe box from the shelf in the closet. She went back to the kitchen, fixed a cup of coffee, and added a stick of oak to the fire.

Sipping at her coffee, she stared at the box, remembering the strange thing that had happened to her sometime in the middle of the night. Usually she slept straight through, but this time she did not. She had awakened, and for some reason an old memory came to her, a memory of a letter her father once showed her and a picture that accompanied it. She opened the box and fished around for the photo.

"This letter," her father had said, "is the last one I got from an old aunt of mine who lives in Sallisaw, Oklahoma. She must be gettin' on now. Here's her picture."

The picture, an old tintype, was faded and brown, but still clear. A small woman stood beside a tall man who wore a big sombrero and a gun on his hip. He had a star on his vest. "This is my Aunt Kezia

Pearl," her father said. "She was my father's only sister. That's her second husband there. He was a lawman in Texas. I only met her once, but she was a pistol! She sure enough believed in sayin' what she thought!"

Lanie stared at the picture, trying to read the small woman's face. She stood erect and wore old-fashioned clothes—a black dress pinned up high at the neck and a small hat. Both she and the man stared without smiles into the camera.

The photo had captured an air of determination about the woman that had not faded with the image.

Lanie picked up the letter and read the thin handwriting:

Dear Nephew,

This is to inform you that my husband has died. The fool spent all his money on a hussy from Muskogee. I'd a shot him if I had caught him, and her, too. He didn't leave a cent, and I am living in a room in a run-down boarding house full of idiots. I got a little money but when that plays out they'll put me in some kind of an old-folks home. Bah! I'll shoot myself before I put up with that!

I hope all is well with you and your family. I remember your pa with affection.

Kezia Pearl Pettigrew

Lanie remembered being rather shocked and questioning her father about his aunt.

"Well, she's always been kind of a renegade, from what I understand," he had said. "Went over the Oregon Trail, and when her first husband died, she married this lawman. She married a dentist named Pettigrew after that. Like I say, she was quite a caution."

Suddenly a thought came to Lanie, complete and total and as clear as if it were carved in stone.

"Why, she's my relative! She's a Freeman! Her maiden name was Kezia Pearl Freeman, and she's probably in a nursing home by now."

In that moment, Lanie realized that God had awakened her in the night and called her attention to this letter. She said, "Lord, I believe You're in this. We've got to have an adult relative to stay with us, or we'll get sent to foster homes." She stared at the letter. "Sounds like my Aunt Kezia is adult enough, and she's about to get quite a shock if she's still alive!"

CHAPTER 24

Orrin Pierce sat at his desk gazing at Lanie, who had burst into his office, her eyes flashing with excitement. He was struck by how she had matured in the past year. It seemed she had moved from the awkward coltish stage of adolescence into young womanhood almost overnight.

"The prayer meeting worked, Mr. Pierce," Lanie was saying. She fidgeted in the chair and nervously ran her hand over her auburn hair. "I think God told me something in a dream."

Apprehension touched Pierce instantly, for he did not want this young girl who had endured such hardship to expose herself to more of the same. "What kind of a dream?"

"I dreamed about a letter and a picture that my daddy showed me about two years ago. I'd forgotten all about it, but it came to me real clear, so I went and read it. Here it is, Mr. Pierce."

Orrin took the letter Lanie handed him and read the return address. "Mrs. Kezia Pearl Pettigrew. Now who is she?"

"She's my daddy's aunt on his daddy's side. Her maiden name is Freeman, but she married a man named Pettigrew and she lives in Sallisaw, Oklahoma."

Orrin's apprehension fell away. "So she's really your great-aunt."

"I guess so, Mr. Pierce, but if I could talk her into living with us, wouldn't that satisfy the people who want to separate us?"

Orrin's mind worked rapidly. He hated to nurture false hope, but this hope was real. "I think it would, Lanie, but she's a pretty old lady by now, isn't she?"

"Yes, sir, she is, but daddy always said she was real peppery. Of course that was a couple of years ago. By now she may be in that nursing home she talked about."

"It's worth a try, Lanie. Why don't you write her a letter."

"All right, Mr. Pierce, I will." Bright-eyed, Lanie rose. "I really think this is the way the Lord's going to help us."

When Lanie stepped outside, the piercing blast of the eleven-forty westbound train came to her. She glanced toward the Missouri Pacific Station and without an instant's pause broke into a run. At the station, the sharp, acrid smell of the black smoke boiling out of the engine made her sneeze, and she watched as Emmett Oz said a few words to the brakeman, then she followed him into the station house. Emmett Oz, a stooped and thin man, made a good station agent and could work the Morse telegraph key, but those were his only practical achievements. He was otherwise known as the most accomplished male gossip in Fairhope. Few females could compete with his tongue.

"Lanie. What are you doing here?"

"I need to find out if there's a train that goes to Sallisaw, Oklahoma."

"Sallisaw? No, I don't believe there is. Not a Mo Pac run anyway. Why? You need to go to Sallisaw?"

"I sure do. What's the closest town to Sallisaw?"

"I reckon that'd be Broken Bow. You'd still have a ways to go. Why you want to go to Sallisaw?"

"I found out I've got a relative there, Mr. Oz. I need to go see her."

"A relative? Who is she?"

"It's an old lady, my daddy's aunt."

Emmett perked up at once. "Oh, sure, I reckon you'd like for her to come and live with you!"

"That's right. Well, I've got to go, Mr. Oz, but I don't guess I can take the train. Thank you."

As soon as Lanie left, Emmett went to the phone. He turned the crank, and when Henrietta Green said, "Number please," he said, "Henrietta, guess what? That oldest Freeman girl has dug up a relative!"

⊙━⋊⊷

"Well, I must say you're the best-looking patient I've had all day." Dr. Owen Merritt greeted Louise Langley, struck again by what a beauty she was. Her complexion was smooth and creamy, and her eyes were large and expressive. He assumed a serious look, but his eyes were glinting. "And now, Miss Langley, I'd better examine you."

"You keep your hands off me, Owen Merritt!" Louise laughed, pushing him away as he put his hands on her shoulders. "There's nothing wrong with me."

She leaned forward and kissed him on the cheek. "There, I hope none of the other lady patients take that kind of liberty."

"No, I must say I don't extract that kind of payment. Of course, none of them are as pretty as you are."

"I came to ask you a favor."

"Your wish is my command. What is it?"

"I need for you to go with me to Fort Smith tomorrow. I need to do some shopping, and I thought we could make a day of it. We could have dinner at the Majestic Hotel, and there's a musical at the Elite Theatre. Probably won't be very good, but we could go."

"I'm not sure I can take the day off."

"Dr. Givens can take care of the office calls." Louise straightened his tie and smiled at him winningly. "You can make your house calls the next day."

"Well, I suppose I can work it out. I haven't had a day off in some time. Hang on here and let me go talk to Nurse Pickens." He winked. "You know she really runs this place. Treats Dr. Givens and me like dogs."

He stepped out and found his sassy assistant. "Bertha, you think you could handle things tomorrow with maybe half a day from Dr. Givens?"

"What do you want the day off for?" Bertha demanded. She stood to her full height, though she was short, stocky, and had a bulldog look about her. "That's the trouble with you young doctors. You're afraid of work!"

"Oh, come on, Bertha, don't be like that." Owen had formed an admiration for this woman. She was sharp, often gruff, but he had discovered a warm heart beneath the rough exterior. "I really need to take a break."

Bertha stared at him critically. "Where are you going?"

"Well, Miss Langley needs to go shopping in Fort Smith, and afterward we thought we'd have dinner together. Just a little break, you know."

"If you're going to take the day off, you could do something better than throw your money away and go to one of those sinful moving pictures."

"What can I possibly do that's better than taking a charming young lady out to enjoy herself?"

"You could take that Freeman girl to Sallisaw. That's what you could do."

This sudden turn perplexed Owen. "Why would I want to do that?"

"I just been talking to Margaret Simmons. She's cousin to Henrietta, the telephone operator, you know. And Henrietta told Margaret that Lanie has found a relative over in Sallisaw. She needs to get over there and see if she can get the woman to come and live with them." Bertha sniffed and stared at him with direct gray eyes. "That would be doing a good deed and would please the Lord a lot better than what you got on your mind!"

Owen considered this, his mind working quickly. "You know, Bertha, I think you might be right about that. So I take it you can handle the office without me?"

Bertha seemed surprised. "I was handling it before you got here, wasn't I? Now you take care of that child. God's done promised to do something, and if you do the right thing, you just might get to be a part of it."

Owen grinned, patted the woman on the shoulder, then returned to Louise. No one knew better than Owen Merritt how spoiled Louise was, but he had decided that she had good things in her. Any young woman with as much beauty and money as she had couldn't help being spoiled.

"Louise, I know it will be a disappointment to you, but I'm going to have to postpone my part of the shopping trip."

"Why would you do that?" Louise said, her lips forming a pout. "You practically promised me."

"Well, it's something Bertha just told me." He explained, and ended by saying, "Those kids need all the help they can get. You know the trouble they're in."

Louise could not directly argue with this, for she knew that Owen felt strongly about the Freeman children, but she said, "Owen, you don't need to be putting yourself in a bad light."

"Bad light? What are you talking about?"

"A man in your position shouldn't take another woman on a trip to another town. It wouldn't look right."

Owen was genuinely amazed. "What wouldn't look right?"

Louise could not bring herself to say what she thought, so she shrugged. "It makes you very vulnerable taking young women on a trip to another town."

"Why, that's foolish! She's just a child."

"She's sixteen, a woman where these hill people are concerned."

"Well, why don't you come along then?" he said. He took her hand and squeezed it. "You could be our chaperone."

"I wouldn't care to do that," Louise said primly, withdrawing her hand. "But I can see you've got your mind made up. I'll put my trip off until you're able to go. Good-bye." She left the office, leaving Owen staring after her.

"Someday maybe I'll understand women—but I doubt it."

<hr />

"Hey, Lanie, Doc Merritt's here!" Cody called, sticking his head inside the door.

"Shut that door, you're letting all the warm air out!" Lanie said. She was cooking supper and had worked hard all day so she was a mess. She tried to smooth her hair, but found it useless to try to put on an appearance. "Hello, Doctor. Did you come for supper?"

"No, Lanie, I came to tell you that I'm taking you to Sallisaw tomorrow."

Lanie's eyes widened, and she cried out with delight. "Dr. Merritt, how did you know I needed to get there?"

Owen grinned. "You told Emmett Oz, didn't you? You might as well have put it on the front page of the paper. What time do you want to leave?"

Lanie could barely contain her excitement. "Any time you say, I'll be ready. Maeva can watch Corliss."

"All right. Let's get an early start. I'll pick you up at seven. We'll go down to The Dew Drop so you don't have to cook breakfast, then we'll be on our way."

A lump rose in Lanie's throat. She stared at the tall doctor and tried to find words. Finally she was able to say, "I-I sure do thank you, Dr. Merritt. I don't know why you're so good to us."

Merritt winked and said, "I really just want a day off, that's all there is to it. I'll see you at seven." He left whistling "Those Wedding Bells Are Breaking Up That Old Gang of Mine."

As they pulled into the small town of Sallisaw, Oklahoma, Lanie said, "I don't believe I've ever talked so much in all my life, Dr. Merritt."

"I guess with a family like yours you have to fight to get a word in. It's been a good trip. Good to be out of the office."

Lanie wanted to thank him again for bringing her, but he had strictly forbidden her to mention the thing. "I'm purely selfish," he said. "Just like to get out of work and travel with an attractive young lady to another state. Sounds exciting and it is. We'll pull in at that station and get some gas, and maybe we'll find out where your aunt lives."

Dr. Merritt pulled up to the gas pump and got out. A lanky man with a salubrious face came forward and said, "Help ya?"

"Need to fill up with gas, please, and we're looking for a lady named Mrs. Pettigrew."

"Oh, you mean Kezia."

"I believe that is her name. You know her?"

"Of course I know her," the man said, offended. "Why wouldn't I?"

Lanie exclaimed, "She's my aunt! Can you tell us where she lives?"

"Why wouldn't I be able to tell you a thing like that?" the man said. He poked the nozzle into the gas tank and began to turn the crank that forced the gasoline out of the storage tank. "How much you want?"

"Fill it up."

Apparently the man could not think of two things at once, for he filled the gas tank up in silence. "That'll be a dollar and eighty-nine cents."

Dr. Merritt paid him and took his change. "Where was that you said Mrs. Pettigrew lives?"

"I've got her address here. It's on Oak Street," Lanie said. "Three thirteen Oak."

"You think I don't know that? I don't reckon you'd trust any directions I'd give you if you think I'm that dumb."

"Didn't mean to offend you, sir." Owen smiled. "If you'd just tell us how to get there, we'd be most grateful."

Somewhat mollified, the attendant said, "You go down Main Street until you come to the First State Bank. You turn right there and go three blocks, then you turn left, and right there on the right is a big old white house, an old mansion it was. Belonged to Colonel Skeffington, who got killed in the Battle of Franklin, Tennessee. The army was commanded by General Hood at that time and—"

"Thank you very much, sir. We appreciate the information." Dr. Merritt and Lanie made their escape and started laughing. "He acted like we hurt his feelings," Lanie said.

"Well, we know where your aunt is." Dr. Merritt drove slowly down Main Street, which was unimpressive, and soon pulled up in front of the old two-story white house with six gables. "You mustn't be too disappointed, Lanie, if this doesn't work out. I know you think it's the Lord, but sometimes we make mistakes about things like that."

Lanie turned to face him. She had come to feel such admiration for this man that she hardly knew how to answer. He seemed so wise and everyone respected him. "I believe it's the Lord."

"Well, we'll soon find out. Come along."

The two got out of the car and mounted the steps that led to the wide wraparound porch. Dr. Merritt knocked on the door, and a short, dumpy woman with her hair pulled back in a bun stared at them. "Are you looking for a place to stay?"

"No, ma'am, we're looking for Mrs. Pettigrew."

"Oh, well, come in. I'm Mrs. Stowe. This is my boarding house." Her glasses sat up on her hair, and she pulled them down and stared at them carefully. "I don't suppose you'd be relatives of Kezia?"

"We just need to speak with her, Mrs. Stowe." Dr. Merritt saw no reason to justify their visit to the landlady. "Could you get her for us?"

"She's right down there in that parlor on the left. If you got any influence, I hope you'll tell her she's gonna have to behave herself better if she wants to stay here."

"Thank you. Come along, Lanie." The two walked down the broad hall, and Lanie glanced back to see the woman watching them. "What's she so mad about?"

"I think landladies get that way," Owen said. They turned into the big room. A fire in the fireplace was sending out waves of heat and made a cheerful crackling sound. In front of it in a rocking chair sat an old woman. Lanie could see only a little of her profile, for she was wearing a bonnet that covered most of her face.

"Mrs. Pettigrew?" Dr. Merritt said. The woman turned and looked up at them. "I'm Dr. Owen Merritt, and this is Lanie Freeman."

The woman rose and tossed her knitting onto the seat. She was a small woman, lean with iron gray hair, and her cheeks were wrinkled, but her black eyes were sharp as she studied them. "You're a doctor? I didn't send for no doctor."

"No, ma'am, we came to see you about something else. Do you have a few minutes?"

"A few minutes? I got the rest of my life. Where you think I'm goin'—out squirrel huntin'?"

Dr. Merritt could not help smiling. "We came to talk to you about a family matter."

The old woman's eyes went to Lanie. "You say your name be Freeman? You must be Forrest's girl. I forget your name."

"I'm Lanie, ma'am. Forrest is my daddy."

"Do you tell me that! Well, I wrote him a letter, and he wrote back. But I guess neither one of us is much for writin' regular." She looked at the two and said, "Well, pull up a couple of chairs. Hit's colder'n a well-digger's rear today!"

"Thank you, Mrs. Pettigrew." Dr. Merritt pulled two chairs in closer, and the old woman sat again.

Lanie cleared her throat. "I found the letter you wrote to my daddy two years ago, Mrs. Pettigrew. That was when your husband died."

"Small loss." The old lady snorted. "Forrest ain't dead, is he?"

"Oh, no! He's not dead, but he's in bad trouble. He got sent to the penitentiary."

"What'd he do—kill somebody?"

"There was a man killed," Dr. Merritt said, "but I knew you'd be sorry to hear that."

"You ain't none of my kin. You any kin to this girl?"

"No, but she needed to come to talk to you, so I—"

"He brought me here to ask you something, Mrs. Pettigrew, but I'll have to take some time to explain. It may sound funny to you."

Kezia Pettigrew stared at the girl and smiled briefly. "Well, that's good. I need to hear somethin' funny, livin' here with a bunch of idjits that eat like hogs and never had a thought in their life except the next meal. Go on with your story and take your time."

Lanie took a deep breath and began. She told the whole story about her mother's death and her efforts to raise the other children. Then she narrated the story of her father's misfortune.

Finally the old woman interrupted her. "So you had to be mama to them kids, did you? I can't stand young'uns myself."

This assertion took the wind out of Lanie's sails. She glanced at Dr. Merritt, who nodded encouragement. "Well, I hate to hear that, Mrs. Pettigrew, because the next part of this story is going be a little hard."

"Say what you mean, Lanie. Nobody ever made money beatin' around the bush."

"Well, the State is going to separate us and put us out in foster homes if"—tears threatened Lanie's courage for a moment—"if we don't get an adult to come live with us."

The old woman's eyes seemed to grow sharper. "So you've come to get me out of this nice place here to come and live with a bunch of squallin', pullin' young'uns who would drive me crazy?"

"It wouldn't be like that, Mrs. Pettigrew," Dr. Merritt said. "They're wonderful children, all of them, and your nephew Forrest is a good man. He just got caught in a bad situation. You'd be doing the children a great service, and the whole town would appreciate it."

"What do I keer about the whole town? I've got my comfort to think of!"

Lanie resisted the despair that threatened to overtake her. "I know it's asking a lot to give up your life here, but we'd make things as good for you as we could. I'm a good cook, and you'd have your own room. We'd do the washing for you." She tried to think of other enticements. "We've even got a radio that you could listen to anytime you wanted."

"And what would I listen to, tell me that? Those jackass politicians makin' speeches?"

Dr. Merritt said, "They live in a fine old house on a beautiful piece of land, Mrs. Pettigrew, and I think you'd grow used to the children. They are very affectionate and a lot of fun too."

"Well, I do need some fun!"

"Would you think about coming back and staying with us?" Lanie said. "I hate to beg, but I can't stand the thought of our family being split up. My littlest sister is only two years old. I wish you'd think about it."

Kezia Pettigrew sighed and set down her knitting. "Don't be tryin' your wiles on me, girl. They probably work pretty good on your daddy and on the young fellows who follow you around, but I didn't get to be ninety years old by bein' fooled by a bunch of tears. You two can go now."

"You mean you won't even think about it?" Dr. Merritt said, appalled at the woman's callousness.

"You can go, and I'll think about it."

"When can we come back, Mrs. Pettigrew?"

"Pettigrew, how I hate that name! Never did care for Mr. Pettigrew. He was the worst of my three husbands." The old lady waved a hand at Lanie. "I don't know how long it will take me to make up my mind. Hurry on back to that town, whatever it was, where you live."

"But Mrs. Pettigrew, we don't have much time."

"We'll stay overnight," Dr. Merritt said. "That'll give you a little time to think about it."

"You get on your way now, but I'll give it some thought. I done lived in Oregon and Texas, and I'll have to ponder afore movin' to a place like Arkansas." She gave the pair a sharp look that reminded Lanie of a red-tailed hawk.

"Come along, Lanie," Dr. Merritt said, rising. He bowed to Mrs. Pettigrew and said, "We'll be staying over tonight. Hope you sleep well. I appreciate your time, ma'am."

The old woman nodded and then put her eyes on Lanie. "Go along, girl. I got me some thinkin' to do."

⚬══◦

Dr. Merritt secured two rooms at the only hotel in town, and Lanie was glad she had brought a change of clothes. She hadn't brought a nightgown and supposed she'd have to sleep in what she wore, but at least she had a fresh dress for tomorrow.

They dined at a restaurant and then saw a movie called *Franken-stein*. Lanie had no desire to see it, but Dr. Merritt convinced her there was little else to do.

"You didn't like the movie much, did you?" Dr. Merritt said afterward. "I must admit it was pretty wild. That monster was scary."

"I felt sorry for him."

"Sorry for him? You're supposed to be afraid of him."

"His condition wasn't his fault, Dr. Merritt. He was all alone. There was nobody else like him."

Dr. Merritt laughed. "You are a caution, Lanie Freeman! Of course there was nobody like him, but why'd you feel sorry for him?"

Lanie didn't answer for a time. "What if you were different from everybody else and nobody liked you? Wouldn't you feel bad?"

Owen Merritt was surprised at this young woman. True, he thought of her more as a child, but now he studied her in a new light. "I suppose you have a point there."

"But I thank you for taking me." They reached the hotel. "I guess I'll go to bed now."

"I hope you sleep well."

"Whatever happens, Dr. Merritt, you did your best, and I am grateful."

"Don't give up, Lanie. The old woman may decide to go with us in the end." He chuckled. "I don't know if that'd be a blessing or not. She's as sharp as a sack full of tacks. Be hard to live with."

"I'd live with that monster in that movie if it'd keep my family together!"

Dr. Merritt's respect for Lanie grew. "You would, too, wouldn't you?"

"I sure would. Good night, Doctor."

⚬══⚬

At breakfast, Owen noticed that Lanie could not eat much. He knew she was worried, and he kept up a line of talk until finally they left the hotel. They drove to the boarding house and found Mrs. Stowe waiting for them. "She's up in her room. It's the second door on the right up the stairs."

"Thank you, Mrs. Stowe."

They climbed the stairs. Lanie's face was set and fixed.

Owen knocked on the door and heard the old woman say, "Well, don't just stand there, come in."

Owen winked at Lanie and opened the door. The two entered and found Mrs. Pettigrew standing in the middle of the floor. "It took you long enough to get here," she said. "What did you do last night?"

"We had supper and then we went to see a movie," Owen said.

"What was the name of it?"

"*Frankenstein.*"

"I heard about that. I'd like to see it myself. That's one of my conditions."

"Conditions?" Lanie said, and hope began to grow within her. "Have you decided to go with us?"

"Certainly I've decided to go with you! A bunch of squallin' kids can't be any worse than the idjits here in this place, but I got my conditions."

"Anything!" Lanie cried. "Just anything you want!"

The old woman had put her "conditions" in writing, and they were extensive. "One, I will have my own room. And two, somebody will keep it clean. Three, I made a list of foods I won't eat, because I'm ailin'."

"Well, what's your trouble, Mrs. Pettigrew? Since I'm a doctor you can tell me."

"I don't put no faith in doctors! I doctor myself. I take Buffalo Lithia Water every day of my life! That's what's kept me goin'. And I always take Beecham's pills, and if I ever get diarrhea, I take some of Dr. Stonebreaker's Indian Gum Syrup."

"It sounds like you've got all the bases covered, Mrs. Pettigrew, but I'll be handy if you need any medical care."

The old lady sniffed. "That'll be as is. Another condition. I git to go to a movie once a week and I git to pick the movie."

"That's fine, Mrs. Pettigrew." Lanie listened as the old woman read what seemed to be an interminable list, but finally she got to the end. "I'm keepin' this list, and I'm postin' it on the wall when we get to our house. Now, how do you propose to get all my stuff to Fairhope?"

"Well, we can put your luggage in the car with us," Owen said.

"Luggage my foot! I got all the stuff that came out of my house packed and stored away. It would take a big truck to haul it, and I ain't leavin' without my stuff!"

Owen coughed. "I'll make the necessary arrangements. Probably I'll hire a truck to come over and pick it up."

The old woman softened ever so slightly. "Well, fer a doctor you're a pretty handy feller, I guess. I'm ready to go."

"You mean right now?"

"I put up with these idjits as long as I propose to. Now, you take me to Fairhope as quick as we can git there. It'll take me a while to get settled in and to get all you kids educated as to my needs."

Owen stifled a grin. "We'll be right on our way then. Are these bags going?"

"You don't reckon I'm going to leave them here, do you?"

"No, I suppose not. Lanie, let's load up Mrs. Pettigrew's things, and we'll be on our way."

CHAPTER 25

Lanie never forgot the trip from Sallisaw, Oklahoma, back to Fairhope. Aunt Kezia talked most of the way. She had apparently decided that they needed to know about her history, for she looked back at the old town of Sallisaw and said, "Thank the good Lord I don't ever have to look at that boardin' house or that old Lady Stowe's sour face again!"

"You weren't really happy there, Mrs. Pettigrew?" Lanie asked.

"Call me Aunt Kezia, child." Kezia sat bolt upright in the center of the Oldsmobile's front seat. The windows were up, but it was a cold November day, and she had brought one of her blankets and wrapped it around her knees. She turned to look at Lanie and said, "Happy livin' in a crazy house?"

"It wasn't really that bad, was it?" Dr. Merritt said. "I mean, the other boarders weren't really crazy, were they, Mrs. Pettigrew?"

"Who says they're not crazy? Do you know 'em?"

"Well, no. But—"

"Then you don't know nothin' about it! Watch out! You're gonna run off the road!"

"I was just trying to dodge a bump."

"I don't like to be shifted around like that. You go straight on. Don't jostle me, you hear?"

"Yes, ma'am."

"I think my daddy told me you went to Oregon in a covered wagon," Lanie said.

"Of course I did! There wasn't no other way to get there!"

"How old were you?"

"Fifteen and just married."

"Why, that's a year younger than I am! Were you afraid?"

"Afraid? Of course I was afraid! Who wouldn't be afraid with a bunch of wild Indians out to get your scalp and people dyin' of cholera right and left?"

"What was your husband like?"

"My first husband was named Jediah Smith. He was a farmer in Georgia. He come through our town and courted me and I married him. Three days after we married, we started for Oregon." She contemplated the memory. "That was a hard life. All those big trees had to be cut down and cleared."

"Did you and your husband have children?"

"Two. Lost 'em both to diphtheria."

"I'm sorry," Lanie said. "That must have been hard."

"Life's hard, girl. Well, after that Jediah died, and I moved to Texas, married Calvin Butterworth."

"Was he a farmer?"

"No, he weren't no farmer. He was a peace officer."

"Really! Did you ever meet any of those famous outlaws?"

"I met Hickok and Calamity Jane, and I met Cody once too."

"Buffalo Bill Cody?"

"They ain't no other one, is they?"

"My youngest brother is called Cody."

"Well, he'd better hope that's all they got in common. I never knew when Calvin was gonna turn up dead, and he did finally one day. Killed by Bat Masterson."

"I thought Masterson was a peace officer," Dr. Merritt said.

"He was a dirty rotten crook! No better than Jesse James or any of the rest of that trash! Shot my husband in the back. Stepped out of an alley and shot him. Claimed it was self-defense. I'd a kilt that man myself, but he left town 'fore I got my chance." She went on for some time about the wild and woolly West before announcing, "And then I married Wilbur Pettigrew, a dentist."

"What was he like?"

"He was the most boring man I ever knew. Hit's a wonder I didn't die of boredom married to that man! He took me to Sallisaw, the most boring town in Oklahoma, and it's the most boring state I was ever in."

"I take it you weren't happy with Mr. Pettigrew."

"Every day was misery. He took him a woman, a red-headed hussy, and planned to run off with her. He gave almost all our money to her.

The rest he gambled on some stocks and lost. All I got left is the stuff you promised to come back and get, Merritt."

She fell silent after that. Dr. Merritt said gently, "I guess you're getting tired, Mrs. Pettigrew."

"I've been tired a long time, Merritt. I ain't as old as Methuselah, but I don't feel much younger either." She turned to Lanie, and her eyes twinkled. "Wouldn't it be somethin' if you went to all this trouble to get me there jist in time to save that passel of brothers and sisters of yours—wouldn't it be somethin' if I jist up and died when we got there?" She cackled. "That'd be a joke on you, wouldn't it?"

Lanie laughed. "Don't do that, please, Aunt Kezia. We need you."

Kezia Pearl Pettigrew did not speak for a time, and then finally she whispered, "Well, I ain't been needed in a long spell."

❧

As they pulled into the yard, the Freeman kids came boiling out of the house. Lanie got out and said quickly, "Now back off! Aunt Kezia is tired, and you don't want to be pestering her."

"Is she going to stay here and keep us from gettin' adopted?" Cody demanded.

"Yes, she's going to stay here. Now, you be respectful."

Dr. Merritt helped the old lady down from the car. She had managed the trip marvelously well and began examining the children. "This is Davis," Lanie explained, "and this is Cody—and Maeva—and this is Corliss. Everyone, this is our Aunt Kezia."

"They look healthy." Aunt Kezia sniffed. "They's enough of them, ain't they?"

"Come on in the house. It's cold out here."

"I'll get the baggage," Dr. Merritt said. "You take your aunt inside."

Lanie took her aunt by the arm and discovered that she was at least two inches taller than the old lady. The old woman seemed unexpectedly frail. "I know you're tired. We'll get you settled in your room right away."

Aunt Kezia did not answer, and climbing the steps seemed to take most of her strength.

Cody opened the door, staring at his newfound aunt with avid curiosity. Davis said, "We've got a nice, warm fire. You want to warm yourself, lady?"

"Don't call me *lady*. Call me Aunt Kezia." She looked around. "I'm a mite tired now, so I want to go to my room, and I don't want nobody botherin' me. Don't come whinin' to me with your problems."

"We fixed up the best room for you," Maeva said. "Can I show it to you, Aunt?"

Kezia faced Maeva. Something about the girl attracted her. Maeva stood still as the old woman's dark eyes went over every aspect of her face. Finally she demanded, "Are you a hellion, Maeva?"

Maeva laughed with delight. "I sure 'nuff am, Aunt Kezia!"

Kezia cackled. "Well, so was I when I was your age—still am when I feel up to it! Now, you take me up to my room, and you young'uns keep quiet. I don't sleep sound."

"I'll keep them all quiet, Aunt Kezia," Davis said. "Don't worry."

As Maeva and Lanie walked up the stairs, one on each side of the old lady, Kezia said, "I hope you fix a decent dinner. I can't eat much because of my weak stomach."

"We'll fix whatever you want, Aunt Kezia," Lanie said.

⌐━⬩⟩⤙

Aunt Kezia slept like a rock, and she ate like a field hand! She devoured everything that was put before her, and Maeva whispered to Davis, "I swear, I don't see why she ain't as big as an elephant! She looks like a little old skinny thing, but she must be stout. I like her."

Once the children discovered that their aunt had traveled the Oregon Trail and been married to a real gun-fighting sheriff in Texas, they fired questions at her right and left.

Lanie, despite her aunt's protests, could tell that the old woman liked being the center of attention. Lanie had fixed the best meal she knew how, and she was happy to see her aunt eat well.

After supper, Orrin Pierce and Owen Merritt came by, and when Lanie introduced Orrin as a lawyer, Aunt Kezia glowered at him. "I never met an honest lawyer or an honest judge in my life. Most of 'em need to be taken out and shot."

Orrin could not help grinning. "You're pretty hard on us, Mrs. Pettigrew, but I'm doin' the best I can to help your family. I've come over to ask you a question. Don't be offended."

"I'll be offended if I take a notion!" Aunt Kezia reached over and got her purse. She pulled out a pistol, and a gasp went around the room.

"Hey, Aunt Kezia, that's a pistol!" Cody yelped.

"You're mighty right it's a pistol! It's a thirty-eight, and I know how to use it too. My second husband carried it while he was lawin'. I keep it with me all the time, even at church."

"Why would you need it at church?" Maeva said, grinning. "Would you shoot the preacher if he preached a bad sermon?"

"I've heered some sermons that men ought to have been shot for preachin', but I ain't shot one yet." She stared at Pierce, then laughed and put the gun back. "What do you want, lawyer?"

"Would it be possible for you to take your maiden name again?"

Aunt Kezia stared at the lawyer. "Why would I want to do that?"

"It would help our case with the State. If they heard that the children's aunt, Miss Kezia Pearl Freeman, was staying here, that would have a better sound than the name of Pettigrew. There's nothing wrong with the name of Pettigrew, of course."

"They's plenty wrong with it! Never liked hit to begin with. Makes me think of that worthless third husband of mine. Why, shore, I'd be glad to be a Freeman again."

"That's wonderful, Miss Freeman," Orrin said. "I think we can take it from here."

As the two left the house, Dr. Merritt said, "Do you think it's going to work?"

"I don't see why not. It meets all the conditions of the law. You know," he said thoughtfully, "it seems like the whole town has been pulled together by the Freeman family's troubles."

"That's what a town's for, Orrin."

⊙══⊷

"Why, Mr. Gamble. Come in, won't you?"

Lanie Freeman's cheerful welcome caught the social services agent off guard. He had come to give her warning that the final papers were being drawn up. He took off his hat. "I'm afraid I've got some bad news for you—"

"Oh, I want you to meet someone. Please come in."

Mystified, Gamble followed the girl into the living room. An older woman sat in front of the fire, knitting. When Lanie introduced the two, she said, "How do you do, sir?"

"Your name is Freeman?"

"Certainly it is. I'm the aunt of these children. The great-aunt, of course, but I'm a Freeman all the same." She cackled. "Does that throw a monkey wrench in your plan to break this family up, Mr. Gamble?"

Gamble's mind went blank for a moment, and then he swallowed and recovered. "It does change things."

"You reckon it does. I don't guess we'll be meeting again. So good-bye, Mr. Gamble," Aunt Kezia said. Lanie showed him to the door and returned to her aunt.

"I got my gun here," Aunt Kezia said. "I was fixin' to shoot that scamp if he pulled anything funny."

Lanie kissed her aunt's withered but firm cheek. "That would've been all right with me, Aunt Kezia, but I'm glad you didn't have to."

"What do you mean they've got a relative staying with them?"

Millard Gamble looked at Otis Langley. "They found this old lady, and sure enough she's their father's aunt, and it meets the law. She's a relative, and she's staying in the house with them, so there's no reason to send the children away."

"Get out of here! I don't want to hear anymore about this," Langley said. He was aware of the town laughing at him. Almost everyone knew what he had tried to do, and it delighted them that he had failed.

Aunt Kezia settled in quickly, her list of conditions posted on the wall in a prominent place. In truth, her conditions turned out to be less severe than they sounded. Two weeks after her arrival, Lanie said, "I hope you're happy living with us, Aunt Kezia. We love having you."

"You don't mind my sharp tongue then?"

"No, we don't mind it at all. We know your bark's worse than your bite."

"I reckon most folks would rather be bit once than barked at all the time. But it's better than that crazy house in Sallisaw."

Lanie smiled, for she knew the old woman had trouble saying anything sweet. "I'm glad you're here. I'm a little bit worried though."

"About what?"

"Well, the note's due again, and we've worked hard, but we don't have enough money to pay it."

"We can sell some of my things."

"No, we're not going to do that. We'll find a way."

Lanie took her aunt to her room and went downstairs. Maeva was sitting at the kitchen table, staring into space. "What are you thinking about so serious?"

"Where we going to get the money to pay that note?"

"I don't know, but God will send it."

"I don't know about that," Maeva said.

"He sent us an aunt, didn't He, that kept us from getting farmed out."

"This is different. We've got to meet this note every month, Lanie. I don't know if we can do it."

⊶⊷

The twenty-ninth of November came, the day the note was due. Breakfast was a subdued affair, and Aunt Kezia demanded, "What's the matter? The cat got your tongues?"

"I guess we're all worried about how to pay the bank," Cody said.

"Why, that ain't nothin' to worry about," Aunt Kezia said. She had eaten three eggs with great gusto. "I don't mind if I have one more of those eggs. It would go down right good, Lanie."

"I'll fix it for you."

Beau barked outside. "What's he barkin' at?" Cody said.

"Go see," Lanie said. "Could be one of those pesky coons gettin' into the trash again."

Cody left, but he returned almost at once. "Looky here! Looky here!"

"What is it, Cody?" Lanie asked. She saw he was holding up a glass Mason jar.

"It's money! It's the angel again!"

All the kids gathered around Lanie as she opened the jar and counted out the wrinkled bills and the change. "It's twenty-six dollars and fifty cents. Just what we needed."

"It's the angel," Cody said. "That's what it is."

"What angel? What are you talking about?" Aunt Kezia said.

Lanie explained that on several occasions when they just had to have money, it had appeared in this fashion in a Mason jar on the front porch.

"It ain't no angel," Maeva said. "It's somebody. Dogs don't bark at angels."

"Why wouldn't they bark at an angel?" Aunt Kezia said. "They're pretty scary creatures. Every time one of them appears in the Scripture, the first thing they say is, 'Now don't be afraid.'" She held up the jar. Then she looked at the bank notes. "I didn't know they used bank notes in heaven." A smile touched her withered lips and her eyes sparkled. "I'd like to meet this here angel. I've got a few matters I'd like to take up with him. Maybe you could set a bear trap out there and catch him."

The kids all found this hilarious, and Lanie leaned over and hugged her aunt. "I don't think you catch angels in bear traps, Aunt Kezia."

"I'd mighty like to see one of them angel critters," Aunt Kezia said. "Now that'd be right interesting."

Lanie smiled. "I guess it would—and I think one of them might look just like you!"

PART FIVE

The Woman

⇀≈ CHAPTER 26 ≈⇀

A chilling blast of wind cut through Forrest Freeman's thin shirt, paralyzing him for a moment. His ax half-raised, a shiver went through him. He lowered the ax and buttoned the top button of his denim jacket. He saw that Oscar Beecham, one of the other inmates, was staring at the ground and his body was shaking violently. Glancing toward the guard, Forrest said, "Mr. Thornby, Oscar's about to fall over. You got to get him out of this weather."

Bent Thornby, warmly dressed in a fleece-lined jacket and a cap with flaps that buttoned under his chin, carried a shotgun loosely in the crook of his right arm. "You do look pretty bad, Oscar. You two come on to the fire and have your dinner. Maybe that'll help."

"He needs to be in the hospital, Mr. Thornby," Forrest said. His lips were so numb he had to frame the words carefully. The wind swept across the flat delta country. In the summer the blistering sun beat down on the inmates as they planted and hoed and picked cotton, and in the winter they cleared new land in icy blasts that seemed more typical of Canada than Arkansas.

Mr. Thornby nodded, moved to the back of a pickup, and jerked a sack out. "Hey, Ray, get the guys in! It's time for dinner."

The shivering inmates came quickly, taking the cold pork sandwiches and more willingly the steaming cups of coffee dished out by the guards. They moved in close to the fire that snapped and crackled, throwing its heat out. Forrest glanced around and wondered if he looked as bad as everyone else.

Taking his friend's sandwich and coffee, he said, "Here, sit down, Oscar. Eat."

"I ain't hungry."

"You got to eat something, and here, drink some of this coffee. It'll thaw your innards out." In his sixties, Oscar was a lifer. Freeman suspected that he had TB. He watched as Oscar listlessly took a bite of his sandwich, then broke into a fit of coughing as he tried to swallow it. He slapped the older man gently on the back until Beecham recovered. "Here, sip this coffee. It'll be good for you."

The two huddled close with the other inmates, all of them slumped down on the frozen earth. The guards, Freeman thought, didn't need shotguns. None of these convicts were capable of escaping. It was late in the afternoon, and the gray skies threatened snow and more cold.

"How's them young'uns of yours, Forrest?" Mr. Thornby looked down at him. The guard was a thick-set, red-faced man, and he sipped his coffee cautiously.

"They're doin' pretty fine, sir. That oldest girl of mine writes every week, and the rest of the kids add a few sentences to her letters. She won't talk about how hard things are, but I know they are."

"Things are hard everywhere," Mr. Thornby said. He studied Forrest and said, "I guess you feel bad you're not out there to help 'em."

"Really bad, Mr. Thornby."

Forrest nursed his sandwich and drank another cup of coffee, and too soon Mr. Thornby said, "Okay, get them axes."

"Mr. Thornby, Oscar really ought to be in the hospital. You know it just like I do."

"They'd just send him out again." Thornby sipped his own coffee and considered Forrest for a moment. "The warden be needin' him a man to take care of his horse and bloodhounds. You know anything about horses and dogs?"

"Don't like to brag, but I don't reckon that you got anybody in this place that knows more."

"I like a man that knows his worth. Reckon you can get along with them?"

"Yes, sir, I can."

"All right." Mr. Thornby got up. "I'll speak to the warden 'bout you. You'll be a trustee if he assigns you, and you'll have to be eating up at the big house where he lives. I reckon that'll put some meat on your bones."

"I sure thank you. I'll do my best with the warden's horse and dogs."

"I know you will, Forrest."

Forrest went back to the work site, picked up his ax, and began swinging at the scrub pines. As he tried to ignore the freezing wind, he began to pray, just as he had ever since arriving at Cummings Prison. *It's mighty hard to have faith, Lord, but I still believe in You. I can't do nothin' for my children in here, so I'm askin' You in the name of Jesus to take care of them, please!*

◁══╍▸

Lanie's room was cold, for there was no fire upstairs. She put on an old coat that had been her mother's but was now too small. It was outdated and the fake fur had mostly fallen off, but at least it was warm. Sitting down at the table she used as a desk, she opened her journal and began writing in it. A poem had been moving around in her mind, and she wanted to put it down.

Lanie could not understand how her poems came to her. She did not deliberately try to make them up, she just had a desire to write in a way that mystified her. Her greatest pleasure had become her work on the series of biblical poems. Each featured one of the individuals Jesus had met and their reaction to Him. She had begun studying the Bible for information for the poems and was amazed to realize how few people understood Jesus.

John the Baptist caught her attention, but it was hard for her to put herself into his character. How can a sixteen-year-old girl know what a prophet who lived so long ago felt? But then she considered that old poets wrote poems about young people, so she had persevered, emerging with a rather long poem that nearly pleased her.

Baptizer

So now the Lamb of God is come, but I,
John Baptist, knew Him not!
Since first Jehovah showed Himself to me
I've stood hip deep in Jordan's silt-brown stream
And plunged the penitents so deep their heads
Almost took root in sand, their flailing legs
Like scrawny weeds of papyrus in a storm!

Sometimes my words cut and nearly stripping
Flesh from bone— even Pharisees
Cried out to be baptized! O hypocrites,

255

Not Jordan's water, nor the ocean deeps
Could purify the stench of your foul hearts!
Your fathers slew the prophets; now you come
That I may feel the venom of your fangs.

A thousand days I've stood, and every face
I've searched, looking for the Lord's anointed,
But knew Him not when first He came to me.
We look for our desires so hard, that when
They come to hand our eyes are fixed afar.
So yesterday He whom I sought
Stood quietly beside me in the stream
While busily my eyes touched every face
On shore. And then, I gave a sigh and turned,
But as I touched His arm my hand recoiled,
For there, one foot away, I saw those eyes
That I had seen in dreams since God
In deep Judean desert sealed my task.
At first I thought it could not be, for He
Was smaller than my thought of Him — He stood
Beneath my height, His quiet eyes looking up
To watch my face. Confused, I cried inside:
How can I tower over God's own Son?
O foolish thought! God ever did delight
In unexpected forms to pour Himself!

When heart and earth at last stood still, I asked:
Why do You come to me? O rather plunge
Me by Your hand beneath the cleansing flood!
For deep in muddy waters, I had found
The purity of God's own righteousness.
He gave command, so deep in watery grave
I buried Him. But then (I know not how)
As He arose, all noises seemed to fade
Like hum of bees in some far distant field.
But out of silence came a clarion call:
This is My Son in whom I am well pleased.
Out of the burning sun there dropped a dove
So white it glittered in the upper air
Like burning snow — until on Him

I held with my arms he came to rest,
And then—I could not see to see.

So now, I've seen the Hope of Israel,
The promised one, resting in these hands.
But strange it is that He who made these hands
Should rest in them—that God should trust a man!

A few more days, and then I must decrease.
My task is now to point men to Messiah
As I have ever done. He will increase
Until earth's very stones will hear God's call:
This is My Son, in whom I am well pleased.

She shook her head. "It's not exactly right, but I'll work on it." She opened the single drawer to put the journal in, and as she did, she saw the picture of Owen Merritt. It was a newspaper clipping that had appeared in the Fairhope *Sentinel* when he first came to town. The story was rather simple, giving a little background on the physician come to help Doc Givens. Picking up the picture, she stared at it. It was not a clear shot, but it brought him before her almost as if he were standing there.

She was gazing at the picture when the door burst open, and before Lanie could move, she heard Maeva's voice, and an arm shot across her shoulder and plucked the picture up.

"Well, look at this!"

"Give that back, Maeva!"

Maeva laughed and held the photo in her right hand behind her back while fending off Lanie's attempts to regain it. "I knew you was lovesick!" Her eyes were dancing. "I just been wondering which fellow you been moonin' around about. Now I know it's Dr. Merritt."

Though Lanie was a year older than Maeva, she was not as strong. Finally Maeva saw that her sister was upset, so she brought the picture around and said, "Here's your ol' picture! No sense frettin' yourself about it."

Lanie snatched the picture, put it back in the drawer, and slammed it shut. "Did you ever hear of knocking before you come into somebody's room?"

"Well, I didn't expect you'd be actin' like this. Shame on you, Lanie, fallin' for an old man like that when you got lots of young fellas chasin' around after ya."

"You hush, Maeva, and get out of here!" Lanie was furious and Maeva allowed herself to be shoved out the door. "You're not foolin' me, Lanie! You got a bad case of the lovebug bite."

"You just keep your mouth shut!" Lanie cried. She slammed the door and turned her back against it, her breath heaving and her face red. "She's nothing but a busybody, that's what she is!"

The door behind her moved and struck her in the back. She thought it was Maeva and whirled to jerk it open. "I told you—" She stopped, for Aunt Kezia stood there wrapped in what seemed like all the clothing she had, her thin body distorted by a large wool overcoat that had belonged to Forrest.

"What's all the yellin' about?" she said. She shoved her way into the room and looked around. "You know I need my rest! I can't sleep with all that yowlin' goin' on."

Lanie had already discovered, as had the rest of the family, that despite Aunt Kezia's protests, she could actually sleep through an artillery barrage. "I'm sorry, Aunt Kezia. I didn't mean to disturb you."

Aunt Kezia looked at Lanie and pulled at the old coat, which was unfastened. "You're poppin' outta yer clothes, girl" she cackled, and her eyes danced. "You'll have the men poppin' their eyeballs at that figure of yours."

"I certainly won't!"

Aunt Kezia was a torment at times. "Which one of them fellers that comes callin' on you do you like the best? I bet it's the one with the big feet, the one who plays the fiddle."

"That's Nelson. He's just a friend."

"A friend, my foot!" she chortled. "I seen him a kissin' you when you two come home after that frolic at Geyer Springs. I didn't notice you fightin' very hard to get loose."

"He surprised me."

"Did he now?" Kezia seemed to enjoy Lanie's embarrassment. "I heard somebody talkin' about Merritt. What was you a sayin'?" Aunt Kezia's eyes were fixed on Lanie, and suddenly Lanie's eyes narrowed. "Oh, that's the way of it, is it!"

"I don't know what you're talking about!"

"Well, by granny, you done went and fell for that doctor!"

"I have not! You're just being awful! I wish you'd leave."

"What are you so stirred up about? There ain't nothin' wrong with a girl likin' a man."

"Dr. Merritt is courting Louise Langley."

Aunt Kezia moved closer and whispered loudly, "I'll tell you how to get him, honey. I could always get any fella I wanted when I was your age."

"I don't want to hear it."

"What you have to do—"

At this point Lanie simply pushed her aunt out of the room, something she had never done. But even after she shut the door, her aunt's voice was loud enough to be heard throughout the whole house. "What you got to do is just poke a curve at him and flutter them long eyelashes of yours. Men ain't got no sense at all when it comes to things like that. You mind what I tell ya, and you can catch him as sure as God made little apples!"

☞

After Lanie regained her composure, she changed clothes, put on a brown dress, and went downstairs. It was a relief to get into the warm kitchen and also a relief that her Aunt Kezia was in the living room listening to *The Lone Ranger* on the radio. She could hear the announcer say in his rich bass voice, "A fiery horse with the speed of light, a cloud of dust and a hearty 'Hi ho, Silver!' the Lone Ranger rides again!"

Beau nudged her with his nose, and she patted his broad head. "Beau, I'm sure glad you can't talk like Aunt Kezia. Two like her and Maeva are enough. Are you hungry?"

"Woof!"

"You're always hungry." She went over to the icebox, opened the door, pulled out a chunk of the raw beef she had cut up for a stew, and tossed it to him. He caught it expertly, bolted it, and barked. "No, that's all you get."

Beau stared at her in disbelief and then lay down facing the corner where the walls intersected. "That's right. You just stay there with your hurt feelings."

Lanie started fixing the evening meal, but she had not gotten very far when she heard a knock on the back door. She went to open it and saw a man standing there, obviously a hobo. He was a smallish man beyond middle age with a seamed face and faded blue eyes. His pants were too large for him, and his coat was too small. His arms stuck out, exposing lean, bare wrists.

"Pardon me, miss, but could I work for something to eat? I can chop wood—anything."

"I'll find something. Come on in, and I'll fix you a plate."

"Thank you, miss. That's right kind of you."

The man pulled his hat off as he stepped in through the door. Gray streaks ran through his black hair. He looked at the stove and said, "That warm stove looks mighty good."

"Go over and warm yourself. I've got some leftovers from dinner."

"That'd be mighty fine. My name's Leo."

"I am glad to know you, Mr. Leo. My name's Lanie Freeman."

Lanie at first had been afraid of the hobos that got off the train as it slowed and made their way to the back porches asking for food. Some looked rough and fierce, but this one didn't. As he held his hands out, absorbing the warmth of the stove, Lanie felt a pang of sorrow for him. She pulled out a plate and opened the warming compartment of the stove. She filled the plate with leftover boiled potatoes, green beans, fried squash, and a large chunk of ham. She piled three biscuits on top of this and set it down on the table. "Here. I'll get you some coffee."

The man sat and stared at the food. When Lanie brought him a big mug of steaming black coffee and a knife and fork, he bowed his head and said a silent thanks. The act touched Lanie, and she got herself a cup of coffee and sat down across from him. "Go ahead and eat," she said. "I'll just have some coffee." The man nodded, then began to eat. He ate slowly, chewing every morsel for what seemed like a very long time.

"Have you been traveling long?"

"About six months, miss. I worked in a laundry but it went under. After that I worked in the wood yard, but I wasn't able to do the heavy work."

"Do you have a family?"

"No, ma'am, don't have nobody."

Lanie sipped at her coffee and wondered what it would be like to be one of the hobos. She knew that there were thousands of them all over America. She had seen the pictures of the bread lines in the big cities, people stretched out in a line that seemed to go on forever, cold, hungry men with caps pulled down over their foreheads as they waited for a bowl of soup and a piece of bread.

The man finished his meal, sopping up the juices with a morsel of biscuit. "I got a little piece of apple pie left," Lanie said. She got it for him, and he ate it in the same thoughtful way, sipping his coffee. "It must be hard riding on the railroad like you do."

"It ain't easy," Leo said. "Sometimes yard bulls catch us, and they carry sticks. I seen a man killed just outside of St. Louis like that."

"How terrible!"

"We always try to work for money, and sometimes there isn't any work." A look of pain crossed the man's eyes. "That's all I want," he whispered, "is to work."

Lanie's pity for the man grew, and she fetched him more coffee. "How do you know which houses to go to? Or do you just go to all of them?"

Leo smiled. "No, not all. We have a code."

"A code? What kind of code?"

"You got a piece of paper?"

"Of course." Lanie went to the kitchen table, opened the drawer, and pulled out a small tablet. She put it before him, and Leo began to make marks. "You see this plus? If we chalk or cut it into a post, that means it's a good place for a handout. The next bo that comes along knows what it means. Here, this one means you can sleep in this farmer's barn. This one, a cross, means religious people." He smiled slyly and winked. "Be sanctimonious."

"This one right here means these people will help you if you are sick, and this means a police officer lives here."

The man went on about his experiences on the road, some of them harsh, even cruel.

Lanie studied the man. *What will happen to him? He has nobody. Will it always be like this?*

Finally she said, "We don't really have any work to do, but I'm going to make you up a sack of food to take with you."

"I don't mind workin', miss. I'd really rather work."

Lanie saw that the man had some pride. "Well, there are a few chores. Come, I'll show you. And while you're doing them, I'll fix you up a sack of goodies."

Thirty minutes later, Leo, carrying a large flour sack full of food, whispered to Lanie, "If everybody in the world was as kind as you, miss, it would be a good world. God bless you."

"God bless you. And remember, Jesus loves you."

"I believe that, miss. Times are hard, but He'll take care of me."

Lanie watched him walk down the street and then shook her head and went back to cooking. Her mind stayed on the poor man the rest of the day.

At supper that night Lanie said, "I've decided something. We're all going to see Daddy this Christmas."

"We don't have any money to do that, do we?" Davis asked.

"It'll just take gas money, and maybe we'll have to stay all night in a hotel, but we can't let Daddy be there at that place all by himself. Not on Christmas. If it takes every dime we got, we're going." She looked at their aunt. "Aunt Kezia, we'll have to get someone to stay with you."

Aunt Kezia was nibbling on a dill pickle, which she dearly loved. She waved the large pickle as if it were a baton. "I'll be dipped if I'm not a goin' with you!"

"But you haven't been approved to get in."

"I don't reckon it's as hard to break into a jail as it is to break out. You get that lawyer feller to call the governor. If that lawyer can't get me in to see my own nephew, why he ain't worth dried spit!"

⚬━⤙

"I'm a little bit worried about the Freeman children, Dr. Merritt." Effie Johnson had stopped Owen in the lobby of the bank. "They're determined to see their father, and I don't think they have the money to do it. They made their last payment in pennies and nickels and dimes. They work like slaves to save their place."

Owen dropped his head and stared at his feet. He was quiet for so long that Effie wondered if she had offended him. But when he looked up, determination filled his eyes. "I'll see about this. Thank you for telling me, Miss Johnson." He left, and Effie thought with satisfaction, *Well, I hit a nerve that time! I'll be bound that he'll do something too.*

Owen drove to the Freeman house. He knocked on the door and was greeted by none other than Miss Kezia herself.

"Hello, Miss Freeman," he said.

"Hello, Doc Merritt. Come on in out of the weather. You out treatin' sick folk?"

"A little bit of that. What's going on? It seems like a lot of activity."

"We're all gettin' ready to go see Forrest. Come on in. The kids are in the kitchen makin' goodies."

Owen followed the small woman into the kitchen, which was filled with the aroma of fresh-baked cookies. "That smells good," he called out. "Can a poor doctor get a bite of a cookie?"

"Hi, Dr. Merritt," Maeva said. "You'll have to sweet talk Lanie over there." Her eyes sparkled mischievously. "Maybe if you put your arm around her and tell her how pretty she is, she'll let you have one of them cookies."

Lanie's face flamed. "He doesn't have to do that! Here, try some of these. They're fresh out of the oven."

Owen took one of the cookies and bit into it. "That's the best cookie I ever had in my life!"

"We're all going to see Daddy," Cody said. "We're taking him a bunch of stuff too."

"That's right," Davis said. "Look, we went out and picked up pecans, and they're all shelled. Daddy loves pecans. Taste 'em."

Owen tried one of the pecans. "That is absolutely a good pecan!"

"We've got fudge and cookies and cake," Maeva said, "and we've got some shaving cream, soap, and razor blades and toothbrushes and toothpaste and things like that."

"Does your dad know you're coming?"

"No, it's going to be a surprise," Lanie said.

"And I'm going with 'em too," Aunt Kezia piped up. "That lawyer fella, he got me a pass to get in."

"Be a pretty cold trip. The weather's been bad."

"Here," Lanie said, "sit down by the fire. I'll make some chocolate."

Owen sat and nibbled at the cookies and the cake that the family pressed on him. Their determination impressed him. He knew they would leave with no money except for exactly enough, perhaps, to buy gas. Finally he said, "Well, Miss Kezia, if you'll show me out, I'll say good-bye."

"Never seen a man that was worth shootin'," Aunt Kezia grumbled. "Come on. I'll put you out."

"I'll see you later," Owen said. "I hope you have a good trip."

"Thanks for stopping by, Doctor," Lanie said, her eyes warm.

Owen smiled and waved and followed Aunt Kezia down the hall. At the door, he reached into his pocket and pulled out a billfold. He removed two bills and pressed them into Aunt Kezia's palm. "Miss Freeman, I hope you know how to be devious."

Aunt Kezia smiled up at the tall doctor. "I can be as crooked as a snake. What do you want me to do?"

"I want you to use this money on the trip. It'll pay for the gas and for food and for a night for all of you in a hotel. But I don't want you to tell anybody where you got it. This will be just between me and you, all right?"

She fastened her jet-black eyes on the doctor's face, observing him so closely that Owen's nerves were a bit rattled. "For a doctor you ain't a bad feller."

Owen laughed and released her hand. "Did you ever know any good doctors?"

"Well, I knowed a dentist once. His name was Doc Holliday. Cold-blooded killer, that one. I don't reckon I'd have ever let him touch my teeth."

"You really knew Doc Holliday, the gunman?"

"He weren't nothin' but a two-bit thug. Wyatt Earp, now, he was a good feller, but that Doc Holliday was nothin' but an imitation bad man." She suddenly blinked and said, "Are you gonna marry that woman you been courtin'?"

"Well, it might turn out that way. Only she's rich and I'm not."

"Well, you better look around before you jump."

"What do you mean, Miss Freeman?"

"I mean it's easier to get a fish hook in than it is to get it out."

Owen grinned. "Don't you like Miss Louise?"

"Don't even know her, but I ain't thinkin' about marryin' her either." She examined the bills, then folded them and stuck them into the pocket of her apron. "You know, I'm worried a bit about Lanie."

"Worried? What's the matter?"

"Well, there's lots of these young fellers campin' on the front steps, come callin' on her. Comin' like moths to a candle."

"She's too young to get serious. Besides that, she's got a lot of sense."

"You know, you're kind of ignorant even for a doctor. Ain't you ever seen a young girl hide all her sense under the porch when some sleek-lookin' fella does some sweet talkin'?"

"I guess I have."

"That girl needs somebody to talk to her about such things. She ain't got no mama."

"Well, you're the one to do that, Miss Freeman."

"Shoot, she won't listen to me! I'm older than pyramids to her. I reckon you'd better do it."

"Me!"

"You got a hearin' problem? You tell her about the birds and the bees and all about how young girls need to be takin' care of their treasure."

Owen felt his cheeks warm, and he chuckled. "I couldn't do that!"

"Yep, I think you'd better. I won't tell 'em about the money, but you'd better think about havin' that talk with that girl. She needs a friend. Now leave."

Thus dismissed, Owen went through the door. He heard it shut firmly behind him and stood there thinking hard. *I hate to see Lanie make a mistake. It would be her mother's place, but since she's gone I guess old Aunt Kezia's right. I'd better have a talk with her.* He got into the car and drove away, mulling over what would be appropriate words for the young girl who had come to mean so much to him.

⇜ CHAPTER 27 ⇝

Christmas week of 1930 brought warm breezes in from the south, thawing the snow and scattering the bitter weather. Lanie had been nervous about driving all the way to Cummings Prison without a man along, but her fears proved groundless. The sun shone brightly, and unlike other trips, when she had nearly frozen as cold air had filtered in through the ancient Ford's many cracks and crevices, heavy clothes and blankets kept the Freeman family comfortable. Lanie packed enough food for everyone for the trip there and back, and they washed down their meals with sodas from country stores along the way.

Aunt Kezia performed well, correcting Lanie's driving and navigating even though she had never made the trip in her life. By the time Lanie pulled into the prison, she had learned to tune out her aunt.

"We have to go in here to be admitted," she said, stopping the car in front of a long, rectangular wooden building. "Now, you all behave," she warned. "We've got special permission from the warden for all of us to visit Daddy, but we have to behave ourselves."

A murmur went around the group, and Lanie kept her eye on her Aunt Kezia as they entered the building. The guards looked up in surprise, and one of them said, "Well, you brought the whole crew, did you, Lanie?"

"Yes, I did, Mr. Pote. Merry Christmas to you."

"And to all of you. These are all your brothers and sisters?"

"Are you blind?" Aunt Kezia piped up. "Do I look like her sister?"

Pote blinked with surprise. "Well, pardon me, ma'am, I didn't notice you there."

"Well, notice me now!"

Pote winked at another guard. "I'll sure do that, ma'am." He riffled through some papers and said, "You must be Miss Kezia Pearl Freeman."

He towered over the old woman. "You're all clear to go. None of you are packin' any drugs or firearms, are you?"

".I am," Aunt Kezia said. "What about it?"

Pote stared at her. "What do you mean?"

Kezia rammed her hand down into the big purse and pulled out the thirty-eight. "I keep this for my own protection."

Pote cleared his throat. "Well, ma'am, you can't take it inside. Here, let me hold it for you."

Kezia reversed the thirty-eight and handed it over. "You be careful with that. It was my husband's. I used it one time and put a bullet in the Sundance Kid's derrière."

Pote blinked with surprise.

"That varmint thought he could come into our town and shoot it up, but he found out better. He insulted me. It's a good thing I did shoot him in the derrière. My husband would have shot him in the head."

The guards, by that time, had gathered around and begun peppering her with questions. Aunt Kezia obviously enjoyed being the center of attention, and finally it was Lanie who said, "Mr. Pote, do you think we could go see Daddy now?"

"Why sure, Lanie. You're not carrying a gun, are you?"

"No, sir, of course not."

"Come along then." He looked at the various sacks and boxes that the children were carrying. "What's all this?"

"It's Christmas presents for Daddy."

"No guns in there or anything like that?"

"No, sir."

"Well, come along."

⚓──⊹⊱

As soon as Forrest came into the room, he found himself swarmed. The children rushed at him and wrapped themselves around him, calling his name. Only Lanie stood off to one side with Aunt Kezia and watched as they pulled at him and patted his cheeks, and her eyes grew misty as she saw him pick up Corliss and look at her face and kiss her cheek.

"Hello, Daddy," she said.

"Lanie! Here, you kids let me get over there and give this girl a hug." He hugged Lanie so hard it took her breath. "Howdy, Aunt Kezia. Lanie told me you were comin'."

"Hello, Forrest. It grates on me to see you in this here place, but give me a hug anyway."

Forrest put his arms around Aunt Kezia's tiny form. She kissed him on the cheek. "You look peaked, but we done brung enough food to feed the whole regiment."

The children began pulling at Forrest. "Open your presents, Daddy. It's all Merry Christmas for you."

"Well, I wish to my never!" Forrest smiled. "You sure done it up right."

For the next thirty minutes the visitors' room was bedlam. Lanie and Kezia had conspired together to bring everything a man in prison could possibly use. There was so much food that Forrest quickly said, "I'll have to share this with some of my friends. A man couldn't eat all this." He took a bite of the chocolate cake and shook his head. "Did you make this cake, Maeva?"

"No, Aunt Kezia, she made it."

"Well, it's mighty good, Aunt Kezia."

"That's my special recipe." She watched the proceedings with obvious enjoyment. "I mind once when we was lawin' in Texas. We had a place just outside of town, and my husband rode in every day to shoot anybody that needed it. One day a bandit rode by."

"A real bandit, Aunt Kezia?" Cody demanded, his eyes round as saucers.

"He wasn't nothin' else. I'd just finished makin' a cake like this, and he come in and waved his gun around and made me cook him a meal."

"Was you scared?" Davis demanded.

"With a two-bit hoodlum like that? I don't reckon! It just made me a little riled."

The kids fired questions at her, but she threw up her hands and said, "Well, I fed him his meal, and he gave me a silver dollar and then kissed me and rode off. He didn't last long. Got shot down robbin' a bank. Didn't even have sense enough to know how to rob a bank! Shows you how dumb he was!"

Everyone laughed, but Forrest was filled with a bittersweet joy, for he hated this place and longed for the day when he would be seeing them again.

"This ought to be enough books to keep you going, Lanie."

Cassandra Sue Pruitt smiled as she pushed the stack of books over toward Lanie. She was wearing a white blouse and a pale blue jacket, and she waited for Lanie to pick up the books and leave. She was somewhat surprised when Lanie said, "Can I talk to you a minute, Miss Pruitt?"

"Why, sure, go ahead."

"Not here," Lanie said. "Somewhere where we can talk."

"Come on back into my office. It'll be quiet enough there."

Lanie followed the librarian through the stacks into the small office. Cassandra waved to a seat and shut the door. She took her own seat and considered the girl. "What is it you want to talk about, Lanie?"

"Well, I want to ask you if there's a book that tells how to grow up."

Cassandra shook her head. "I don't know exactly what you mean."

"Well, Miss Cass, I'm gettin' bigger. I'm big as a full-grown woman now, but I don't know how to handle things."

"What kind of things?"

Lanie blushed and she wrung her hands. "I don't know how to treat fellas who like me. Some of them sometimes . . . well, they try to make me do things that aren't right. How do I make them act right?"

Cassandra was stunned. "Well, I don't know exactly."

"What do you do when a fella gets too familiar?"

Cassandra Sue Pruitt could answer many questions about books, but this issue tied her tongue. "I . . . I don't really have that problem."

Lanie stared at the woman. She had always thought Miss Pruitt one of the prettiest women she had ever seen. "Don't you like fellas, Miss Pruitt?"

Cassandra suddenly wished that this interview was not taking place. "Well, not . . . in that way."

"They sure like you. The sheriff, he thinks you're real pretty. He told me so."

Now it was Cassandra Sue Pruitt's turn to grow red. "He has asked me out, but I've never gone."

"Why not? He's such a nice man and good-looking, too, don't you think?"

"I suppose so, but he's older than I am."

"I don't see that that makes any difference, he's not that much older. But anyway, I need a book that tells me how to get a man to like me."

"Who? Which man?"

Lanie swallowed, then shook her head. "I'd rather not say. He's a little older than I am and real genteel, but, Miss Pruitt, he thinks I'm only a little girl. How do I get him to see I'm a grown woman now?"

Cassandra Sue Pruitt fumbled for an answer, and Lanie saw that she had asked the wrong person. Finally she said, "Well, I thank you for listening to me. Is there a book that might tell me what I need to know?"

"I don't think so, Lanie. I'm sorry."

❦

Doc Givens and his assistant hit a gap in the steady flow of patients. Givens was looking at the paper and commenting on it. "It says here there's four million people unemployed in this here country, and there's bound to be worse."

"That's bad," Owen murmured. He disliked being read to out of the paper, but Givens loved it.

"More than thirteen hundred banks closed this year. I don't know what's happenin' to this country, but it's not good."

"It's good for H. L. Hunt. I see he bought out that oil business. Made him the richest man in America."

That was Owen's only contribution to the conversation, and in time Givens lowered the paper and looked over it. "I'm not boring you, am I?"

"Well, I've got a problem."

"What's the matter? You're not sick, are you?"

"No, it's kind of a responsibility I have. How would you advise a young girl about the dangers of being . . . of, well . . . of being a young girl?"

"What young girl?"

"Oh, just any young girl," Owen said.

"What kind of dangers? You mean like falling down a well?"

"No, Dr. Givens, you know. With men."

"Tell her the truth. Scare the daylights out of her."

"I don't know. She's a sensitive girl. She doesn't have any parents."

"Why do you have to take this on, Owen?"

"She needs help."

Givens put his paper down and leaned forward. He flexed his foot and his leg, which was much better now, but still gave him problems. "Son, don't you get mixed up with some female."

"Oh, it's not like that at all!"

"Uh huh. How many times have I heard that? You want my opinion, I'd stay out of it."

Owen nodded. "Maybe you're right." But he thought otherwise.

For the rest of the day Owen performed his duties perfunctorily. When he set out to make house calls, he began at Butcher Knife Annie's, and he was surprised to see Lanie going toward the house. He watched her enter and muttered, "Well, this may be as good a time as any." He parked the car, grabbed his black bag, and walked to the door. When he knocked, Lanie answered. Her face lit up when she saw him, and he smiled. "Why, hello, Lanie."

"Come in, Doctor. Did you come to see Annie?"

"Thought I might look her over a little bit. She's not quite over that flu she had."

The two went in, and Annie, who was sitting on a couch decorated with cats of various sizes and colors, seemed glad to see him. "I hope you brought somethin' for my misery, Doctor."

"That's what I've come for, Annie. Let me check you over." As he went through his routine of listening to her heart and lungs and asking her questions and taking her temperature, he thought about what he would say to Lanie. Finally he gave Annie some mild sleeping medicine and told her to stay in bed and rest.

"Could I give you a lift somewhere, Lanie?" he asked.

"I'm just going home."

"Why don't you come with me? I've got to make a call over to the Sixkillers."

"Are they ailing?" Lanie asked.

"The kids may have chicken pox. I hope not, though. You'll have to stay outside. I wouldn't want you to get it."

"I've already had it."

"Well, that's good." He looked at her face and said, "It didn't leave you marked any. You've got a smooth complexion there." He saw her flush and did not answer. "Well, anyway, their daddy told me he's got a brand-new litter of cocker spaniel puppies. Maybe you'd like to see them while I'm doctoring."

"Oh, I'd like that!"

They left Annie's house and all the way out to the Sixkillers' place, which was one mile out of town, Owen tried to think of some way to begin his speech. He could not, and when they arrived at the veterinarian's home, he left Lanie on the floor covered with puppies. "You can't have them all," he said with a grin.

"You can have one of them," Matthew Sixkiller said.

"No, sir, we don't need any more dogs. Beau would be jealous."

⌗⋆⟩

By the time Owen was ready to leave the Sixkillers, he had a plan. "Let's see how high the river is." He pulled up on top of the levee and shut the engine off. "Not too high. I understand it flooded the town one time."

"Daddy told me about that. He was just a boy then. He said water was in all the houses and all the businesses."

Owen turned to face her in the seat and was impressed at how smooth her skin was. She had beautiful auburn hair that was long and fell over her shoulders, and her eyes were wide-spaced and clear. Her lips were full and round and very expressive, and he was aware that she was no longer the gangling fifteen-year-old girl that he had first known. "I've wondered maybe if I ought to talk to you, Lanie."

Lanie looked at him with surprise. "Have I done something wrong?"

"Oh, no, of course you haven't."

Lanie stared at him. "What would you like to talk about?"

"Well, I think you need to give consideration about young fellows. You know boys take advantage of girls sometimes."

Lanie was dumbfounded. "Do you think I'm not a good girl, Dr. Merritt?"

"Great Scott, I didn't mean that! No! I think just the opposite, but you're getting to be such a beautiful girl, Lanie. Why, if I was seventeen years old, I'd be camped on your doorstep."

"Would you really?"

"Of course I would, but I feel more like a . . . like a father to you."

Lanie huffed indignantly. "You're not old enough to be my father!"

"Well, an older brother then."

Lanie's tone went flat. "You're not my brother, Dr. Merritt."

"I know that, but what I meant was that an attractive girl like you will draw young men, and they'll try to get you to do wrong things."

"Like what?"

Owen Merritt was floundering out of his depths. "Well, you know what I mean."

Lanie knew exactly what he meant. Her offense turned to amusement and she felt humor bubbling in her. "Tell me about it. What sort of things do I need to be careful about?"

The next ten minutes were as hard as any that Owen Merritt had ever experienced. As generally as possible, he told her about the wiles that young men used to overcome the virtue of young girls. She watched him quietly, and he could not understand the expression on her face. Finally he threw up his hands and said, "I don't know why I'm telling you all this, but it's just because I . . . well, I think a lot of you, Lanie."

Lanie turned and looked out the far window. She did not move for a long time, and he reached out and touched her shoulder. "Lanie, what is it?" When she turned, he was shocked to see tears in her eyes. "Oh, great guns, I've hurt your feelings!"

And then Lanie Freeman touched Dr. Owen Merritt for the first time. She put her hand on his arm and whispered, "No, Owen Merritt, you made me feel just fine."

<hr>

January 14, 1931. I can't get Owen's "talk" out of my mind. That was nearly a week ago, and I've been going over it until I'm almost crazy. He means so well—but he has no idea of how I feel about him! And I'll never tell him! I couldn't do that. Some things you just can't say to people. I guess we all have secrets from each other—even good friends. I wish we could just come right out and tell people what's in our heart, but only Aunt Kezia can do that.

I tried to put all this into a poem—about how we like to know what's in people's hearts and would like for them to know what's in our heart—but it just won't come out right. Maybe I'll make this poem say what I want it to, but right now I just can't.

The Secret
We keep close watch but almost never see
The things concealed; they're buried too deep down,
The secret life of friend and stream and tree.

They're plated with a fine duplicity
Heart-haven, running brooks, peopled towns.
We keep close watch but almost never see

Beneath bright foliage to reality.
Oh, buried deep like rivers underground
The secret life of friend and stream and tree!

For just one act of country charity
Unassuming as a cotton gown
We keep close watch but almost never see.

We crave the ripe, the rare virginity
Of love unseen which strongly castles round
The secret life of friend and stream and tree.

So many things die slowly, silently
Like dusty blossoms in some minor field.
We keep close watch but almost never see
The secret life of friend and stream and tree.

⊶ CHAPTER 28 ⊶

For the third time Lanie added up the money from the coffee can. She stared at the wrinkled bills and the change as if by concentration she could increase the amount. Cap'n Brown leaped up on the table, arched his back, then nudged at Lanie's arm with his head. "Get away, Cap'n Brown!" Lanie said. "I don't feel like petting anybody."

Shoving Cap'n Brown away, she slowly put the money back in the can, and a sense of despair seized her. *We're never going to get the money to pay this house off. The bank will take it away from us. I know they will!* The coins made a tinny sound as they hit the bottom of the can. Outside she could hear the voices of the boys as they played some sort of game. February had brought bitter weather. It took all their efforts to keep enough wood chopped for the house to be halfway warm. Glancing at the old clock, she saw it was time to start thinking about supper, but the gloom that had been with her all day long, the foreboding of habitual struggle, drained her. Aunt Kezia came through the door, startling Lanie. "Lanie, it's Wednesday."

Aunt Kezia was wearing the old overcoat of Lanie's mother, which brought back many memories. She had seen her mother put on that coat so many times that the sight of it resurrected her loss. "I know it's Wednesday," she said. "What about it?"

"I want to go to that movie show tonight," Kezia said. "It's a good un."

"We can't go to the movies tonight, Aunt Kezia."

Kezia plopped herself down in the chair opposite Lanie. "Maybe you forgot about my conditions," she said. "You promised me I'd get to go to the movies every week and that I'd get to pick it. Well, there's one on tonight I been waitin' for. It's called *Dracula*. It's about a blood-sucking vampire. That Jinks boy done seen it, and he told me about it. Said it scared the pants off of him. I want to go tonight."

"You can't go."

"I purely got no respect for a girl who won't keep her promises. That was one of my conditions—"

"There's no money!" Lanie struck the table with her fist. "There's no money, and we're going to lose this place!" To her dismay, tears flooded her eyes, and a sob escaped from her chest. She whirled and ran out of the room.

Aunt Kezia got up and followed Lanie to the base of the stairs. She shook her head and walked down the hall, turning in to the living room. Maeva was playing on the floor with Corliss. "What's the matter with that sister of yours, Maeva? She just about bit my head off when all I asked her to do was to go to the movies."

Maeva shrugged. "She's scared, Aunt Kezia."

"Scared of what?"

"She's scared we're gonna lose our place, and besides that she's got a crush on Dr. Merritt. She won't tell anybody, but I know she keeps his picture up in her room."

Aunt Kezia frowned. "Maeva, you keep your mouth shut."

Maeva looked up with shock. "What are you talkin' about? What'd I say?"

"If your sister's got a problem, you don't need to go blabbin' it all over the place. How'd you like it if somebody blabbed about how you smoke store-bought cigarettes out behind the barn?"

"How'd you know that?"

"Never you mind how I know it, I do. You leave Lanie alone and keep your mouth shut about her problem, you hear me?"

"I didn't mean anything by it, Aunt Kezia. I was just tellin' you."

"Well, you told me, now don't say nothin' more about it." Aunt Kezia turned and walked toward the stairs. She held onto the railing and toiled upward. As she did, she thought about her youth, when she would have been able to bound up those stairs as Maeva and the boys always did. "Gettin' so old I can't hardly get around," she muttered. She reached the top and limped to Lanie's door. She knocked on it. Lanie's muffled voice replied, "Who is it?"

"It's me, Aunt Kezia."

"Go away."

"I ain't goin' away. You might as well let me in."

"I don't want to talk to you."

"Well you're goin' to. Now, can I come in?"

After a long silence, Lanie said. "Well, come on in if you've got to."

Aunt Kezia opened the door and saw Lanie sitting on the side of her bed, her fingers twined. The room was cold. "It's too cold in here. Come on down where it's warm."

"I don't want to."

"You're stubborn as a bluenosed mule, Lanie!" She sat next to Lanie. The bed sagged. "I don't care about goin' to that old movie."

Lanie gave her a startled look. Her face was stained with tears. "I know I promised you could go to the movies, and you might as well. We're not going to have enough money to pay the note anyway."

"I know you feel bad, Lanie, but we spend so much time worryin' about things that never happen, we don't have time to take care of the things that are happenin'. Now, you look at it this way. We're all right for today. We got food down there in the cupboard. We got a roof over our heads and clothes to wear."

"But what about when that note's due and we can't pay it? That old Mr. Langley has already been at Miss Johnson to foreclose, and he'll do it too."

"Where's your faith, girl?" Aunt Kezia said. "You done told me about how that angel brought some money more than once when you didn't have it. I don't know much about angels, but I know they come around once in a while."

Lanie did not answer. She was struggling against her tears. "Oh, Aunt Kezia, what are we going to do?"

"We're gonna just trust the Lord." Aunt Kezia took Lanie's hand and held it in both of hers. "You know, I recollect once when we was on the trails headed for Oregon. I was only a girl, just fifteen, hadn't been married but a month. It was rough going. The roughest part," she said slowly, "was when my man got the cholera."

"You never told me that."

"Well, he did. You can't imagine how it was. We passed little markers all along the trail. Sometimes whole families was buried with just little wooden crosses there, with the husband, the mama, and little kids. As soon as somebody got the cholera, we started thinkin' of the funerals."

Lanie sat entranced by her aunt's story. "What happened?"

"Well, everybody gave my husband up for dead, and he was powerful sick. I was sittin' with him, and everybody said he wouldn't last until mornin'. It must have been three o'clock or so in the middle of the night. I recollect how the stars were shinin' brighter than I'd ever seen 'em, but I was plum scared to death just like are now."

Lanie studied the old woman's face.

"I was too scared even to pray. I was just settin' by the fire holdin' Jediah's hand, just like I'm holdin' yours. And then I plum give up almost. I prayed until I couldn't pray no more, and all of a sudden this feller came in out of the night. We was a big train, more than thirty wagons, scattered all over creation. I knowed most folks, but I'd never seen him. Well, he come over and said, 'How's your man?' I looked up at him and said, 'I reckon he's not gonna make it.'

"He said, 'I come to pray for him.' And that's what he done. He prayed a simple prayer, and he looked at me and said, 'Woman, you've got your husband back again.' He went off into the dark, and I just sat there starin' after him."

"What happened, Aunt Kezia?"

"Well, by the time mornin' came, Jediah's fever was broke. Everybody was shocked out of their boots. He got better and better, and finally he got well."

"What about that man?"

Kezia's eyes grew soft. "I don't know about him. I went over the whole train askin' about him, but nobody knew the likes of him. I always reckoned he was an angel."

"That's a wonderful story, Aunt Kezia." Lanie summoned a smile. "I guess I'm not a very good Christian. My faith is pretty weak right now."

"Don't you worry, it's gonna get better." Aunt Kezia studied the girl. "You got any more problems we need to talk about?"

Lanie dropped her head and did not answer.

"You can tell me," Aunt Kezia said. "I won't tell nobody."

"Well, did you ever care for somebody who didn't—"

Lanie broke off and Aunt Kezia squeezed her hand. "Who didn't care for me? I shore did. I never told you about how I got married to Mr. Butterworth, my second husband, did I?"

"No, you never did."

"Well, I think about it a lot. Jediah died, you knowed that, and I moved to Texas to live with some relatives of mine. There was this fella there called Calvin Butterworth. He was a lawman. My goodness if he wasn't a handsome fella, tall and broad-shouldered, with hair about the color of yours that he wore long. Oh, every woman he passed by looked at him. Well, I had lots of fellas that come courtin' me, and I liked bein' married, but none of 'em suited me. Then when I saw Calvin somethin' happened. I'd read them romance stories about love at first sight and never believed 'em, but I did then."

"Did he come courtin' you?"

"Courtin' me? I reckon not! He was runnin' around with rich women, the daughter of the attorney general of Texas for one. Everybody said they was gonna get married. Well, I done everything I could to make him notice me, but I was just one of about a hundred. And you know what I done?"

"What?"

"I up and asked God to give me a husband. Of course I didn't specify. I figured God could take care of that."

"And what happened then?"

"Well, I was woke up one night, and the Lord spoke to me, and He said, 'You're gonna get married. I'm gonna give you a husband if you'll believe me.' And, of course, I told the Lord I would, so He said, 'I want you to tell your aunt and your uncle that you're gonna get married.'

"Married to who, Lord?" I asked.

"'You just tell 'em,' He said. Well, it didn't make much sense to me, but I didn't doubt what the Lord had spoke, so I told my uncle and aunt the next day that I was gonna get married, and, of course, they wanted to know who I was marryin'. I said 'I don't know yet, but I am.'

"Well, my uncle he made fun of me and said I was just a silly girl, which I guess I was. But I believed the Lord, and then about a week later the Lord come to me again. I guess it was a dream, but it was just as clear as this room, and He said, 'I want you to get some bridesmaids.' Why, I had three good friends, and the next day I went to ask 'em if they'd be my bridesmaids." Aunt Kezia laughed heartily. "Of course they was just dyin' to know who my fiancé was, and I said I didn't know, but the Lord told me to get my bridesmaids picked. They laughed at me, but I didn't care."

"Aunt Kezia, didn't you feel funny telling all these things?"

"Well, I felt pretty silly, but I was followin' the Lord."

"What happened next?"

"He told me to set a date and go tell the preacher I was gonna get married. It was about a month away, so I did. And, of course, the preacher he wanted to know who the groom would be, and I had to go through the whole thing again. Well, it got out, of course. Them girls couldn't keep quiet, and the preacher he was a blabbermouth too. Everybody was talkin' about how I was losin' my mind."

Lanie stared at her aunt with amazement. "I wouldn't have done a thing like that!"

"Well, I don't know how come, but I did. And then the next time the Lord spoke, He said, 'You gonna marry Calvin Butterworth.' Well, that's where my faith nearly broke down. Every girl in Texas, it seemed like, wanted to marry that man."

"Did you tell him?"

"Didn't say a word to him, but one day I was walkin' along the streets of Abilene. I went into a store, and when I came out, I ran right into him. I mean I bumped right into Calvin Butterworth's own self. He was a big, tall man, and I dropped my packages. He started helpin' me pick 'em up, and he smiled at me. Goodness me, I thought my heart would melt! He said, 'I'm gonna help you carry these here packages.' Well, he did, and by the time we got to my folk's house, he had done asked me out, and he said, 'I hear you're tellin' folks I'm gonna marry you.'"

"He said that?"

"He shore did, and his eyes was laughin'. Oh, that man had laughin' eyes! Of course I couldn't do nothin' but turn red and couldn't say a word. Well, he took me to a social that night, and two weeks later he asked me to marry him. And so we got married. He was a good man."

"That's a wonderful story, Aunt Kezia!"

"So you see, God can give you a man if you ask Him real hard." She pushed a lock of Lanie's hair off her forehead. "I don't really care nothin' about goin' to see that old movie."

"Yes, you do, and we'll go tonight." Lanie hugged her aunt. "You always make me feel better, Aunt Kezia."

"You never know what God will do. Don't you ever give up on Him, you hear me, girl?" She left the room, and Lanie went over to her desk, pulled out her journal, and began to write.

⌖

"Oh, I've had such a wonderful evening, Owen!" Louise said. She threw her coat across the room, where it missed the chair. She put her hands on his shoulders, and her eyes were sparkling. "I wish we could have such a good time every night."

"A poor country doctor can't afford an evening like this very often." Owen put his arms around her and held her lightly. "But it was fun, wasn't it?" The two of them had gone to Fort Smith for an opera, a rather rare occurrence in the hills of Arkansas. True enough, the opera company was not the Metropolitan, but still it had been entertaining. "I didn't understand a word they said, but they sure made the chandeliers rattle, didn't they?"

"Yes. Thank you so much for taking me." Louise leaned forward and kissed him firmly, and Owen held her tightly. She sensed the desires that revealed themselves in the strength of his arms and the demand of his lips. His lips were firm as they pressed against her own. When she pulled back she whispered, "Owen, you're so sweet!"

Up until this time no other woman had stirred Owen Merritt as this one did. She was rich in a way that a woman should be rich, at times gay and reckless, but at other times with the deep, mysterious glow of a softer mood. "You know, Louise," he whispered, pulling her close so that his face was only inches away from hers, "you're like that music we heard tonight. Makes a man feel strong enough to whip the world."

Louise knew she was beautiful, and she knew she was a picture framed before his hungry glance. At that instant the heat of something rash and timeless and thoughtless touched her, and she knew with certainty that it touched him also. He embraced her and she did not resist, for she gloried in this power she had to stir him, to deepen his hungers and the sense of loneliness she saw in him.

The two stood there for a long time, and she waited until she understood that she must make the first move. With her hands pressed against his neck, she asked, "Do you care for me at all, Owen?"

"You know I do."

His words encouraged her, and she said, "I care for you too."

A silence grew between them, and he said, "I can't let myself care for you too much, Louise."

"Why not?" she cried. "Why not, Owen?"

"Because I'm a poor man, and you're used to better things than I can give you."

"Oh, Owen," Louise whispered, "that doesn't matter!" She kissed him again and then shook her head slightly. Her eyes were large and luminous. "If two people love each other, they can make a life. And money and things like that don't matter."

"I always thought they did," Owen said. "I think it's a serious thing to take someone into your life forever, or at least for a lifetime."

"Is that what you want to do, Owen?"

Louise waited for his reply, and when it came, he spoke urgently. "I do care for you, but I've been afraid to let myself say anything."

"Say it, Owen! Say whatever you wish."

"All right then, I will," Owen had an impulse then, and although he had not planned to do this thing, he said, "I'd like for you to be my wife, Louise. I'd like to care for you."

"Owen!" she cried, and her lips were tremulous. "Do you mean it?"

"Yes, of course I mean it. A man doesn't joke about things like that. But, Louise, it will have to be a long engagement, a very long engagement. I'll have to establish myself."

"That doesn't matter. I'll help you. Daddy will help you. You can do anything, Owen. I've always known that."

Owen felt surrounded by her beauty and by her excitement. The future seemed a long way off, but he had taken the first step, and now he knew that it was the sort of step a man takes and cannot turn back on. He put that from his mind, and as she drew him over to the couch and they sat down together, he smiled at the excitement he saw in her as she began making plans.

⚯

As Owen pulled into Doc Givens' driveway, he saw with some surprise that Pardue Jessup's car was parked in front of the house. "Hello, Pardue. You're out pretty late."

"Need to talk with you, Doc."

"Why, sure. Come on inside."

Pardue shook his head. "No, I can't stay. Got to go corral a bunch of drunks over at the Green Door." The sheriff's face had a serious cast. "It's about Forrest Freeman, Doc. I've got a tip that might mean something."

Owen straightened. "What about Forrest?"

"Well, I got a call from Birdie Pickett, the deputy over at Blakely. We're fishing partners, and I've done him a good turn once or twice. He told me he picked up Alvin Biggins."

"On what charge?"

"Oh, drunk and disorderly—nothin' serious. But he said that Alvin was drunk as Cooter Brown when he put him in the cell. Birdie got to talking to him, and Alvin got to braggin' on how him and his brother Duke had put the run on Forrest."

"What exactly did he say, Pardue?"

"Lots that didn't mean anything—but mainly that him and Willie and Ethel wasn't the only witnesses to the shooting."

"That's just what we need!"

"Maybe," Pardue said cautiously. He rubbed his chin. "Alvin said there was a woman named Thelma Mays there. I know her, Doc. She's really low rent!"

"And she saw the shooting?"

"Alvin talked like she did."

"Why didn't Forrest ever mention her?"

"Apparently she was in another room, but the door was open."

Owen felt deflated. "Then she might not have seen anything."

"That's right—and Alvin could be lying about it all. But I thought it was worth looking into—so I did." Pardue shifted his weight and chewed his lower lip. "I tried to locate the woman, but she's flown the coop. Gone to California."

"What part of California?"

"Someplace in Los Angeles. Might as well have gone to the moon. That's a humongous big place. But I hear you gotta brother there?"

"Yes, my brother Dave. He's a policeman in L.A. I'll see if he can find her. Do you have an address?"

"Nope, nothing but a name. Way I got it she was going to work at some saloon called The Black Lily."

Owen took out his notebook and wrote down the information. "I'll ask Dave to see if he can help with this."

"Hope it works out, Doc. Sure would like to see Forrest out of Cummings. Well, I got to go corral the drunks."

"Thanks, Pardue," Owen said, and as Pardue drove away, he stared at the slip of paper, then muttered, "Think I'll call Dave instead of writing. This might mean something!"

❦

As Lanie entered Stockwell's General Store, she almost collided with a couple. "I'm sorry," she said, "I didn't—" And then she broke off for she saw that it was Owen Merritt and Louise Langley.

"Why, hello, Lanie," Louise said. The two stepped aside, and Louise said, "Come on in out of the cold."

Lanie saw that Louise was smiling and believed there was something of triumph in it.

"I'm glad we've run into you, Lanie," Owen said. "I wanted to ask how that gash Cody got in his knee is doing."

"Oh, it's healing fine, Dr. Merritt." Cody had run into a stob during one of the wild games he played with Max Jinks and laid his knee open in a wicked gash that required several stitches. "You'd never know anything was wrong."

"Well, I'd better drop by and take a look at it anyway. And how's the rest of your family?"

"We're all right, Doctor, thank you."

"I'm glad we ran into you too, Lanie," Louise said. Her eyes sparkled and the corners of her mouth turned upward. "I'm the happiest woman in the world. Can you guess why?"

Suddenly Lanie knew exactly what made Louise Langley so happy. She glanced quickly toward Owen and saw that he was smiling mildly and watching Louise.

"You can't guess?" Louise said. "Well, I'm going to be married, and I'll bet you can guess who the groom will be."

Lanie felt an emptiness grow inside her and a heaviness, but she managed to cover it. "Congratulations, Miss Langley, and to you, Doctor. I hope you'll be very happy."

"Of course we will," Louise said. "We were just made for each other. And we'll want you to come to the wedding."

"Of course it'll be quite a while," Owen said quickly.

"That's what he says," Louise grabbed his arm and held on possessively. "But it won't be as long as he thinks."

Lanie could not think of a single thing to say, but she managed to murmur, "I'm sure you'll both be very happy."

"Of course we will. Come along, Owen."

Lanie turned to watch them go, and as the door closed behind them, she felt that a door in her own life had closed.

CHAPTER 29

For a moment Lanie paused outside Planter's Bank. She stiffened against the cool March breeze and stared at the building, which had a blank, unadorned face except for the words "Planter's Bank" etched into the marble. The impulse came to her to turn and run away, but she had fought that battle already. The payment was due, and there was not enough money to pay it, and that was that.

Taking a deep breath, Lanie stepped inside. There were only three customers, and Lanie waited until the one seated at Cora Johnson's desk got up and left. Cora smiled and motioned toward her and said, "Hello, Lanie, good to see you."

"Hello, Miss Johnson."

Cora caught the dead tone of the girl's voice. "What's the matter?"

"I . . . I don't have the money to make the payment on our place."

Cora nodded. "Come on in. We'll talk to Effie about it. Maybe we can do something."

The two headed for Effie's office. Cora tapped on the door and Lanie heard the older woman say, "Come in!"

Effie Johnson was sitting at her desk going over papers. "Hello, Lanie."

"Effie, Lanie has a problem."

"We worked hard, Miss Johnson, but we just don't have the money. We had some doctor bills this month, and it took nearly everything to pay for them and for the doctor and the medicine."

Effie carefully replaced the pen in its holder and folded her hands. "I'm sorry to hear that, Lanie."

"We did our best, ma'am, we really did."

"I'm sure you did."

Lanie could not help asking. "What's going to happen? Are we going to lose our place?"

"We'll hope that won't happen. Try not to worry about it, Lanie. The board is meeting this week. I'll make a special plea for you."

"Thank you, ma'am. I know you've always tried your best to help us."

"It's a heavy burden for a young girl like you." Effie got up and walked around the desk. She came and stood directly in front of Lanie. She put her hands on the girl's shoulders and said quietly, "You run along home now. Try not to worry about it. Come by and see me tomorrow. Maybe I'll have good news for you. I'll do my best."

After Lanie left, Cora said, "Surely there's something that can be done."

"I'm not optimistic, Cora. They've missed two payments now, and that's all Otis Langley will want."

"But he's not the whole board."

"The board's been balanced, but one vote will sway it. I've got an idea that Otis has been putting pressure on our mayor."

"Mr. Delaughter's a good man."

"He's a good man, but his business has been going down, and he's depending on help from the bank to make it. I'm pretty sure Otis has promised to help if he changes his vote."

Cora dropped her eyes. "I hope it doesn't happen. Those children have tried so hard."

"We'll just have to see, but as I said, I'm not very hopeful."

⚙️⚘

The sun coming through the window touched Lanie's eyes, and she woke up. She felt groggy and listless, for she had slept little the previous night. Several times she had awakened, and the fear of losing the only home she had ever known gripped her. She prayed, but this time it seemed that prayer did little good.

Throwing the covers back, she dressed swiftly and then lifted her eyes toward the calendar handed out by Brewton's Funeral Home. The picture for March 1931 must have been reprinted a million times. Two small children were about to step off a broken bridge into a deep pit, while overhead a bright and shining angel was moving in to be sure they didn't. When she was a very small girl, Lanie asked her mother if angels looked like that, and she remembered clearly how her mother had smiled and said, "Oh, I'm sure they're much more impressive than that."

Her eyes fell on the number thirteen, which was heavily circled. "Today I am seventeen."

Lanie spoke the words aloud, and her voice seemed to reverberate in the silence of the room. The whole house seemed to be silent. Lanie sat on the chair in front of the dresser and looked into the small mirror. She studied the face that she saw every day and whispered, "Well, so you're seventeen years old. How does it feel?" She touched her cheeks and saw no trace of the child that had first looked into this mirror in this very room.

I don't feel any different. Seventeen is just like sixteen. The thought brushed against her mind. *But sixteen is a child and seventeen is a woman. I've always thought that.* She knew that she was somehow disappointed, for she had thought that the magical age of seventeen would mark the beginning of something wonderful, and yet she felt just the same, just as vulnerable, just as touched by fears and apprehensions as when she was sixteen.

"You're a foolish girl," Lanie said aloud, "to think that one day would make any difference!" She got up abruptly and went downstairs and started the fire. While it caught and she pulled the elements of the breakfast together, she saw that the sun was no brighter and the trees were no more beautiful than they were yesterday. The world was just the same as it had always been—and she had to struggle against the fear that seemed to rise from deep within.

Lanie pulled herself up straight. "I can't let everybody see how scared I am," she whispered. She walked to the foot of the stairs and called, "Everybody get up!" She heard the cries of protest but insisted, "Everybody up now! It's time to get up!" She turned back and took out a frying pan and began scrambling eggs. She concentrated fully on not letting the others see any of her fears. She knew they suspected, but the possibility of losing the house had become an unapproachable topic. Her brother Davis said that when a pitcher was pitching what looked like a no-hitter, nobody would say so. It was a jinx. It couldn't be touched. Everybody ignored it. That was the way their family had been about the payment at the bank for the past weeks. They did not mention it, but she could see the fear lurking in their eyes as it lurked in her own.

⊶

"Well, I'm sure we all feel for the Freeman children," Otis Langley said. "But business is business."

"I don't see why we can't give them a little more time, Otis," Orrin Pierce said. "It's not like the bank is going to go broke if they're a few months late."

"Oh, come now, Orrin, you know better than that! If there were any chance at all for the Freemans to settle this debt, I'd be as anxious as the rest of you to give them more time. But their record is getting worse. It won't be any better next month. It'll be worse. This Depression is not going to go away."

Elspeth Patton sat at the table, her back upright. Her eyes were fixed on Otis. "Everyone else is afraid to mention it, but I will. The word is that you want the Freeman property, Otis. That's the reason you're so anxious for the bank to foreclose."

Langley's face flushed. "That's an insult, Elspeth!"

"Then you don't want the property?" Elspeth said, not wavering under his angry gaze.

"Of course it's good property, and someone's going to get it, but not necessarily me. I would be interested, but the bank will have to take over the sale of the property."

"We pretty well know who will get first shot: the only man who has the money!" Pierce said harshly.

"Orrin, you're not a businessman! Anyway, it's time for the vote."

This was the moment that Effie Johnson had dreaded, but she had no choice. "All in favor of extending their loan, raise your hand." Every eye was fixed on Delaughter, for it was his vote that had held off the foreclosure so far. He sat there, his head bowed, not moving. His face was a dusky red.

"Well," Effie said, "there's no sense asking for those in favor."

"Well, I'll ask for it," Otis said loudly. "Those in favor."

The vote was in favor of foreclosure.

"Well, I'm glad that's out of the way. Now we can get on to other business," Otis said.

"I don't feel up to other business." Elspeth Patton got up and left the room.

"I don't feel up to it myself," Effie said grimly. "This board is dismissed."

Otis Langley shot her an astonished glance, but when he saw the light in her eyes and the line of her set lips, he muttered, "Well, perhaps we can handle the other business at our next meeting."

⚓

"There was nothing you could do, Effie," Elspeth said. The two women stood in Effie's office. "You did everything you could. Otis Langley is a hard man."

"He hasn't always been that way. When he was a younger man, there was a gentleness in him, but he lost it somewhere along the way."

"He lost it all right," Elspeth said. "What now?"

"I've got to go tell the Freemans the bad news, and I'd rather be shot."

"I'll go with you," Elspeth said.

"That'll be good of you. Two bearers of evil tidings won't make it any better for the Freemans, but I need your support."

Neither woman spoke as they walked to the front porch. They climbed the steps, and Effie knocked. The door opened, and Maeva greeted them. "Hello, Miss Johnson, Miss Patton. Won't you come in?"

"Thank you, Maeva."

"Everybody's in the living room. We're popping corn on the stove."

"Haven't done that in a long time," Elspeth said.

"It's real good," Maeva said. Apprehension was in her eyes. She led the two women into the living room. Lanie was sitting in the rocking chair holding two-year-old Corliss, and the two boys stood stiffly as if called to attention.

As a rule, Effie Johnson had little trouble saying her mind, but she wished at this moment that she were anywhere in the world but in this place. "Hello, everyone. Miss Patton drove me over. My driving is not as reliable as it used to be."

"Won't you have some popcorn?" Davis said.

"No, thank you, Davis," Effie said. "It gets in my teeth."

"How about you, Miss Patton?"

"None for me, thank you." Elspeth was staring at a clock over the fireplace. She walked to the mantel. "What a marvelous old clock."

"Why, it's just an old clock that belonged to our grandma," Davis said.

Elspeth drew her fingers across the mahogany clock. "This is a John Evans bracket clock."

"What does that mean?" Maeva asked.

"John Evans made some of the finest clocks in England at one time."

"Well, it doesn't run very good anymore," Cody said. "I tried to fix it, but I couldn't make it work."

"It's a very fine old piece. I like to see the old things. That's all I have in my house. I think the new furniture is pretty ugly."

The talk went on for some time, but the tension rose in the room. Finally Effie took a deep breath and said, "I'm afraid I don't have any good news for you." She forced herself to say the words. "The board met, and Miss Patton and I did all we could, and Mr. Pierce, but we were outvoted."

"What does that mean?" Cody demanded. "Does it mean we have to leave here?"

"I'm afraid it does," Effie said. She saw her words strike against every face except the baby's. She had seen fear like this before. Since the stock market crash she had delivered similar bad news to a great many people. It was the worst part of being a banker, and there was nothing she could say that would make things any better.

Lanie stood up and put Corliss down. Corliss toddled over to Davis, holding up her arms. He picked her up, and she began to touch his face, seeing that he was frowning. She began to whimper.

"Don't cry, Corliss, it'll be all right," Davis whispered.

Lanie knew that there was nothing to be done. "Miss Johnson, we all thank you for all the times you helped us when we couldn't make our payments, and I know if you had your way, it would be different."

Effie Johnson looked down. She could not meet the steady gaze of the young woman who, barely out of girlhood brushing against the mysteries of womanhood, had to bear the load for them all. "We'll be going now."

The two women murmured their good-byes and left. They didn't say a word to each other until they were in the car. After Effie slammed the door harder than necessary, she said, "I'll get the Baptist folks to praying, and you see what you can do with your Presbyterian bunch."

"And I think we'd better go by and tell Sister Myrtle to get her Pentecostals praying."

"And the colored church. They're very fond of these children too."

"We'll see. It's going to take a miracle if I know Otis Langley!"

○══◆══

The birthday party was quiet enough, just the family except for Butcher Knife Annie. Davis had brought her, and Maeva made a cake, and all helped make ice cream. But it was a feeble attempt. The presents were small, and everyone was thinking about the last birthday party when everything looked so much brighter.

Finally Annie said, "It's gettin' late. I'd better get home."

"I'll walk home with you, Annie," Davis said.

Suddenly Cody said, "You got to remember that we might get out of this thing yet."

"No, we won't," Lanie said heavily. "It's all over, Cody."

"Don't you remember before how the angel brought the money? I'll bet he'll bring more."

Annie, who had turned to go, paused. She was wearing the same ratty old coat and oversized boots that she always wore, and she looked frail, and her expression was filled with pain. "There ain't gonna be no angel, Cody."

"You don't know that, Annie."

"Yes, I do." Everyone turned to look at Annie, and she dropped her head.

"It was you, Annie, wasn't it?" Lanie said. "You're the one who left the gifts for me and has been putting money out so that we could make our payments. You're the one!"

"I wanted to help you," Annie said in a whisper. She looked up, and they saw the wishes in her eyes. "You've been so good to me, but I don't have no more money."

"Don't you feel bad about that, Annie," Davis said, putting his arm around her. "We shore appreciate what you done."

"I wish I was an angel." Butcher Knife Annie looked very little like an angel of any sort, but there was love in her eyes. "You've been the only people that ever cared about me. If I was an angel, I'd give you this whole blasted town."

"I don't want the whole blasted town," Maeva burst out. "I just want this place." She gave a gulping sob, then whirled and left the room.

"I ain't seen Maeva cry since she was five years old!" Cody said in awe. "Things are bad to make her squall."

"I'd squall myself if it'd help," Lanie said, "but it won't. But the Lord's still the Lord, and He'll take care of us some way or another." Her words did not make much of an impression, and she knew they were feeble comfort. "You go ahead and take Annie home, Davis. The rest of us will clean up."

"That was pretty nice of old Annie to give us her money," Cody said after she left. "She ain't got much."

"She may not be an angel of the regular kind," Lanie said, "but she's something very special."

CHAPTER 30

As Roger Langley listened to the conversation his family carried on during dinner, he was struck by a strange impression that he could not explain. Later, as he examined this feeling, he could only describe it as feeling as though he was eating in the family dining room for the first time, though he had eaten hundreds of meals there since childhood. Perhaps his being away at college for a time, and now returning for the spring break, had brought about this strange effect.

Roger toyed with the steak that he had cut up into tiny fragments, aware that his father was speaking of the Freeman situation. The subject interested him, and he attempted to pull himself out of his alien mood. He glanced around the dining room and was struck by the richness of the furnishings. The enormous room boasted mullioned glass windows at one end that let in the light during the daylight hours. The enormous chandelier over the table served as a surrogate sun during the night. This evening, the golden sunlight illuminated the richness of the Persian carpet beneath the table, which was large enough to seat twelve people with ease. "Well, this carpet cost three thousand dollars," his father once said, "but it's worth it. It will last for a lifetime and it could be resold easily enough."

Three thousand dollars for a single carpet!

Roger had put his feet on that carpet hundreds of times and never once thought of how much money he was treading underfoot. His eyes swept the rest of the dining room and paused at the seventeenth-century oak baking cupboard filled with china and silverware, a piece he remembered cost two thousand dollars. An ostentatious gold pattern rimmed the showcased china, imported from France. He did not know the cost of it, but a maid who once broke a piece had been dismissed without references. His eyes moved from the ornate plastered ceiling to the floral curtains to the rich mahogany furniture. The mahogany grandfather clock that boomed out the hours and chimed delicately on the quarter hours caught his attention, and he stared at it. It seemed to transform itself into stacked gold coins. He looked down at the heavy silver fork he was holding in his hand and wondered how much it would cost to replace.

"I don't think you should worry about it, dear. Things like that happen during a depression," his mother said. She was tall and stately in an expensive dress with her fair hair done up in the latest style. Roger stared at his mother and wondered, *Have you ever gone without a meal or had to put off buying something because you didn't have the money?* He knew that she never had. She had been born into a wealthy family and married a wealthy husband.

"Of course you shouldn't worry about it, Father," Louise said. "Their situation was impossible from the beginning. How could a group of children keep a household without any parent? You had no other choice."

Roger studied his sister. They had always been close, there being only a two-year difference in their ages, and he knew of Louise's total selfishness. *But am I any different? I knew the Freemans were in trouble, but I didn't do a thing to help them.*

He could keep silent no longer. "I think you ought to reconsider your decision about foreclosure, Dad."

Every head at the table turned, and Roger felt like a bug under a microscope. He raised his head defiantly. "After all, it doesn't mean much to us, but that house is everything to Lanie and her little family."

"I can sympathize with the children," his mother said, "but as Louise said, it's impossible for them to keep it up. You've led a sheltered life, Roger."

"I've led a sheltered life?" Anger touched Roger. "What about you, Louise? You've never wanted for anything in your life."

"That's enough, Roger! Don't speak to your sister that way," Otis said. A frown marred his face, and a vein throbbed in the right side of his nose. "You know nothing about the situation."

"I know that 'bunch of kids,' as you call them, have worked themselves to death trying to make those payments. I know that much. And I think it wouldn't hurt to show a little Christian charity here. After all, a few late payments won't break the bank."

"That's enough!" Otis said, an immovable finality in his voice. "You're not in the real world, Roger. You're off in college, studying. When you've had a little bit of experience, you'll understand these things better."

Roger recalled a picture of a cow and her calf surrounded by a bunch of wolves. It was called *Last Stand*, and the end was in sight. Though Roger was an easygoing fellow who usually gave in for the sake of family peace, a rebellious streak seemed to touch him now. "I've always been proud of our family and proud of your accomplishments, Dad. But I'm not proud of you now."

The red vein in Otis Langley's nose seemed about to burst. He jumped to his feet and shouted, "I'll not have any of your insolence at this table or anywhere else! You're excused, Roger!"

Roger stood, his face pale. "Thank you, Dad, it's good to be excused from a situation like this."

He walked toward the door and did not even pause when his father shouted, "And don't you come back until you've changed your attitude, do you hear me?"

Otis heard the front door slam, and he stood there for a moment trying to regain his composure. "What's got into that boy?"

"Oh, he'll be all right, Father. He's just young and idealistic," Louise said. "Now sit down and finish your dinner."

"That's right, dear," his wife said. "You were probably the same way when you were his age."

"He's had everything handed to him. No one ever gave me anything," Otis said. "He'll have to change his ways and grow up a little bit before he gets out in the world."

❦

The March wind brushed red strokes across Roger's face. He had left the house furious and walked, waiting for his anger to subside, but if anything he grew more upset. He reviewed the explosion—for he could call it no less—numerous times and knew that when he faced his father again an apology would be expected.

"He'll wait a long time if he waits for me to apologize," Roger muttered. Even as he spoke, a solution came into his mind. "It's one thing to talk, but that's all I've ever done. Now I'm going to do something!" He changed direction and walked swiftly across town, thinking hard until he arrived at the Freeman house. Without pausing, he walked right up on the front porch and knocked firmly on the front door. He could hear voices from within, and finally the door opened. He found himself facing Lanie, who was holding Corliss, wrapped in a blanket. "Why—Roger!"

"Lanie, I need to talk to you. Can I come in?"

"Of course." Stepping back, Lanie allowed him to pass. "I should tell you though that Corliss is sick. It may be contagious."

"I'll take the chance. What seems to be the matter with her?" Roger came closer. "She looks like she's got a fever."

"She has, and it's getting worse."

"What does the doctor say?"

"We haven't called the doctor yet."

"Why not?"

Lanie did not answer, and Roger understood it was a matter of money. "Look, she needs to see a doctor. Which doctor do you want?"

"No, Roger, we don't have the money."

"Well, I do," Roger said firmly. "Which doctor would you like?"

"Dr. Merritt, but I couldn't let you pay the bill."

"I doubt if he would charge you, but if he does, I've got the money to pay it. But before I go, I want to talk to you about something."

"Come on into the living room. It's warmer in there." The two walked into the living room, and Roger saw an elderly lady whom he did not know. He had heard about her, though, and when Lanie introduced her as her Aunt Kezia, he nodded and smiled. "I've heard about you, Miss Freeman."

"What have you heard?"

The question came so sharply that Roger could not answer. "Well, nothing much."

"I guess you heard I was an eccentric old lady. Well, I am. Your name's Roger?"

"Yes, ma'am."

"How old are you?"

Roger blinked. "Nineteen, ma'am."

"Where do you work?"

"I'm not working right now. I'm in college."

"Oh, what are you gonna do when you get out of that place?"

"I suppose I'll go to work in my father's business."

"Is that what you want to do?"

"No, it's not."

The answer was out before Roger could evaluate it, and he stood there shocked by his own honesty. He had never said as much to a living soul, but the old lady's aggressiveness disarmed him. "Well, that is, I don't think I'd like it very much."

"Do what you want to, boy. It's your life, not your father's."

"Aunt Kezia, stop telling people what to do," Lanie said.

"That boy needs some help. Don't you see it? Look at him. He don't know whether to run in circles, scream, or shout."

Roger laughed. "That's right, Miss Freeman. I have been thinking a lot about my life lately, and I appreciate your input."

"What did you want to talk to me about, Roger? Would you like to talk to me alone?"

"Why would he want to talk to you alone?" Aunt Kezia demanded. "Anything he can say to you, he can say to me." She turned to Roger and said, "You wasn't aimin' to speak rudely, were you?"

"Oh, no!" Roger said. "And I don't mind speaking in front of you, Miss Freeman. The fact is, Lanie, I've got some money. Enough, at least, to make one payment on this house."

Lanie stared at Roger. For him to make this offer after his father had behaved so badly touched her greatly. "That's so sweet of you, Roger." She smiled warmly. "And it's like you. I don't know anybody else who would do such a thing."

"Oh, lots of fellows would do it."

"What would your family think about this?"

Roger thought about the anger in his father's voice and knew it would be magnified a hundredfold if word of Roger's plan reached his ears. He smiled wanly. "Well, Dad and I don't see eye-to-eye on this thing. I've talked to him and tried to get him to be more lenient, but . . ."

Lanie saw the whole situation then, and she held Corliss tighter and said, "I think it's wonderful of you to take our side."

Roger looked down at the floor. "You know," he said quietly, "it's the first time I ever stood against my father in my whole life."

"It's good to obey your parents, boy, as long as your parents are right," Aunt Kezia said. "But if they ain't, smash 'em in the mouth! Not really, of course. What I mean is be sure you're right, then go ahead. That was Crockett that said that, the fellow that died in the Alamo."

"That's a good motto, Miss Freeman," Roger said. "What about it, Lanie?"

Lanie was tempted, but she knew it must not be. "No, I can't let you do it. It wouldn't solve the problem, Roger. Next month we'll face the same thing all over again. But it's wonderful that you made the offer."

Roger tried to persuade Lanie, but he saw that it was impossible. "I can at least do one thing. I'm going to get the doctor."

"Get Merritt, not that old fogy," Aunt Kezia commanded.

"Yes, ma'am." Roger smiled. "Merritt it is."

⊂══×∾

As soon as Roger stepped inside the door, he was accosted by Nurse Bertha Pickens. "What's wrong with you, Roger?"

"I need to see the doctor."

"Have you got a pain somewhere?"

"It's private."

"You can tell me," Bertha said. "I've heard everything."

Roger smiled. "Not this time, Miss Bertha. It's not really my affair, but I do need to see Dr. Merritt."

"I'll see if he'll talk to you." Bertha walked into the inner office. She came back almost at once and sniffed. "You can go see him now, but I still say you could've told me what the problem is."

Roger stepped through the door and halted, for his sister Louise was standing inside. "Why, Roger, what are you doing here?" she asked.

"I need to talk to Dr. Merritt for a moment."

"What's the matter? Are you sick?" She placed the back of her hand on his forehead. "You haven't said anything."

"No, I'm not sick."

"Well, I wouldn't be surprised if you were after the way you behaved at the dinner table."

Roger clamped his lips together, resolved to say nothing, at least not in front of Louise. Finally he gave Owen Merritt a look, and Owen said, "Would you excuse us, Louise?"

"Now really, Owen, he is my brother. If he's sick, we need to know about it."

Resentment boiled up in Roger. Ignoring her, he said, "Dr. Merritt, Corliss Freeman is very sick."

"Sick? What's wrong with her?" Owen asked with surprise. "I didn't know anything about this."

300

"I was just there," Roger said, aware of the displeasure that had come to mar Louise's smile, "and she needs a doctor."

"Well, why didn't Lanie bring her in?"

"She says she doesn't have the money."

"Well, what foolishness that is!" Owen exclaimed. "She ought to know better than that."

"She's very proud, Dr. Merritt," Roger said, "and, as a matter of fact, I want to pay you for your call."

"Forget about it, Roger. I'll go right over. There'll be no fee for this."

Louise glared at Roger and set her lips in a prim line. "You've lost your balance, Roger! Father will be unhappy over your obsession with that family. He already is."

"What's all this about?" Owen demanded, turning to face Louise.

"Roger got into a fight with Father about his foreclosing on the mortgage on the Freeman place. After all, he is responsible to the stockholders of the bank and didn't have any choice."

"He had plenty of choice," Roger said grimly.

Owen saw the trouble brewing between the two. "Well, I'm going out to see Corliss."

"Could I go with you, Doctor?" Roger asked.

"Sure. Let me get my bag." Owen began equipping his bag.

"I'll be going now," Louise said.

"I'll see you later, Louise," Owen said in a preoccupied fashion. He closed his bag and started out the door, followed by Roger.

"Don't forget. Supper's at seven."

"I may be a little late, Louise. I have several calls to make. Start without me if I don't make it on time."

Louise Langley stood there with a petulant look on her face. Her eyes narrowed, and she formulated a plan. "Wait until Father hears about this. He'll really have a fit!"

⚬═⚬

Lanie opened the door and saw Owen Merritt and Roger standing there. "Roger, I told you not to do this."

"I'm glad he did. Don't be foolish, Lanie. You're too wise a girl for that. Where's Corliss?"

"She's in her bedroom."

"I'll wait here," Roger said. "I usually don't interfere, Lanie, but I was worried about her."

Lanie passed a hand over her forehead. "That's all right, Roger. I'm sorry I was so short. It's just that, well, I've been real worried."

She led Dr. Merritt down the hall into the bedroom on the first floor. Merritt went in, put his bag down, and rubbed his hands together to warm them. "I hate to put cold hands on her, but I need to examine her."

"Here, let me help you." Lanie slipped off Corliss's gown, and the little girl woke up and began crying. "It's all right, sweetheart," Lanie said. "The doctor's going to help you." She held the baby while Merritt examined her.

"It's some kind of upper respiratory problem, but I'm not sure exactly what," he said.

"She'll be all right, won't she?"

"I'm sure she will be. We just have to take very good care of her. I don't have exactly what she needs, but I'll go down to the drugstore and pick it up."

Lanie finished buttoning Corliss's gown and held her against her chest. "I . . . I hate to be such a bother."

"How could you be that?" Dr. Merritt said gravely. He studied the young woman's face. She had a beautiful face, all its features generous and capable of robust emotions, all of them graceful. He saw a hint of her will and her pride in the corners of her lips and eyes and felt a sudden sense of possession. *I've got to take care of these kids, but I've also got to let Lanie keep her pride. She hates charity.* "I'll be back later on in the evening. In the meantime, keep her out of the drafts. She's got a fever now, and we may have to do something about that."

"What is it?"

"It could be something just passing, but there's always a chance of flu. And the one thing we want to avoid is pneumonia."

"I'll do anything you say, Dr. Merritt."

"I know you will." He closed his bag. "That young fellow is pretty determined, isn't he? Roger, I mean."

"I've always thought he was the best of that family." She suddenly caught herself. "I didn't mean to say anything against Louise."

"That's all right." He smiled. "It's only natural that a young girl would think highly of a good-looking chap like Roger. I imagine half the girls in the high school had a crush on him."

"A lot of them did."

"What about you?"

Lanie fussed with Corliss's gown. "Oh, I was too busy to think about things like that."

"He's a fine young fellow." Owen started to say something about the quarrel but immediately knew it would not do. "I'll be going now."

"Thank you for coming, Doctor. I appreciate it."

"Now, Lanie, you let this be a lesson to you. Anytime any of you get sick, you call me at once. You forget about money and things like that. I wish you'd think of me as a member of the family, a dad, perhaps, or an older brother."

Lanie smiled. "All right, Brother Merritt."

Merritt picked up his bag and walked from the room, and Lanie followed him.

"Is she going to be all right?" Roger said.

"Oh, yes. With good care, which she'll get, she'll be fine. I've got to make some more calls. Where can I drop you, Roger?"

"I'll just walk home."

"Stay a while, Roger," Lanie said suddenly. "I want to hear some more about what you've been doing at school."

Roger looked surprised. "All right, I will."

"I'll see you later," Merritt said.

As soon as the door closed, Lanie said, "I made some gingerbread, and we've got coffee."

"That sounds good. I can resist anything except temptation and gingerbread." Roger smiled.

Lanie led him into the kitchen, and he ate several slices of gingerbread and drank the rest of the coffee, talking mostly about his time at school. "Where are all the kids?" he asked.

"They're all at school." She was standing beside a window, and the sunlight coming in from the side illuminated her face.

"I hated that you had to drop out of school, but I admire you for it, Lanie."

"It was something I had to do."

"Most girls wouldn't have looked at it that way. You've missed out on so much." He came over to where she was standing. "Most girls would get bitter if they had to give up school and parties and all that sort of thing."

"I didn't mind missing the parties, but I hated missing the classes. I've been studying a lot at home. I get all the books I can from the library, and I get to read a lot when I'm not working or taking care of the others."

Roger studied Lanie. "You know, I got mad when you beat me out for that grand prize award."

Lanie looked up, her eyes wide. "Why, I didn't know that! You didn't act it."

"Well, I've got a little pride, I guess, and to be beaten out by a girl, especially a freshman! You'll never know the ribbing I took."

"I'm so sorry."

Roger laughed. "Didn't hurt me a bit, and I'm proud you won, Lanie. If you had finished, I'm sure you'd be delivering the valedictorian address."

"Oh, no, I could never do that."

Roger looked at her so closely that Lanie became nervous. "What is it?"

"I was just thinking how you've changed."

"Well, I'm older."

"Yes, you're older. You were just a kid then, and now you're a grown woman." Roger suddenly reached out and put his hands on her shoulders. Lanie looked up, shocked and surprised. He studied her with such an odd expression that she could not imagine what was on his mind. She waited for him to speak, and finally he said, "You're the finest young woman I've ever known, Lanie. You've given up everything for your family, and I admire that."

Lanie was so overwhelmed she could not say a word. She was shocked when he said, "And furthermore you've flowered into one of the most beautiful young women in town, or anywhere else for that matter." He leaned forward and without warning kissed Lanie on the lips. "There," he said, grinning. "Now that's all the kisses you get for today."

Lanie saw that his eyes were dancing, and she could not help but laugh. "You're awful, Roger, just awful!"

"No, I'm not. I'm really a fine chap. You'll like me a lot better when you get to know me."

The two talked lightly, and finally Roger left. She went to the window and watched him as he walked down the sidewalk whistling, his hands in his pockets. He stopped once to look up in a tree at something. As he stood there, she examined his clean, sharp profile. *I got a kiss from Roger Langley. That's something, I guess.*

Over the next two days, Corliss did not improve. Instead, she grew steadily worse. Lanie was almost out of her mind. So were the boys and Maeva. They asked Lanie a hundred times a day, it seemed, "Is she going to be all right?" and finally she grew short with them.

On Wednesday, a cool March evening, Dr. Merritt came by very late, almost nine o'clock. As soon as he stepped inside, he did not need to ask how Corliss was. "I'm glad you came," Lanie said, and there was fear in her voice. "She's worse."

"Let me take a look."

Dr. Merritt followed her into the living room, where she had been rocking Corliss. The boys had built a fire that was now a glowing bed of hot coals with yellow and red flames flickering occasionally. From time to time the wind outside drew the flames up and seemed to utter a wailing cry.

After Dr. Merritt made his examination, he said, "We've got to get this fever down."

"What can we do?" Lanie asked.

"We'll have to put cold cloths on her. I'll hold her while you get a pan and some cool water."

⊂━≺⊱

"What time is it?" Dr. Merritt said sleepily.

Lanie looked at the clock on the wall. "It's almost four in the morning." She was exhausted. Bringing down the stubborn fever had taken all their efforts. Lanie laid her hand on Corliss's brow. The girl slept on the couch. The fire had gone out, and Lanie shivered.

"I think she'll be all right now, Lanie. The fever's broken."

"I'm so worried about her, Dr. Merritt."

"Well, I was, too, to tell the truth. There's not much we can do for things like this. The old herb women have about as much success as all of us doctors."

Lanie turned to him. "I don't know what I would have done if you hadn't come by," she whispered.

Owen Merritt did not answer. He was studying her as he had several times before, but now by the dim light of the single lamp, he admired the richness of her lips. She had a ripe and self-possessed curve in her mouth, and he was, without being conscious of it, comparing her to other women he had known. Where her blouse fell away from her throat, her skin was a smooth ivory, and her auburn hair gave off glints of gold. She had clean-running physical lines. Her shoulders were strong and rounded, and he admired the lines of her throat. He remembered when he first met her. Her hips had been straight as a boy's, and now they were rounded, and his awareness of the lovely curves of her body gave him a start.

She thanked him again, and her lips made a small change at the corners and softened. She made little gestures with her shoulders as she spoke to him. He had thought much about this girl, especially lately, and now he saw in her face an expression that he could not name, though it stirred his curiosity. It was something like the gravity that comes when someone has seen too much. She was looking at him silently, and a great compassion rose up in him. He saw that she was exhausted, and he said gently, "Lanie, you've had too much for a young woman to bear." He was shocked when he saw the tears start in her eyes and then run down her cheeks. "Oh, Lanie, there's no need to cry." He put his arms around her, and she laid her head down on his chest. He felt the tremors in her body as she wept. She was utterly vulnerable then, and when she lifted her face it was only inches from his.

"It's all right," he said. And then almost without volition, out of the compassion that he felt for her but also something more, he leaned forward and kissed her. A shock ran through him for her lips were softer than he had dreamed, and he felt her arms tightening as she clung to him almost fiercely. It was not the kiss that he had meant to give, and as he held her, the heat of something thoughtless brushed against his spirit. Then she suddenly pulled away from him, and he saw that she was trembling. "You shouldn't have done that," she whispered.

"I . . . I'm sorry." But inwardly he knew that he did not in any way regret what he had done. The caress had shaken him, for he had stepped across a line that he had not known existed. "I didn't intend to do that." He struggled to find the words. "It's just that I admire you so much."

"You must never do it again. You're a promised man, Dr. Merritt."

He felt the sting of her words and saw that somehow he had hurt her deeply. "I'm sorry, Lanie. Just forget it."

He left the Freeman house, but he knew that he would carry the memory of that kiss for longer than he might have wished.

⤏ CHAPTER 31 ⤐

The quarrel seemed to explode without warning. Owen arrived at the Langley household for dinner and noticed that a cool air pervaded the household. Roger had devised plenty of schemes to avoid the family since his run-in with his father, and Helen was visiting a friend. Louise and her parents spoke mainly to one another. He tried to join in the conversation but got little response.

After dinner they all moved into the drawing room and listened to the radio, but Otis and Martha soon found an excuse to leave. Louise got up to turn the radio off and put a record on. "I seem to be in the doghouse, Louise."

Louise was holding a gramophone record in her hand, and she put it down and then clasped her hands together in an angry motion. "My parents are very unhappy with you."

"About what?"

"I think you know. You've been spending entirely too much time at the Freeman house."

Surprise washed across Owen's face. "What are you talking about? They have a sick child over there."

"This is a small town, Owen," Louise said. "It doesn't look right for you to spend the entire night at a patient's house, especially a woman patient."

"A woman? Corliss is not even three years old!"

Louise made a frustrated gesture. "I'm not talking about the baby! I'm talking about Lanie!"

A touch of anger brushed across Owen Merritt. He was being punished by the Langleys for doing his job. He got to his feet. "Louise, I'm willing to listen to you and your family when you have something to say about my personal life, but when it comes to my profession, I'm not."

It was the strictest tone he had ever taken with Louise, and she knew that she had gone too far. "Well, it's just that—"

"We might as well settle this right now. If what my job requires bothers you—and your family—so much, then it wouldn't be a good idea for us to marry." His voice was even, and Louise knew she had stirred up a side of Owen Merritt she had not known existed.

"But, Owen, can't you see—"

"I can see that you're jealous of one of the finest girls I've ever known. She's straight as a string, Louise, and she's got enough character to stock a seminary. There's nothing going on between Lanie Freeman and me and there never will be, but as a doctor I will be calling on homes, and there'll be women in those homes. I've seen some good marriages break up because doctors' wives couldn't understand that this is part of our responsibility."

"I'm sorry, Owen," she said, and forced herself to speak gently. "I was wrong."

Owen studied her. "Yes, you were, and I think you'd better consider what it would be like to be married to a doctor. There are some unpleasant sides to it for wives. Doctors aren't their own masters at times. They're the servants of their patients. I'll be gone for long periods of time. I'll be called out at night. At times you'll have to attend parties alone."

Louise sought some way to repair the damage. She put her hands on his shoulders and lifted her head. "I am sorry," she whispered and put herself against him. This had always worked before, but now he was unyielding.

"I'll be going," he said. "You think about what I've said. Good night, Louise."

Louise stood there unable to think of a single appeal that might make him stop. She heard the front door close and found herself trembling, for she was a proud woman and had always been able to control the men she liked. But she understood that Owen was deeply hurt by her behavior. She knew she would have to speak to her family, and she knew also that she would have to, in effect, win him back. She made her way upstairs and knocked on her parents' bedroom door. When she walked in, her parents were getting ready for bed. "I have to talk to you. It's about Owen."

Aunt Kezia looked at the kitchen calendar, at the circle around March twenty-sixth. Lanie was seated at the table staring listlessly at her hands. The house was quiet. The boys and Maeva were outside and Corliss was asleep. "Well, it ain't the end of the world, Lanie."

"It seems like it to me." Lanie looked around the kitchen with longing. "This is the only home we've ever known. Now we'll have to be split up. I don't see any way out."

"It irritates me," Aunt Kezia said as she sat down across from Lanie. "If that idjit husband of mine hadn't spent all our money on that hussy, I could pay off that note!"

"I know you would, Aunt Kezia." Lanie enclosed her aunt's hands in both of hers. "I was looking at an old house that we could have for only ten dollars a month. It's not much, but we've got to go somewhere."

Aunt Kezia felt Lanie's strong and capable hands. "We're gonna be all right, honey. I don't know how, but God's done give me a promise."

"What kind of a promise?"

"It wasn't nothin' very definite, but I got skeered last night. I felt like I did the time we was in Oregon and the Injuns went on the rampage. They was burnin' houses, scalpin' men, attackin' women, and carryin' off children and all sorts of devilment. We was right in the middle of it. I was so skeered I couldn't even swallow, and I cried out to the Lord. He didn't say nothin' in no words, but all of a sudden all my fear went away." The old woman's eyes dimmed with tears. "I ain't never forgot that. God took all that fear away, and the same thing has been happenin' to me lately. Every time I try to tell God how to handle this business and tell Him how skeered we all are, He don't answer me, but the fear and the aggravation just all goes away. It's kind of like He has me inside a big ball. Outside there are storms and wind and meanness and all kinds of bad things, but inside there's just me and the good Lord."

Lanie smiled. "That's wonderful, Aunt Kezia."

"Yes it is. You just hang on now. God's gonna rear back and do a miracle!"

"We won't be havin' many more meals in this house."

It was Maeva who spoke. They were gathered for breakfast, but none of them had much appetite except Aunt Kezia. As usual, she ate like a field hand. With her mouth full of scrambled eggs, she said, "You don't know that, Maeva."

"This is the day that they're gonna foreclose, ain't it?" Maeva muttered.

"Maybe so, maybe not. There ain't no sense you sittin' there lookin' like you et green persimmons."

"What are we going to do, Lanie?" Davis said. "Where are we gonna live?"

"We're probably going to move into that house by the stockyards, out by the siding."

"That old shack!" Cody said. "Why, a good wind would blow it away. It ain't been lived in in years."

"It'll have to do," Lanie said calmly. To her amazement she awakened on this day, the worst of her life, the day they were scheduled to lose their home, and a sense of peace had come to her. She thought at once of how God had shielded Aunt Kezia emotionally during the Indian attack, and now she was able to smile and say, "There's a whole new tomorrow out there that hasn't been touched yet. God hasn't given up on us."

"If we only had the money to pay that durned old note!" Cody exclaimed.

Aunt Kezia dug into the strawberry jam with a spoon and liberally layered a biscuit with it. "If a toady frog had wings, he wouldn't bump his rear!" She grunted. "Now you hush up, Cody!"

They finished breakfast, but they sat at the table talking about how they would have to get someone to move their furniture to the shack. Maeva lifted her head. She was holding Corliss in her lap. "Somebody's comin'. I hear a car."

"Probably that danged old Langley come to get his pound of flesh," Davis said.

Lanie got up. "Now you be nice no matter who comes or what they say." She walked to the window and looked out, then said with surprise, "Why, it's not the bank! It's Miss Patton, and there's a man with her."

"Who is it?" Aunt Kezia demanded. "Does he look like law?"

"No, he doesn't look it."

The man was short and fat and he had a dark complexion.

"You all remember—no complaining."

She walked to the door and opened it before Miss Patton could knock. "Come in, Miss Patton. You're just in time to have breakfast. There's plenty left."

Elspeth Patton stepped inside and smiled. "No, we didn't come for breakfast, but we have business."

"Well, come in."

Miss Patton did not introduce the man with her. He wore a dark suit with a snow-white shirt and a solid gold watch chain spanned his generous belly. He had thick hands with stubby fingers. His nails were manicured and he smelled like the barber shop, with some sort of lotion.

In the kitchen, Miss Patton said, "Good morning, children. I want you all to meet someone. This is Mr. Otto Franz."

Mr. Franz had taken off his hat and now bowed slightly. "I am glad to meet you all." Mr. Franz was some sort of a Yankee. He spoke with an accent that none of them recognized.

"Let me fix you some coffee at least," Lanie said.

"No, we're here on business." Every eye turned to the man beside Elspeth. "I'd like for you to let Mr. Franz look over your house."

"Why, of course, Miss Patton," Lanie said. "Mr. Franz, you're thinking about buying the house?"

"The house? No, I don't buy houses. I buy furniture."

Miss Patton said, "Mr. Franz owns one of the largest antique stores in St. Louis. When I was here the last time I noticed the clock over the mantel in the living room, and I also saw that you had a great many old pieces."

"We sure do," Davis said. "All of it's old. We never get to buy no new stuff."

"That may be a very fortunate thing, young man," Mr. Franz said with a smile.

"We can't sell our furniture. It's all old and used, but it's all we have," Lanie said.

Miss Patton laughed. "Oh, I think you may be able to come to some sort of terms. Is it all right if we look around?"

"Why sure, but like I said, we've got to hang onto our furniture."

"Come along, Otto." The two left the room, and Aunt Kezia said, "Maybe we can sell enough of the furniture to make the payments for a couple of months. I think they might put up with that."

"I don't think so. Even if we made our payments that are past due, we couldn't keep them up. But maybe we can sell some of the things for enough to fix that old house up."

They waited, but apparently Otto Franz was not in any hurry. Finally they did the dishes and started their chores, but Otto and Miss Patton continued to walk around the house, going into every room.

Finally they came out, and Miss Patton said, "Don't you have some furniture stored out in the barn?"

"Yes, up in the loft. It's just old dressers and stuff like that," Lanie said.

"We'd better look at it," Mr. Franz said. He was smiling broadly, and he winked at Lanie. "You never know when you find a treasure."

"You won't find any treasures in that loft," Davis said. "Come on and I'll show you."

"I'll wait here," Miss Patton said. "You go with Davis, Otto. I think I'll take that coffee now if I may."

"Oh, yes, there's plenty. You sure you won't have some eggs or a biscuit or something?"

"No, thank you."

Lanie poured the cup full of coffee and put it in front of Elspeth. She sat down and watched as the woman put sugar and cream in it. "It was real nice of you, Miss Patton, to think of us like this."

"We've had every church in town praying for you, and when I saw that clock, I thought of my friend Otto. He knows antiques like no man I ever saw. As a matter of fact, I would like to buy some of your furniture myself."

"Oh, yes, anything you want!"

"Better wait." Elspeth's eyes were dancing. "This furniture may be worth more than you think."

⚬⛌⚬

Otto Franz returned with Davis and insisted that the family gather in the living room. He waited until they were all seated, rubbed his hands together, and nodded three times. "Yes, yes, yes! You have many fine things here, and I would like to make you an offer on all of it."

"Remember, Otto, I know a little bit about prices myself." Miss Patton smiled. "You're not going to give these children a bad price."

"Would I do such a thing?" Otto Franz rolled his eyes. He walked to the clock that Elspeth had admired. "If I were buying this by the piece, I would make you an offer on this. I would offer you two hundred dollars."

"Two hundred dollars!" Maeva yelled. "We'll take it."

"Not so fast!" Miss Patton laughed. "That clock is worth more than that."

"I have to make a profit, Elspeth," Otto protested, "but maybe I could go as high as three."

"For that old clock! Why, it don't even run," Cody said.

"You don't understand antiques," Miss Patton explained. "The thing that makes this furniture valuable is how many are available. This clock is very rare, so it's worth a lot of money."

"You see that table over there?" Otto gestured at a table that bore a lamp beside the settee. "That's a Majolica Jardiniere stand. It's worth at least four hundred dollars."

"We'll take six!" Aunt Kezia yelped.

Otto's eyes widened, and he grinned. "I see you have a bargainer here. He pulled a piece of paper out of his pocket. "Well, I have made a list of the things I can use and put a price beside each one. As I say, I would like to take the whole lot. There are some pieces out in the barn that would have to be restored, but they are good pieces."

"How much?" Maeva demanded.

"Yes, how much?" Aunt Kezia said.

Otto Franz looked around the room and smiled. "I cannot offer you more than seven thousand for the whole lot."

Silence took over the room until Aunt Kezia yelped, "Well, hallelujah, God's done come through again!"

Then they were all talking and yelling. Davis and Maeva were doing a dance around the living room floor, and Cody grabbed Corliss and was swinging her around. Lanie felt herself trembling all over. "That's enough to pay off all the loan and have enough left to buy furniture."

"Let's get new stuff," Maeva said. "I'm tired of this old junk."

Elspeth Patton laughed. "I think it's a fair price. I've gone over it with Otto. Lanie, I think you and I need to make a trip to the bank. Otto, if you'll write a check, we'll take it with us."

"Of course. You're getting a good deal, but then, so am I." Mr. Franz laughed. He whipped out a checkbook, sat down at the table, and made out a check for $7,000. He handed it to Lanie. "There you are, Miss."

"Thank you, Mr. Franz." Lanie stared at the check, and the others gathered around her. She handed it to Aunt Kezia, who studied it and said, "You know what? I think we'd better stop right now and thank the good Lord for deliverin' us. I see His hand in this."

"That's a good idea," Lanie said. They all bowed their heads, even Mr. Franz and Miss Patton, and Lanie prayed a simple prayer. "Lord, we all thank You for sending Mr. Franz and Miss Patton to help us. It's Your doing. You used these good people, and we all thank You for it. And we continue to pray that You would deliver our daddy from prison. You've done so many miracles, and we ask for one more. In Jesus' name. Amen."

The news of the Freeman family's great deliverance went all over Fairhope. In almost every house the telephones were ringing, and every church in town that had a bell began ringing it.

One house, however, didn't share in the celebrations. Otis Langley received a call from Effie Johnson. "The loan is paid in full, Otis. I know you'll be sorry to hear that."

Otis was unable to answer. He went home that night and shared the news.

"Roger will be glad to hear it," his wife said, "and I think it is a good thing. I know you wanted that property, Otis, but it is the children's home."

Louise said little. She had been waiting to see Owen when the news came by way of the nurse, and Owen's face glowed with joy. He turned and hugged Bertha, lifting her clear up off the floor, and shouted, "Hallelujah!"

Louise tried to play her role. "I'm so happy for them. Nobody really wanted to see them lose their place."

Owen scarcely heard. "I've got to get over there and congratulate them." He seemed to notice Louise for the first time. "Would you like to come along?"

"No, you go along. I'll see them later."

At the Freeman house, Owen found a celebration in progress. He hugged every one of them, including Aunt Kezia, but when he came to Lanie, he found himself filled with inhibitions. She looked up at him, and he knew she was thinking of the kiss he had given her. Instead of hugging her, he stuck out his hand, and when she took it, he enclosed it with both of his. "I'm so happy for you, Lanie."

"Thank you, Dr. Merritt."

"Don't you think you could call me something besides Dr. Merritt?"

"Like what?"

"Like Owen."

"Maybe someday." Lanie smiled. "It is wonderful, isn't it?"

"It's a glorious miracle."

"Doc Merritt," Aunt Kezia said, "you done hugged everybody including this old woman. Now give that gal a hug."

Owen's face suddenly flushed. "I can't do that, Miss Freeman. She's a grown woman now. One of her boyfriends might get jealous and beat me up."

Aunt Kezia cackled. "That fiancée of yours has already got you under her thumb. You just missed a mighty good huggin' is all I've got to say."

"You hush, Aunt Kezia," Lanie said. Her hand was still in Owen's grip, and she looked up at him and smiled. "You'll have to come over for supper and bring Miss Langley with you sometime. We've got a home now."

"Yes you have, and I thank God for it." He grew conscious of her hand in his and dropped it suddenly. "Well, I've got to be going."

As soon as the door closed behind him, Maeva whispered, "You're still stuck on him, ain't you?"

"Hush, Maeva!" Lanie said.

"I can tell. And you can take him away from that stuck-up Louise Langley."

"Don't be saying such things!"

Maeva winked at her. "You can do it. He likes you. I can tell."

Aunt Kezia had been taking all this in. "That's right. I know how to get men. You and me will have to have some lessons together."

"You're both being foolish!" Lanie said and angrily turned away. "Don't ever mention such a thing again."

⚬⚬⚬

The house was different now, for a big truck had backed up and emptied it of all of its antiques. Cash in hand erased any regrets about the old furniture, and Lanie and the others had fun buying replacements. Much of what they got was secondhand, but Lanie was thrilled with a brand-new electric icebox that made its own ice. Cody was even more thrilled. "Now I won't have to empty that dumb ol' drip pan anymore!" he said exultantly.

The furniture arrived, yet Lanie could not take it all in. They went to church the following Sunday, and everyone applauded when she and her family entered. Pastor Prince declared a day of thanksgiving for God's deliverance of one of their own. Lanie heard later that the same sort of celebration took place in the Presbyterian church, in the Pentecostal church, and in the Methodist Episcopal church as well.

On Thursday, Orrin Pierce dropped by for a visit. Lanie was cooking supper, and she wiped her hands on her apron and invited him in. "I've got the papers from the bank," he said, handing her an envelope. "This place is paid for and in the clear. Congratulations again, Lanie."

"It was the Lord that did it, but, of course, He used Miss Patton and Mr. Franz."

"Have you told your father yet?"

"Not yet. We're going to see him tomorrow, all of us."

Orrin hesitated. "I've got some news, and I'm not sure your father needs to hear it just yet. But I'm going to tell you, and you can decide."

Lanie set the papers on the counter and sat down with a sense of foreboding. "What is it, Mr. Pierce?"

"Pardue found out that there was another witness to the shooting of Duke Biggins, a Thelma Mays. She left town and Pardue was told she went to Los Angeles. Doc Merritt's brother Dave is a policeman in Los Angeles. He's on the hunt for this woman."

"What does it mean?" Lanie said.

"It means we've got a witness who might tell us the truth about what happened on the day Duke Biggins was shot. I've never believed Alvin or Ethel. They'd perjure themselves in a minute."

"You mean there's hope my daddy might get out of prison?"

Pierce hesitated. "It's just a chance, Lanie. Dave's working on it, so don't give up."

"I'll never give up, Mr. Pierce."

"Do you think you'll tell your daddy?"

"I think I will. He needs all the hope he can get. Thank you so much for trying to help us like this."

"Then you tell him I'm working on it."

"I will, Mr. Pierce."

Forrest was sitting on a bench stroking the silky ears of Booger, his favorite of the warden's bloodhounds. He knew the dogs were used to run down escaped prisoners, but he couldn't help loving them. The big dog rested his chin on Forrest's knee and looked up at him with soulful eyes. Warden Gladden stuck his head out the back door. "Forrest, you've got visitors! The whole bunch of 'em, even the old woman. She's threatened to shoot me if I didn't get you there."

"Well, she might do it, Warden." He chuckled and put Booger back in the pen with the rest of the bloodhounds. He went to the visiting room and was swarmed, as always, by the children. Maeva held him tightly. "You look good, Daddy. You're all tanned, and you've gained weight."

"It's a pretty good job I've got, just taking care of a bunch of dogs and one horse. It doesn't pay much, but it's easy."

The warden had come in with Forrest, and he sat to one side talking with Cody, who wanted to know all about the prison, "You got any cold-blooded killers here, Warden?"

The question amused Gladden. "Well, I ain't taken the temperature of their blood, but we've got some men who are here because they killed folks."

"I'd like to meet the meanest one you got."

The warden laughed. "Why in the world would you want to do that?"

"I may want to become a lawyer, and I need to know what they're like."

"Well, I think you'd make a good one, boy. But I'll tell you, instead of meeting a killer, why don't you come on with me. I'll introduce you to our dogs. You like dogs?"

"Sure."

"I do too," Davis said. "Can I go, Warden?"

"Anybody can go that wants to."

"I want to see them dogs," Maeva said.

"I'm gonna take these three young'uns with me to see the dogs, Forrest. I'll bring 'em back in good shape."

"Thanks, Warden." Forrest had Corliss on his lap, and she was stroking his face. "She sure looks like her mama, doesn't she, Lanie?"

"Just like her, Daddy."

"Now, tell me all about how you managed to save the place."

"It wasn't me, Daddy. It was the Lord." Lanie related the full story to him, and she took an envelope out of the purse. "Here's the mortgage. You see, it says 'Canceled.' It's all paid for. When you get out, you can come right home to your own place."

Forrest Freeman ran his hand over the paper. He did not look up for a long time, and when he did, Lanie was somewhat shocked to see tears glimmering in his eyes. "I never was much of a crybaby, but this sure touches me. You done fine, Lanie."

"It wasn't me."

"Yes, it was. You're the one who's held this family together, and I'm mighty proud of you, Muff." He held his arms out, and Lanie hugged him. "You're a grown woman," he whispered, his face against her smooth cheek. "Beautiful like your mama and tough like me."

Lanie held onto her father and then drew back and took a deep breath. "I've got somethin' else to tell you. It's something Mr. Pierce told me." She proceeded to tell him about the missing witness. "Did you know that she was in the next room?"

"No, I didn't have no idea, but I know Thelma Mays. She's about as worthless as Duke and Alvin."

"But if they find her, and she tells the truth, Mr. Pierce says that'll make a difference. Then he could get you a new trial."

Hope came into Forrest's eyes. "That would be a miracle, but God's done miracles before, hasn't He?"

"And He'll get you out of here too. I know He will, Daddy."

The two talked quietly for a while, and finally he asked, "How's that Dr. Merritt?"

Something changed in Lanie's face, and he did not miss it. "He's engaged to Louise Langley."

"I know. Aunt Kezia told me. Listen, I don't know any man who deserves you, but this doctor sounds like he comes close."

"Oh, Daddy, I'm just a little girl to him!"

"You ain't no little girl no more, and if he's as smart as Aunt Kezia says he is, God's gonna open his eyes. And when he looks at you, he's gonna see a full-grown woman that's got love to offer such as he's never dreamed of."

Lanie dropped her head and stared down at her hands.

Forrest laughed. "I believe God's going to get me out of this place, honey, and I think He's gonna do somethin' with you. Now, come on.

I want you to see those dogs. The best one is one called Booger. He reminds me of you in a way."

"I remind you of a dog called Booger? That's awful, Daddy!"

"He's the pick of the litter, hon. He's loyal and just filled up with affection. Just lookin' for a place to put it." He squeezed her, then kissed her cheek. "Just like you. Come on now. Let's go see old Booger."

CHAPTER 32

Getting everyone to bed took longer than Lanie had anticipated. Even Corliss Jeanne seemed to have caught the excitement of the day, and it took more than an hour before she went to sleep.

Finally Lanie tiptoed out of the baby's room, leaving the door open so she could hear if she cried. Lanie realized she was very tired. She went into the kitchen. The fire had burned down to coals in the cookstove, but the coffee pot was still on. Getting a cup, she poured it full and then sat on a kitchen chair and let the silence of the house soak into her. A good feeling came to her. For months she had been living on the edge of fear—fear of losing the house, of the children being put in foster homes, of so many other things. She sipped the coffee and let herself relax and felt the weariness seep into her bones.

Beau came over and plopped his big legs down in her lap. She grunted and laughed. "You want something good to eat? You always want something. Let's see if we've got any biscuits."

She found two overlooked biscuits that were rather hard. She broke these into quarters and tossed one of the morsels to Beau, who snapped it out of the air. He swallowed it in one gulp and nudged her with his nose.

"Don't be so greedy. You're going to get them all. I declare, Beau, I believe you'd eat rocks if I fed them to you."

Beau had just finished the last of the biscuits when Lanie heard a tap on the front door. Beau growled low, and Lanie wondered who would possibly call at this time of night.

She turned on the front light and looked through the glass. Roger Langley was standing outside. She opened the door and stepped out. "Roger, what are you doing here? It's late."

"I had to see you, Lanie."

"Everybody's asleep. If we're going to talk, we'd better stay out here."

"That's all right. I just came by to tell you something." Roger seemed agitated. He was wearing his football jacket with a big "F" on it for Fairhope, and his fair hair was mussed as if he had forgotten to comb it. He bit his lower lip nervously.

"What's wrong, Roger? Is someone ill?"

"No, it's not that, but . . . well, to make a long story short, I've had a run-in with my dad."

"About what?"

"Well, actually it was about you and your family. A while back I tried to talk Dad out of foreclosing on you. He got angry about it so he told me to leave the house."

Lanie stared at him. "The bank didn't foreclose, so you can go home."

"No, I'm not going to do that," Roger said. He ran his hand across his lean cheek, and then words began pouring out of him. "We've been at it again. See, when all this came up, I realized I'd never done anything on my own, Lanie. Everything I've done has been to please my dad."

"That's not a bad thing, to want to please your father."

"It can be. I'm a man now, and I've decided it's time for me to make it on my own. I'm never going to take any more help from my family. I've got some college left, and I'm going to save money so I can pay my own tuition."

"Are you sure that's what you want to do? It may take a while."

Roger grinned. "I know what you're thinking. You're thinking I'm too soft, that I've had it easy and, well, I've been thinking the same thing myself. Do I really have the right stuff or not?" His lips tightened and he nodded. "That's what I've got to find out. Am I a man or just a kid living off his family?"

Lanie was surprised. Though she'd never had a similar problem, she knew Roger needed encouragement. "I think that's wonderful, Roger," she said firmly, "and you can do it too. I know you can."

"Do you really think so, Lanie?"

"Of course I do!"

"While I was making this decision I thought about you. I'm going to get a job here for at least six months to save enough money to go back to school in the fall." He hesitated, then said, "And what I'd like is for us to see more of each other."

Lanie could not answer for a moment. "You mean like you want to come courting?"

"That's what I mean, Lanie. I think you're the finest girl I've ever known." He reached out and touched her cheek and smiled. "You're not the skinny little freshman that beat me out for the award. You're a grown woman now. What about it? Will it be all right?"

Lanie could not think for a moment. It never once had occurred to her that Roger Langley would ever be interested in her this way.

"Why, Roger, I never thought of you like that."

"Well, start." Roger's grin widened. "I'm just saying we could take in a movie once in a while, go for walks. I'd enjoy someone like you to talk to."

"Yes, I think I could do that, Roger, but do you—" The sound of an automobile broke the silence of the night. She turned to see a car pull up. "That's Dr. Merritt. What's he doing here this time of the night?"

"You didn't send for him? Nobody's sick?"

"No."

They both waited until Owen Merritt came up the steps. "Hello, Roger."

"Hello, Dr. Merritt."

"What's wrong?" Lanie asked.

"I came over to talk to you. What are you doing here, Roger? Your dad's waiting for you."

"He'll wait a long time," Roger said.

Owen stared at him. "What does that mean?"

"It means I'm moving out. I'm going to make my own way. I've just been telling Lanie about it."

Owen shook his head. "Don't be foolish. You've got to finish your education."

"I will, but I've decided that for once, I'm going to do something on my own."

Owen's eyes narrowed, "And you came over to tell Lanie about it?"

"That and to ask her if she'd be willing to see me. I'll be working here for at least a few months, so I asked if I could call on her now and then."

"Well, you can't," Owen said.

Lanie looked surprised and started to say something, but Owen said, "She doesn't need any more problems."

Roger Langley stared at Owen for a long time, then said, "I know what your problem is, Dr. Merritt. You're in love with Lanie yourself."

"That's ridiculous! Now you go home and make up with your father."

Lanie saw by the porch light that Roger's accusation had shaken Dr. Merritt. He refused to look at her and raised his voice. "You go on home now. Don't be a fool." And then for emphasis, he gave Roger a slight push.

Roger pushed back. "You go home and make up with Louise. You're engaged to my sister, and here you are coming to see another woman!"

"You can leave right now! Stop pushing me." Owen gave Roger another shove and soon the two men were engaged in a wrestling match.

Suddenly Lanie cried out, "Both of you, leave!"

When they stopped struggling and turned to her, she said, "You're acting like kids. Now go home."

Roger straightened his jacket. "I'm sorry it came to this, Lanie. I didn't come to argue." He gave her a faint smile and winked, "How about going to the movies tomorrow night?"

"That'll be fine, Roger. You go along now."

"See you tomorrow."

As soon as Roger left, Owen said, "Good, he needs to go home. And I need to talk to you."

But Lanie said, "So, it's ridiculous to think that you'd be interested in me."

"I didn't mean it that way."

Tears came to Lanie's eyes. She could not explain them, and she hated for him to see them. In a tight voice she said, "Go on back to Louise, Owen."

"Yeah, go on back to that dishwater blonde."

Startled, both Lanie and Owen looked up. They saw Aunt Kezia in her nightgown and a nightcap leaning out of an upstairs bedroom window. She did not turn the volume of her voice down. "Doc Merritt, go someplace and grow up. You come up here, Lanie, and I'll tell you about what worthless critters men are!"

Lanie turned to go, but Owen took her arm. "Wait! I don't think it's ridiculous that a man would be interested in you. I . . . I think you're the sweetest girl I've ever known."

"You're an engaged man. It's not proper for you to talk to me like that."

Owen made a face and shrugged his shoulders. "I may not be engaged any longer." He reached out and put his hand on her shoulder and turned her to face him. "I'm sorry this all happened." He put his hand under her chin and lifted her face. "Don't cry," he whispered. "We can't let anything come between us. You and I," he said quietly, "I believe we could be something pretty special." He waited for her to speak and saw that she could not. "Good night. I'll see you tomorrow."

Lanie watched him leave and then went inside the house. The lights came on, startling her, and the whole family applauded and cheered. Davis put his two fingers in his mouth and gave a piercing whistle.

"What are you all doing up?" Lanie demanded.

"We came to see the show," Maeva said. "You are something, Lanie. You man-killer, you." Her voice was filled with merriment, and she could not control the grin that came to her lips. "You've got a doctor and the son of the richest man in town chasing you."

"Yeah, I vote for Roger," Cody yelped. "He's rich!"

"No," Davis said, "you'd better take Dr. Merritt. He's already got it made. Besides, we'll have all of our doctor bills paid."

Lanie's face turned crimson. "You go to bed, every one of you. You should be ashamed, listening in on private conversations!"

As she ran up the stairs, Maeva called after her, "You ought not to play love scenes on the front porch at the top of your lungs."

"You children go to bed," Aunt Kezia said. Her eyes were flashing. "I'll go up there and tell Lanie how the cow ate the cabbage."

Aunt Kezia gave several more dire warnings and went upstairs. She paused outside of Lanie's door and knocked.

"Go away!"

"Let me in, Lanie, I need to talk."

"I don't want to talk."

But Aunt Kezia persisted and finally said, "If you don't let me in, I'll stand here all night."

A muffled "Come on in" came through the door.

Lanie was seated on the bed, tears streaming down her cheeks. "That was just awful," she said.

"No, it was fine."

"Fine! How can you say that?"

"Well, I enjoyed every bit of it. You need to let both them fellows dangle a little while."

"I don't want any men dangling."

Aunt Kezia sat down on the bed and put her thin arm around Lanie's shoulders. "Sure you do, honey. That's part of growin' up. A fine girl like you is gonna have fellas comin' around. And it does a fellow good to dangle. I was hopin' they'd get into a real fist fight and bloody each other up."

"Why in the world would you wish that?"

"Because you could tell which one of them was serious. Whichever one fought the hardest, that'd be the one to tie to."

Lanie sighed and laughed ruefully. "One is engaged and the other has a family that hates me. He doesn't even have a job."

"Oh, that's fine. Mighty fine," Aunt Kezia said. "You don't have to decide nothin' tonight. Like I say, let 'em dangle." She pulled Lanie's head close and kissed her on the cheek. "Let God have a little time to work. He'll sort it out." She went to the door, then turned around and winked. "It may not be either one of them, Lanie. I can't wait to see what God's got in store for you." She shut the door softly, and Lanie listened to her footsteps going down the hall. Then she heard the bedroom door close.

For a long time Lanie sat on the bed. Finally she got up, undressed, put on her gown, and got into bed. She lay there for a few moments, and then Cap'n Brown leaped on the bed and shoved his head against hers. She reached over and stroked his fur, trying to sort out her heart. The moon was silver, a perfect disk. She could see it clearly, and she watched it as she stroked the big cat.

"There are so many problems," she whispered. "Daddy's still in prison and may not get out anytime soon. Davis still can't read. I don't know what we're gonna do about that. And Maeva—she's just a stick of dynamite waiting to explode." She weighed the problems that stretched out ahead of her and wondered how to get this family raised.

"I wish Mama were here, and I wish Daddy weren't in prison." But wishful thinking didn't help. She lay there for a long time and finally started growing sleepy. More than once she thought of what would happen to the Freemans of Fairhope in the days to come, but she prayed, and God gave her a strong sense of freedom and ease.

Her thoughts turned to the scene that had taken place on the front porch, and she smiled. Finally she whispered, "Mrs. Lanie Belle Merritt. How do you like that, Cap'n Brown?"

"Wow!"

"You like it? What about this? Mrs. Lanie Belle Langley."

Cap'n Brown began to purr like a small engine. He curled up next to her, and as Lanie Belle Freeman dropped off to sleep, the moon cast its argent beams on the face of the sleeping girl and then suddenly was covered by a drifting cloud.

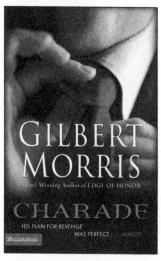

The Spider Catcher

Gilbert Morris

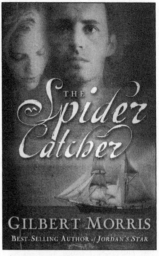

He is a young Welshman who forsook the family shipbuilding business to study medicine . . . until, poised at the brink of a brilliant career, tragedy broke his heart and shattered his dreams.

She is a daughter of London's inner city, a woman-child weaned on life's harsh realities who has learned much about fending for her living and her virtue but little of what it means to be loved.

Thrown together by circumstance, Rees Kenyon and Callie Summers head across the ocean toward a new life during the stormy beginnings of the American Revolution. As a new nation struggles for independence, Rees employs his medical knowledge to save lives, and his shipbuilder's skills to build the potent fighting vessel known as the "spider catcher."

But it is Callie, whom Rees scooped from the mud of the London streets, on whom his own life will soon depend . . . and who can help him find for himself the faith, hope, and love he has taught her.

Softcover: 0-310-24698-9

Pick up a copy today at your favorite bookstore!

ZONDERVAN™

GRAND RAPIDS, MICHIGAN 49530 USA

WWW.ZONDERVAN.COM

The Ultimate Journey.
The Impossible Decision.

Jordan's Star

Gilbert Morris

Bound for the Oregon frontier, Jordan Bryce and her new husband, Colin, a dashing ex-mariner, face danger from both man and nature: a deadly buffalo stampede ... tragedy at a river crossing ... hostile Indians ... and hatred within their wagon train, escalating from bitter words to the point of bloodshed. All that separates the Bryce's party from disaster is seasoned leadership, the skillful guidance of Ty Sublette, and the hand of God.

For Jordan, the journey west is more than a trip into an untamed land. It is a passage from a teenage girl's romantic fantasies to the wisdom and character of womanhood. But nothing can prepare Jordan for the testing that awaits her beyond the journey's end. There, in the face of staggering circumstances, she will face an impossible decision ... as two good men—one wounded by past grief, the other branded by his own impetuousness—struggle with the demands of faith and honor on behalf of the woman they love.

Softcover: 0-310-22754-2

Pick up a copy today at your favorite bookstore!

ZONDERVAN™

GRAND RAPIDS, MICHIGAN 49530 USA

WWW.ZONDERVAN.COM

Jacob's Way

Gilbert Morris

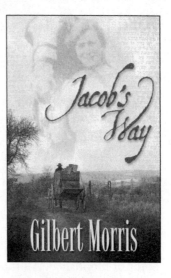

Fleeing a bloody pogrom that threatens their tiny Russian village, Reisa Dimitri and her grandfather, Jacob, sail the ocean to a new life in America. They are swiftly embraced by New York's Jewish community. But God has other plans that will call them far from the familiar warmth and ways of their culture.

Accompanied by their huge, gentle friend, Dov, Reisa and Jacob set out to make their living as traveling merchants in the post–Civil War South. There, as new and unexpected friendships unfold, the aged Jacob searches for answers concerning the nature of the Messiah he has spent a lifetime looking and longing for. And there, the beautiful Reisa finds herself strangely drawn to Ben Driver—a man with a checkered past, a painful present, and a deadly enemy who will stop at nothing to destroy him.

Softcover: 0-310-22696-1

Pick up a copy today at your favorite bookstore!

ZONDERVAN™

GRAND RAPIDS, MICHIGAN 49530 USA

WWW.ZONDERVAN.COM

Edge of Honor

Gilbert Morris

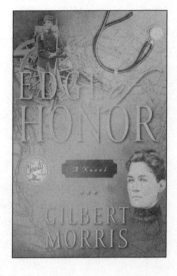

Quentin Larribee is a surgeon—one of the best. But in the confusion of one of the Civil War's last, desperate skirmishes, the hands devoted to healing bring death to William Breckenridge, an enemy soldier in the act of surrendering. Now the deed haunts Quentin.

A bright future lies before him, with marriage to the lovely Irene Chambers and eventual ownership of her father's prosperous medical practice. But it cannot ease Quentin's troubled conscience. Honor compels him to see to the welfare of the dead man's family. Quentin moves from New York City to the little town of Helena, Arkansas, where he attempts to save the wife of Breckenridge and her children from financial ruin.

Edge of Honor is an unforgettable novel of redemption and honor, where good is found in the unlikeliest places and God's unseen hand weaves a masterful tapestry of human hearts and lives.

Softcover: 0-310-24302-5

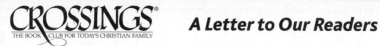

CROSSINGS®
THE BOOK CLUB FOR TODAY'S CHRISTIAN FAMILY

A Letter to Our Readers

Dear Reader:

In order that we might better contribute to your reading enjoyment, we would appreciate your taking a few minutes to respond to the following questions. When completed, please return to the following:

Andrea Doering, Editor-in-Chief
Crossings Book Club
401 Franklin Avenue, Garden City, NY 11530

You can post your review online! Go to www.crossings.com and rate this book.

Title _____ Author _____

1 Did you enjoy reading this book?

☐ Very much. I would like to see more books by this author!

☐ I really liked_____

☐ Moderately. I would have enjoyed it more if_____

2 What influenced your decision to purchase this book? Check all that apply.

☐ Cover
☐ Title
☐ Publicity
☐ Catalog description
☐ Friends
☐ Enjoyed other books by this author
☐ Other _____

3 Please check your age range:

☐ Under 18   ☐ 18-24
☐ 25-34   ☐ 35-45
☐ 46-55   ☐ Over 55

4 How many hours per week do you read? _____

5 How would you rate this book, on a scale from 1 (poor) to 5 (superior)?
_____

Name_____

Occupation_____

Address_____

City_____ State_____ Zip_____